.

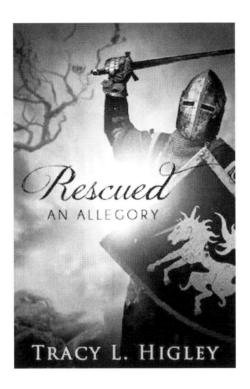

STAR OF
WONDER

THE INCENSE ROAD

BOOK ONE

TRACY
HIGLEY

STAR OF WONDER

THE INCENSE ROAD

BOOK ONE

MISHA'S STORY

CHAPTER ONE

MISHA

*F*rom that first night nine months ago, a sickness had been growing in me, like some hideous creature wanting to be birthed. I knew its cause. That damnable, beautiful star.

Tonight on the palace roof I tried to look away, to stop my ears to the endless musings and sharp-tongued arguments of my fellow scholars. They bickered over the portent of that silver-white specter wandering the charred field of Sin, god of the night. But it was the night before my final examinations and I could not afford distraction.

Only a few hours remained until dawn, and I must retrieve the one thing that would assure my place among them, that would give me an edge over Navid and all his advantages.

One chance. I had one chance to redeem last month's disaster.

I glanced at Navid, his dark head bent to the shorter Zahir, who served as mentor to us both. Zahir's finger traced a star chart, weighted with amulets and spread upon the roof's ledge, as he explained some hidden knowledge to Navid. A stab of jealousy delayed me. Navid was born into the Kasdim, as I was, and would also face examinations tomorrow. But that was where the likeness ended.

Navid flicked a condescending glance at me, and in that glance was all the superiority he wielded like a club in his privileged hand.

"Shouldn't you be practicing your presentation, Misha?" His nasal voice arched over the rooftop, loud enough to draw the attention of every studious mage. "Perhaps a good meal to strengthen you, eh?" He glanced left and right, ensuring he had an audience. "Ah, but I forgot, you are likely to present your last meal to the Kasdim along with your lessons." He snorted. "Perhaps you should arrive hungry."

The snickering response proved that no one had forgotten last month. My lifelong fear of speaking before a crowd had gotten the best of me, in front of every first- through fourth-level palace mage.

I shrugged one shoulder and smiled. "I have no worries, Navid. Even the contents of my stomach are more impressive than the contents of your mind."

Navid's eyes darkened with a flash of insecurity. He gave a half bow. "We shall see, my friend. By this time tomorrow I expect to have acquired a most troublesome assistant."

One slot for this year's second level. It would belong to either Navid or me, and the one who did not achieve it would serve the other as assistant for the year.

The idea of a year under Navid's thumb propelled me from the roof without further comment. I must not fail tomorrow. The star hung behind me, whispering its usual curse on my head if I would listen, but I ignored its threats.

Shadowy steps led down to the next level, and the temperature increased as I descended. King Phraates liked a warm palace, and no expenditure of fuel was too great. But I would go much deeper still, past the granary and down beyond the wine cellars. I reached the lowest level, deep beneath the streets of Nisa.

A place, a deep and secret place, existed far beneath the palace floors, where only the initiated were allowed to enter, where the elements and instruments saved for the practice of the most important magic were kept. It would be many years before I would be invited to enter this hallowed cave.

Tonight I did not wait for an invitation.

Only one small torch flickered at the end of a narrow passageway, and one guard stood in its shadow. A dreary post, waiting for hours for intruders who never dared to come.

I waited at the intersection of two passageways, body hidden but eyes watching the guard. He was alert despite the late hour, dropping silver coins from one hand into the other palm, a game to amuse away the hours. The coins jangled in the corridor, the only sound.

It would have been easiest to face him straight. I'd seen my share of street fights. I was born poor and foreign and raised in a palace as part of a despised sect. I could get the best of one slow-witted guard.

But he'd remember me, and I couldn't take that chance. I'd have to kill him, and I never would, not even to avoid a year of groveling before Navid.

I dug my fingers along the rough stone of the wall at my back, found some loose and crumbling, transferred them to my other hand, and scrabbled for more. When it was enough, I stepped backward, away from the joint in the passageways, and tossed the first handful down my own corridor, past the intersection.

The guard shifted his position, the clink of metal on stone echoed.

I threw the other handful.

His measured steps moved toward me, a soft scrape of sandal on pavers. He rounded the corner, away from me and toward the scattered debris.

Barefoot now, I slipped around the corner, ran for the guard's abandoned post—a narrow arch cut roughly into the wall and a splintered door. The latch held and stuck. Was it locked? It rattled under my white-knuckled grip, then gave. I slipped in, swept it closed behind me, and leaned against the wall, holding my breath. At the guard's grunting lean against the door, I released a slow breath.

I had never been inside the Vault. How far did its walls extend? Where would I find a light? I pulled two packets of powder—one a silvery gray and the other snowy white—from a pouch belted around my tunic and found a solid surface. I poured a bit of the powders on it, then a drop of acid from a small vial also pulled from my pouch.

The two powders merged in the acid with a puff of bluish smoke and a slight pop that made me grin, despite the danger. I touched the end of a loose wick to the spark as it sputtered. It caught. With this small light, soon to burn my fingertips, I searched the cave's walls for a torch. Heart pounding, for there was little time.

There! Mounted in a socket, a tar-soaked torch. One touch of my burning wick and it blazed. I squinted in the light and took in the Vault.

The treasury of the Kasdim shone and sparkled with a king's hoard, but it was not gold or even bronze that assaulted my eyes. It was the accumulated wealth of generations of knowledge, stored in ordinary amphorae, wooden crates, and earthenware jars. I scanned the treasures, looking for the box I sought. The box I had seen Zahir open on several occasions with a mere wave of his hand over the lid.

I did not know if I would even be able to open it, but within that box lay the power I needed to pass my examinations in the morning, to prove to my father that I was worthy to be called his son and to prove to the Kasdim that I was not Jewish trash.

The Kasdim were an old and proud race, tracing lineage backward into the shadowy times before the Parthians took power over the land. Before the Seleucids had their brief burst of rulership. Even before the glorious and mighty Persian Empire—all the way back to advisorship to the great kings of the Babylonians.

I was one of the Kasdim, and yet I was not.

There were many boxes such as the one I had seen contain the black *khemeia* powder, created in Egypt, where the learned worked in secrecy to transmute one element to another. I took the torch in hand, careful not to allow its light to spill from the cracks around the door. Each treasure, each secret, shone under the wave of the torch. My palm around the torch's shaft grew sweaty and my tongue and throat were dry.

But then I saw it, innocuous as a lady's jewel box, with the mark of earth, air, fire, and water upon it, as I remembered. I took it up with one hand, replaced the torch in its socket, and set the box on a table near the wall.

I passed my hand over it, expecting nothing but it seemed worth trying. The box lay still, its lock unsprung.

How had Zahir opened it? The Kasdim own many tricks, many illusions, held in reserve and in deepest secrecy, to be used in the times when their natural power does not appear at will. Was it one of these illusions that opened the box, or was it the true power that I did not yet possess?

My numb fingers shook. And I would swear I heard that star whispering. If I gave it notice, it would repeat its single message: *You must leave. The leaving will unmake you.* A repeated message that I must heed, but was I doomed for destruction if I did? Madness. Perhaps I had served our ghost-plagued king for too long.

I took a deep breath and waved a palm over the lid once more. My right hand disguised the action of my left as I did. Feeling along the underside, the tiniest indentation and protrusion revealed itself to my probing fingers. I lifted the box above the level of my eyes. The mechanism was not a simple lever as I had hoped. I would not turn the box on its head, not knowing how the contents were arranged, so I worked at what was clearly a small puzzle with it still above my head, arms shaking with fatigue and anxiety after only a minute.

But it should be able to be released with one hand. Quickly. With the box on the edge of a table. I set it down again and felt under the lip, eyes closed, picturing the puzzle of dials and lever.

With a soft click and a sound like an escaping sigh, the lock yielded under my fingers and the lid opened.

The khemeia lay within, folded into a tattered piece of parchment, which had probably come from its native Egypt with the powder. I tucked the packet into my belt, tugged my robe over it and replaced the box. It was not stealing, not in the strict sense. Zahir gave winking approval to his protégés who employed whatever means necessary for success, even considered it an unofficial part of their initiation. But neither could he sanction my actions before the other Kasdim. To be discovered would bring worse than a failed examination. Thieves were hanged for less than this.

I would waste no more time in exploring the Vault. The next challenge—escaping the room undetected—awaited.

For this feat I had brought yet another item in my pouch. I squared my shoulders, assumed an authoritarian air, and yanked the door open.

The guard bolted from his leaning position against the wall and turned on me, wide-eyed and snarling.

I stared him down. He was a large Hun, with thick hair cut severely across a heavy forehead and eyebrows like bristling caterpillars.

His hand went to the dagger on his belt. "What—?"

"Ah, I see you have awakened." I laced my tone with angry condescension. "Perhaps I shall not report to Zahir that his guards find this post too tedious to remain awake."

He straightened his back as though before the king himself. "I have never slept on watch in my life!"

I laughed, my hand sneaking into my pouch. "No? That is not what it looked like when I stepped over you to enter the Vault." I pushed past him before he could think too deeply under that large head.

But his glance was already darting down the passage, where he had followed the sound of my scattered pebbles.

I slapped his cheek lightly. "Do not fear, my friend. Your secret is safe."

The oily residue smeared on my fingertips left a slight imprint that glistened in the torchlight. His eyes flickered and rolled briefly with his first intake of the scent I had smeared there.

I took a few paces, then half-turned. "Perhaps you only dreamed of being on watch, of chasing intruders down passageways, while you dozed at the wall."

Again the dazed blinking, then a slow nod of agreement.

I leaned in conspiratorially. "I have done the same myself, on the palace roof while I was supposed to be studying the stars. You are not the only one who fears to displease Zahir." I gave him a wink to seal our pact, then a wave of farewell. I would be in my chamber before his mind had cleared.

My gaze was trained at the floor as I headed for the end of the passageway. I did not see Kamillah standing there, arms crossed, until I had nearly run her down.

My pulse yammered in my throat. Had she seen?

Her look—those cool dark eyes—were at once amused and knowing.

And if she knew, then I was as good as dead.

CHAPTER TWO

MISHA

"*I* was not made aware that you had been initiated, Misha-aku." Kamillah's voice was smooth as warm oil, low and silky, in the passageway.

She was one of the Kasdim. Though a woman, she was one of the rare few allowed into their ranks. She was perhaps twenty-and-five years, only slightly older than me. But she had come as a princess from Egypt years ago, come with all manner of dark lore and Egyptian secrets and the wisdom of a hundred sacred generations flowing in her veins, glowing behind her dark skin. She was beautiful as the Nile and mysterious as the sphinxes of her deserts, and she had never spoken to me.

I did not know which startled me more—that she had caught me in my errand or that she knew my name. Not my given name, of course, for I never used it among the Kasdim. But the Persian variant my father abhorred.

I smiled and bowed, wiping the oils from my fingertips on the tunic I wore under my unbelted black robe. "Simply hoping to meet a beautiful woman in a quiet place."

She huffed, her posture erect and condescending. "I do not know if you speak of me or one of the dozens of servant girls who seem to follow you like chickens after a hen."

I shrugged. "Your choice."

"Hmmm, well, your charms won't save you from the noose if you're caught."

"Then I'll have to be sure I'm not." But we both knew my fate was in her hands.

"Whatever you've taken, I doubt you'll need it. Navid is an idiot."

I looked away to hide my surprise. "I appreciate your confidence in me. Navid has the advantages of birth, of course."

"Ah, but you have the advantage of wit and good looks, do you not?"

I still avoided her eyes, for they disturbed me in a way servant girls' eyes did not. But I smiled. "If you say so. You keep careful track of the minor examinations of first-level magi."

She shrugged a narrow and elegant shoulder. "There are a few I watch more carefully than others." A smile at last, still haughty but with a touch of admiration.

Her familiarity gave me boldness. I raised an eyebrow. "Then do not take your eyes from me. You will be amazed."

The superiority returned. She rolled her eyes, flicked a glance to the narrow door at the end of the hall, then to the pouch at my waist. "Oh, I am certain I will."

I risked a look at her lovely face, her sensuous lips. "You will not speak of this—"

She held up a hand. "I am not your keeper." Her eyes flickered with distaste. "You have Zahir for that."

Our gazes connected for several suspended seconds. We had each other's secrets now, for no one spoke against the Chief Mage.

Kamillah stepped aside and turned her body to let me pass.

I bowed and made as graceful an exit as a gutter-born pretender could make. Her perfume, exotic as a distant Nile sphinx, washed over me as I brushed past her, my head down. She was nearly taller than me, and a woman to be respected. But I had no time for pursuing women, even beguiling Egyptian ones.

In the upper levels at last, I escaped to my bedchamber and passed three fitful hours until it was time to appear before the Kasdim Council and prove myself.

I dressed carefully in the black robe stitched with white moons of a first-level and belted it, regrettably, but it was an examination after all. A knock at my door interrupted the final knot. I opened it to a palace servant, his gaze respectfully lowered to my chest. "Your presence is requested in the throne room, my lord."

My chin lifted a bit at the title, my hands still fumbling at the belt. I had gained little honor yet in my life, except from kitchen slaves and chamber-pot emptiers, but one must take it where it comes. "The Hall, you mean. Before the Council."

He shook his head. "No, my lord. The throne room." His gaze lifted briefly, connected with mine. "There is some sort of—trouble."

I saw a warning in his eyes and smoothed my hair. "Very well."

I closed the door on him, if only for a moment to gain composure. She had claimed she would keep my secret, but had Kamillah told Zahir, or worse—the king—about my visit to the Vault?

A few deep breaths, and I crossed through the palace—two green courtyards, a silk-draped corridor, to twin double doors, twice the height of a man.

The Council was indeed convened in the throne room. Surely, I had worried for nothing. It was only the examinations, to be held here instead of the Hall.

But Phraates was pacing before his throne, his complexion a sickly pale, his forehead sheened with sweat.

Zahir stood at the foot of the throne, nodding. "Yes, my king. You are most wise in your decision."

Decision? I felt my own sweat building on the back of my neck.

Zahir seemed to feel my entrance and turned. His eyes were blacker than basalt, and a jerk of his ever-present diviner's rod ushered me toward the Council and the other initiates. Was I the last to be summoned?

I strode to the left of the throne room, toward the cluster of Kasdim. Navid stood among the older fourth-level magi, and his smug, knowing smile washed over me in a nauseous chill.

It was not until I attempted to bury myself at the back of the group that I saw my father, numbered among his strange and tiny sect within the Kasdim, called the Chakkiym. He signaled me with a quick shake of his head, as though trying to communicate some message. But it had been many years since I could understand anything the man tried to tell me.

And I knew what had happened. I had ignored the star and now its threats would harden into truth. Somehow I had been found out. I braced sweating fists against my thighs and willed my back to remain straight.

Eyes wild, King Phraates stopped before Zahir and twisted meaty fingers into the mage's robes. He was shorter by a head than his Chief Mage but with a thicker build. A man who commanded attention, if not respect, with the intensity of his bearing. "You know how it is with me, Zahir. I must find a way to be cured of this sickness. Every night, every night they torment me."

Zahir tapped his diviner's rod three times against the marble floor and placed one of his own delicate hands upon the king's and tilted his head, silent. The king's oiled curls and jeweled headpiece gleamed in the morning sunlight.

The king's posture relaxed at once under the power of Zahir's restraining touch, his hypnotic gaze.

My own fear subsided, draining into the marble flagstones at my feet.

Zahir's voice was smooth. "You have a collection like no other, my king. Ready for any need that arises within your kingdom. But this piece, this Nehushtan, will be its crown and will assure your reign forever."

The Nehushtan!

My glance shot to my father's. His brows were drawn together, forehead furrowed. The darkness in his eyes seemed to accuse me, as though I were the one who betrayed knowledge of the ancient piece to the Parthian king we both served.

The king was pacing again. "And the star, you say? The star is a warning?"

Zahir bowed at the waist. "The teachings of Zoroaster are clear, my king. A World Savior will come. Whether this star signifies that end of time or whether it is another, perhaps a strong ruler, who is rising against you is unknown. But I have no doubt—"

"You will take your best, Zahir." Phraates waved a vague hand in our direction. "The best of the Kasdim. And soldiers, of course. For protection."

The captain of Phraates's personal guard, already a general, emerged from the shadows with a two-step march of military boots. Chest out and chin up, Reza looked fierce even to me, who had been his friend since childhood.

Phraates acknowledged him only slightly. The nightly dreams that had haunted his sleep of late were taking their toll. His fleshy face sagged and his listless eyes could barely fix on anything. "Yes. Yes, Zahir. Find me the Nehushtan. Then all will be well."

Zahir bowed again and took a step backward.

"And I shall offer a prize to the man who brings it to me, yes?"

Zahir smiled.

Phraates's gaze skimmed the room and landed on Kamillah, observing among the Kasdim. "A princess of Egypt. Given as a wife to whoever brings me the piece."

Kamillah's eyes widened, then darkened. She lifted her chin to stare at the king but said nothing.

Phraates's attention wandered to the rest of us Kasdim, then to his contingent of guards and the slaves who awaited his next move. As though he could not decide his next action.

Zahir spoke softly, like a cajoling parent with a distraught child, and held a palm toward the arch at the head of the throne room. "Perhaps the king would find sleep more pleasant, now that the sun has risen."

Phraates nodded once and whirled. The royal scarlet-and-gold robes billowed, then settled as he scuffed from the room.

The hush of subjection ruled the chamber for the space of several heartbeats, and then chatter erupted, mostly among the Kasdim. The soldiers were disciplined enough to hold their tongues, and the slaves as well. But the Kasdim, always we must debate.

My father was at my side in an instant. His eyes were as tired as the king's. My mother had not been well. He wore the purple robes of the Kasdim, stitched with gold stars, though we both knew they covered a traitorous heart. "Is this your doing?" His voice was quiet but still accusatory.

I laughed, humorless. "Why? Because the Nehushtan is an artifact of your people, you assume that I could begin this?" I waved a hand to take in the activity in the throne room. "You give me too much credit."

"*My* people?"

I sighed. "Our people."

My father's gaze slid toward Zahir. "You know how I feel about this obsession of the king's. And Zahir only encourages it."

"Not all of us have your faith in the unseen, Father." My hand went to the pouch at my waist. "Some of us prefer our magic to have a tangible source."

It was Father's turn to laugh. "My life has witnessed evidence of your 'source,' my son. Trust me, you do not want it to be tangible."

It was an old argument, and one best left alone.

I saw myself through his eyes, rebellious and disappointing. Wished his censure did not sting. Still, I felt the need to justify myself. "The Nehushtan is a tale for children, not for men and not for scholars."

At the note of disrespect in my voice, he snarled. "You are so hungry to be accepted by them, Misha-el. When will you see—?"

"That I will never be worthy?"

His eyes blazed and he took a step toward me, grabbed my arm below the sleeve of my tunic. His voice was low and hard. "It is *they* who are not worthy, son."

I blinked, confused. Was this a rare commendation?

But Zahir was coordinating a plan, and I would not be left out. I pulled away, shouldered toward the front of the group, and raised a hand at a pause in his speech. "Zahir, what of this morning's examinations?"

His gaze fell on me with none of his usual warmth. "Eager to display your—newly acquired—skills, Misha?" The glance dropped to my pouch.

My stomach clenched. How—?

Kamillah. She had betrayed me to Zahir. I searched for her and found her watching the exchange.

She gave a slight shake of her head, as if to deny it.

"You have skills, Misha-aku." Zahir glanced toward Navid, still smirking in the shadows. "But you have always been overconfident. Underestimate your opposition's strengths."

Strengths? What did the weak-minded Navid possess that I did not?

Money.

I saw it at once, those silver *tetradrachm* in the guard's hand, clinking and glinting in the torchlight. Where had a palace guard gotten such a treasure?

"There will be no examinations today, Misha."

The nausea returned.

Navid sauntered to us. "Perhaps your last words before an audience will be your last words in this life, Misha. Will you die with dignity or with vomit at your feet?"

Sweat beading on my neck and running down my spine, I turned back to Zahir. Surely he would approve me. I had never understood why he chose me, the poor son of a Chakkiym, as a protégé, but was he not fond of me?

Zahir turned back to the group. "We will meet at the usual time tonight, on the roof. I will give instructions then." He struck his rod twice against the floor. We were dismissed.

The group began to disperse but Navid remained, shoulders thrown back as if prepared to receive his new title.

Zahir grabbed my arm as my father had done.

"Forget your examination, Misha. It would have been a cheat anyway, yes? This I would have known, and you would have failed."

I flattened slick palms against my robes.

"To break into the Vault, to steal the khemeia—"

"Zahir, I—"

He silenced me with a hiss of his tongue. "These are skills that will serve me well on the quest we undertake."

It took a moment for his meaning to penetrate my fear.

"Navid will remain in the palace and take the position of second level. You will come with us."

My head swam. No execution, but no examination. Navid would have the coveted place, but I would not be his assistant.

Navid seemed to be spinning through the consequences in his mind as well, and he crossed tight arms over his chest, his brow creased. "Zahir, you honor him when you should be—"

Zahir held up a palm. "Yes, I honor him, Navid. It is true that you have the power of riches at your disposal. But money runs out." He turned to me, his gaze approving. "Cunning never does."

Navid sputtered, his face reddening.

Zahir's smile on Navid was cold. "Perhaps if you hadn't been so pampered, you would have developed a thicker hide and a faster mind."

I warmed to the praise, but in the recesses of my thought was a single phrase.

You must leave. The leaving will unmake you.

Zahir patted my cheek. "Gather your belongings and say your good-byes, Misha. We leave at dawn."

So the cursed star would have its way with me after all.

CHAPTER THREE

MISHA

"I have no time for arguments, Father."

I whispered the words in the early morning darkness of my parents' small home, with the rasping breath of my mother scraping against the warm air, against my heart.

Everywhere in this place were touches of her. She trailed beauty wherever she moved, and the tiny home could have been a bedchamber in the palace, with its abundance of gold-tasseled and red-jeweled cushions, its silky fabrics in lavenders and pale green wafting across the walls and looped from the planked roof. In this Persian land ruled by Parthians, Mama's half-Greek blood brought stone pedestals and flowered greenery, nurtured by her artistry, and all the color and pageantry of her Egyptian heritage. But it was her Judean blood that made the place a home.

The slight hitch in her breath turned us both to the bed. My father reached her first.

"Is it time?" Mother's voice was small, rolling over the syllables lightly as though it demanded effort to pronounce them. "Is he leaving?"

I took her pale, long-fingered hand in my own. "I am here, Mama."

On the other side of the bed, my father clutched her other hand.

She connected us, as she always had. As little else did.

Mama looked to him, into his eyes. "Will he take them?"

Father gave a slight shake of his head, jaw muscles bulging and tight.

The sigh that escaped her lips nearly broke my heart.

"Mama, you are my first concern. I will find the Nehushtan and bring it back for you. To make you well."

It was Father who answered. "Superstitious and idolatrous artifacts are not your destiny, Misha-el."

"Ha! You speak to me of—" At my father's glare, I lowered my voice, for Mama's sake. "Your precious scrolls—handed down like some sort of magical charm over a dozen generations. How are these any different than the Nehushtan's power to heal?"

Father's right hand was twined with Mama's, and his left stroked her forehead, where wisps of her still-dark hair clung to her damp skin. "Your mother risked her life for those scrolls more than once, son."

I knew the stories. Knew every particle of how they had met, how my father had failed his duty and it was Lydia who brought the scrolls back to the Chakkiym, some of whom were Jewish and some not, though it ceased to matter years ago. There the scrolls remained, where they could be guarded until the time was right.

As though he read my thoughts, Father's words were a pronouncement. "And this is the time. Though you refuse to acknowledge it, the star confirms—"

"The star." The words were a growl in my throat. What would Simon say if he knew my refusal stemmed from a fear of madness?

"Yes, the star! For nearly six hundred years our people have watched the skies, whispered the prophecies, trained and studied for this time. We have kept our place among the Kasdim despite their ridicule, remained advisors to kings. And now, now it is finally time to bring the scrolls and the Chakkiym back to our land. I have convinced the Chakkiym that it must be you."

"That is *your* destiny, Father. Yours and Mama's." But my voice caught at the edges of this declaration, and my hand tightened around my mother's weak fingers.

Clearly, Mama could make no journey to Judea, to bring back the prized scrolls they had secreted out of Jerusalem in the year before my birth. But neither could I do it. Zahir would never allow me to break off from the caravan and travel with the Chakkiym sect, forsaking the quest for the Nehushtan. I would never attain even second level if I defied him.

I repeated his last statement. "Yes, of course you convinced them. The Chakkiym would do anything you said, even rely on your wayward son." The words escaped tinged with disdain, but in truth my father commanded the respect of his entire sect and had rightly earned it. He was a virtuous man, bold and intelligent, and everyone knew it and loved him for it. Including me, though I could never seem to say it right.

"Why must you turn everything into an argument between us, Misha? Can't you simply do what is required—?"

"What *you* require!"

"What the One God requires! You are called to be the man you must be. Would you defy Him as well as me?"

"Stop!" Lydia's voice cracked over both of us like a whip.

I sucked in a breath at the force of it and leaned over her pale face. The anger drained, leaving me weak and hollow.

A low moan escaped my father's lips, and his head dropped to where his hand still clutched hers.

She reached to touch my cheek. "Why must you always hurt each other?"

"Mama, we are sorry."

My father was kissing her hand.

The loss of her would kill him.

I saw it in that moment, saw it clearly like a vision. They had traveled a dangerous and uncertain road together for so many years, their passion for each other and for their cause never abating. He could not live without her.

From the day of my birth two ways of life had warred within my soul.

I acknowledged I was born of one land, one people. Yet another pounded so fiercely in my blood that I could, at times, hear it scream along my veins, feel its elemental pull toward other gods, other lands.

My mother was old when she bore me. Nearly thirty-one, bearing her first child at a time when other mothers dandled grandchildren upon their knees. When she saw I was a boy, her dream of grandchildren must have evaporated into a misty belief she would not live to see the next generation born.

But the other mothers—those with the brats of their own children chasing around their feet—they were the ones who envied my mother. She served as handmaid to two queens before her marriage.

Served them, yes. But outlived them both.

No, my father could not live without her. But nor could I. She was the only person under the stars who believed anything good of me.

"I must go." The walls were closing in on me, and outside the door the sounds of hoofbeats and jangling harnesses in the street warned that time was short.

"Misha-el," Mama summoned breath and words from somewhere. "Know that I love you, no matter what choices you make."

I nodded, not trusting my voice.

"But also know that the One God will not let you go. Not until you have grasped His truth for your own."

They were final words, parting words. Good-bye words. But I would be back.

"I will bring the Nehushtan to you, Mama, and you will be well."

"Our deliverance is at the door, Misha. But it will not come in such a way."

I leaned over her, kissed her fever-warmed forehead. "Wait for me, Mama." The salt of tears tickled my lips and I dashed it away. Her fingers slipped from my hand and I escaped the house, taking up my bulging pouch at the door.

My father trailed me into the early morning. The warmth of the day was building, a dry heat that filtered from the east. But we would set our eyes west. Where the star still hovered.

I did not pause to speak with my father. He would follow me to the caravan, to say good-bye to his fellow Chakkiym.

The caravan stretched from the palace steps all the way to the narrow residential streets. The Kasdim were well represented, with Zahir at their lead. The tolerated magi sect of Chakkiym kept to one side, and one of them acknowledged my father with an upraised chin. Soldiers bolstered the numbers, enough for two of them to guard every mage. A large retinue of traders joined us, taking advantage of the protection offered by the soldiers to travel the Incense Road without fear. Their camels snorted and stamped, as though impatient to get moving, perhaps to ease the load of bulging packs slung over them.

I weaved my way through to Zahir, sensing my father still on my heels.

"Ah, there is my thief." Zahir's lean frame tilted toward me, his dark curls brushing his shoulders. He held his diviner's rod, which I was certain he would manage to strap to his beast and bring along.

I cringed. Father had not heard that part of yesterday's call to join this quest.

"Glad to escape Navid, I would think, eh, Misha?" Zahir's laugh was as oily as his curls. He gave his camel a firm-handed pat on the rump and stepped away, revealing another figure just behind him.

Kamillah.

"But I wouldn't want you without supervision completely, would I?" Zahir inclined his head to Kamillah. "You'll be under her pretty thumb for the duration of our adventure."

I opened my mouth but nothing emerged.

Kamillah looked as surprised as I. "Zahir, Misha is his own man. He does not need—"

Zahir held up a hand, "It is decided."

I half-bowed to Kamillah, signaling at least an external accord with the arrangement.

Her eyes were narrowed and unfriendly, with no trace of our earlier banter. No doubt she resented having to look after the Kasdim's rebel.

There was little time for thought. The Kasdim and traders were mounting their camels, the soldiers forming into ranks behind Reza.

Reza stalked the line, examining his men, until he reached my father and me.

He had an embrace for Simon, who also pounded his back with affection.

"Keep these men in check, Reza." His voice held all the affection of a father for a son.

"I will, sir." Reza gave me a sly smile. "And this one, too."

Father laughed. "Ah, you will need help from on high for that, I fear."

Their easy camaraderie had always been a mystery to me. I had followed Father's second path to power—the pursuits of a scholar—and yet he seemed to have more respect for Reza, who was a soldier as he had once been, long ago. But Reza had all the traits I did not: a steady, dependable nobility and an innate sense of what was right and good.

I turned to my own beast, ready to mount.

Father caught my arm and turned me to himself, pulled me into a tight embrace. His voice was low against my neck, ruffling my hair. "Do what you must, Misha-el. What you know must be done. Do not return until you have fulfilled your destiny."

"I will bring it back, Father. She will be well."

His grip on me tightened further and then released. He blinked away tears.

I felt my own emotion rising again and fought to tamp it down. Not here, in front of Reza and Zahir. And Kamillah.

Ahead, Reza barked out a sharp signal, and his men began marching. Here in the streets of Nisa, their boots clacked in a sharp-heeled rhythm. Soon enough men and camels would be ankle-deep in soft sand, wishing for the unyielding paving stones.

Father held my leg, just above the ankle, and looked up into my eyes a final time.

I met his gaze. "Do not let her go, Father. Not until I return."

For all our arguments, for all our conflicting ambitions and contrary qualities, on this one thing we would always agree.

He nodded. "Be safe, Misha-el. May the One God protect your steps and bring you home."

He released my leg and I used both heels to goad Abu into a slow walk, falling in behind the others.

The people of Nisa had emerged into the dawn to see us off and stood quiet and watchful at their doors. We did not ride for any benefit to them, and they were not a people to cheer simply at the sight of a large party setting out across the killing sands. Many had sons on camel or on foot and did not know if they would ever be seen again.

Somewhere behind me Kamillah followed as well. I should be at her left flank, slightly behind, as tradition dictated.

Tradition be damned.

This journey, this quest—it was a chance to prove myself. I would follow no man. Nor woman.

I would make my own way and show them all.

CHAPTER FOUR

MISHA

*W*hat were they doing, heads together under the blaze of the midday sun?

Kamillah's glance flicked left and right.

I lowered my own gaze, fiddled with the saddle I was supposedly repairing under the paltry shade of my makeshift tent.

Reza grabbed her elbow. His scowl deepened and he spoke something quick and clipped into Kamillah's ear. I knew that tone, even without hearing it. Reza had a way of making his wishes sound like royal decree.

She shook her head, a clear refusal.

The rest of the caravan was spread over the camel-colored sands, sleeping off the heat of the day under poled canvases, waiting for the sun to look sideways at us before we covered a few more tedious miles. The camels themselves would have been camouflaged against the pale sand and white sky were it not for their leather packs and jeweled saddles. The only color in the desert came from the blood-red and glinting-gold ornamented camels of the traders. Some of the women, brought to cook and carry for them all, stirred even in the heat, preparing food for their evening meal.

I was waiting too, but not for the sun's descent. For Kamillah.

There. She broke free of Reza, pulled herself from his grasp, and headed for her own shelter.

I reached the enclosure before she did.

Her eyes narrowed. "What is it?"

I shrugged. "What were you and Reza—?"

"None of your concern." Sharp words, sharp eyes. She dropped beneath her canvas with a huff.

I joined her, ignoring the upraised brows. "How long will it take to reach our destination, do you suppose?"

It was a casual question, with calculated intent. We had been traveling all morning without knowledge of anything but that we plodded mostly south and slightly west. I was betting Kamillah had more information. I put a mask over my uncharacteristic nervousness with her to try to gain it.

She looked slant-eyed at me once more. "There is more to that question."

I laughed and dragged a finger-wide trench through the gritty sand beside my sandal. "I am only trying to predict our course, to see if my nightly alignment with the stars is correct." At my own mention of the stars, I nearly winced. It was all I could do to ignore the single star that was never far from my imagination.

"You are planning something."

My laugh was forced this time, a little choke of guilt. "From the looks of you and Reza, I am not the one with plans."

She shifted as if to stand.

I grabbed her arm.

The look she turned on me was fierce and unfriendly.

How had we gotten to this point? Zahir's ridiculous placement of me as her assistant meant nothing, but she had seemed resentful since we left, as if every glimpse of me interfered with her plans, her life.

She yanked her arm from my grasp. "Find your information elsewhere, Misha. I will not help you find your prize."

She left me under her tent and stalked toward the supply wagons.

I kicked at my sand line drawing.

Had she discerned my intent already? But how could she know I meant to find the Nehushtan first, and steal it back to Nisa to heal my mother? Unless—unless she believed I was after the prize Phraates had offered. Her.

I had tried, the gods knew, to find my information elsewhere. I questioned Zahir about our destination before we'd put Nisa twenty miles behind us, about where we would find the Nehushtan. He knew my heritage. The Hebrew artifact—a bronze snake lifted in a desert such as this one for the healing of the Jews as they escaped enslavement in Egypt —had been a legend of my people for more than a thousand years. It had become an object of idolatrous worship, believed to still carry power. But it had supposedly been destroyed by King Hezekiah after his victory over the Assyrians seven hundred years ago. The rumor that it still existed, still had power to heal, belonged to me in a way Zahir must acknowledge.

Did he also see through my supposed curiosity to my true intent? If I could, I would snatch the Nehushtan before anyone had a chance to place it under guard and return to the city. It would only be a loan—I would hand it over to the king once my mother was healed. But if I let Zahir get to it first, she would never see its benefit.

Whether Zahir knew my heart or not, he was displeased with my questions and had turned nothing but coldness toward me since I asked it. Even relegated me to the tents of the Chakkiym. "Since you are so committed to your heritage," he said.

By nightfall I had gotten no further in my inquiries. Straying from the plodding group of Chakkiym to the third- and fourth-level Kasdim, even to the cluster of traders who surely would know our destination, had yielded nothing. Chakkiym shrugged and smiled at their revered leader Simon's little son, Kasdim looked down their noses and heeled their camels to outpace me, and traders grinned black-toothed smiles and spoke in terms too general to be of help. There was only one more place to seek it, and the thought goaded me enough to keep me on Abu's back, slugging southward as the day waned.

When the sun's final slice of orange fell below the lip of the desert, we navigated by starlight until it was too cold to travel and the camels faltered. I assisted the older Chakkiym in the setup of our shared tent and dragged my bedroll and belongings in from Abu's pack.

Sixteen Chakkiym there were, with myself the seventeenth if my father had convinced them of that. Not one was younger than my father, and they patted my shoulder or my head when they passed me in the tent, as though I still ran between their legs in their hushed meetings or was learning to read from their strange writings.

I opened my pouch and removed the few personal items I had brought. A knife for shaving. An extra wineskin of water, in case the shared supply ran low. The pair of metal rings whose illusion I had mastered. An alternate tunic should we find a place to wash the ones that already clung in less-than-pleasant scents.

Gaspar snapped his bedroll open beside me. He was a stout man, with wiry hair he could never seem to tame. "We are all glad you have joined us, Misha-el. Glad, but surprised."

"None more surprised than me, Gaspar."

"It is an exciting time to be Chakkiym, yes? After nearly six hundred years, finally, we are on the move!"

This sect that was a splinter from the larger pool of diviners, sorcerers, and priests that formed the Kasdim, had been meeting in secret since the days of the Jewish Daniel, when he had been Chief Mage in the palaces of both the Babylonian Nebuchadnezzar and his successor, the Median Darius. Daniel instructed Jew and Persian alike—anyone who would listen—about the coming Jewish Messiah who would somehow be for all people. It was Daniel's scrolls, kept sealed until the right time, that my father wished me to carry back to Jerusalem from whence he had stolen them. He believed, as did Gaspar beside me, that the time had come.

And it was the star that told them so.

The self-same star that whispered nothing but torture and destruction in my ears.

"I hope you find what you are seeking in Judea, Gaspar." I reached for my own bedroll, wrapped and twine tied, but not before seeing the narrowing of his eyes.

"You do not intend to be part of the northward journey?"

"My father's aims are not my own." I loosened the bindings on the sleeping mat. "I have another quest that calls my name."

You must leave. The leaving will unmake you.

I shook my head, as though to dislodge the whispered words. Outside our tent, the star must be climbing. I gripped the edge of my bedroll and flung it outward against the sand.

Something *clunked* as it unrolled. Bounced and rested in the wavering torchlight.

A wooden box, similar to the one that held the khemeia I had stolen from the Vault. It was not the same. But I had seen this box before.

Gaspar raised his eyebrows, but it was not surprise etched on his face. It was disapproval. "Your father believed you worthy to carry the scrolls, Misha-el. I should think you would take better care than this."

My father believed me worthy—

The balm that could have been in that phrase evaporated against the heat of anger.

I had refused him! Told him I would not be responsible for the precious scrolls he and my mother had risked their lives to protect.

I snatched up the box and shoved it into Gaspar's gnarled hands. "You should have them, then. You are much more qualified. Deserving. And you are going to Judea."

Something passed over him in that moment, something like new knowledge imparted to him from outside himself. He laid the box gently at the head of my mat and turned away.

The torch within the tent was extinguished, the old men said their prayers—some in Aramaic, some in Hebrew—and settled to their beds with the grunts and moans of bones and muscles unused to days of hard travel.

I placed the box back in my pouch, wrapped inside my extra tunic, stretched out on my mat, and used the pouch to pillow my head. What would Father say to that? Probably find hope that its secret words would somehow burrow into my mind while I slept.

But sleep did not come. The star was loud tonight. Loud and angry. It spoke its paradoxical message in two different voices, split into cajoling and condemning, sweet and spiteful. I closed my eyes but could not close my ears. Finally, sometime in the center of the night, I slipped from the tent, sweaty with unrest and seeking the coolness of desert air, even if it meant the cold eye of the star on me.

Only the guards tasked with patrolling while others slept stirred at the boundaries of our caravan camp. One of them flicked a glance in my direction, gave a nod of acknowledgment, and continued his rounds.

By the gods, it was beautiful, that star.

I could not look away.

At the edge of my vision a whiteness fluttered. I turned to see who had joined my night watch. But there was no one. Some strange trick of the torchlight. I returned to my unwilling study of the star.

But there it was again—that wavering light just beyond my sight line. And then gone when I turned my head. A tiny thread of cold snaked its way along my veins. Did the star now move among us, ready to destroy me? Mad thoughts.

You will be destroyed.

It came from the wavering light. Not from the star above. Somehow I knew this. I swiveled, fists raised to my chest. Nothing there.

Look away. I am not for you to see. Not fully. Look away.

The flesh on my arms, the hair on my neck, all raised in response.

"Who are you?"

"The Watchers. Those who warn."

That he spoke of himself in the plural wormed itself into my stomach and gripped. I could think of nothing to say. Nothing.

"You should not have left Nisa. The leaving will destroy you."

"You told me to leave!" More madness, to be arguing with someone I could not see. Was it one of Phraates's ghostly brothers? The king had murdered thirty of them to take the throne, and he swore to royal and commoner alike that one visited him each night of the month.

A low laugh. Did ghosts laugh?

"That was not us. We warned you not to leave."

The split voice I heard in my tent tonight. Had it always been thus? I could not be sure. Had there always been two, speaking two different messages? A command to leave and a warning to stay?

"Who then?"

The apparition was silent. Silent, but not still. I could sense an increase in the trembling activity, a frantic fluttering. I risked a look.

Straight on, the vision disappeared once more. But in that fraction before, when my eyes were still half-turned, I saw them.

Yes, two of them. Fighting.

Coldness tunneled through my limbs.

I ran. Shameful, but I ran like a coward from the battling spirit realm.

The camp had formed itself into natural alleys and paths between the tents of mage, soldier, and trader. I plunged into the heart of it, careful to avoid hidden ropes that tethered tents to sand.

Not careful enough.

Around the corner of one faintly lit tent, I tripped and met the sand with my face.

Pausing, breathing, recollecting, I heard the soft murmur of voices within the tent.

"He is still reticent. Does not believe it is time yet."

"How much longer must we wait? The king has gone to madness with his ghosts and his magic—tasking us to guard these fools as they search for yet another potion or charm to fix what cannot be repaired!"

The words were urgent, tight.

I pushed myself to my knees in the sand. Stood beside the entrance to the tent.

"There are enough of us now, and this journey is the perfect time to make our plan. When we return, we can be ready to place him on the throne."

An errant breeze, perhaps the work of my infernal haunting spirits, blew the tent flap open.

More than a dozen sets of eyes lifted at once and met my own.

Soldiers. All of them.

The breath of a heartbeat passed and they were on their feet.

I stepped away. But not before I saw them lunge as one.

"Take him!"

A plot to overthrow Phraates was no idle talk of bored troops. An eavesdropper would not live to tell what he heard.

I ran again, the soft sand sucking at my feet, betraying me.

Behind me, the near-silent chase of armed men. The vicious whisper of unseen spirits. The cold condemnation of the beautiful star.

And where, under all that purple-black desert sky, was there for me to run?

CHAPTER FIVE

MISHA

I ran into the chest of Reza.

With a grunt and thud we gripped each other's arms, took in each other's faces.

"What is it?" Reza's words were clipped. He shot a look over my shoulder.

I followed his look. Behind me, my pursuers gathered like a sandstorm.

Reza pushed me aside to face his men. "What is going on?"

"He was listening at our tent. He heard things—"

"Get back to your beds. All of you." Reza's hand was around my upper arm. The glances of his men followed that grip, looked to Reza in trust, and backed away into the night.

The clamp on my arm was not a show for the men. Reza dragged me across the sand wordlessly. He grabbed a small lighted torch from the sand and shoved me past a posted guard at his own tent. A flick of the head dismissed the guard who had a look of suspicion for me before leaving.

"Reza, they are right. I did hear things."

He pulled me into the tent, used the torch to light a tiny brazier in the center, then returned the torch to its sand support and reentered the tent. Every movement terse and abrupt, a soldier on the march.

"Best to forget anything you heard, Misha. The idle talk of sleepless soldiers is—"

I shook my head. "They were not trading stories of scandalous escapades, Reza!" I lowered my voice and stepped nearer.

He turned his back to me, adjusted the brazier.

"They spoke of revolt. Of a usurper they think to place on the throne of Phraates—"

"It is me." The words were spoken quietly, directed to the sand at our feet.

The revelation felt like a slap.

Reza's gaze found my own. "I am the one they want to put on the throne."

I closed the gap between us. "You are planning a coup?"

"They are planning. I am only their figurehead."

"What? But why you?" I lifted an apologetic palm at the seeming insult. "You are an exemplary soldier of course, but—"

"Because it is my birthright." Reza's eyes were tired, more tired than a man of his few years had a right to. "Because if the Parthians had not come, I would be king."

I searched my learning, the histories. "If they had not come? Two hundred years ago?"

"To some two hundred years is nothing."

Yes, the Chakkiym would agree. "You are telling me that you are the heir to the Persian throne and I have never known it? Since we played at dice as children you have never told me?"

"I have only known for three months. Apparently it is the way with my people. To guard the heir and keep him oblivious until it is determined if he is ready, if the people are ready."

"And now?"

He shrugged. "And now the factions that would overthrow the Parthian scourge and return our land to its Persian glory believe they are strong enough—believe I am strong enough—to see it happen."

A surge of pride in my friend found its way into my voice. "You do not agree?"

He smiled at my confidence and gripped my arm once more. "I do not know what I think. A revolt would be bloody and there are no guarantees. I would not lead people into disaster if I could avoid it."

A flash of imagination, of Reza on the throne in place of Phraates, fired my blood. "It is your birthright."

"Ah, Misha. Always ready to take on the next impossible challenge, aren't you?"

The Nehushtan. "If Zahir finds the Nehushtan—if it truly holds power and he gives it to Phraates—there will be no defeating him."

Reza kicked at his bedroll. "I care little for this quest."

I circled the rumpled bedding. "No, no you must." My mind raced through possibilities. I already intended to steal the Nehushtan from under Zahir, albeit temporarily. "It must be destroyed."

With the words my future as Kasdim began to bleed away. If Zahir ever suspected that I destroyed his artifact, I would be relegated to scrubbing floors in the Hall. The only way to retain my dream would be to steal the Nehushtan, see my mother healed, and then destroy it without Zahir ever learning I had it.

Reza grabbed up a jug of water and swigged from it. "Such serious words. Is this my sweet-stealing Misha?"

His words pricked. He had relied on me as a child, to swipe honey pastries from the palace kitchens for us to divide under the stairs. But did I have what it would take for such a serious undertaking? I would have to learn the location of the Nehushtan, then race ahead of the caravan to retrieve it.

You must leave.

The leaving will unmake you.

I heard the distinction now. The two warring voices. The star and the spirits. But was the latter a kindly warning or a threat? Which voice spoke for my good?

"Zahir will not be pleased." I grinned. "I am guessing he will not retain his place as Chief Mage if you take the throne?"

"Ha! My first royal act would be to replace him. With your father."

My amusement flagged for a moment. But of course Reza would elevate my father. And the honor would be well deserved.

"Then we will get rid of it. After my mother is healed."

"Are you certain you don't wish to present it to Phraates, to win yourself a wife?" His voice held humor but also a tightness.

I waved away the awkwardness. "She would sooner drink poison than subject herself to me, I believe." I slapped him on the back. "In the meantime, find Zahir. Keep him occupied."

"What are you going to do?" His voice followed me from the tent.

I raced to my own tent, found what I needed, and was creeping along the alley near the center of camp within minutes. My black turban was wound around my head and lower face, leaving only the sliver of my eyes exposed.

A central square was standard in every caravan camp. A place to meet, to cook over a shared fire, to discuss plans for the coming day. I slipped across an open space between tents, long enough to spot Reza talking with Zahir. Good man.

Two minutes later I slunk along the side of Zahir's private enclosure.

As expected, a guard stood at its entrance.

I sucked in a breath, remembered my training. First-level magi did not typically outmatch soldiers, but my father believed every man should be master of his body, and I had surprise and stealth on my side.

One swipe of my leg from behind felled him. I caught his neck as he fell, applied the right pressure. His mouth opened and closed like a struggling fish. He took the measure of my eyes, but only my eyes.

His body went limp and I dragged him backward, into Zahir's tent.

If maps of our destination and the plans for the Nehushtan's retrieval existed, they would be in this tent.

I swiveled to take in the space, search it in a glance.

The sudden intake of breath and flurried movement from the corner sent a jolt of heat through me. But I was still swathed in my turban, unrecognizable.

"Misha!"

"Kamillah?" I breathed out her name, the sound deflating my chest. From only my eyes she knew me?

Hands behind her back, face white in the lamplight, her glance shot to the guard at my feet. "What in the heavens are you doing?"

I choked over an excuse, faltered, and managed only a strangled sigh.

She was beside me in a moment, her body and voice hot at my side. "Did you kill him?"

"Of course not! He will only be unconscious for a few minutes."

"Unconscious!" Her beautiful lips tightened in disapproval after that single word.

"What are you doing in here, Kamillah?"

Her eyes widened and searched my face. "You are asking *me* this question?"

But I sensed evasion, even fear. Did she have goals as disreputable as my own?

I pulled her close and hissed an answer against her ear. "I have no time to argue nor explain. I am looking for something."

The smell of her hair was like cinnamon. Why did I believe she would keep my secret? Because she had come to my defense over the khemeia?

She turned her head slightly, her body brushing mine. "Tell me what you seek."

"I must know where the Nehushtan is to be found."

"Will Zahir not tell you when he needs you to know?"

"That is not soon enough."

She took a step backward, searched my eyes again. "You want it for yourself."

I advanced on her again. "Not myself. But I must reach it first. You must trust me."

"I have always thought you trustworthy, Misha. It is you who does not trust himself, nor believe in your own ability."

I eyed the tent entrance. How long would Reza keep Zahir from his lodging? "I do not know what that means."

She waved away the argument. "Of course you do not."

It was my turn to study her. "Does Zahir share his secrets with you? Is there a map or writings here that are guiding him?"

She flushed, the warm pink rising from her throat into her face, and pulled away. "You should know better than anyone. He has deep knowledge that comes from beyond the workings of the physical world. And he keeps it locked in the darkness of his mind, where no thief can find it." She arched an eyebrow. "No matter how skilled."

Behind me, the tent flap swished.

"What is this?"

"Zahir." I pulled the turban away from the lower half of my face.

He seemed unsurprised to see Kamillah in his tent. The thought stabbed at me.

Over me, his brow furrowed. "You are looking for me?"

Kamillah's laugh was low and amused, drawing his attention smoothly to herself. "I am afraid Misha-aku was looking for me, Zahir. He is always anxious to please, as you know. It seems I have not given my new assistant enough to do on this quest. He grows bored."

Zahir grunted. Then saw the guard at his feet.

"I found him asleep at his post." Kamillah's lies came as easily as pouring water. "I tried to wake him, but it would appear he had been drinking before duty. I had Misha drag him in here."

I mentally apologized to the defamed soldier. But when he awoke, he would have a defense. What tale would he tell of the attack from behind?

"Misha," Kamillah snapped her fingers at me, "perhaps you had better get to work on that piece of translation I gave you earlier, yes?" She lifted her chin. "And feel free to report to me in the morning. I will be eager to hear how you fared."

The two watched me with an air of dismissal, and there was nothing to do but nod, bow, and back my way out of the tent.

Reza met me halfway back to the tent of the Chakkiym. "Now will you tell me what that was about?"

"It was about you!" I stalked away, leaving him bewildered, and reached the outskirts of the camp where I fell upon the sand and avoided the stars.

I pounded at the sand under my fists, but it gave way too easily to satisfy.

Pulled in too many directions. Everyone wanted something different from me. From Nisa I could hear my father urging me to follow the star, to take the scrolls and lead the elderly Chakkiym to Judea to find their Messiah. Zahir would have me bow and scrape my way to the next level of the magi by finding the Nehushtan for Phraates. If I found it first, it would be for my mother, and then I could destroy it for the sake of Reza and his hopes for the throne.

Or perhaps it was Kamillah whose advice I should follow. Would she think more highly of me if I were to pursue my own goals?

I laughed under my breath, humorless. What goals would those be? When, in all my years, had I ever thought beyond what others wanted for me?

The Nehushtan or the scrolls? The burning star or terrifying spirit-beings?

Father or Zahir? Kamillah or Reza?

Oh, how I would give anything for a simple stomach-roiling examination before the fourth-level magi right now.

CHAPTER SIX

REZA

"*Y*ou there!" Reza shouted from the saddle of his horse and pointed to three men marching on his right flank.

They snapped to attention in his direction.

He jutted his chin toward the wavering copse of palms in the distance. The dust of a thousand years hung in the heat. "Take horses and ride ahead. Report back."

The eyes could not be trusted in heat like this. Six days out, and they needed to reach the Wadi Lama. But the oasis ahead looked smaller than he remembered. Had they gotten off course?

Zahir's camel broke away from the pack of Kasdim and plodded over. His too-smooth voice filtered through the hot air. "Concerned?"

Reza shrugged. In one word Zahir could imply both condescension and control. Reza could learn from him. "Not yet. But we need water."

"And I trust you'll find it for us." He nudged his beast's head back toward his men.

Reza glanced across, met the gaze of Misha, and sighed.

His friend's relentless pressure was only an addition to what he already felt from his soldiers. Misha and his Nehushtan were convincing. Tempting, even. And Kamillah…

But Reza had more important concerns.

Starting with how to stop his men from getting him, and themselves, killed.

Already, only six nights out on this journey, and they had been indiscreet enough that Misha overheard their plans. And their attempts to turn thirty rebels into a hundred before the journey ended would only spill dangerous information into the ears of many who may not hear it kindly.

Could they truly succeed in putting him on the throne? Restore Persian glory? His father had been working for two generations to see it happen.

An artifact of great power, if it were real and if they found it, could mean the difference between crushing defeat and guaranteed victory. Misha thought it must be destroyed. But could it not guarantee Reza's victory?

He'd known Misha nearly all his life. If this Nehushtan were only one of his pranks, it would be easy to dismiss. But from his conversation at the camp's central fire last night, Zahir seemed intent, even crazed, to see it found. And with Kamillah set up as the prize, Zahir's reasons would include more than just power and influence.

The three soldiers were already on their way back. If they had not found water, they would have known not to push their horses so hard. Reza heeled his mount's flank and rode ahead to meet them.

The first, Bassam, spoke quickly. He was a squirrely man, with large teeth. "It is not the Lama I have heard tales of—it's shrunken into itself and with trees browned or fallen on its former perimeter. But it will suffice."

Reza nodded once, turned, and delivered the news to the troops. The Kasdim, their strange little Chakkiym, and the traders received the news at the edges of the military contingent that was Reza's alone.

The caravan urged harder now. It took only the prospect of a little water and the paltry shade of straggling palms to inject them with energy. And halfway to Yathrib, with nothing but desert in every direction, the Wadi Lama was as close to pleasure as they were likely to find.

The traders with their loaded camels, some mounted and some rope led, lagged behind. Reza nodded permission to his men to pull away. Little danger existed in this wide vista of raiders or nomadic tribes intent on thievery.

He hung back, falling into the ranks of the Kasdim, until Kamillah's beast drew even with his own. She was properly swathed for the heat in head covering and flowing robes with little more than her eyes visible, but she was the only woman of her rank and easy to find.

She paid him little heed, kept her face to the water, so all he saw was the defiant blink of her eyes.

"You have not reconsidered."

She was silent a moment, then breathed out a sigh that puffed the whiteness of her head scarf about her lips. "Is that a question?"

Ahead, his men were beginning to reach the oasis. He would welcome the shade himself. They would spend the afternoon here, and perhaps Kamillah would talk further with him under his tent.

"I suppose not. I know the answer."

"Then do not waste your breath."

She had never let him command her, the way he could his men or even any women he chose. It aggravated him, at the same time that it drew his admiration. And now that thoughts of kingship were never far from his mind, would Kamillah not make an excellent choice for a royal wife?

A fierce cry echoed over the desert sand.

Reza shot higher on his mount, squinted into the haze.

The first knot of traders had reached the water's paltry edge.

Kamillah leaned forward. "What is it? An attack?" The words were laced with fear.

He had told her before they left, the desert was no place for a woman.

He left her wondering and clucked his horse into action. The ground was too soft for a full gallop, and he risked injury to the horse if they went too fast.

"Spread out!" His troops moved into familiar positions and pressed forward.

He reached the first glut of mounted soldiers ringing the oasis.

Since that first outcry, there had been only silence. No sounds of a raiding party.

"Let me through, stand aside."

The soldiers parted and he passed through the sandy edge of the Wadi Lama. A dozen soldiers stood in a cluster, with as many traders facing them. The rest of the traders held back. Were they restraining their animals?

Reza's tribune scuffed toward him over the grit, avoiding a small pile of bleached bones—all that remained of a jackal or hyena, perhaps.

His face grim, Bassam looked up to where Reza sat above him. "Poison."

Reza growled. "The water?"

Bassam inclined his head to the traders. "When they reached us, they were quick to point out the dying trees." He waved a hand around the perimeter. "And the quantity of bones. Animals that drank and died."

One of the traders, Mahdi if Reza remembered correctly, approached. "It happens when a spring begins to go dry. The level goes down and the water sickens with impurities." He dropped his head. "We should have warned you when we saw the faltering trees from a distance."

Reza eyed the group of soldiers near the oasis, then looked back to Bassam. "How many drank?"

"Probably fifty." Bassam closed his eyes briefly. "Including myself."

"Mazda's bones." Reza hissed the curse under his breath, but loud enough for Bassam to cringe. He called another tribune, Jabari, forward. "Pull everyone back from the water. Make certain no one else drinks. We will camp here until the sun lowers." He looked down on Bassam. "Take the men who drank and get them settled in comfort. We will wait it out and hope for the best."

But by late afternoon the sickness had overtaken. Men moaned in their tents, staggered to the outskirts of the camp for privacy, and called out to the gods for mercy.

"We cannot move on." Reza took council with Zahir in the filtered shade of a palm.

Zahir huffed. "You expect the entire caravan to wait for your men to die?"

"Mage!" Reza glanced toward the sick tents. "Hold your tongue."

"We need water, and we need to keep moving. You know this as well as I. It is not safe to stay in one place too long."

"One night."

"We lose hours of travel—"

"One night." The cold determination in his voice finally silenced Zahir.

The decisions regarding travel belonged to Reza and clearly Zahir was angry.

The mage shrugged and turned away.

Reza avoided company through the afternoon. The fault of his men's sickness lay with him and brought questions of how he could ever lead a kingdom. His thoughts drew him beyond the camp, to a rise on the western side.

Perhaps he could lead if he had something to back his power. Something like the Nehushtan.

As the sun dropped away and the stars flickered to life, a light too large for a star bobbed along the horizon. Traders, perhaps? Coming to the Wadi Lama as they had done?

Within the hour they reached the camp, a band of merchants, with low-slung pouches and fitful torches.

They pushed through to the center of camp and ringed the fire.

Soldiers, magi, and traders alike filtered through the tents to hear news. Reza stood apart, and Kamillah came to join him. He half-bowed in greeting to the small band.

One of them, the skinniest, stepped forward. "We saw your camp-fires and thought to warn you that the water is sick."

Reza ground his heel into the sand. "Too late, I fear. Half of our men have taken ill already."

The half-starved-looking merchant, his hair in greasy strands, gave Kamillah a leering smile and jabbed a thumb in the direction they had come. "We are camped by a small spring we came upon. Very little marks it, but there is water enough for your group."

Reza bowed again. "I thank you for your generosity and your assistance. We will pack up in the morning and come across."

The man who would be their mouthpiece shrugged. "The night has not grown too cold yet. Why not send some to refill skins and bring clean water back for your ailing men?"

Reza glanced toward his healthy men. They were fewer in number already, and to send others away would leave the camp vulnerable.

The merchant spoke to one of those who had come from Nisa. "We are traveling the Incense Road to the east, bearing all manner of spices and jewels. But we would be happy to exchange silks for fresh fruits."

There were glances and nods all around. Omari, the chief of his traders, eyed Reza. "We will go. Send us with goods and camels and we will bring back water with our purchases."

The merchant swung an arm toward the distant camp. "They are welcome in our tents for the night. By morning you will have fresh water."

It was quickly arranged. The mixed group of traders set out together, against the purpling sky.

When they were only a series of specks across the dark sand, Reza began to pace. Through the camp, past his soldiers' camp and the sick men, beyond the whispers and muttering of the Kasdim within their enclosures and the silent darkness of the traders' tents. He made the circuit, then started back again.

Something felt wrong. Half his soldiers lay weak, all of the traders gone. He had learned to trust his instincts in his years of soldiering, and this night was nagging at his thoughts, leaving him clammy in the desert night air.

He slowed at Kamillah's tent, nodded to the guard he had placed there to keep her safe from unscrupulous men.

Through the fabric he saw her combing out her hair. He lifted a hand to sweep the tent flap aside, then let it drop.

Halfway through the night watch, when Reza had finally settled to an uneasy sleep, his premonition exploded to reality.

Raiders.

Reza shot upright from his mat. Grabbed his sword.

Guards had raised the alarm, shouted the news.

He bolted from his tent while the horde was still pouring in from the east.

The camp erupted. Soldiers appeared from every tent, materialized from darkness.

Not enough. They were not enough.

To his left, Kamillah emerged from her tent. Her dark hair was loose and swung about her shoulders.

"Get back inside!" He yelled as he ran toward the black-robed invaders. They pushed through to the center of camp where the traders had left goods for transport.

Chaos everywhere. Raiders and soldiers clashed, sword against sword. The clank of metal outshouted battle cries, left a burning in the ears and on the tongue. Reza engaged one of the black robes, crossed swords with him only twice, then ran him through. He yanked his sword from the raider's gut and turned for the next.

They were armed and they were many, but they were untrained. Surely his men had a chance, even with their numbers halved.

He caught a glimpse of a Kasdim here and there, snatching the sword of a fallen raider and joining the fray.

How long did they fight? It seemed hours before his men had the central camp ringed two deep. The elderly Kasdim huddled beside the huge fire, and the pack camels pulled as close as they could be coaxed.

From the shadows, one of the raiders stepped forward, his men behind him. "We will take what we came for."

Reza lifted his chest. "You will die trying."

He inclined his head toward the western desert. "Then your traders with our men will die as well."

It had been a trick. The friendly merchants from across the sand offering water. It had been a ploy to whittle down their numbers, separate the wealth from those who carried it, and give these scoundrels the advantage of hostages.

Reza cursed the man to his face.

The leader of the raiders ranged his eyes over the grouping behind Reza. His eyes came to rest on Kamillah. He inclined his head, as though the sight of a woman of her beauty and birth here in a merchant caravan was a puzzle to him. His face split with a smile. He directed one of his men to pull her out. "She is the first treasure we will take."

Reza raised a sword, but Kamillah stilled him with a look and came willingly from safety.

At that moment a mighty shout went up from the distant perimeter of the camp, and several dozen torches blazed in a circle.

Reza's chest constricted, his breath died in his throat. They could never outfight so many. His fist tightened around his sword, slick with sweat and blood, and he raised an arm to stay his men.

But the raiders were glancing left and right, eyes wide, mouths agape.

A rival raiding party?

The ring of torches held at the perimeter, but one torch bobbed nearer, until close enough for its bearer to be revealed.

Misha?

He stood erect, stone-faced. And he wore the leathers of a soldier. "General, we've put the rest of their pathetic band across the sands to the sword." He thrust a torch toward the leader of the raiders. "Our merchants who traveled to them await your permission to return to camp." He smiled coldly. "And they've taken a bit of a haul themselves."

Misha, always the trickster.

Reza puffed his chest, faced the raiders with a sly smile, but spoke to his friend. "Tell the men it is time to dispatch with these fools as well."

Their leader glanced again at the ring of torches around the camp. He would know there could be a dozen men for every torch he saw.

Misha let out a whoop, as Reza himself had done at the start of many a battle.

From around the camp, the answering cry lifted.

Caught between the two halves of Reza's small army, the raiders did the only logical thing.

They fled.

From the inner circle of the camp, Reza's men chased them through the maze of tents, past Misha's torches.

Reza rounded his men, put as many as possible on horses with the rest on foot to charge into the desert and recover their traders before the cursed lot had a chance to regroup and join their colleagues.

On the way out of the camp he passed Misha, still on foot, helping a sick soldier back to the physician's tent. A burning torch remained upright in the sand, a broken pot beside it.

He slowed only long enough to grasp Misha's hand and shake his head.

Misha grinned, that childhood grin from their escapades long ago in the palace halls. "A little trick I learned from my father's stories of his ancestors."

Reza released his hand and turned his face toward the campfire across the desert. "Well, you would have made him proud today."

CHAPTER SEVEN

MISHA

I pressed myself farther into the stone wall, then leaned only a fraction of my head, just enough for half an eye to see past the crumbling corner to the entrance of the Temple of Amun-Re in the center of Yathrib.

The streets were busy here even at the edge of the city, busy everywhere in this major trading crossroads of Arabia.

In the days of traveling from Nisa, the Nehushtan's location had built itself into a strange and mysterious desert outpost in my mind. Or perhaps a lost cave of the nomads, tunneling into a forlorn rocky cliff.

Never did I imagine it would reside within a pagan temple to an Egyptian god in a city primarily inhabited by Jews.

Now to successfully liberate the piece, convince Zahir I'd failed, and then get it back to Nisa and my mother somehow.

A band of Jews passed the temple, arguing and gesturing, no doubt on their way to synagogue.

I drew back until their heated words faded into the paving stones, then darted around the corner and slipped across the street, to the alley beside the temple.

Why could it not be on a high place, as most temples to gods were, away from the eyes and ears of crowds? But the street crowds were easy to avoid. The priests and penitents inside would be hardest to deceive.

I crept along the south wall of the temple, to the elevated portico fronting it, and climbed to the platform with the stealth of a mountain cat. At least, I liked to think of myself that way.

Five quick steps and I was inside, pulled into shadows and watching.

Priests crisscrossed the open chamber, disappearing through the heavy columns that formed a double row of support under the lofty roof. The temple smelled of incense and smoke, and a low intoning of prayers echoed from somewhere deep within.

Under the statue of Amun, Zahir said. Steps leading into the earth. A cavern dug beneath the god's temple to hide a Jewish artifact that had become a pagan thing in the eyes of the Jews' God and his ancestors. Supposedly destroyed in the days of King Hezekiah, after the people of Judah began to worship it for what it had accomplished in the past. But here it waited. For others less scrupulous to use its power to further their ambition.

Could I time it correctly? I counted the steps between myself and the huge statue and a small doorway behind it. Roughly thirty. I needed only fifteen seconds to cross the temple and get below. Fifteen seconds of backs turned.

What lay below? Did they know the treasure they held? Would a guard and a sword await me in the darkness under the Temple of Amun-Re?

The priest was filling an incense burner, his back to me. Should give me the required time.

I waited, counted. Then ran.

A familiar jolt of excitement shot through me. I was at my best in these situations.

I reached the statue in twenty-four steps. Not quick enough.

Another priest emerged from the shadows. "You there!"

Surprisingly loud—and forceful—for a priest.

I skidded to a stop before the dark entrance, more ramp than stairs, and turned.

The priest, swathed in white and draped with a lion's hide, waddled toward me, brows drawn together. "Where are you going, boy?"

I took a breath, waiting for an excuse to form on my lips.

Before I had a chance, a voice called from the temple's portico. "He is studying."

The priest and I followed the honeyed voice to Kamillah, striding across the temple.

"Forgive his inquisitiveness, honored one. I have been schooling him in the ways of Amun-Re, but he is often too eager."

I looked her over with narrowed eyes. What was she doing here? A chip of resentment hardened in my chest. I did not need her rescuing me. Again.

"And you are?" The priest looked her up and down, wary but clearly admiring what he saw.

Kamillah half-bowed. "Kamillah of Alexandria, honored one. I have spent these many years in Nisa, studying the ways of the Persian magi to add to my knowledge of Egypt, where I was born and first trained."

The priest harrumphed. "And this miscreant is your student?"

"A first-level mage." Kamillah turned an indulgent eye on me, in every way the patronizing tutor. "Newly assigned under me. We are traveling through the area, and I wished to take advantage of the wonderful Temple of Amun-Re here to teach him a bit of the learned world beyond his narrow borders."

The priest puffed a bit at this, his lips forming a satisfied pucker.

"Perhaps, high priest, you could show me the deeper cella? The kitchens of the god, even?" She led the priest by the arm toward the shadowy corridor beyond the fat-bellied columns and tossed a pointed look over her shoulder at me as she went.

Fine. She had given me an opportunity. I owed her a favor, perhaps.

With the priest drawn into the shadows by Kamillah's smooth flattery, I half-slid down the ramp, hands scraping against the rough stone on my way.

A narrow-cut slot at the bottom led into complete darkness.

"A door half the height of a man, with only a notch to betray it," Zahir had said. Where he got his information, I did not ask.

I slid my right hand along the wall, pushing into the darkness. Some sort of corridor proceeded ahead. The left wall was too far to reach. After a few steps, I walked forward in a crouch, feeling for some kind of notch.

My hands grew clammy in the damp air, and my legs burned. How far did this corridor go? Were there other tunnels branching away on my left, tunnels that would confuse me as I returned?

But there—there was a strange hole cut into the wall, just above the level of my knee.

Heart thumping, I knelt and poked a finger through the hole. Nothing.

I pushed against the stone around it with both hands. It gave a little under the pressure. Jaw clenched, I shoved my shoulder against the stone, putting my weight behind it.

A small, square portion of the wall swung inward. From somewhere within a light reached out to reassure me.

Sweat beaded down my back, despite the underground coolness. I squeezed through the opening, left it ajar for my return, and crept toward the light. The roof of the tunnel was too low to stand, and it scraped painfully against my scalp. Ahead, another narrow corridor ended in a blank wall, but the light shone from around a bend.

I turned the corner at last, to a sight as unexpected as a waterfall in the desert.

Stone steps, wide as a man, led downward into a huge cavern. In the center, a bronze brazier burned bright and hot. All manner of treasure—vessels of burnished gold and mottled ivory, massive chests of inlaid cedarwood were piled against the walls. The firelight glinted off the polished surfaces, even reflected off the walls, which themselves were painted and sketched in deep reds and charcoals, highlighted with the mirrored patina of gold leaf.

My breath caught in my chest. My gaze wandered to take it all in at once. Impossible. It was the treasure trove of a fable, the lair of some long-dead king or jinni who had stored the wealth of a thousand generations before his exile, guarded only by the brazier whose light never extinguished.

I exhaled and the trembling in my legs increased.

A quick tour around the cavern revealed treasures from a dozen different civilizations, etched and engraved and painted with the languages and images of gods of every land. I could not even tell how far the cavern stretched into the shadows. Did all of Yathrib sit atop this fortune?

And how was I ever to find the Nehushtan among this collection?

A stab of panic propelled me forward, examining each item I

encountered. If I wanted to get out of Yathrib with the eastbound traders I had bargained with yesterday, I had to find it before dawn. And I still had not thought of a suitable ruse to convince Zahir that I had failed.

But was I not looking at the very answer? How could Zahir fault me when I returned empty-handed from this?

And perhaps it would be the truth. Perhaps the artifact had lain buried in this muddle for seven hundred years because no one could find it.

I picked up a Greek rhyton, examined its underside, set it down. My mother had its replica at home, made from more common material.

My mother. I fought back the fear for the sake of focus. For her.

"Guarded by the lamp, cursed by the gods." I spoke aloud the words Zahir had given me for guidance. The silent mounds of plunder muffled and absorbed the words as though they were all buried together.

An hour later I had progressed through only a fraction of the cavern. Jewel-encrusted lamps, engraved chests, and golden statues. But nothing that looked like a bronze snake wound around a staff, lifted in the wilderness for the healing of a band of rebellious Israelites fleeing Egypt.

Concern had turned to a tightness in my neck and shoulders and was now a breathless sort of fear. I could search for a decade and not find it. Dust coated my tongue and the smoke of the brazier burned my eyes. I would not have imagined my fingers could grow weary of the touch of gold and ivory, but I would give anything for the dull sheen of some ordinary bronze.

"Guarded by the lamp."

I turned to the brazier. It was not an otherworldly fire, burning through eternity, as I had first thought. Only an ordinary ring of bronze, fed by a wide wick of twisted flax that drew oil slowly into its basin. Not a brazier at all, which would be filled with charcoal. Only a large lamp.

And the jug that fed it was practically empty. I pushed down the thought that someone kept that oil supply filled. Perhaps a priest who could appear at any moment.

Under the brazier, around it, above it—I examined every measure of stone and metal and air.

Nothing.

I straightened and flexed my shoulders, wiped the stone dust from my fingers, throbbing from the attempt to pry up the stones of the floor.

I closed my eyes and breathed. Counted my heartbeats to focus.

"Cursed by the gods."

Could the curse be written?

I snatched up one of the many lamps I had found, used a pottery shard to scoop a bit of oil from the brazier's supply, and touched the wick to the flame. Lamp in hand, I began an examination of the walls.

The myriad languages baffled me. If there was a curse, I would only find it if it was in one of four languages.

I found the back of the cavern. Splashes of light and streaks of darkness danced along the wall, lit only by my light.

The drawings and paintings here grew more familiar. Hebrew words painted in small figures. A seven-pronged lampstand, like the one in the Temple in Jerusalem. Had I found the section of the cavern dedicated to the Jews?

A lampstand.

I held my light aloft, until the gold leaf painted onto the lampstand seemed to glow with its own flame. The language above it was not Hebrew, but the lampstand surely was. I traced each of the seven branches with my gaze, followed the center shaft downward.

The base was oddly shaped. Not wide and stabilizing as it should be, but pointed. Like a spike that would drive it into the earth.

Like a finger pointing downward.

My heart picked up and I licked my lips against the dusty dryness.

Beneath the painted lampstand, an ordinary chest, unmarked and simple, nestled among a stack of golden bowls. I cast aside my lamp, dove for the chest, and knelt before it, fingers trembling.

Perhaps there was still time to make this happen.

The chest had no lock, no latch even. Could it be this simple?

I hesitated. What if it was filled with vipers? Poisoned air? Some other horrible death I could not imagine?

With a deep breath, caught and held in my chest, I lifted the lid.

A shriek at my back sent my heart into my throat and exploded lights behind my eyes.

"What are you doing?"

I dropped the lid. Swiveled. Blinked against the lamp between myself and a solitary figure.

Kamillah.

CHAPTER EIGHT

KAMILLAH

*K*amillah tried to breathe, tried to swallow against the crushing dread.

Misha stood beneath the curse with wide eyes and a dropped jaw, as if she were the one who was mad.

He jumped to his feet, took a step toward her.

She backed away. Better to get farther from him, from the words.

"You followed me?" He issued the words through clenched teeth, fists at his sides.

"I—I wanted to help—"

"Help?" Misha advanced on her again.

She slid backward, hands behind her to feel for obstacles.

"You are going to get me caught!"

She shook her head. Her lips felt numb. "I was careful. They didn't see me."

"I don't need your help."

With his defiant words, a bit of her old self returned. "You certainly needed it up there." She lifted her eyes to where the temple spread far above them.

Misha raked a hand through his short-cropped dark hair and growled. "You were a convenient distraction at the right time, but I could have done it alone." His eyes bore into hers, then he waved a hand of dismissal and turned back to the wall.

"Wait!"

The growl again. That little sound in his throat he always made when frustrated.

"Have you not read the words?" She pointed above his head, to the black-etched pictorials above the Hebrew lampstand.

He glanced up, then shrugged.

"You can't read it, can you? Haven't learned Egyptian Demotic?"

Those eyes again, dark and angry. "It wasn't considered important to my education."

She bit back an angry reply. "Well, it was important to mine. And I can tell you that everything on the floor below that lampstand has been cursed."

He blinked, scowled, but seemed to believe her. "What does it say?"

She laughed but the sound was harsh. "All the gold in this cavern could not induce me to repeat the words."

He seemed to consider them, and she pressed into his hesitation. "Misha, please. Leave with me now, before—"

"You know nothing about it, Kamillah. I must find the piece."

She knew that desperation. It was the same desperation that had driven her under this temple. Did she truly wish to abandon her cause now?

"Why are you here, Kamillah?"

"I told you—"

"You are not here to help me."

She must make him believe it. Must make him trust her.

He huffed in her direction and turned away. "I will count to twelve before I open this chest. Out of respect for you and your fear. If you run, you can probably reach the steps." A note of amusement crept into his voice. "Perhaps you can outrun your gods."

Her blood surged. "Must you always make light of everything, Misha-aku?"

He swiveled toward her, covered the distance between them in an instant, brought his face close to hers. The golden flecks in his brown eyes were barely visible in the shadows. Or had they darkened in his anger?

"Is that what you think? That this"—he spread his hands to take in the cavern—"that it is some sort of game to me?"

She looked away. "I—"

He stood even closer. "That *you* are some sort of game to me?"

Her breath caught. "Misha—"

"My mother is dying."

Of course. He wanted the fabled piece for his mother. Not for any political gain. Or anything that involved her. She should have known. Her own deceit mocked her in the face of his love for Lydia.

"Get out, Kamillah. I will get what I came for and you will not stop me."

He was finished with her. Turned back to the little chest that held some manner of disaster for him.

She should run, as he suggested.

But there was no outrunning the gods. She had learned that long ago.

She skimmed cold fingers over the pouch secreted beneath her robe. She was going to fail this task.

And there was no outrunning Zahir, either.

Indecision rooted her to the stone floor.

Misha lifted the chest's lid.

Silence.

His wide shoulders bent over the chest. The sheen of his skin, his muscled arms, glowed from the small lamp beside him. The corded tightness of his neck, the dampness just above the neckline of his tunic, all stood out as though in relief.

Did this increased awareness come for everyone just before they died?

But then he was lifting something wrapped in rough fabric, lifting it reverently from the chest. Sucking in a breath.

She fought for air as well, but for a different reason. The gods were pressing in on her, squeezing her.

He turned, held it aloft. The wonder in his eyes belonged to a child, to a boy seeing magic for the very first time.

"I—I cannot believe that it was truly here." He glanced back at the chest. "Simply sitting here, not buried, not hidden."

She dared not speak the reason. If only he could read it, written above his head.

The Nehushtan was a wriggling worm on the hook of the gods.

"Misha, we must leave. Before it is too late." Zahir's strict instructions warred with her humanity. How could she leave him here, under that curse? He was not the shallow and selfish would-be mage she once thought, and she cared for him, even if she would never admit it.

He stood, still cradling the fabric-wrapped object. "It is smaller than I imagined."

She could see only the top of it, the sinewy head of a bronze snake, coiled around a central shaft, but the entire piece was shorter than his forearm.

"There is time for wondering later. Come!"

But it was already too late. The vibration under her feet was slight but unmistakable.

Misha glanced at her, as if to ask if she felt it.

The dust and smoke of the cavern choked her. Powdery stone sifted from the roof far above them and fell like an ashy curtain between them, catching evil glints of lamplight.

Misha walked toward her slowly, his glance flicking left and right. He held the Nehushtan like a babe in his arms.

Another rumble, this one stronger. Stone amphorae tumbled from their perches and shattered. Piled treasure slid and shifted.

His eyes widened. "Earthquake!"

Yes, yes, and only the beginning. Did he not see?

He transferred his treasure to under one arm, grabbed her hand with his free one. "This place is coming down!"

They ran for the wide steps at the other end of the cavern, but another surge rocked them from their feet.

Kamillah's elbow slammed the stone floor and the breath exploded from her chest.

Everywhere the cavern was collapsing around them. Precious objects slid and flowed and flattened like water seeking its own level.

Misha hovered over her. His gaze ran the length of her body. "Are you hurt?"

She shook her head, grabbed his arm for support, and climbed to her feet.

The dust in the air thickened impossibly.

Smoke.

They half-stumbled, half-ran toward the entrance. A pool of fire, an inferno too large to be the brazier she had seen on the way in, blazed ahead.

Misha pulled her to his side, his free arm firm around her waist as they circled the flames.

The jug of oil that fed the brazier had toppled and cracked. The oil that was left burned along the stones. The fire lapped it like a starving beast.

The few paces to the steps that led to fresh air seemed a Roman mile. Her blood pounded with the beat of a hundred god-fearing generations of her people.

The earth roared. The bellow of a herd of oxen, of rocks thrown from heaven. Of the gods of the underworld, Osiris, Anubis, and Thoth, wrestling beneath their feet.

And the stairs collapsed.

Sucked downward into nothingness. The lintel of support above the entry followed. It cracked down the middle and plunged into the chasm.

The wide space where she had paused to take in the cavern when she first followed Misha vanished, replaced by a pile of ruinous rock.

And then silence.

She turned on Misha and beat her fists against his chest. "I told you! Why did you not listen? We will die here among your treasures, our eyes eaten by worms while we watch!"

It was only part of the curse. She would not speak the rest.

Misha trapped her wrists against his chest with one hand. Pulled her to him. "I will not let that happen, Kamillah."

Her frantic heart slowed, but she shook her head. "Even you are powerless here."

As if to punctuate her words, the flames exhausted their supply and blinked out, leaving them in darkness like a heavy blanket of suffocation.

She dragged in a desperate breath of stale air, as if she could fill her lungs and store it against the future.

All around them rocks and jars, chests and vases still shifted and cracked.

But they were blind now. The roof could collapse upon them and they would not see it coming.

No, that would not happen. It would be too merciful a death, and the gods had much worse planned for them.

A sticky wetness warmed under her hands, still pinned to Misha's chest. She pulled away. "Are you—are you bleeding?"

He hesitated. "Yes, perhaps."

"Misha!"

"A cut across my chest. Nothing serious."

Even without light she could hear that teasing tone creep into his words. She resisted the desire to beat against him again.

"You are a fool, Misha." The words came out harsher than she intended and were met with silence. "Have you ever heeded a warning in your life?"

"Reza once warned me to stay away from you."

Reza. Too protective. She huffed and turned away, even though he could not see her face.

"Don't be angry, Kamillah. There must be a way out of this place."

"And you will find it in the dark?"

"I could find a black cat in the dark."

She smiled despite her anger, glad he could not see it. "Well then, where shall we start?"

Her question was met with silence.

"Misha?"

Nothing.

Had the gods spirited him away to a horrible fate so soon?

"Misha!"

She cast about with her hands in the darkness, finding only empty space.

"I am here." His voice was fainter, farther.

She followed it and found him, leaning against broken stone. "Your injury—"

"Just needed to rest a moment. I will be fine. We should search for another way out."

She could feel his struggle to stand under her hand and pushed back against him gently. "No. We should wait. Zahir knows that we are here. He will—"

"We? Zahir knows that *we* are here?"

Kamillah exhaled and closed her eyes against her own stupidity.

"He sent you? Why?" Misha's voice pitched higher. "Did he not believe I could find it?"

"No—he knew—"

"What?" He wrapped his hand around her wrist. "Tell me the truth."

She wrested her arm from his grip. "'Use a thief,' Zahir said. 'Never trust one.'"

"So you came to make certain I would not steal it for myself?"

If that was what he chose to believe, she would let him. Better he not know what the pouch at her waist held. What Zahir's plans for him held, and her part in it. Not now, when it would make no difference.

"Or perhaps it was you who told Zahir I was not to be trusted, eh?" His voice hardened into anger. "And I am all the more the fool for trusting *you*."

CHAPTER NINE

MISHA

*T*he pain in my chest came partly from the gash that had ripped apart my tunic and skin. But the fiercer sting lodged inside, at the site of Kamillah's betrayal.

I held the Nehushtan against myself, as though she would take it from me even now and disappear into the darkness.

"Misha—you must understand—"

"It makes no difference. What you do is nothing to me."

My words were met with inky silence. Was she capable of feeling hurt? She had made it clear she needed nothing from me, not even friendship.

The taste of grit and smoke was like ashes in my mouth. "All that matters is that we get out of here." Yes, and that Zahir believe the Nehushtan was never found, or at least was lost. And that I escaped in time to meet the trading caravan heading back to Nisa in the morning. Neither seemed possible now.

Kamillah shifted in the darkness. "It seems unlikely another passage would be easy to find, even if we had light." The practical scholar's tone had emerged in her voice. No more talk of broken trust, apparently.

"We'll make a circuit of the cavern. Perhaps walls or treasure have shifted to reveal a way out."

She groaned. "Always the optimist."

"Better than to live without hope."

"Do you speak of me?" Anger now. "Because you know nothing about me."

"And why is that, Kamillah? Perhaps because you will tell nothing of yourself. You prefer shadows and hiding. I should think this place suited you well."

Strange argument without faces. I could not read her in the darkness, could not see whether her sensitive mouth was downturned in anger or soft with hurt. Whether those dark eyes that always seemed to see into the truth of everything flashed with fury, or if tears sparkled on the lashes. Did she push her hair behind her ear, as she always did when self-conscious? Or raise her chin and fold her arms across her chest?

"You know nothing about me," she said again.

Ah, the voice. The voice gave her away. Quiet and focused toward the floor.

I cursed the shades of black and gray and deepest blue that kept her face hidden. "Then tell me. Tell me why you serve Zahir when it is clear you hate him. Why you are here in this cavern with me." I found her arms, limp at her sides, and clutched her elbow with my free hand. "Are you my friend or my enemy, Kamillah of Alexandria?"

She did not answer at once.

I felt her inhalation, felt the beginning of a confession.

Her voice, when it came, was a whisper. "I do not know."

I dropped her arm. Turned away from her. Turned toward the coldness that grew in my body. She did not find me worthy of her trust. Very well, then.

"I am going to walk around the cavern. Come with me if you wish." I shifted the wrapped Nehushtan to my left hand. My fingers were growing numb. Blood loss, perhaps. But the cavern was cooling rapidly as well. Did night fall so soon?

"I thought that piece was supposed to heal. Will it not repair your wound?"

I paused. The idea had not occurred to me. I pulled the fabric away from the piece and held it aloft, invisible in the darkness. I felt nothing but the pain and the blood. "Ironic, I suppose. It has to be looked upon to achieve healing. Now that I have it, and need it, I cannot see it."

I rewrapped it and held it under my arm, leaving my right hand free to search the shifting rubble as I walked. I could feel Kamillah follow.

"Let me hold it, Misha. You cannot keep it safe and search for a way out."

I snorted. "Thank you, but I think not."

Silence again.

"I suppose you think I should have heeded your curse, left it where I found it." A skidding of pebbles, or perhaps the slide of a hoard of coins, echoed my words. I tried to sense a draft in the unknowable space around me but felt nothing. "But I have my own curses, you know. Breathing down on me from the night sky, flitting at the edges of my vision."

Her small cry turned me to her in concern.

"What do you mean, Misha? What do you see in the sky?"

I turned to her, closed the space between until I could feel the heat of her body. "What do I see? I see what everyone sees—that hideous star."

"But you spoke of curses. Of seeing things—"

"What difference does it make?"

"Please, Misha." Her voice trembled with a hint of something—fear, perhaps—weakness I had never witnessed in her. "Please, tell me the truth."

The truth. It was rarely a commodity shared between us.

"The star. It speaks to me."

I heard her quick intake of breath.

"What does it say?"

No ridicule, no disbelief entered her voice. Only a dread-filled question.

"It told me to leave Nisa. I thought for a while it also told me I would be destroyed by leaving, but now—now I think perhaps those were other voices."

"Voices at the edges of your vision?"

I hesitated. Certainly she would find the truth to be madness. "Yes."

She pulled away from me, and I sensed she turned her back.

"I see them, too." Her voice was tiny and low like an evening dove.

Words fled from me. Did we truly see the same apparitions? Hear the same voices?

"What do they say to you?"

Her answer was long in coming. "They say nothing. They only stand in the way."

"In the way of what?"

"Of my leaving."

I shook my head, invisible though the gesture might be. "I don't understand. Leaving what?"

"The palace. Nisa. I have long desired to return to my homeland. But he has placed them in my way and will not let me go until he has used me for whatever he needs."

"Zahir." Somehow, it explained much and nothing at all. "Kamillah, you must resist. They can be resisted—even fought—I have seen it. Do not let Zahir reduce you to his pet. You are strong and brilliant and capable of so much more."

Her laugh was brief and disbelieving. "If that is true, you are the only who sees it. The rest of the magi tolerate me at best."

"Ridiculous! I have met no one who does not respect you, who does not walk in awe of your abilities and your knowledge."

Her breath released more slowly now, like a soft sigh in the breeze. "You are kind, Misha. But you see through blinded eyes."

I said nothing to this. We both knew what she meant. My admiration of her had been written more plainly than the circle of the zodiac in the sky.

"So what will you do?"

"I am here, aren't I?"

Yes, that answered my question. She was in this cavern at Zahir's command. Spying on me, perhaps stealing from me. What else? Did she and Zahir even intend to let me live? "You trust him more than you can believe in me."

"Trust! How can you speak of it? I trust no one, Misha. Nothing. Except myself and my ability to find a way home on my own."

"Even if it means doing the bidding of Zahir."

"Yes, even that! I know you cannot understand—you have never yielded to another's demands. Even your own father, who loves you more than life."

"Do not speak of my father!" I barked the words, tasting the sting that she felt as he did, that I was not worth trusting. That I was an obstinate fool.

"Well, if I am not to speak of your father, then you will keep silent on my relationship with Zahir!"

"Relationship? Exactly what does he require of you, Kamillah?"

She said nothing, leaving me to imagine.

"I thought you were stronger than this. Perhaps I was wrong. You will never let yourself believe, so you will always be alone."

My harsh words did not have time to be returned before another horrific sound—like the rending of the mighty earth itself—shuddered through the cavern. The floor rippled and tilted. Thunder cracked beneath my feet, then a sudden *whoosh* of coldness and air and fear sucked at my chest.

I reached for Kamillah. Shouted her name above the din. Heard nothing.

Two steps forward and my toes tipped over emptiness.

The floor had given way, exactly where she had been standing.

"Kamillah!" I waved an arm through the space, as though she might hover impossibly above the yawning mouth.

I dropped to my belly, laid the Nehushtan aside, and reached down into the hole with both arms. Stone scraped at the gash on my chest and stole my breath. My fingers touched nothing. I heard nothing now but the gentle slide of pebbles. "Kamillah!"

No desperate grasp of my fingers, no panting breath, no moans of one injured yet still breathing.

She had been swallowed by the earth, as though she never existed.

I lay on my belly still but turned my head toward the back of the cavern, toward the Demotic script on the wall where I found the Nehushtan.

She had never told me the entirety of the curse, but I suspected I knew another part of it now.

And what could one fool do in the face of the wrath of gods?

CHAPTER TEN

ZAHIR

"*H*it him again."

Zahir turned away from the strung-up piece of man-flesh, toward the sunlight streaming through the front window of the mud-brick home at the ragged edge of Yathrib. With a narrow index finger, he stroked the daintily painted vines on the glazed mug that held his wine, then took a sip. He grimaced. He had helped himself to the wine after paying the poor homeowner a fortune to use his empty house for the afternoon. As the sun sank lower and the soldier refused cooperation, he had grown thirsty and not a little irritable.

Sami drove a fist into the soldier's ribs for perhaps the tenth time. Zahir had lost count.

He swiveled to examine the multicolored bruises on the soldier's face.

"Still you will not speak?"

Arms bound above his head, the soldier blinked one eye. The other was swollen shut, a fat clot welling up under the skin and purpling the cheekbone. "You. Will kill. Me. Either way."

Zahir could not deny the truth of this. He would pay any price to hear whatever truth lay behind the rumors.

A new king on the throne. A usurper to take the place of Phraates.

Zahir would have treated the rumors as nothing more than fable if it weren't for that cursed star, screaming the same message at him every night.

And if Phraates were displaced, what of Zahir? He had carefully composed the king's utter dependence on him. His thirty ghostly brothers were only part of the way Zahir kept him bound.

When Zahir returned with the Nehushtan, he would "cure" Phraates of the visitations he had engineered and convince the king that only Zahir could wield the artifact's power. He must have the Nehushtan to ensure the star's threatened world-ruler could not steal the position that was rightfully his.

But if these rumors came to pass, he could not be assured of success.

He leaned into the soldier's swelling face, squinted at the broken vessels in the whites of the man's eyes, shot through with lightning streaks of fiery red. The sun inched lower in the west, fell upon the hideous face with a beneficent warmth, and the soldier lifted his head as if to receive its blessing.

Zahir stepped between the soldier and the window and cast a shadow over him. "You stink." He spat the words at the man, not that he would care. The heat of the afternoon sun brought out the odors of sweat and blood and all manner of bodily excretions that occurred under torture.

The soldier remained silent. He had long ago given up insisting that he knew nothing, that his involvement in the whispered rumors was nothing more than the idle talk of bored men.

Zahir cursed. Perhaps it was the truth. Or perhaps—what was even more dangerous—the rumors were true, and this soldier was part of a rebellious faction so strong and so committed to their cause that he was willing to die denying it.

Zahir would have much preferred a confession and the names of a paltry few who had hopes of a coup. Silence left too many unanswered questions.

He snatched up his rod and struck the next blow himself. But the rod's first impact and the next accomplished nothing but flying blood and spittle, and the cracking of a few more ribs.

Zahir swirled the contents of his pretty cup and watched the light catch the inferior wine, a color similar to the rising purple-red blooming across the soldier's chest.

If disloyalty to Phraates lay within the army camp, it had to originate somewhere, have its nucleus within one person. Reza? Did he have designs on the throne?

The Chakkiym were never to be trusted. Perhaps one of them.

The grinning face of Misha-aku bobbed in his thoughts. Part trained monkey and part Chakkiym. Was he more loyal to his cursed father's cause than he admitted? He could be a powerful mage one day—the potential was certainly there. But his Jew blood ran thick, and his loyalty could not be assumed. It was good that Zahir had sent Kamillah to retrieve the Nehushtan and leave Misha behind. Anyone, even a mage, with that much connection to the Chakkiym should not be trusted with anything so important.

And Kamillah... The restless conflict that always accompanied thoughts of her soured his stomach. He could love her, or he could use her. But not both. He learned long ago that love and power cannot coexist. He would choose power.

Zahir took a final sip of the wine, then tossed the remaining half cup at the face of the whimpering soldier.

He screamed with the sting of it. Zahir huffed a brief laugh.

Yes, Kamillah was no more to be trusted than Misha. She too had the potential for great power, and as soon as she figured out how to turn it against him, he would lose his hold on her.

He was still envisioning her lovely face, twisted with fear under his control, when the first wave of shifting rock erupted under his feet. The mud-brick house came down around his ears.

CHAPTER ELEVEN

KAMILLAH

*D*arkness pressed upon Kamillah like a black sea, deep and cold. She tried to move a limb, open an eye, but all was muffled, leaded, heavy.

Again—just a slight movement—how long had it been?—a finger twitch, then her arm. Eyelids fluttering, opening to more darkness. The smell of rotting flesh.

Something jagged poked at her shoulder blades. She shifted away from it but still lay upon chilled stone. The throbbing in her head, in her ears, was an audible drumbeat. She struggled to a sitting position.

A cave-in. She had been arguing with Misha, and then the horrific noise and the falling, and then nothing. How long had she lain here?

She stretched her arms and legs, flexed her ankles. Soreness but nothing broken, amazingly. Her right wrist had taken the worst of it, and she winced at the flexing, but it would heal.

But her head—a gentle probing revealed warm wetness on the back of her skull, her hair already matted with blood.

"Misha!"

The call came out like a half-strangled cry.

"Misha!"

Had he left her?

No, regardless of their trading angry words, he would not have left.

They were always at odds, but they were both rebels at heart, connected by their refusal to do what was expected. Besides, he was not capable of abandoning even an enemy.

Had he fallen into the hole with her?

She waved her arms along the surface of the floor, shifted to hands and knees, and crawled in random directions, calling his name, feeling for the warmth of him. Her wrist gave out under her and she tried to use only the left for support.

Why had she stayed? She should have taken the Nehushtan, left Misha asleep and unharmed in the cave as she had planned, then escaped to Zahir, fulfilling their bargain. Now Zahir would never release her, never allow her to go home. If she ever escaped this pit.

But even as she berated herself for foolishness, the desperation to find Misha grew. Did he live?

She needed to be more systematic in her search. Even if Misha was not here, she must find a way out. She tried to ignore the dizzy waves of nausea. The head injury would grow no better if she rested. Better to push on.

On her feet now, she made a careful circuit of her pit, feeling for tunnels or drafts and finding nothing but a floor littered with chunks of rock and ragged walls of rock. How could the cave have yet another cave underneath with no way out? The rotten smell of death assured her that something living had once found its way in—could she not find her way out? The warmth of her blood ran in a trickle down her back now. She pulled her ripped gown closer to stop its flow on her skin but dared not probe the wound with her hand again. She needed her wits about her.

Clearly, her hopes that the cavern above would be one of the Centers of Power had been misplaced. Her studies had revealed that special places existed—locations where heaven and earth came close, touched each other in unseen ways, and opened gateways of power for those who understood. One of the places could supply what she needed to break the invisible bonds Zahir used to keep her enslaved—the whispering and threatening apparitions at the edges of her vision. It was why she had come on this journey, why she had agreed to follow Misha into the cave.

"Misha..."

Where had he gone? He did not fall through with her, that much she had discovered. If he did not abandon her, it left only one possibility. He was still above but deaf to her cries.

How far above?

The darkness was total. She had no sense of depth, only of width now that she had traveled the circumference of her dungeon several times.

But surely if she had fallen very far, she would have sustained worse injuries. Or be dead.

She breathed in a deep and dusty breath. It was time to stop calling out for someone who would not come to her rescue and find her own way out. She lived life alone, and she could take care of herself.

First, the wrist.

She crawled until she found what she needed—a sliver of rock the length of her hand and somewhat flat. She found a rip near the bottom of her robe and widened it, tearing a strip as long as she could from the edge of the fabric. Her wrist stabbed, watering her eyes for a moment, but she blinked away the pain and ripped the final threads, then used the flat rock to fasten a splint to stabilize her wrist.

Now, the rocks.

How long would it take to build a pile large enough to climb out of her hole? Did enough rocks even exist? And if she did get back to the cavern, what then?

Asking questions was pointless. She set her attention to the rocks, choosing a spot at the edge of the pit, then pushing, rolling, and lifting every chunk of rock and piece of the fallen cavern floor from above to the central pile. The work raised more dust and burned her eyes. She tried to work with her eyes closed, since she could see nothing in the darkness, but it made her feel even more vulnerable.

Vulnerable. Yes, that was the condition she tried most to avoid, wasn't it?

It had kept her apart from the Kasdim who barely tolerated having a woman among them, apart from Misha who had never shown her derision but left her unsteady with his teasing wit and unbounded energy. Even apart from the rocklike Reza, who would have protected her if she asked for it but who did not understand her.

Since her first days in Nisa, she had kept her distance, never trusting, always testing. Her father had willingly given her to Caesar Augustus to be a political gift to King Phraates, just as the king's slave-turned-wife had been. Kamillah had spent the years ignoring men who seemed universally bent on exploitation and following her ambition, which had served her well.

The rock pile grew, but the supply was getting low. She heaved and pushed a large flat slate toward the pile but could not lift it.

Well, she had gotten her wish. She was truly alone.

The words of the curse on the wall burrowed into her soul. Were the gods to make an end of her in this pit, then?

The pile was as large as it would be. She climbed unsteadily to the top of it, braced her legs as wide as she dared, and reached above her head for a lip of paving stone, a handhold, anything to pull herself to the next level. She clawed nothing but empty air.

Her wrist throbbed, her eyes burned, but it was her hollowed heart that finally got the best of her, bringing her to a hopeless heap on her rock pile and threatening to cave her courage.

If she were to die alone, a victim of the gods and this pit, then so be it.

But the thought that she would go unmourned, it stuck in her throat and ached in her chest.

Back in Nisa, she was feared, disliked, or dismissed, but she never let anyone know the pain she felt at the isolation.

If by some miracle she escaped, she would not go on as she had. Untrusting, unwilling to open herself even to friendship. In this, Zahir would have less power over her, even if his demons still did his bidding in trapping her.

No, if she escaped this pit, she would take some chances with her heart, instead of merely her life.

A moment later, her resolve mocked her and her rock pile collapsed.

CHAPTER TWELVE

MISHA

The Nehushtan banged against the gash in my chest but I kept pushing forward. Toward the shard of light half-choked with dust. Kamillah's cave-in had shifted something—rocks, wall, treasures— I didn't know what, but I was scrambling toward the light, the treasure strapped to my chest with a makeshift sling tied from my robe to leave my hands free.

I had wasted little time at the edge of the cavern that had opened beneath Kamillah. A few minutes of frantic calling, reaching, trying to find a way to climb down to her yielded no sound from the pit. Not a breath, not a moan answered my hoarse yells. Her only chance was for me to find a way out, to find help to get her out of whatever the gods had sucked her into.

Did she still live? Our last words had been in anger. The idea that she could die, without knowing how I felt, propelled me as if the gods themselves chased me out of that cave. *"You will always be alone,"* I had said to her. But it was I who would always be alone, because I was worth little more.

How had it come to this? I had undertaken this quest to help my mother, to impress my father, to please my mentor, to outdo my rival, to support my best friend, even perhaps a little bit to win Kamillah. Everyone wanted something from me. Even the star and the whispery voices at the edges of my sight pressured me to do their bidding. Every part of me, every action I took, was for others—to be seen by others as worthy of something. Of anything.

And what had all my scrabbling for love and admiration gotten me? Trapped in a cave, with Kamillah badly hurt or worse.

I swore under my breath. If I survived this, if we *both* survived this, things would be different. I would make my own choices.

I heaved rocks from my path, but the slice of light above me barely grew. I was close, then. I climbed a pile of rubble, trying to get an idea of which direction I climbed. It seemed to be where the wide staircase had been. Did I scramble up its remains, toward the tunnel I'd descended? But there would be no light where the winding tunnel had ended.

At last my fingers pushed into the crack itself, out into the heat of the day.

The sun on my skin had never been so welcome.

I could do nothing to widen the gap with my hands. I lay on my back and kicked both heels against the stone.

Again and again I kicked, yelling curses at the effort, until my feet were bloody within my sandals.

The stone gave way with another rumble and hail of rock shards.

I covered my head with my arms and waited for the death blow, but the raining of stones ceased and now I could hear the chaos in the streets of Yathrib.

Somehow I had climbed high enough to reach an outer wall of the temple. The street lay before me, slaves and nobility, animals and children, churning like foam upon the sea. The narrow channel I had managed to cleave in the wall would barely allow me to pass. Its jagged edges would likely tear me apart. I rocked back onto my heels, and my supporting hand touched something rough and textiled.

The beam of sunlight revealed a rug. Woven tightly in jeweled colors and delicately thin, with four golden tassels at its corners. I snatched it up, wrapped it around my body, and wriggled through the hole, my carpet aiding and protecting my escape as though it had appeared by magic to do so. I pulled myself through the narrow channel and tumbled to the hard-packed dirt.

At the end of the street a house burned—from an overturned oil lamp perhaps, or a cooking fire that had overflowed its borders when the earthquake struck.

I got to my feet, gave a cursory glance at the wound on my chest. It was deep, but it would wait.

I needed rope. And I needed help.

I grabbed the first man to run past me. "Please, there is a girl—"

He yanked his arm from my grasp. "We are all searching!" His last words were lost to me, as he was already running toward the burning house.

My thoughts spun. I must get back to Kamillah. Another quake would entomb her in that pit.

The market. Surely someone there would have rope to spare.

The Nehushtan bobbed against my chest again as I ran around the corner to the front of the temple. The pain slowed me, and the sling was unreliable. The fleeting thought that I must choose between the piece and Kamillah's safety was only that—a fleeting thought. I would stash the piece somewhere until she was safe, but if I had to give it up, so be it.

I darted inside the temple. A glance revealed that the priests had fled. I yanked the knotted fabric from the back of my neck, found a large statue of Isis in the corner, and jammed the piece behind it.

Wait... Now that I could *see* it, I could use the piece to heal my own wound and better help Kamillah. I pulled it out from behind Isis and peeled away the fabric covering to get my first look.

Bronze scales formed a thick snake wrapped around a wooden shaft. The wood was somehow preserved, though splintering, and the bronze felt cold to the touch.

I waited for the pain to cease, for the skin to mesh, for the blood to dry.

I felt nothing.

I could waste no more time. I returned the piece to its hiding place and sprinted from the dim temple onto its portico. Was it only a few hours ago that I hid here, waiting for my chance? The sun was setting behind the dusty houses of Yathrib, but it seemed to me that a day and a night should have passed.

"Misha-aku!"

I searched the crowded street for the one who shouted my name.

Zahir.

He drew up near my feet, his dark eyes stormy. "Where is it? Did you find it?"

"Kamillah is trapped down there! She fell into a pit and I cannot reach her."

Zahir's eyes flicked toward the temple's interior but registered no surprise that she had been with me.

I slapped his arm as I sprinted toward the market square. "We must find some rope. Come, I need your help!"

Whatever his relationship with Kamillah, and his designs for me, he appeared willing to help. Within a few minutes we had secured a sturdy coil of rope and a torch from a Yathrib merchant still packing up his wares and had run back toward the temple wall where I emerged.

"Can we not simply go in the other way?" Zahir's voice grated against my impatience.

"It is blocked. This is the fastest way to her. Come!"

I grabbed Zahir's diviner's rod and knocked the blunt end against the pieces of rock still poking into the opening. He yelped a protest, but the rock gave way more easily from the outside, and I soon returned his rod. I dove through the hole.

Zahir hesitated in the opening.

"Zahir! The rocks will shift and kill her!"

With a grunt he followed me through, rod in hand, and we half-slid, half-scrambled down the pile of rubble. The torch revealed what I had suspected—the great cavern was in ruins, but its treasures were ripe for plunder by anyone who breached the wall as we had.

I ignored Zahir's intake of breath at the wealth.

"Did you find it? Where is the Nehushtan?"

I growled under my breath. "I found it, yes. But it was lost in the cave-in. It is somewhere here, under all of this mess. You are welcome to search for it—after we get Kamillah!"

"So noble." His tone was honeyed but sarcastic. "Perhaps you do not know your lovely Kamillah as well as you think."

I continued down the slanting pile, reached level ground at last, and pushed toward where I remembered Kamillah's pit to be, all the while carefully waving the torch to reveal any unexpected fissures. "I know you keep her on a leash and sent her here to follow me to ensure I would not cross you."

"Follow you?" Zahir's laugh echoed from the cavern walls. "Is that what she told you?"

I slowed and turned to him, a fierce and unspoken question in my eyes.

He laughed again. "I have little use for you once it's been found, Misha. A first-level mage who cannot hold his dignity in front of his peers."

"You expect me to believe Kamillah followed me here to kill me?"

"Kill you? No. I don't think even I could convince her to murder. But you would have had a wonderful sleep down here among the treasures, and not awakened for several days. Long after our caravan had moved on."

She knew why I wanted the Nehushtan. Why I *needed* it. And yet she would have taken it from me to give it to Zahir?

I returned to my search for the pit where she had fallen. "It matters little now. The piece is buried somewhere, and my only concern is in retrieving Kamillah."

"Then I say again—how very noble."

The torchlight played over a huge gap in the flooring. "Here!"

I flattened myself to my belly and waved the torch down into the hole. "Kamillah! Kamillah, can you hear me?"

The voice that returned was weak but infinitely welcome. "Misha?"

I breathed again, a rush of relief, and dropped my head for a moment against my forearm. "Are you hurt?"

"No. Some bruises only. But it is too deep to climb out."

"I've brought rope. And Zahir is with me. We will get you out."

It took only a few minutes to drop her the end of the rope, instruct her in how to secure it around her waist and under her arms, to anchor the end, and to haul her out.

She climbed over the lip, staggered to her feet, and embraced me. "I feared you had abandoned me."

My single word was a whisper against her ear. "Never."

She pulled away to examine the cut on my chest. "You must get—"

"A pity the Nehushtan was buried in the earthquake, or I could have used it to repair us both."

She searched my eyes for only a moment, then nodded. "Yes, a pity."

"We should get you back to camp. One of the healers can tend to us there."

I left Zahir to handle the torch and supported Kamillah on the way out, though it seemed to mainly be her wrist that was injured. No matter. It was a good excuse to keep my arm around her waist.

Zahir led us out, tossed the torch, and the three of us wove through Yathrib back to where our party camped at the desert's beginning.

Reza met us at the edge of camp, his frantic gaze playing over my bloody tunic and Kamillah's disheveled appearance. "Were you trapped?" He reached for Kamillah, pulled her from me. "Where are you hurt?"

"I am well, Reza. It is Misha who requires attention."

Zahir allowed the three of us to move toward the healer's tent, but he tossed a threat in my direction as we did. "Meet me within the hour, Misha-aku. We have things to discuss."

Reza and I both insisted the healer tend to Kamillah first. He checked her over carefully and declared her wrist to have no fracture, only pain that would soon heal. When he turned to me he dismissed the others, but Kamillah shook her head. "I want to stay until I am sure Misha is well."

I turned my head from the healer's ministrations and beckoned Kamillah closer.

She pulled away from Reza to join me.

"Kamillah, the words I spoke earlier—"

She held up a palm. "It is better forgotten, things we both said."

Her words should have brought relief, but a serious, almost dismissive, tone entered her voice. Whatever closeness had been growing between us had disappeared amongst the cursed treasures, angry arguments, and shattering rock.

Reza slipped an arm around her waist and frowned at her. "You should rest."

She leaned her head against his shoulder briefly and smiled up at him. "Perhaps I will."

The healer finished his work on my chest and left within minutes of Kamillah, leaving Reza and me alone.

His eyes held the question his lips did not speak.

I nodded once and spoke softly. "I found it."

He exhaled and closed his eyes. "Will it—does it—?"

I shrugged, then winced at the pain. "Obviously not for me. But perhaps there is more we do not know."

"We could ask the Chakkiym."

"No. It is too great a risk to bring it here to the camp, to arouse curiosity. I must take it back to Nisa for my mother immediately. When you return with your troops, we will be ready to help." Reza's numbers had been diminished by the plagued water, but thanks to Kamillah's medical knowledge, not as badly as they could have been.

"Help...with the Nehushtan?"

Ah, then he wanted it, too. Not to see it destroyed to keep its power from Zahir and Phraates, but to aid his own cause. I shrugged. "My father will know what to do."

"You will leave tonight?"

I eyed the entrance to the tent. Zahir awaited my report. The man had powers to see beyond the spoken word. It would be better to avoid him altogether.

And Kamillah? The warmth in her eyes for Reza was unmistakable. I knew when I was beaten. And even if she preferred me, I would not take her from him.

No, my path was clear, as it had been since I left Nisa.

I am coming, Mother. Hold on, but a few more days.

CHAPTER THIRTEEN

MISHA

*T*he dark and spacious desert beckoned, with only a few flickering fires on the horizon to indicate the caravan that would lead me back to Nisa in the morning. With the Nehushtan safely strapped against my chest once more, I bent my head to the road out of Yathrib and steered my course away from my own encampment, where Kamillah and Reza would cover for me should Zahir come looking.

Though I had wished to avoid Zahir, in the end, I had needed to speak with him after all. Only a few minutes, and I kept my face in the shadows. A casual conversation about exactly where I believed the precious artifact to be buried in all that rubble, and how I believed I could lead Zahir directly to it if we returned under the temple with torches and muscle. When he found me missing, I needed him to have a reason to stay, a reason to delay that would allow me at least a day or two ahead of him. The smaller trading party I had found should move quickly back toward Nisa. As long as we were not met by bandits.

Besides the Nehushtan, I carried only my lightweight pouch into the silent sands. I brought little more than my clothing and my metal rings of illusion. If only I could pass through the danger of the desert as easily as I could make one metal ring appear to pass through the other.

My pouch was lighter still than when I arrived, as I had left my father's box of scrolls tucked beside the sleeping head of Gaspar before I left. Gaspar would know what to do with them, after he traveled north to Judea following his star.

Your star.

I pushed the words away. Not tonight.

Yathrib winked behind me now and the campfires ahead. I strode through shifting sand in the deep darkness that only the desert knew. It was the night of the new moon, and I blessed Sin for hiding his face and better hiding me.

A low sound carried to me on the breeze and raised the hair on my arms. A cool chuckle, full of condescension.

I slowed and searched the sky and the edges of my vision for night visitors.

But it was not the unearthly spirits that laughed at me.

Zahir.

Gliding out of the darkness so complete, he was nearly full upon me before I even saw his face. His face filled with loathing, etched with malice, twisted with disdain.

Why had I not thought to bring a weapon?

"Leaving us so soon, Misha? When we are on the verge of a discovery unlike any the world has seen?"

I backed away, my gaze trained on his eyes. "My mother is ill. As you know. I thought it best to return to her, in case I was needed—"

"I am certain *you* are not needed. But perhaps—" He pointed to the sling against my chest. "Perhaps you have something of far greater value than your miserable life?"

He knew.

Perhaps he had me followed. Perhaps his voices whispered my fate in his ear. It did not matter. Zahir knew, and he was going to kill me for it.

I clutched it to me, nevertheless. "You will not have it. Not until I've done what is needed."

A glint in the feeble starlight revealed a sword, held in his right hand. Did I have a chance to outrun him in the darkness?

Another glimmer to my left halted my flight. Had he brought others?

But Zahir's face turned in surprise as well.

The faint white flicker all but disappeared when I turned to it. A chill not borne of the desert night snaked across my skin.

"Ah, here they are." Zahir's voice was soothing, as one spoke to a child or a pet. "My Watchers. But they will do more than watch tonight."

Kamillah had spoken of her inability to get free of the spirit beings who came when Zahir summoned. Could they also trap me, until the point of Zahir's sword found me? I shuddered, repulsion rippling through me. I would prefer to have it end quickly than to be gripped by one of the specters that refused to be fully seen.

Summoning courage I did not feel, I turned on Zahir, pulled the sling from around my neck, and gripped the fabric-wrapped shaft. "I will break it into pieces if you set them upon me, Zahir. I swear to you I will do it."

Even in the blackness I saw a flicker of uncertainty in his eyes.

"What have you done?" He stared at my bundle. "Already you have broken it? It is too small—too small to be what I seek!"

Yes, I had wondered the same thing in the cave under the temple. The stories at my father's knee gave me visions of a large staff, set upright in the desert for thousands to look upon and be healed. Not this piece no longer than my arm.

"But perhaps—" His gaze shifted toward his left, lost to thought. "Perhaps this is what the words mean…"

"What words?"

He continued, but as if to himself. "Have I been a fool, then? Understood nothing?"

"That would not surprise me."

His momentary musing ended. His attention returned and he rushed me, murder in his eyes.

I flung the fabric from the Nehushtan and brandished it like a weapon. He would not dare strike his sword against it. And I yelled into the utter silence of the desert, the first thing to come into my mind. "If the One God gives this thing power, then you are not worthy of any power it holds!"

A silvery coldness, colder than the grave, swirled around my head. It burrowed into my ears and mouth and nostrils. I choked on the cold but did not let the shaft waver.

Most High God, give me strength to stand against them!

Alone in the desert with Zahir and his minions, and yet suddenly— not alone.

A rush like the beating of wings. A thick and salty warmth in the air, humid as the distant sea, cloying as sacrificial blood. The taste of metal in my mouth, like summer lightning and yet no lightning struck. My palms grew slick around the shaft and my breath shallowed.

A flourish of more of the silvery whiteness all around. Above my head, on either side, behind me. Tens of them. Perhaps a hundred.

They did not so much as arrive as simply *appear*. As though they had always been there, hovering, waiting, and then stepped through some invisible barrier in the air to make themselves known.

Zahir saw them, too. But the condescension was gone, replaced by terror.

He did not control them. They were not here at his bidding.

They were here for me. For my defense.

There in the desert sand and air and under the starlight they battled against Zahir's spirits in a silent, bloodless death match. Though we could see them, we heard nothing and stood with mouths agape as the celestial fought the underworld.

"How—?" Zahir's question lingered in the air. He turned a slow circle. "How have you done this?" His voice shook and his sword was half lowered to the ground.

I said nothing. I would not claim to have summoned my defense, but neither would I admit ignorance.

The voiceless battle raged. The weapons made no sound as they struck but flashed gold and orange like sparks from a smith's forge.

I pressed into Zahir's momentary weakness. "Do not think that I am powerless, Zahir." I waved the Nehushtan at the fantastic battle around us. "You have underestimated me too long."

I would make good my escape, but there was one more piece of business. "You will call off your demons from their hindrance of Kamillah. Leave her in peace."

At this Zahir seemed to come back to himself. The old light came into his eyes. "Who is the fool now? You think I can tell them what to do? Look at them! They do as they please. If they desire to trap Kamillah, there is nothing I can do about it!"

The hovering battle raged around our heads, the flickering silver-blue and silent crack of orange illuminating the night, making it impossible to tell which way the advantage went. Did all these beings truly battle on my behalf, either for or against me? It was heady stuff to take in.

There seemed to be less of them now, but where did the fallen lay? Could they be killed?

Zahir still stood apart, as though unwilling to come against me while my defenders hovered.

But I was eager to move. I circled behind him, waited for his gaze to stray heavenward. Darted forward and cracked the Nehushtan against his wrist.

Not hard enough to harm the artifact—but sharp enough to knock the sword from Zahir's hand. In his moment of shock I scooped it up, took three paces back, and pointed both toward his face.

Just that quickly, the ghostly battle ended.

Not in a victory, not with my defenders raising fists of triumph. It just blinked out, like a candle snuffed, like a heavy blanket dropped over a window.

If Zahir had doubts that the army had come to my defense, their sudden departure the moment I had the upper hand left doubts vanquished. His lips parted once more, and a breath of hatred escaped, but he said nothing.

"I am leaving, Zahir. Taking it with me. You can do nothing to stop me. As you have seen." I could not resist this last bit.

He blinked and sneered. "Go ahead. Take your worthless piece. It will do you no good, broken as it is."

Still aiming the sword at his belly, I tried to get a better look at the Nehushtan, but the darkness was too solid now that we were alone.

"You spoke of words—'this is what the words meant.'" I flourished the sword and took a step forward.

He shrugged, as though he did not care to keep his secret. "The writings. Ancient texts from the days of your father Moses. They have led me here."

"And?"

"And there were parts I did not understand. I thought perhaps—" He broke off and exhaled heavily.

"Speak it all, Zahir!"

"I thought there were three objects. Three pieces that held power.

This one for healing. But I think now it was only this object. In three pieces."

I slid my hand along the shaft to the top, ran my fingers along the edge. I had believed I found the ornamental part of Moses's piece, that it was the only part that mattered. But my fingers told me otherwise. The top edge was sharp where it had been broken. The bottom was the same.

But that cavern under the temple! Could I ever find the other pieces in all that rubble?

My gaze must have shifted toward Yathrib, for Zahir shook his head. "They are not in the cavern."

"Then where?"

Once again he shrugged, but this time not with indifference—in confusion. "I have tried to ascertain where the other two objects—pieces—might be, but I have never been able to comprehend the pious mutterings of your people."

I half-smiled, cold and determined. "Then it is fortunate you have a first-level mage to teach you."

CHAPTER FOURTEEN

MISHA

We bent over the charts and scrolls like old friends, Zahir and I, but the Nehushtan fragment was safely strapped to my chest once more. My vague threat of calling in my spirit allies kept Zahir's hands from it. For now. An oil lamp at the corner of the table danced shadows across the writing and the words seemed to join the dance.

Reza had been summoned, and he arrived looking ghostly white himself.

At a nod from me that I was well, a bit of color returned to his face. "What is happening here?"

Zahir lifted his head from the parchment. "Your *friend* is no more loyal than your troops, I fear." He skewered me with a hateful look. "He was planning to steal the piece we have all come to retrieve."

"Misha's mother is ill—"

"Yes, yes, we all know that the lovely Lydia awaits her heroic son." He sneered at Reza. "But are you so certain that is the only reason he wishes to obtain the piece?"

"You spoke of loyalty. Of my troops."

Zahir straightened now and came around the table to confront Reza. He crossed his arms in front of his chest and leaned back against the table. "So you do not even know what goes on under your nose? I suspected as much. Your men are disloyal, Reza. They seek to rise up against Phraates, to put another man on the throne. And you can be certain that when they start attacking those above them to get what they want, you will be the first in line."

I cleared my throat. "This has nothing to do with me—"

Zahir whirled. "Does it not? The Jews have long contended that they would bring the world a ruler to conquer nations. How better to empower this new leader than with a piece that can bring healing to any who look upon it? An army with this power—it would be more invincible than a thousand chariots, ten thousand mounted archers." He rounded the table to jab a finger in my chest. "And perhaps my first-level Jew-mage believes he is the very man himself."

"And why not?" I glared at Zahir. "Would I not make a better ruler than the madman who sees visions of his thirty dead brothers? But you have no need for fear, my lord." I bowed my head, my disdain heavy in the words. "I am more Persian than Jewish, as even my father would attest."

Kamillah slipped into the tent, eyes wide and gaze darting between the three of us.

"Ah, Kamillah, good." Zahir circled back to stand beside me at the table. "Your proficiency with languages will serve us well here. You can assure me that our little Misha is not misinterpreting these writings."

I exhaled but bit back a retort. He was forgetting who had the power now. "There is no misinterpretation, Zahir. Whoever penned these words did so against the express wishes of King Hezekiah. The Nehushtan has always been thought to have been destroyed beyond repair. Though the books of the law say only that it was broken into pieces. But those entrusted with the task, as you know, violated the king's decree—"

"Yes, yes I know all that. But the three pieces that are spoken of—"

"Three parts of the one whole, as you suspected. It was broken and scattered." I patted the piece at my chest. "It appears we have only the middle section."

Kamillah's arm brushed mine as she leaned over the parchment. "What has happened to the other two?"

And therein lay my dilemma.

There were clues in the writings, to be sure. But would I give them to Zahir? I had no desire to see him put them together, but my best chance in retrieving them was in keeping the caravan together—Reza's troops, the Chakkiym, the rest of the Kasdim, and even the traders all afforded protection and security if I was to complete my quest.

"Yes, Misha-aku. What has happened to the other two?" Zahir's hands were fisted at his sides and his voice was tight.

"I cannot focus with you breathing down my neck. Leave me space to read more carefully."

Zahir snorted and threw himself to a pile of cushions at the side of his tent.

At Reza's attempt to leave, he grunted again. "Where are you going? This concerns you as well. Or are you indifferent to this supposed world leader your men are trying to crown?"

Reza's glance met mine for a brief moment, and then he lowered himself to wait beside Zahir.

Kamillah spoke softly, for my ears only. "It is clear from this writing that the three pieces were scattered. I did not realize that Zahir's Hebrew was so rudimentary."

I gave her a half grin. "He's much less capable than you'd think." I glanced at Zahir but he was engaged with Reza. "We'll have you home before the next Inundation."

She touched my arm and smiled, then returned to the writings.

We studied in silence for some time, each of us puzzling through the cryptic words clearly meant to obfuscate the locations of the pieces, even as they recorded them for future generations.

It was all here—the prophecies of the world leader that had been known across various cultures for centuries. It was easy to see how Zahir had put this document together with the positioning of the regal star and its indication of a birth unlike any the world had seen. *A ruler to rule the nations.*

And yet… Where Zahir had interpreted the Nehushtan as the object imbuing the leader with supernatural power, I saw something different.

Not a ruler *holding an object of power*, but a ruler who was Power itself. Dominion over all people and all of creation, not because of what He possessed, but because of who He was.

Messiah.

Long had my people held to hope that the Messiah would free us from the tyranny that plagued us through all the millennia of our existence, a Messiah to make us a strong and mighty nation once more. But this was more, so much more. A Messiah to rule the entire world.

I sucked in a breath, heart pounding with a strange exhilaration.

Did Kamillah see it, too?

Had the star been whispering truth all along? The prospect chased a chill along my veins.

"What is it?" Zahir bent forward from his place on the cushions. "You have deciphered the meaning?"

I swallowed. "Three pieces. I have found the first, the most important. But the other two are necessary as well, and they are hidden in places renowned for the intersection of heaven and earth. Places where the other world touches this one, and the divide between grows thin, thin enough even to travel through."

"Yes, and where are these places?" Zahir was on his feet now.

"Of that I am not sure. I need more time to study what is written here, and to consult the holy writings of my own people in comparison." I rolled up the parchment.

"If you think I am going to—"

"Yes?" I took up the parchment and advanced on Zahir. "Did you have something else to say?"

He took a step back.

And in that moment, I knew I had won.

Somehow the spirit beings, the star, and perhaps the One God Himself had given me power over this man I had so long feared. It was mine now to make my choices, to take my stand. To do what I must.

"I will inform you when it is time to move again, Zahir." I bowed to Reza and crossed to the tent's entrance. "Come, Kamillah. I am sure these two will wish to confer."

In truth, I did not want to leave her with them. Either of them.

Zahir laughed. "Still fascinates you, does she? Even after I told you she meant to betray you underground?"

Kamillah's eyes went wide and her lips parted. She looked to me. "You knew?"

I shrugged. "I do not count on loyalty from any corner. Including yours."

She swallowed hard and blinked. Then strode from the tent.

"Kamillah!" I swept the flap aside but she had already vanished into the night. With a last glare at Zahir and a self-conscious avoidance of Reza's eyes, I followed her out.

CHAPTER FIFTEEN

KAMILLAH

*M*isha had known.

Kamillah's thoughts pounded in rhythm with her sandals on the well-trodden sand, out toward the edges of the encampment.

Misha knew she found him in that cavern to drug him, to leave him behind and give Zahir the Nehushtan. And still he returned to pull her from the pit, to keep her safe.

How could she continue to mistrust him in the face of his obvious affection for her?

And Reza—she had seen how desperate his searching eyes had been as they traveled over her, looking for injuries. Was he not a good man as well? Why did she refuse to give either one a place in her heart?

The midnight moon glared down on the desert with its single, unblinking eye, chilling the air as surely as the sun heated it during the scorching daylight hours. The desert held on to nothing—not the sun's heat when the day waned, nor the moon's coolness when the sun outshone it. Her heart was stronger than even the desert—holding on to past grudges, past hurts, that in turn fired her blood and then turned it cold. When would she be free?

When I am free of Zahir.

Yes, it would take more than what Misha or Reza could give her, more than the security of a friend or even a husband. She needed freedom, and she needed Egypt.

They journeyed toward the Centers of Power now. She had seen the message as clearly as Misha had in the writings, even if he stalled Zahir by giving him vague half-truths and speculation. Two sacred locations, at the top and the bottom of Judea, where the links between this world and the unseen were forged so tightly that passage between became a possibility.

In one of those places she would find the power she needed to break Zahir.

And until then?

Whether friend or enemy, she would keep them all close. Close enough for her to watch. Never close enough for them to harm.

CHAPTER SIXTEEN

ZAHIR

Zahir let Misha run after the girl, let him maintain the delusion that he was in control.

Reza, too, he dismissed from his tent with a disgruntled wave of the hand. The soldier was too stupid to see traitors in his ranks and useful only as a disposable defense against marauders as they traveled.

They would pull up stakes in the morning. Misha had better have his answers by then, wrestled from the cryptic writings and the wizened heads of his beloved Chakkiym.

Zahir poured himself a cup of wine and stood at the entrance to his tent, divining rod reassuringly in his hand, his gaze pulled toward the star as it always was.

It would be westward, toward Judea, he had no doubt.

He would allow Misha to lead the expedition, to believe he held the reins of power. But only until Zahir was finished with him. Until he had used him for both his cunning and his knowledge of his people's history and prophecies. He had let the boy believe he had no power over the spirits. But despite the troublesome events of the night, Zahir felt assured they would aid him when needed. Well, reasonably assured.

The wine was too warm. He tossed it into the night, and it pelted the sand like drops of red rain. Like the waters of Egypt that had turned to blood under the Jewish prophet Moses.

Yes, he knew his history, too.

And he was poised to take his place in it. The prophecies and the stars were aligned—a new world leader rising out of Judea. And an object of power that could sway the course of nations.

One way or another, Zahir would be part of this new world. Advisor to this new king—or his destroyer. But there was no turning back now.

The spirits had spoken.

CHAPTER SEVENTEEN

MISHA

*I*n the end, it was Kamillah who found me. Long after I had searched the night-settled camp without finding her, and after I had spent an hour huddled over the parchment with Gaspar.

Gaspar called in Balthazar—an expert in the geography of Judea, though neither of them had ever set foot on its soil—to muse over the places named in the writings.

"Dan, certainly." Balthazar nodded and stroked the dark and pointed beard that poked from his chin. "At the foot of Mount Hermon, where the fallen angels descended." He leaned over the text again. "Panais, perhaps?"

"Fitting." Gaspar cleared his throat and stretched the tension from his neck.

I joined him in standing upright to stretch. The single oil lamp smoked, burning the eyes and thickening the voice.

Balthazar poked a thick finger at the parchment. "Whoever penned these words knew they preserved an object with great potential, but one that could be used as a tool of either the heavens or the darkness. They left a piece near Dan to remind any who found it of its dangers."

"And the other piece?" I looked to Gaspar. "Do you agree? Bethel?"

"It would make sense, though the reference is more obscure. The two places where Jeroboam placed his golden calves. Dan in the north and Bethel in the south, two centers of power, flanking the land."

Balthazar shook his head. "But then, why Yathrib?" He used the finger to poke now at my chest. "Why place the centerpiece, arguably the most important, in Yathrib?"

I shrugged. "Perhaps those who hid the top and bottom came here afterward, brought it with them in hopes that removing it from Judea would keep it safe."

Balthazar grunted, the frustrated sound of a scholar without answers.

Gaspar rolled the parchment and handed it to me. "One thing is certain. The scrolls that your father entrusted to you must return to Jerusalem."

I thanked the men and ducked from the tent of the Chakkiym with the parchment held closely to the broken Nehushtan, into the starry night. Beyond the tent, at the edge of the camp, a dark figure stood against the night sky, her profile making her identity obvious, her stance clearly waiting.

I went to her slowly. Perhaps because I feared what she might say. Or perhaps because I wanted to remember this moment, to place it in my mind to keep for later—Kamillah's beautiful form silhouetted against the desert night, her silky dark hair blowing gently behind her shoulders, her face upturned to the stars.

She did not acknowledge my approach, only continued her night watch. But we stood in companionable silence under the messenger that had brought us to this place.

Finally, I spoke. "You were disturbed by what Zahir said—"

"Not disturbed. Surprised. Perhaps confused." She turned to me at last. "He told you why he had sent me to that cavern to find you. But you came back for me despite my treachery. Why?"

I took a step nearer but paused. It was not time yet. Not yet.

"Because I know you are a good woman and did only what you felt you must—to survive. As we all do."

"And would you betray me to survive, Misha-aku?"

I inhaled the chilled air and looked away.

"Your silence proves your words wrong, for I know you would not.

You say I am a good woman, but it is you who are a good man, Misha. Destined to be a great man, I believe."

She should save her admiration for men like those I had just left in the tent of the Chakkiym. I was destined only to disappoint. But I did not tell her this. Instead, I placed the parchment on the ground, took her hands in mine, and turned her to look into my eyes.

"And you, Kamillah, are worth far more than the price that has been put on your head. While you are a great prize any man would be honored to receive, you do not deserve to be *given* as a prize in a contest for greedy men."

She half-smiled and gazed into the dark once more. "Well, we shall see—"

"No. I am making a promise to you. Here, this night." I clutched her hands to the sling across my chest. "A promise on the Nehushtan."

Her glance returned to me, her lips trembling slightly.

"We will find the pieces, and with them the power to break Zahir. Where we are headed—"

"There is power in these places."

"Great power, I believe. And I am promising you that I will find a way for you to return to Egypt."

She smiled fully now, and I almost felt she believed me. Even more, that she believed *in* me, as no woman ever had.

Nearly as numerous as the sands at our feet, the stars above our heads shone down on our pact. But the one star, the star I had been avoiding for so long, was silent tonight. No ghostly visitors hovered at the edge of our pocket of stillness.

I kept Kamillah's hands bound up in my own, and I set my eyes toward Judea. Toward Jerusalem, where my father had said the true source of power was to be found. And the whispering star seemed less bent on my destruction than I had once thought. The Nehushtan, the spirits, the scrolls—all of them bound up inexplicably, all of them both beckoning and threatening.

Perhaps I was a fool. Perhaps I journeyed still toward my own ruin. Time would tell if Reza would find power enough to be king, if Zahir would remain in control, or if Kamillah would reach her home. They all had a purpose, borne of great desire.

But as for me, only one choice remained.
I would follow the star.

EPILOGUE

HEROD

*I*n the center of Jerusalem, beside the Temple Mount he had rebuilt along with countless other projects across Judea, the king of the Jews looked out over his city and scowled.

Herod the Idumaean, self-styled as "Herod the Great," had spent the last twenty-five years watching and waiting.

A dark figure joined him at the window.

"Pain again, my brother?" Salome placed a soothing hand at his back and kept her voice low.

He did not answer. She knew the answer.

The pain had begun the moment they cut Mariamme down from the gallows. Just a niggling discomfort then, with the roaring anguish in his heart and his mind tamping down the physical pain until he barely noticed it.

But all it grew as the years passed. The corrosion of his skin and the pain in his mind, which sometimes screamed obscenities at him and sometimes mocked and sometimes, late at night, cried with a despair too deep for words.

He heard the whispers around the palace. They believed he was mad.

They did not know that the voices were real. That the voices were stronger than any of them.

The voices owned them all.

But for now, for today, he was still king. Salome had told him of the cursed scrolls that had eluded her grasp and been carried off by his dead wife's handmaid, Lydia, and his palace manager, Simon. Scrolls that promised a new king—one who would topple him from his throne.

And so he watched. And he waited.

Above the palace, the stars swirled and converged and danced their messages across the blackened sky. Herod leaned his forehead against the window's ragged stone edge and studied the Eastern Gate of the Temple Mount, with the purplish line of the Mount of Olives looming behind it. Beyond the mountain, farther east, the Jordan River chased along the edge of Judea, then the cities of the Decapolis in the Transjordan, and farther even, the eastern lands where Simon and Lydia had no doubt fled, with the traitorous words inked on parchment secreted in their belongings.

Yes, if trouble came, it would come from the east.

And Herod would be ready.

STAR OF NIGHT

THE INCENSE ROAD

BOOK TWO

TRACY HIGLEY

STAR OF NIGHT

THE INCENSE ROAD

BOOK TWO

REZA'S STORY

CHAPTER ONE

REZA

*I*n the twelve days since we left Yathrib, I lost sight of who I was, as a man and as a general.

Perhaps our stop in the city of Petra would help me regain my focus.

But my men had other ideas of what a few days in Petra could mean.

We pushed through the Siq—that narrow, rock-cut channel into a city so well protected by rosy cliffs that a caravan could pass it by without ever knowing of its existence—into the pleasantly cool shade of Petra's bustling market. The cliffs soared on all sides, giving one the impression that this massive oasis in the center was all that existed. But I had passed this way before and knew that around that bend to the west lay the rest of the carved city, awaiting my men with more distractions than the market's smoked meats and silk fabrics.

"Fahim," I yelled a sharp rebuke to the young soldier, who had swatted the backside of a less-than-respectable girl swinging past him.

Fahim only laughed, a sure sign that my men believed themselves on holiday now and not subject to the command of their general.

My pulse thumped at his casual response. Indiscretion, this far into our journey, could mean disaster.

A slap on *my* back made me whirl in anger at the soldier who had taken too much liberty.

Misha held up two palms, mock fear on his face. "Whoa, General, I'm not the advancing Romans."

"Good thing, then." I jutted my chin toward my men. "They'd probably welcome you in and buy you a meal."

Misha grinned. "This city didn't become the crossroads of the trading routes for nothing, Reza." He scanned the cliffs, lingering on the immense yet intricate carving against the west wall behind us.

Like the façade of a many-cultured temple, the gods of numerous peoples had been carved into the rock face atop columns, pediments, and niches. It was a wonder, truly, with more wonders to come in the city itself. But Misha spoke of the city's defenses, not its architecture.

"No raiders. No armies, Reza. Take a few days to rest. We've all earned it after these hundreds of dusty miles."

"I'll rest when we are back in Nisa with all of the Nehushtan."

Misha's grin faded and he nodded once. "In this we are brothers."

There were a thousand reasons why defying Zahir was foolish. But in truth, our resolve had only hardened on the trek northward from Yathrib to Petra. The Nehushtan, that ancient artifact of Misha's people that his forefather Moses had raised in the sands outside Egypt to heal the people of Israel, would serve us both in Nisa. Misha would see his lovely mother healed of the sickness that had weakened her for months.

And I would see my destiny revealed.

Kamillah approached, an equal smile for both of us, as always.

"Just like a woman." Misha pointed to her pouch. "Wasting no time in shopping."

Her eyes darkened in response.

I took a step forward. "What have you purchased?" I spoke quickly, whether to distract her from Misha's comment or from Misha himself, I could not say.

Her fingers brushed the pouch and she smiled slightly. "Some perfumes."

Misha's ever-present grin returned at the answer, but he was wise enough to keep silent.

In that silence, the shout of Walid, a newly ranked soldier under my command, rang out nearby.

We turned, all three, to his hailing of me.

"We have found the gift for you, General!" He stood at the table of a fabric merchant and held something aloft in two meaty fingers. "This will serve you well very soon, eh?"" He wriggled the silk, a royal purple that glistened in the sunlight, then flung it around his shoulders like a robe.

Around him, a few other soldiers guffawed, then bowed in sham obeisance.

I stalked to the cluster of idiots and yanked the fabric from Walid's shoulders. "What do you think you are doing?"

Walid's cheeks paled, though he tried to maintain his humor. "Just a bit of fun—"

"Do you think your jest is subtle?" I swung an arm to the rest of the market. "That no other fool will catch its meaning?""

I wadded up the fabric and threw it at the old merchant, whose rheumy eyes betrayed surprise and not a little annoyance. "Forgive my men, sir." I fished out a few coins for the man's trouble. "They have been too long in the company of only each other."

He pocketed the coins with a gummy smile.

I growled at Walid. "Find something useful to do with yourself."

Zahir sauntered over. "Your men are a bit rowdy already, General, with only a half-day's holiday behind them. Perhaps a sign they are kept on too tight a leash, yes?"

The anger at my loud-mouthed soldiers turned to something else under Zahir's rebuke. I led him away from the merchant's table. Misha and Kamillah followed. "On the contrary, Zahir. It is this leave of duty that is the problem. They require a firm hand to be in control at all times."

Zahir's half smirk said more than words.

I jabbed a thumb toward the city around the cliff bend. "How long do you expect to remain here doing nothing? We are wasting time."

Misha slid between the two of us. "Inactivity is not your strength, Reza, we know. But we are not 'doing nothing' as you say."" He lowered his voice. "Besides the necessary trading that our caravan came for, we hope to find valuable information here in Petra."

"Well, we should make it quick and get back to the discipline of the road."

Zahir squinted at the marketplace. "I have been asking a few discreet questions and will continue to do so. If there is information, it passes through this city with the rest of the world's goods." He turned on me and pointed to the cliff above our heads. "Perhaps you can quiet your restless spirit with a climb to the High Place of Sacrifice."

With that he slipped away, thankfully, or I might have removed that smirk.

Twelve days on the road was turning me into a thug, too. Or perhaps it was only this one day of uselessness.

Kamillah touched my elbow. "Why don't we move into the city, find lodging." Her glance took in Misha, making the suggestion less personal. ""Leave your men to their fun. They'll be grateful to see you disappear."

A cluster of traders pushed past, none of them our own men, and one of them jostled Kamillah as he passed.

She stepped aside, but clearly the collision had been intentional.

"Look here, friends." The trader motioned to his fellows. "The finest piece of luxury the market has shown us yet."

I cleared my throat, signaling them to be on their way.

But the fool was too lost in himself. He started to circle Kamillah, eyeing her up and down. "And what does something so fine sell for in Petra these days?"

Kamillah flushed and opened her mouth, no doubt to cut the man into small bits with her verbal skills.

I did not give her the chance. My sword slid from my belt with a smooth *whoosh* and its point tickled the trader's throat before he had blinked twice.

He pulled his head backward, eyes wider than double moons.

"Trust me, friend. You could not afford her."

He raised a hand and backed away. "Not looking for trouble, my lord. Just having a bit of fun."

"Have your fun elsewhere, before I cut it short."

One of his friends grabbed his arm and yanked him from my threat, and the group trotted off toward the city.

Kamillah sighed. "You did not need—"

But Misha was leaning in, watching my eyes. "I have never seen you react to a minor insult with a drawn sword, Reza. What is going on?"

I wished I knew.

The days on this journey, trying to keep my men quiet while I examined my father's plan for me from every possible angle, had not made me more circumspect. If anything, I felt myself becoming a tyrant long before I would become a king.

I returned my sword to my belt and wiped the back of my arm across my forehead. "I need rest. That is all."

But apparently, rest was not to be had. Not yet. Across the market, between a table of pomegranates and peaches and another of potatoes and onions, a knot of my men had started brawling.

"Soldiers!" Once again I stalked across the sand to chastise them like errant boys playing in the streets.

"Tell him, General." A seasoned soldier who should have known better jutted his chin toward a younger. "Tell him you are not afraid to fight for what is yours.""

I surveyed the group quickly. All of them were part of the faction that knew of my heritage, of what my father expected of me. Expected of them.

Yazid continued. "He says when the time is right, when we return, you will be too weak to make your claim."

"Quiet!" I moved to the center of them. Not only were their eyes trained on me, but the eyes of many others as well. "This is not the place. Go find taverns or brothels or beds. You are all half-drunk and fully stupid!" I raised a hand to feign a strike against the nearest of them, and they scattered.

I scanned the marketplace for Zahir. How close had he been when my loose-lipped men had nearly proclaimed me Persian king right here in the Petran marketplace?

CHAPTER TWO

REZA

*T*here was no evidence of Zahir in evidence in the marketplace, but I pulled Misha along toward the city just the same. Better to remove myself from the men than to count on them doing the right thing.

Misha kept to my side around the bend, and I could feel Kamillah following at a more leisurely pace. After the way that trader had accosted her, she should stay closer, but I would not be the one to tell her so.

"You can't run from this forever, Reza." Misha inclined his head back toward the market incident. "Once men have tasted the idea of something different, they are quick to crave it."

We sped through the chasm between the pockmarked cliffs, their caves staring down on us like black eyes.

"My father was a fool to tell anyone but me. Not all soldiers can be trusted to keep silent."

Misha huffed. "A revolution made of one man has little chance for success. You need every sword you can get."

I reached down to grab a handful of Petra's rosy-tan pebbles from underfoot. "I don't want a revolution!" My voice rose too loud, and I glanced back to find Kamillah, her eyebrows raised. Now even I was betraying myself.

We slowed to allow Kamillah to catch up and she moved silently between us. We made an interesting trio to be sure, for all the Petra folk who undoubtedly watched us from their rock-cut homes, deep inside the cliffs' black eyes. Misha in the black-and-white robes of his sect, Kamillah in a white robe that mysteriously stayed pure in the midst of the dust that coated the city, and me in my browned military leathers.

I tossed a pebble against a stone half wall that led toward an amphitheater. "How can my father expect me to lead an uprising, and then to lead a country? Look at only this expedition—I have lost eight men to a poisoned spring, been duped by raiders into leaving our camp unprotected, nearly lost the two of you to a collapsing cave, and still have little idea where we are headed, nor why! What kind of leader—?"

Kamillah's cool hand on my arm stopped the words but brought a painful thickening to my throat.

"You have been in training for this moment your whole life, Reza. Your father—"

"My father should have stepped into this place himself. Why did he wait to have a son who would rather study than fight?"

Misha slapped my back. "At least *your* father believes in you."

The words were spoken lightly, but Kamillah and I both knew the pain that undergird them. I flicked a glance at my friend and saw in his eyes the lifelong tension between us. We had been drawn to each other as boys, become as close as brothers, and realized too late that my relationship with his father, Simon, would always come between us.

And now Kamillah. Another barrier between Misha and me.

The sun was dropping behind the cliffs, and already the cooling of rock began. Smells of the market—both spices and beast—faded, replaced by the scent of cook fires, and I was hungry.

I pointed to a canopy jutting from the bottom of the north cliff we walked along. "Food and drink?"

The other two nodded and followed me to the entrance of a low-ceilinged cave set up as a tavern. My mouth watered at the odor of pheasant on a spit, and the proprietor greeted us by pouring something dark into three cups and pointing us to a squat bench along the wall.

We waited for the plates of smoked meat and lentils that would come, sipping at the wine.

Well, they sipped. I had other plans, and soon signaled the tavern owner to refill mine.

"Reza." Kamillah sighed, disapproval and frustration lacing her voice. "Your men are unwise, but all the more reason for you to keep a clear head.""

I raised my cup in a mock salute. "All the more reason why no one should expect me to."

A young girl approached with a plate in hand, balancing another two along her arm. She distributed them to us, first Kamillah's, then Misha's, and mine last, with a lingering look and a coy smile at me that was more than hospitable.

I watched her turn and walk away, watched her glance back at me again.

Misha jabbed me in the side. "I would swear, brother, that you get invited to share a bed in every city we pass. Even in the middle of the desert, I half-expect some raider's woman to lift your tent flap and invite herself in."

I felt my neck flush and didn't look at Kamillah. "Her invitation is wasted, as you well know"—I couldn't resist a return jab—"but perhaps she'd settle for you instead."

Misha's bark of a laugh lifted the tension.

We talked and drank and ate into the evening hours, but when Misha and Kamillah left, I was not yet finished with my drinking.

Kamillah eyed the serving girl on her way out, and I let myself imagine it was with a bit of possessive envy. Perhaps. The girl was oblivious to Kamillah's attention, as she was cleaning cups alongside a child, most likely her sister.

But she soon attended me with more wine and more smiles, and I instructed her to keep the amphora close.

I was tired. Bone-tired and heart-tired of the act of rough valor required of a man in my position, a mask I had worn like a Greek dramatist for so many years. Perhaps I had worn it too well, convinced even my father of my worthiness. Irony, that in seeking to avoid his displeasure, I had qualified myself for a position even farther from my true desires.

The wine helped to dull the familiar stab of jealousy at the thought of Misha, of his father Simon who wished only for his son to study the knowledge of generations of their people.

Men came and went from the tavern and the night grew blurry around me. I did not notice a figure at my side on the bench until his smooth laugh interrupted my thoughts.

"So this is how a future king prepares himself for an uprising."

I started and lifted my head at both Zahir's smug voice and his frightening words.

His white teeth gleamed in the lamplight, and a narrow smile played about his lips. "I should think you would be planning future strategy, not drowning the day in wine."

"I leave the strategy to you, Zahir. I am only on this expedition to provide safe passage." I casually tossed back the dregs of wine in my cup, but my hand trembled.

"I do not speak of our current quest, and you know it." He studied the entrance to the tavern, his voice low and too calm.

I leaned forward to better hear him, then forced myself back against the wall. "No? Then you must have knowledge of my next orders even before I do."

He laughed. "Yes, I believe you only follow orders, for you are not a man to come up with such a plan yourself." He turned on me, eyes narrowed to slits. "But tell me, is it only the dull-witted thugs who follow you, or is there someone else who has filled your head with delusions of rulership?"

There was no point in maintaining pretense. Word had gotten back to Zahir of at least the incident in the market, if not more. And yet I resisted telling him anything of my heritage, of the secret alliance of Persian men who had convened for generations and had trained me up without my knowledge to claim a birthright that had been stolen from them.

"You mistake the silly ramblings of idle soldiers for something more, Zahir. Even you know I would rather be a student of yours than your king."

He pressed the pads of his fingers together, then touched them to his chin and studied the floor. "Perhaps. But lesser men than you have been persuaded to take up arms in misguided attempts at greatness."

"You needn't fear—"

"Fear!" His derisive laugh turned heads in our direction. "Who said anything about fear?" His words turned to a hiss. "It is you who should fear, General Reza. Fear that word of your—indiscretion—will return to Phraates and you will find yourself not only without an army, but without a head."

The little girl, sister to the woman who had served me several times, approached. "Would you like a plate, my lord? A cup—"

Zahir shoved the girl from him with a forearm across her upper chest. "Leave us, little dog. If I want something from you, I will whistle for you."

The girl stumbled backward and I caught her against my arm and set her upright. Her lips puckered and she eyed me with fear.

I smiled and patted her shoulder. "You make your father proud, I'm sure." I pulled a coin from a pouch that was getting low in supply. ""I will pay your father for the food and drink, but this one is just for you."

Her eyes brightened and she snatched the coin with a grin and ran away.

Zahir huffed a sarcastic laugh and shook his head. "You are better suited to be queen than king, I believe."

"Then as I said, you have nothing to fear."

"I should have you killed right now."

"Then who would lead your protection?"

His nostrils flared and he looked away, then back to me. "You are right. I have need of your men, of their protection, until I have found what I seek. But do not believe that I trust you. If you are foolish enough to return to Nisa, I will speak the truth to Phraates and you will face execution before you can raise more than the handful of supporters you have here in the desert.'" His face was purpling with the force of his words. "In the meantime, you will do what I need or there will be pain."

It was my turn to laugh. "A soldier is well accustomed to pain, Zahir. I would like to see—"

"For Kamillah."

My jaw dropped a fraction and I forced my lips to seal.

"Yes, you see the wisdom in silence now, do you not? Silence and obedience—these are what I require of you, or Kamillah will feel the repercussions. And you know I have the power to do it."

Yes, he had sick power over her. I did not understand it, but I could not deny it.

And he would use it to keep me loyal until he could see me dead.

CHAPTER THREE

REZA

*M*isha had warned me. But I didn't believe him until tonight, as we prepared to head down into Panais to reclaim the next piece of the Nehushtan.

We had left the comforts of Petra fourteen days ago and traveled north beyond Judea, beyond the city of Dan, up into the foothills of Mount Hermon until we hung over the city dedicated to the goat-god Pan, and my men silently strapped on helmets and swords as though the Romans lay in wait.

But on the edge of the camp, on a hill above the sacred grove, it was not Romans that ran my blood cold. It was the apparitions at the edge of my vision, whispering dark suggestions into my mind. Inhuman creatures Misha had warned were following us since Nisa.

There is only death for you here. Do not waste your life on such a cause.

I whirled and brandished my own sword, as if to pin the air. "Who is there?"

They are not worth protecting.

I listened in the stillness for more, heart pounding, but only the gush of water from the mouth of the grotto across the valley sounded in my ears. The smell of wet soil, of rotting decay, seemed to issue forth from the underworld, at whose gates we stood.

Did the voices speak from that underworld, as Misha had said? They tried to turn him back, back to Nisa, he told me. And now they seemed to say the same to me.

No one will know if you pull back your protection. Let the course of nature run.

Pull back?

Misha was heading into the black maw of the Panais cave within the hour, before the crazed followers of Pan returned at dawn and tried to stop him. Kamillah had insisted on accompanying him. I would bring my men to the marble temple at its periphery and stand guard.

If I pulled back, my two friends could be attacked from without by cult followers. Or from within, by whatever dark horrors lay inside the grotto.

Yes, yes, let them go. They are not worth protecting.

The black and white shades of the hillside accentuated the flitting white that winked away like a snuffed candle when I turned. The hilt of my sword grew slick in my hand, palm down, and even the call of a circling raven caused my pulse to leap.

"Do you feel the power?"

I jumped and raised my sword.

Zahir again—always at my elbow. He held up a single hand and wriggled his fingers as if to brush away my sword.

I would swear he took delight in startling me.

"Such a nervous soldier you are, Reza."

I nodded toward the temple and the sacred grove. "This place does not sit easy with me."

He smiled. "Then you do feel it."

"If by power you mean evil, then I suppose I do."

"Ah, evil. Such a vague and inadequate word."

Beads of sweat formed on my neck in spite of the coolness that traveling north had brought. Once the sun rose we would be able to see snow-capped Mount Hermon in the distance. The city was as different from the desert as it could be, and yet I felt no more at ease.

Zahir dipped his head in farewell. "Let us hope you find your courage before the party embarks."

He left me to watch him descend the hilly rise, wishing I could thrust my sword through his back.

Yes, the thought was attractive, as unlike me as it seemed. I would never truly do it—never kill the man without just cause. But the thought pleased me.

I was sick to death of being treated as a coward. As a pretender who had no business claiming kingship, not because my bloodline faltered but because my courage failed.

The voices tried to sway me to abandon my friends. And Zahir believed he could intimidate me into never returning to Nisa.

I raised my sword into the night, and the rising moon glanced off its polished surface. The hilt, carved so intricately by the master metalworker commissioned by my long-dead grandfather, glinted in the night, winking approval.

Something shifted within me in that moment.

I would do whatever it took to protect Kamillah, even to win her. Not as Phraates's prize, but to win her over to the idea of becoming a queen. And I would help Misha find what he sought. But most importantly, to fulfill my destiny and become king of my people.

And if I should pull back my protection from anyone, it would be from Zahir.

Ghostly beings that would not even show themselves would not stop me.

I took a deep breath of the death-scented air, exhaled my determination, and turned to prepare my men for what lie ahead.

I found Misha and Kamillah in her tent, poring over the Hebrew writings yet again.

I returned my sword to its hilt and crossed my arms. "Do you two still believe you will gain information from that parchment you do not already know?"

Misha kept his attention on the words, but Kamillah glanced at me. "We've come all the way north to Dan, and everything points to the cave of Pan here, but there is little more to guide us. If we could find only a bit more direction——"

"Perhaps you should take your Chakkiym with you. They might recognize something important."

"Ha!" Misha pushed away the parchment. "I could barely convince them to get this far. No obedient Jew wants to come near this pagan place, and certainly not into the mouth of Hades itself."

I touched Kamillah's arm. "I do not like you going in there, either."

She shook her head, a slight movement that dismissed my concern. "This place is a Center of Power, I have no doubt. The Hebrew writings speak of a portal on Mount Hermon where the fallen angels of Yahweh were cast down to earth. And the cave—the grotto from whence the spring flows——has long been believed to be an entrance to the underworld."

"All the more reason—"

"To go inside! To absorb whatever power I can find." Her eyes flashed. "I will find a way, Reza."

"I saw your spirits."

Misha's head jerked up to meet my level gaze.

"I think they want me to stop protecting you. Let both of you be destroyed."

"You saw them?" Kamillah grabbed at my tunic.

"And heard them."

Misha's brow furrowed. "I thought you didn't believe me."

"More like I believed you were going mad. Maybe when you wouldn't listen they moved on to me."

"What are you going to do?"

I snorted. "Am I going to do their bidding, do you mean? Of course not."

"Good." Misha returned his attention to the parchment.

The moon was rising. It was time to get my soldiers ready to move.

Outside in the damp air, I waited to hear them speak again, to urge me to keep Misha from his plan. Instead, as I walked toward the edge of the ranks of silent soldiers, I thought I heard a whispered, *Yes*.

Yes, let them come, so we can destroy them.

CHAPTER FOUR

REZA

The temple of Pan clung to the side of the cliff, its four white columns like birch trunks in the moonlight. Carved figures marched across the triangular pediment above, but it was too far to see the details as my four lines of soldiers trotted toward the cliff. The roar of the water pouring out of the cave covered the sound of our hobnailed sandals on the pebbles.

Priests would be in the temple, even at this hour, and perhaps a few of the more devoted followers of the goat-god. But it should not be overly difficult to get Misha and Kamillah into the cave. The Chakkiym of course stayed behind, but they joined the rest of the Kasdim. Only Zahir accompanied the soldiers and the two thieves.

Did the priests know what treasure their grotto held? Had they been tasked to defend and protect the broken piece of the Jews' artifact, or did it rest inside unknown and unmarked? They were more than idle questions running through my mind, for in the answers was also the extent of the battle we were about to face.

Almost to the temple, at the edge of a still pool, I signaled to my men to head into a copse of trees and hold their position.

Zahir joined me at the edge, along with Misha and Kamillah, who were both covered in dark robes and held sturdy walking sticks.

Zahir's face was set toward the cave. "I will be watching more closely this time, little Misha-aku. Do not think you can betray me twice."

Misha adjusted the pouch at his waist and said nothing.

Zahir was not finished. "I would have killed you in Yathrib, if I could have found another of you Jews to help me with this puzzle."

"Not much chance of that."

Misha's tone was light, but I could hear the trace of excitement that was always there before an adventure.

"Trust me, Zahir, I am the only Jew you know who would enter that." He pointed to the cave, its black outlines barely larger than the foamy water churned out by the spring within.

"I do *not* trust you. But I do not need trust. Not when I have a leash to keep you heeled, eh, Kamillah?" He yanked on the back of her hair, causing her to cry out softly.

My hand circled the hilt of my sword, and Misha's eyes flashed even in the darkness.

"Ah," Zahir laughed, "one leash for two dogs." He smoothed Kamillah"s hair with a flat palm. "You are so very useful, my dear."

I glanced at the moon, already rising too high for my liking. "We are wasting time."

Zahir nodded, as if to release us.

I crept ahead, knowing Misha and Kamillah followed. My men would follow behind them, as arranged. No doubt Zahir would remain as far back as he could while still keeping us in his sights.

Along the edge of the pool, then through a grove of gnarled olive trees, we wound past their aged trunks, using their bulk as cover, moving quickly.

I did not know what Misha and Kamillah planned once inside the grotto. They had not made me part of their plans, nor confided the results of their studies with me. No matter. I was only here to provide muscle, not intellect.

Nothing stirred in the grove—not olive leaf nor man—and I signaled to those behind me to stay close. The temple steps and portico loomed now, with the entrance to the cave to the left.

From what I could see, the temple's exterior had been built up against the cliff face, but its interior extended into the cliff itself, into the cave and alongside the rushing water. How much space between the temple wall and deluge would there be for Misha and Kamillah to enter?

Did the Pan followers creep in there or only enter the temple? Would they be swept back out of the cave if they tried to enter?

We were close now. I could hear a priest crooning some sort of prayer inside the temple, which glowed with lamplight from deep within. I nodded once to the two of them. It would be up to them now.

They slipped past me, and Kamillah squeezed my arm as she passed. In gratitude or farewell? I sucked in a breath, jaw clenched.

The shadows at the mouth of the cave swallowed them and they were gone.

Zahir still hung behind me, clearly counting on me to protect him from anyone, or anything, that might be a danger.

A thrumming sound in my head distracted me. No, not my head, more in my blood, in the veins.

I glanced at Zahir. Did he feel it? But he had pulled back toward the grove, and I could barely make out his outline against an olive trunk.

The throbbing increased until it became almost a chant.

Yes, yes, yes.

A bitterness soured in my chest. I flexed my shoulders and tried to shake it loose.

I did not need to focus at the edges of my sight to know they had returned.

As if the spirits had summoned him, a figure appeared on the steps of the temple, turning his head left and right as though listening.

I remained stone-still, but my position was completely exposed. I had not wanted to retreat from the cave in case Misha or Kamillah needed me.

My stillness did nothing to conceal my presence. His gaze fixed on me as though I held a torch in the night.

Something glinted in his hand. A sword.

What kind of priest wandered a temple with sword in hand?

He took two slow steps downward, his gaze still pinning me in place.

Yes, yes, yes.

Did they chant for my demise or for Misha's? Did the priest hear them, too?

I expected him to speak. To ask what business I, a soldier, had in the sacred grove at that hour of the night.

I did not expect him to charge me, sword upraised and a keening shriek on his lips.

I lofted my sword in defense.

His own glanced off mine with a sharp *clang*. Wide and frantic, his eyes glowed white in the darkness.

"Stand down, priest! I wish you no harm!"

"You defile the god and his grove!" He tried to strike again, to drive me through with his sword.

What kind of priest was this? I staved him off, while at the same time signaling my men to remain hidden. There was no wisdom in revealing our strength in the face of only this one crazed priest.

But as he continued to come at me, anger built along my arms and in my chest. The anger that always came over me in the midst of battle. Always I had tried to avoid it, to remain detached and emotionless as I fought necessary conflicts. But something had changed on that hillside above Panais. It was time to absorb the anger, to let it fuel me and take me where I needed to go.

I let it ignite, burn through me, harden my sword arm.

The priest was reeling backward now in the face of my ignited battle passion. His lips pulled back in a grimace of pain or fear.

I drove harder, pushing him toward the temple steps.

A black raven lifted heavy wings from the pediment of the temple and screeched as it circled.

The priest fell upon the steps, one hand bracing his fall, the other still clutching his sword.

The blood of kings ran in my veins at that moment, and I towered over him, sword point to his chest. "Drop your weapon, priest. There is no winning for you here."

He should have released it. Should have let the sword fall to the steps and surrendered. Instead he swung it toward my head. Clutched it with both hands. Screamed a curse upon me.

I ran him through.

The gods help me, I skewered that priest on the steps of his own temple. He had given me no choice.

My sword released easily from his rib cage, his blood black in the moonlight. I staggered backward, breathing heavily. A cold sweat along my neck seemed borne of the curse and not the battle. And the battle still pounded in my body.

There was regret, yes. But also, under the regret or perhaps over it, was the knowledge that in this I had taken one more step toward kingship—had embraced that core of inner strength necessary to follow my destiny.

Yes, yes, yes.

I shook away the chant again. I did not want to think upon what it meant.

"You continually surprise me, General."

"And you would be safer in the shadows, Zahir."

He contemplated the bleeding priest on the steps. "Where there is one, there are others."

I nodded. "I will advance to the cave. Give Bassam the word that he should lead the rest of the men should there be any coordinated defense here."

"If this goes wrong, Reza, it is on your head." Zahir's smooth voice was like honey in the darkness. "I am holding you responsible to get that piece safely out of the grotto."

"The piece alone? What of Misha and Kamillah?"

He shrugged. "Useful, but not vital."

The spirits had prompted me to leave the two to their fate within that cave. Zahir seemed as unconcerned. What if I pulled my protection from Zahir instead? Could another angry priest solve my problems for me?

Surprised at my own traitorous thoughts, I waved him back toward the grove and advanced on the mouth of the cave, creeping low and watchful.

I needn't have been so careful.

As though the priest's death had summoned all of Pan's followers from the depths of the underworld and the entire city of Panais, a swarm of figures crested the hill above the grove with an outcry that matched the priest's attack. Each seemed to wield a weapon of some kind—I could not tell from this distance.

I faced them from the cave's entrance unseen.

But my men knew their business, even without me there to command. They poured from the grove to meet the onslaught of men.

The battle for the second piece of the Nehushtan had begun.

CHAPTER FIVE

MISHA

*M*isha kept to the side of the cave as they entered, testing out the footing before proceeding. The rocks were wet and mildewed—a dangerous combination that could plunge either of them into the rushing water. He passed the unlit torch to Kamillah behind him, switched the flickering oil lamp to his other hand and braced against the interior rock wall with his palm.

The crashing of the water was slightly less deafening inside the cave than just outside.

He moved forward, one hesitating step at a time. "Once we find the piece, you aren't going to push me into the underworld and deliver it to Zahir, are you?"

"I would think I was in more danger than you. I seem to be the only thing standing between you and freedom."

"Ah yes, Zahir's leash." The ledge along the water seemed to widen. He glanced back. Were they deep enough to safely light the torch?

She made a low sound in her throat and did not answer.

"Still, perhaps you could convince him to let you go if you brought him the second piece without me."

"And who would figure out where to find the third?"

It was true, his puzzling over the writings had given them a good clue as to where to look. The veiled reference to this cave, which had been little more than a natural spring and an altar to Pan when the writings were penned, was only discernible because the place had become so established, and even so Zahir had not understood the reference.

Now that they were inside, the direction was less clear. He only knew that the piece would be found in a niche in the stone wall, in the mouth of the lion. Whatever that meant. Was the lion painted on the wall, like the Egyptian curse under the Temple of Amun-Re in Yathrib?

Strange that the first piece had been found in a center of Egyptian worship, and this one in a cave dedicated to a Greek god, but each of them with Hebrew symbols. Did those who were to have destroyed the Nehushtan seek to appease the gods of every nation or to disperse its power among them?

Either way, Misha was all that much closer to putting the artifact back together, then getting it back to Nisa to heal his sweet mother and lend power to his best friend's coup.

Kamillah was close behind him now and spoke loudly over the water. "Although if I brought back the Nehushtan myself, perhaps I would be the one to win Phraates's great prize."

"You would cheat all of us out of our winnings, then?" The words were said in jest. She knew that neither Reza nor he intended to hand the Nehushtan to Phraates and claim her for themselves.

"I would sooner cut my own throat."

Misha pulled up short at the bitter declaration and turned on her. Her face was hidden by shadows. He reached for her hand in the darkness, wrapped around the unlit torch.

They had spent much time together in the journey from Yathrib, discussing the parchment writings, but so much more. Their own histories – both national and personal – their families, their dreams. He had never let any woman see as much of his heart. And she surprised him by opening her own as well.

But still there were times, like the harsh words just uttered, that she drew back into her shell of protection once more.

Misha slid his hand up the length of her torch until he reached the oil-soaked end, then pushed it outward toward the water. A touch of his lamp's wick to the torch and it flared. He tossed the clay lamp into the foamy water.

Her face was as stony as the wall beside them.

"Kamillah—"

She shook her head. "I know."

"I trust you. You need to trust me, remember?"

"I know." She nodded toward the depths of the cave. "We are wasting time."

Misha took the torch from her and led the way forward, watching the walls for any indentation that might hold their piece. The walls were riddled with such niches, carved by dripping water and eons of time. And the cave appeared to travel backward endlessly. It could take a life-time to search it out.

Creeping through a dark cave with Kamillah behind him—it felt so reminiscent of their first adventure under Yathrib. Were they destined to spend all their time alone searching mysterious caves?

If they were successful, they would head south again, back toward Jerusalem. His best guess was that the third piece resided in Bethel, though he hadn't shared that knowledge with Zahir. The older mage would agree to a southward journey, however, because it would put them back in the path prescribed by the star.

A sharp cry behind him turned him around, in time to see Kamillah slip.

He cursed his wandering thoughts and inattention.

The slimy rocks, coated with mildew and moss, had betrayed her. She flung out an arm but found no handhold. Her feet and then her body slid over the edge of their narrow walkway. Into the water.

"Kamillah!"

Misha wedged the torch into the crack where wall met ledge and flung himself toward the place she had gone over.

The water churned below, ready to suck her under.

She clung to the narrowest lip of rock, just below the ledge. Her eyes were upturned and wide, but she did not scream.

Misha flattened his body and thrust an arm toward her. "Grab my hand!"

Her lips parted. She did not release her tenuous hold on the edge of rock.

It would have to be quick. If she didn't catch his hand immediately, she'd be caught in the surge.

Misha pushed farther, dared to lower half his body over the ledge, prayed they wouldn't both be pulled into the water.

His fingers made contact with her hand.

"Now, Kamillah!"

She clutched at his hand.

He circled her wrist with his other hand. Yanked upward without concern for causing her pain.

Hand over hand he pulled her up, until her knees braced the slippery ledge once more.

They both scrambled backward, then leaned against the rock wall, breathing hard.

"I cannot believe I was so clumsy."

Misha puffed out a breath. "I cannot believe I almost lost you."

"We should keep going."

He grabbed the torch and offered her a hand that she did not take.

They kept closer to the wall now and moved more slowly. Misha waved the torch as near his feet as he dared, ensuring that good footing lay ahead before taking each step.

Before too many steps, however, the channel where they walked turned sharply right away from the water, then forked into two distinct tunnels.

They stood side by side, wordless, contemplating the choice.

Kamillah finally spoke. "I say to the right first. Then double back and try left if we find nothing."

Misha shrugged. "Good enough for me."

The ceiling was lower in this section of the cave, almost low enough to force him to duck, and he held the torch higher, concerned for the safety of his head more than his feet.

The tunnel branched again and they took the right-most branch. And then again.

Misha pulled up.

Kamillah bounced against his back with a grunt. "What is it?"

"This place is like a Greek labyrinth. We may never find our way out."

"We'll be fine. Keep moving."

He glanced back at her face, lit with wavering shadows from the torch. "Why so anxious?"

She lifted her shoulders, but tension was there. "I feel—bothered."

Misha raised his eyebrows, waiting for more.

"Like we are being watched. Followed. Maybe chased."

A chill snaked down Misha's back at her words. "Chased?"

"I don't know. Foolish, probably."

"Given all that we have experienced on this journey, it does not seem foolish. Have you seen—?"

"No. No white fluttering. It's only that wind."

"The whistling sound?"

"Does it not sound like whispering to you?"

Misha lifted his head to the ever-present chilled breeze. A wave of near-panic washed over him and he fought it back. "Perhaps."

He would not voice what he suspected—that the Watchers could watch them even in this black place and wished them no goodwill. But the breeze was no longer the simple snaking of wind through empty chambers to him now.

Perhaps the demons rushed out of the underworld through this portal, into the world of men.

Should he have broken away to travel north, away from the star? Perhaps it was only the star that protected him, that sent the defending angels to his side when Zahir would have killed him.

Misha had insisted they travel up the east side of the Jordan, avoiding the more crowded cities on the western side and following established trade routes. But that was only the reason he gave Zahir. In truth, he wanted to avoid Jerusalem, and the return of the scrolls, until he had all the pieces of the Nehushtan. Whatever awaited them there, be it a new king to rule the world or something else, he wanted to be prepared with all the power that any of them needed——Kamillah, Reza, and himself.

But now, now that cold voices nearly choked the air from his chest and Kamillah clutched at his free arm and they wandered a maze of blackness with the sky and the star blotted out… Perhaps he should have continued in the star's path.

"We should have brought Reza with us." Kamillah's voice was hushed, as though she feared calling forth the residents of the underworld.

"Yes, Reza is the only one who can take care of himself."

She squeezed his arm, a little too hard. "Do not be spiteful."

How could he not be, when she continually seemed to prefer the soldier to the scholar?

"It is not spite. I am the first to admit that Reza has – qualities – I do not possess."

"Yes, a propensity to bludgeon his way through any obstacle. Even people." Her hand was still on his arm, softer now. "Reza does not know how to listen. Not like you.'"

Ah, but the general would have heard those words. Heard and been displeased.

As if she read his thoughts, she whispered, "I defended you to him, remember? When he wouldn't believe you about the—the things we see.'"

She was right. Her defense had warmed him, though it only increased the tension between Reza and him.

The tunnel opened suddenly to a cavern, the ceiling lifting above them to a height that gave Misha cause to take a deep breath, relieved of the tightness of the narrow channel they had traveled.

He lifted the torch as well, surveying the walls of the cavern.

"Do you think this is the place?" Kamillah pointed at the various niches and gouges in the rock walls. Most of them looked natural, but perhaps a few had been carved by hand.

"We are looking for something about a lion. You can read it in Aramaic, right?"

"I remember."

They circled the cavern together, Misha's light held as high as he could lift it, then dropped to take in the lower sections of the wall.

Would it be painted? Carved? A word spelled out or a pictorial representation?

"Step back, Misha."

He took in her face, worried that she had seen some danger. But she wore an intrigued expression—that look she got when she was deciphering a bit of puzzling text in a scroll.

"Look at the wall as a whole." She swept her arm in an arc to take in one side of the cavern. "When you try to see all the imperfections, does it not look like a lion?'"

"I can see it. But how—?"

"The mouth of the lion, it said, yes?"

"Do you think we need to dig below it?"

She shook her head slowly, still lost in thought. "No, the wording seemed clear about it being *in* the wall. Not the floor. Not at the base of the wall."

"Wait—it said *in the mouth*. We assumed that meant it would be in some kind of depression or niche in the wall. But what if—?"

But Kamillah was already rushing forward, feeling the stone.

Misha joined her, running his hand over the surface of the wall until his fingertips touched hers, then widening the search and coming back to her searching fingers again.

"What is this?" She slid her hand vertically along a crack, then pushed her fingers into it. "I can feel something!"

Misha searched the cavern floor for anything to use as a lever but found nothing.

"It's wedged too far in there. How did they expect us to get it out?"

"Perhaps they didn't."

She made a face and kept wriggling her fingers deeper into the crack.

If Kamillah's hands couldn't get deep enough, surely Misha's could not. He hated the idea of leaving without it, to return with some kind of tool.

"I have a corner…"

Misha frowned. "Corner of what?"

"I'm not sure." She flattened her body against the rock wall, her cheek pressed to the stone and eyes closed in concentration. ""Some kind of wrapping. Like the first piece we found, I think."

"Pull slowly."

"I know!"

Misha held his breath and watched the muscles of her forearm shift slightly as she eased the find out of its hiding place.

Her hand finally emerged, thumb and forefinger pinched around a scrap of rotting fabric.

Misha reached over her head and took hold of another part of it, keeping it secure between the two of them.

A moment later the entire piece fell into his hands.

He unwrapped it immediately, Kamillah hovering over it.

A bronze snake head, wrapped around a pole. The upper portion.

They had found it.

He had memorized the jagged break at the top of the middle section they'd located in Yathrib and knew already that this piece was a match. He lifted his eyes to Kamillah and found her smiling, such a joyful expression he nearly kissed her.

The wind through the cavern seemed to pick up, raising the hair on the back of his neck.

"Let's get out of here."

He rewrapped the piece and handed it to Kamillah in a show of faith, then poked the torch ahead of them to lead them out.

Many minutes later, he was sure they had taken a wrong turn.

"Misha, we are lost, aren't we?" Kamillah's voice was not quite accusing, but not amused either.

"Not lost. Just taking a different route out of here."

She huffed in response.

"Feel free to make a different suggestion."

But she had nothing to add, and they traveled in silence.

Until they heard something.

Misha drew up to listen more carefully.

Kamillah spoke the word. "Water."

Faster now, toward the sound. He never would have believed that water gushing from the underworld would have sounded more welcome.

And then they were back at their ledge and picked their way carefully along toward the mouth of the cave, catching glimpses of moonlight above the cascade of water that poured into the plain below.

They stumbled from the grotto, and Misha nearly gave a whoop of exultation despite the secrecy of their mission.

Until he saw the grove.

In the crash of water the scene before them played out silently, but there was no mistaking it.

A battle raged.

CHAPTER SIX

REZA

I swung my sword alongside men while the cold night sky looked down on the fiery rage of the sacred grove. Sword met sinew and flesh and bone with the sound of men screaming, men dying.

How had they known to come? Did Pan summon them from bed, warn them?

I had heard of Pan's followers—how they worshipped their god's ability to cause hysteria. They were crazed with lust and madness and opposed to civilization and order.

They believed that the relics in their cave drew power from the underworld. Drew it up and held it here, in this place, where they could call upon it.

And somehow they knew we had come to steal it.

I slashed at a man who held a sheep-shearing blade, pushed him back with the point of my sword. "Go home! Home to your family!"

But he would not heed logic. He came at me again, blade toward my gut.

He met my sword first.

More men, more improvised weapons. This was madness.

Soldiers, townspeople, farmers clashed in a battle while the cacophony of water rushed over us all.

My hand grew slick around my sword, coated with sticky wetness. I switched hands, wiped it clean on the swatch of tunic at my thigh. Even in the chilled night air, my fingers burned hot with the battle.

Were the Kasdim safe? Once again I had left some under my watch unprotected. But surely this canopied grove was the focus of the cultic attack. The old men would be safe in our hilltop camp.

Beside me, one of my men fell at the end of a pike.

I shouted a curse, slashed down the foe about my age, and glanced at Talib. The wound was not mortal, but it would be if he stayed on the ground. I wrapped a hand around his upper arm and yanked him up. Ignored his scream of pain.

"Get to the cover of trees! Can you walk?"

He moaned and would have fallen if not for my grip.

I wasted no time and lifted him like a babe. Arms under him, my sword was nearly useless but there was no changing it. I half-walked, half-ran to the thicker copse of trees and deposited him at the base of one. He leaned back in relief.

"Tie that off." I pointed to his leg. "Do you have the strength?"

He nodded toward the battle we left behind. "Go!"

And so I returned. Into the thick of the fray, feeling the hardness flow into my arms and hands. The cold marble that always came in battle.

And yet this was different. The coldness enveloped more than my limbs. It spread into my chest to meet the oath I had taken on the hill. I became a raging piece of marble, invincible stone with the fires of Hades within.

No battle had ever felt like this.

I lost count of the men I struck down. I whirled and slashed, yelled and trampled on bodies. Hair whipped my face like leather lashes. Blood mixed with sweat and tears, and I spit to clear it. The sounds of battle competed with the water—the hacking of limbs, the gurgle of blood pooling in throats.

And yet it was not a horror. I had let something loose inside myself, finally. And that loosed thing gloried in the destruction. Lost itself in the black and white of battle. The stars winked through the branches of olive trees and the pale moon smiled on me.

Sound and sensation ceased. There was only the movement of my arm and sword. Small details, sharp as pinpricks in my vision—a neck puckered with a pinkish scar before my blade reopened it, a bulging belly tied with a yellow sash that could not hold in life.

And then there was no one nearby to fight.

I circled, growling with bloodlust, looking for an enemy.

Bodies pockmarked the floor of the grove. Soldiers, half-bent still in defense, searched for remaining enemies.

It had been a slaughter. Greek farmers and merchants against a cohort of Parthian-trained soldiers.

I let out a whoop of exhilaration, and my men answered with their own.

And then Misha was there at my left arm, torch in hand.

I slapped him with a bloody palm. "You have missed the entertainment, brother!"

His eyes bore into mine. "Reza! What have you done?"

I looked from him to Kamillah, pale and shaking, who stood behind him. "What have I done? What have *you* done? Nothing! I can tell you that. As usual you are off playing your games while we put ourselves at risk for you."

"Playing games!" He pointed to a wrapped item in Kamillah's hands. "It is more than that and you know it. You are the reason that I—"

"You never do anything for anyone but yourself, Misha-el."

He glared at my use of the name he avoided.

"Oh, except for Kamillah, perhaps." I scowled at her. "I believe you would do anything to gain the attention of the fair Kamillah.'"

Misha took a threatening step toward me. "You should stop your mouth when the battle ends, Reza. You are out of control."

"Ha! Do you know how many men I have just killed?" I waved my sword to take in the grove. "What is a failed Kasdim going to do to me?'"

My men had gathered around this interchange, and I hailed them with words of praise. "Now, half of you stand guard while the others wash in the pool, then trade places."

I had barely finished before they were stripping off battle gear and plunging into the cold water.

Misha and Kamillah still watched me as though I had grown another head.

"I am going to join my men." I shed equipment, and when I began to pull the tunic over my head, Kamillah finally turned away.

She headed toward the hillside camp. "I will be in my tent."

And that was where I found her, after I had cleaned myself and my gear and changed into a gleaming white tunic.

I did not wait to be invited.

She climbed to her feet in surprise at my entrance but recovered herself quickly. "You owe Misha an apology."

I propped my sword at the entrance, crossed the tent in two strides, and towered over her. "Now you are acting as my commander? How many does that make who believe they can order me? Zahir, Misha. You."

Her face clouded. "What is wrong? Did something happen—?"

I grabbed her upper arms. "A battle happened, Kamillah! What do you think happens in battle?"

She pulled her head back, still in my grip. "I have never seen you like this."

"You had better get accustomed to it. This is what it looks like to have the strength to be a king."

"I am not talking of strength, but of anger. Misha and I are not your enemies, Reza."

I let her go with a shove. "You know nothing about what Misha and I are to each other."

"I think I do." Her voice was low, filled with sympathy.

But her pity only angered me. I did not need it.

"Yes, you watch with amusement, I suppose, at the way we compete over everything—over Simon. You."

"There is no competition when it comes to me."

"What does that even mean, woman?" I approached her again, wanting to grab her by the hair this time. Had she given herself already to Misha?

She took a step backward, her shoulders nearly brushing the back wall of her tent. "It means I will not be handed over as a prize to either of you. Or to Zahir. You know this, Reza." Her eyes turned to pleading.

But I did not understand what those pleading eyes asked.

"I do not speak of Phraates's prize, Kamillah." My voice thickened with emotion and another surge of anger as my weakness flooded me. ""I ask you to make your own choice. A rational choice. You have royal blood and you are beautiful. We are well-suited. You would make a fine wife."

She said nothing to this, only turned her face away.

Yes, a fine wife, if she didn't insist on disagreeing with everything he ever said.

"Now you are silent? Now when I am finally bold enough to speak the truth?"

"Truth?" At this her own face flamed. "Neither you nor Misha know anything of truth."

"Bah! A woman's riddles!"

She laughed, sharp and laced with derision. "You know nothing of women, either."

I backed her against the tent wall, took her by the shoulders. "I could have any woman I wanted, Kamillah."

She kept her face to mine, our foreheads nearly touching. "And you take whatever you want? Is that the truth, Reza?"

By the gods, she would drive me mad.

I wrapped my hands around the back of her head and pulled her to me. Something like the battle lust still raged in me. The urge to conquer, to control. I pressed my lips to hers, hungry. Angry.

She did not give way. Did not soften in my embrace or return my kiss.

I felt her struggle in my grip. Hands slapping at my arms. The sound of a cornered animal in her throat.

I did not care. I was finished with the patient weakness of a scholar. I was a general and I would be king.

I swept her down to her sleeping mat and fell to my side along her body.

Only then did I look into her eyes.

I expected a womanly apprehension. But all I saw there was loathing. Saw myself reflected in her eyes, savage and uncaring.

I hesitated and in my weakness she saw her opportunity.

She pummeled the side of my head with a fist. Struggled out of my grip and to her feet. Kicked me in the stomach for good measure.

And fled the tent, flinging my propped sword toward me, where it lay on the woven blanket beside my face.

I took several deep breaths, waiting for the beating in my blood to cease. But it went on and on, an echo to the pounding of battle.

Fingers wrapped around my sword, I pulled myself to sitting and examined its hilt for the thousandth time. It had been my grandfather's, then a gift from my father to me upon my promotion to the rank of general. I shifted the blade in the lamplight until it caught my face reflected in its polished sheen, staring back at me from the lifeless eyes of a man I did not know.

What had that man become?

A hundred emotions warred in my soul.

The need to be a strong general, to win the respect of my men.

The need to protect Kamillah, to win her heart.

Hatred for Zahir and his persecution of her, and yes, even hatred for Misha and the greater hold he had on her with his puzzles and his studies.

But under all of it was that promise of a greater destiny—the lure of power ready to be grasped, calling for me to surrender my nobility in exchange.

I had been pretending for so long. But tonight I had found a new strength, a new fury, in battle. The mask was becoming my real face.

But was it possible that aggression left unchecked, even welcomed, would break out in all directions? How could I have attacked Kamillah, the only good thing in my life?

Shoulders caved over my sword, I studied my reflection again in the blade that had seen such violence.

Could I be a man of brutality on the battlefield, on the throne, and yet remain a man of integrity and gentleness with a woman?

It was a question without an answer, but my soul cried out to make the attempt.

I thrust the sword from me, into the sand at the tent flap. There had to be a way to make a difference in the world, to do what one was called to do, without destiny turning the soul into something corrupt.

Could I find a way?

CHAPTER SEVEN

KAMILLAH

*E*nough.

The single word repeated in Kamillah's head, pounded in her heart, as she ran from her own tent into the north Judean night.

She had waited long enough to be free, to return home. She would wait no longer.

She ran along the edge of the noisy encampment, praying to Isis that she would not encounter Zahir or Misha, then past the ring of tents into the wild meadow on the hill above the Panais grove.

Wind snatched at her hair and sharp grasses snagged her legs, but she did not slow.

The beat of her sandals on the narrow graveled path kept time with her sole thought.

Enough.

For how many years had she longed to return to Egypt? She had absorbed all she could of Babylonian and Persian wisdom, of the teachings of Zoroaster studied by the magi under the Parthian Empire's thumb. She could return to her people with knowledge. Knowledge of a World-Savior that Egypt's worship of the gods and her fascination with death and the afterlife had never afforded her. It was hope she could give her people, and yet she'd had little of it these past years.

How far would she run before Zahir's threatening spirits caught her?

She had never dared face them fully, to see what they could do to her. Perhaps they were no stronger than the air in which they flickered, and she had been a fool all these years to fear them, to allow them to trap her in Nisa when the sands of Egypt called to her.

And yet she could not deny that she had gained power in Nisa. Her time there had trained her in the magic arts, and her power frightened even her at times. She had studied the knowledge, learned the tricks and illusions of the Kasdim, but it was not all sleight of hand. At times she felt the power flow through her, accomplish wonders even she did not know she could work.

In the distance an animal howled over a kill, raising a chill on her arms as she ran. She lifted her eyes to the horizon. A vague, dark line against the night sky marked Mount Hermon to the north. Almost she could pretend the mountain was the outline of one of her beloved pyramids. But she needed to run away from the mount, to the south and west where cities would offer her a chance at finding transportation to Egypt.

She would not dwell on the idea that she was fooling herself and it could not be that easy.

Her breathing grew tight and shallow, and she slowed to a walk finally. How far had she come from the camp? Did they miss her yet? Did Reza emerge from her tent to seek her out, to push her further?

Her fists tightened at her sides at the thought of him, of his dark eyes glazed over with battle. She was not a brothel woman to be so roughly handled.

And this after trying to convince her that she was his best choice for a wife!

Royal blood and beauty, Reza had said. Misha never spoke to her of either of these attributes. Perhaps because he did not see them. Perhaps because whenever together, they were too much occupied with fascinating discussions of philosophy and history and religion.

A rustle in the grasses nearby caused her heart to jump, then race faster than her feet. What dangers lay along this path, even before she reached a city, as a woman traveling alone?

She fought back hot and salty tears and focused on the coolness of the black sky, the white moon, and silver stars.

Which way to the nearest city? The ground was too level ahead to get a sense of how far. Would she eventually see firelight in the distance? It was too late for cook fires, too early for morning lamps to be lit. She could be accosted by any number of fearsome dangers—man, beast, or underworld—long before she reached safety.

As if in answer to her fears, another howl wailed in the distance and the sound of something, something large, moved through the night to her left.

She slowed, then stopped, all senses alert. The smell of animals, wet soil, and decay filled her nostrils, and she rubbed her arms to warm herself, keeping her lips sealed to slow her breathing.

Out of the darkness shone two bright yellow eyes, slitted with black down the center. Wolf? Some kind of large cat? It approached slowly, eyes unblinking.

Panic flooded through her, down to her fingertips.

Run? Back to the camp or toward an unknown city?

She chose the city. She hurtled forward, arms pumping and breath puffing white in the cold air.

Behind her, the padding of feet kept time. Whatever it was, if it chose to run, to pounce, she would have no chance.

Perhaps Zahir had sent the beast to drag her back to him.

A rock twisted her ankle but still she ran, blood hot and eyes streaming.

The sound of her sandals on gravel was now too loud to hear any soft paws. She veered into the grasses. Brambles caught her robe and slowed her flight. She returned to the path.

Any moment she would be torn apart. There was no cover to be had, no weapon to fight it off. Panic turned to cold certainty, as though she were falling from a great height and had simply not yet hit the bottom.

A horrible animal-shriek cracked open the night. She nearly stumbled at the sound, wanting only to curl up on the ground with her arms around her head.

Another terrifying sound—a growl and a snapping of jaws—erupted but the jaws did not close around her flesh.

She risked a slower pace and tried a glance over her shoulder.

She could see nothing in the night. But the noise, the noise was fearsome, as though the hounds of the underworld had been unleashed.

She paused and turned back. Whatever had been chasing her,

hunting her as prey, had drawn the attention of a larger beast. Two of them snarled and twisted in moonlit flashes of teeth and eyes and dripping saliva. A glistening of filthy fur, of dark blood on the white-pebbled path.

She would not wait to see who was the victor. With a shuddering breath of disgust mixed with terror and some relief, she continued her flight through the darkness.

Before long she was forced to slow to a walk. She had not run so far since childhood, and her lungs and heart would not cooperate with her mind.

How far did this path continue? Would it end in a forest or field, without taking her to a major road or a place to rest and find help?

She allowed herself a flicker of hope. She had come so far already without Zahir riding up behind her, without any nightly visions dancing along beside her, forcing her back to her tent.

And ahead, the horizon seemed to twinkle with spots of some kind of light. Too far yet to tell if they were bonfires a great way off, or tiny oil lamps shining through windows of nearby homes. But it was something. People, if nothing more than that.

She walked faster, emboldened and encouraged by the thought of help in the distance.

The ground began a slight rise she could barely feel except for the burning in her legs, an exhaustion she had not felt in all her studied years of palace life. Why had she not better prepared for this moment? Some part of her had always known that when the time came, she would have to run.

And why was this the time? Why tonight did she suddenly decide to risk whatever Zahir and his demons could do?

Reza.

She was too tired now to summon anger. A weary sadness burrowed through her thoughts. For years she had put him off, kept him circling just outside a place of intimacy. Knowing how he felt. She would not allow herself involvement with anyone of the Parthian Empire. She was going home.

And now Misha. Misha with his laughter and wit, his confident and defiant spirit. She would keep him at a distance, too.

As though to commit to the thought, she began to run again, putting more ground between her and the confusion of the two men.

The lights in the distance had grown no closer. Perhaps they were only the fires of shepherds on some distant hill, and she would be frozen long before she reached them. She pushed on, regardless. She would get somewhere, anywhere.

And then the ground fell away.

There came a fleeting moment of weightlessness, as though she ran through air. Then a fall, a jolt. The night sky tumbled to rest beneath her feet, then spun aright and winked out.

She was rolling. Rolling down an incline, with nothing to grab to stop the slide. Scrubby growth scraped her limbs. Dirt in her mouth and rocks sliding alongside, chasing her downward. She squeezed her eyes shut, thrust an arm out. Stopped tumbling and simply slid, down, down.

The bottom, at last.

She welcomed the jolt of hitting bottom, then moaned at the pain that wracked her body.

She lay there, panting, staring up at the pitiless moon.

The tears that had been waiting below the surface would not be denied. They slid in silent paths down her temples, soaking her hair. Then came in choking sobs, cutting off her breath. Would she die here at the bottom of this slope?

Back in Egypt, ceremony would have accompanied her death. Nostalgia rippled through her, a longing for mortuary temples and the clacking tools of the embalmer, of the softly chanted rites spoken over the dead. The spicy scent of myrrh like that which she had bought in Petra, and the wrappings of mummification to keep loved ones safe into the afterlife. It had seemed so peaceful, so simple.

She was too honest, even with herself, to leave her thoughts in that idealized memory. Always in Egypt she had questions, a discontent about the soul's passage, a desire for something more.

But tonight, at the base of a hill that would likely claim her life, she would give anything for even the uncertain comfort of Anubis and the Weighing of the Heart.

The tears had slowed and she wiped her face with her robe, still too weak to rise from where she lay.

A faint light wavered on the horizon. Was the darkness lifting so soon? Surely she did not run through the entire night.

A stab of terror lifted her from the cold ground.

It was not dawn at the edge of her vision.

How? How had they found her all the way out here, at the bottom of a hill? Could they see anywhere and everywhere, follow a person from birth to grave?

She tried to face them, to summon courage to order them back.

What prayer? She should have prepared an amulet while still in Nisa. Should have strung stone on knotted leather and spoken magic words over it as it lay under the stars, calling down power into itself, distilled and potent.

What was that beating sound? Did her heart threaten to pound from her chest?

No, it came from without.

The spirits had never made a sound.

But it was not the flickering apparitions. She knew the sound now. Hoofbeats. The swift approach of a rider on horseback.

And then he was there, as she had known all along that he would be. He pulled up beside where she sat among the rocks, and his horse pawed the earth as if impatient over the delay and eager to race forward.

Zahir.

They would not be moving forward. She saw that in his eyes, even in the darkness.

They would be going back. Back to the camp, back to the two whose friendship she was destroying. Back to bondage under the thumb of the man who tilted his head to study her now with a cool smile, as if she were nothing more than a wayward child.

"Kamillah, dearest. You left without saying good-bye."

CHAPTER EIGHT

ZAHIR

*D*id the foolish girl truly believe she could escape?

Zahir leaned down and reached a hand to help Kamillah onto his horse.

She smacked it away like it was the plague-riddled hand of a leper.

He swung from the horse, stood beside it, still swinging its leather reins in his hand.

"How did you find me?" Her voice fluttered like a silk head scarf in the breeze.

There was fear in that wavering voice, but something else as well. Hatred, perhaps. The desire to gain mastery over not only her own words but over him.

"Kamillah, it must be clear to you after all these years that I will not allow you to stray far from me."

She was on her feet now, arms wrapped around herself. "Why, Zahir?"

Yes, hatred in the voice.

"What do you want with me? Why are you so determined to keep me with you?"

He gave her a quick smile, one that revealed nothing. "My reasons are my own and do not concern you. You have only to be concerned with obedience."

"I am not your trained pet!"

He stepped forward, grazed the back of his hand across her jawline.

She pulled her head to the side.

"Not a pet, no. But you are well trained. Sometimes I believe that not even you know how well I have trained you."

Her eyes flashed. "Apparently not well enough to escape you."

Zahir lowered his eyes so she could see no response that would betray him. He greatly feared the day she discovered the untruth of those words. She was like a jinni kept locked in a bottle, who did not know she had the key to her own freedom. But he would keep his jinni for as long as he could.

"It is time, Kamillah." He inclined his head toward his horse. "You may mount first. I will ride behind you."

"I am not getting on that horse. You will have to kill me."

Ah, this frustrating rebellion was what he loved about her. "I have no intention of killing you, Kamillah." He waved an arm at the darkness around them. "But neither can I leave you here in this wilderness to be attacked by something dreadful."

"It is too late for that. You have already found me."

His amused frustration flared into something more heated. He wrapped a hand around her upper arm, a grip hard enough to leave a bruise, perhaps. But she had forced him to it.

She struggled to release herself from his grasp, beat against his arm.

He circled her shoulders in a tight embrace and pulled her toward the horse. Her hair was loosed and flowed over his arm like dark water. He leaned slightly, to bury his face briefly in all that luxurious hair. She smelled of perfume and spice like the Petran market. Like incense in a temple.

She fought him still, writhing under his hold, kicking at his legs. By the gods, he needed to break her spirit if he was going to keep her close.

"Kamillah!" The stern rebuke did nothing to slow her efforts. Did she not see how important she was to him? Why could she not simply continue as she had been in Nisa, learning under him and content in her pursuit of knowledge?

Despite her hostility he had her mounted on his horse, with himself behind, within moments.

He turned the horse back toward the camp above Panais, keeping the reins in one hand and the other arm wrapped about her waist. They traveled for some minutes at a walk. He was in no hurry to return.

Her body was as rigid as a corpse and nearly as cold.

She shivered in his arms. "My leg is bleeding."

He slowed the horse. "Why did you not tell me you were injured?"

She huffed a sarcastic laugh in answer.

"Kamillah, I am not a fiend. I have a true affection for you, even if you do not see it." He reined in the horse, dismounted, and then pulled her down with him. "Let me see your wound."

She cast her robe aside, revealing a dark gash against the silky tan of her skin.

He bent to better examine the cut to her shin, probing the cool muscles of her calf.

She shuddered under his touch. "It is not broken. Only a deep cut."

Zahir removed a strip of linen from the pouch he wore at all times and wrapped it gently around the injury, pulling the edges together.

She was still shivering, arms wrapped around herself again.

"You are so cold, dearest. I am going to make a fire. Get you warm."

"I am fine. Return me to the camp, to my own tent, and I will get warm there."

He smiled to himself but did not answer. She would not be returning to her own tent. Not tonight.

"Sit." He pointed to one of the larger boulders that littered the field. "There. And do not try to leave. Surely you can see that it is futile.""

She lowered herself to the stone, lips white in the darkness.

The trees at the edge of their field afforded him enough dry fallen twigs to burn for a short time at least, and he had items in his pouch that would assist. He gathered an armful, gaze straying to Kamillah often. The breeze whispered intimately in the branches above his head, soothing his troubled spirit that had plagued since the Watchers first woke him and directed him to Kamillah's empty tent. They had given him a gift tonight—the magic of far-off sight, eyes to see across the hilltop, along a white pebbled path, down into a rocky ravine.

He would do what was best for her, even if she did not yet see it. And she did not belong to Egypt, not when she could still do so much good for Nisa. For him.

She did not try to run again while he gathered fuel, nor when he knelt at her feet and added a few pieces of bitumen from his pouch to the pile of twigs.

The tiny container of bitumen shook slightly in his hand. He pinched a bit of it and sprinkled it onto a flat rock. A few strikes, a wave of his hand, and an incantation and he had it sparking yellow in the darkness. His gathered grasses caught, then the twigs, and finally the lumps of bitumen, which burned hot and soon glowed.

"Come." He pulled her from the rock to sit closer to the fire and she did not resist. Even a woman as obstinate as Kamillah could be bent by a need for simple warmth.

When they were seated side by side, shoulders touching, he studied her face. The golden light of the fire lit her skin until it glowed like sweet honey. The darkness retreated from their silent circle, and it felt as though they were the only people who existed in this tiny world of firelight.

"Why do you keep me, Zahir?"

He sighed. She would not let it go so easily. He must find a way to satisfy her questions and ensure her future cooperation. But not the truth. He would never let her see the truth, for that would be to admit weakness, to admit the fears that scratched at him in the night.

"Because you are strong. You are strong and useful for your insight."

"You have others for that. All of the Kasdim—"

"They do not fight me."

She closed her eyes and her head drooped. "So you keep me in bondage simply because I fight you? Do you mean to say that if I stopped fighting, you would let me go?"

He laughed. "No. But it might be more pleasant for both of us."

"You talk in riddles. In circles."

Yes, she would see through flimsy logic. He would expect no less.

"Your strength makes your knowledge more valuable, my dearest. Someone both brilliant in the ways of learning and gifted in the ways of magic is a valuable ally to those in power."

"And you would have more of this power, always."

"Yes, always!" He fought to control his voice. It would only reveal his commitment to never tread backward, back to a life where he had little knowledge, and therefore little power. He had been weak and despised once. Before he met his Watchers. Before they came to serve his needs. He could accept being despised. But he would never again be weak.

There were times, moments when the darkness seemed to creep across his soul like a slow-working venom, and he feared it would consume him. That it would blot out the scholar and leave only the power-mad sorcerer, the purity of knowledge forgotten.

That was why he needed Kamillah, though he would never tell her. She was all that was pure about the knowledge, about the learning. She kept him grounded in it, anchored to it. A reminder that knowledge could be prized and handled gently, without being abused to gain power over those weaker.

If the darkness was a venom in his blood, then Kamillah was the antidote. And for that reason alone, he would never let her go.

"Whatever it is you are trying achieve, Zahir, I will never be your ally."

He laid a palm across her skin.

She flinched but did not pull away.

Her skin was growing warmer. He traced the beauty of her brow line with a single finger, outlined her delicate ear, trailed his hand down her neck, then cupped her jaw against his palm.

Her eyes were so much colder than her skin.

Did she sense how he desired her, not only as an asset in a quest for power, but for herself, for the beauty that she was?

It was a battle he had often fought within. He would keep her close, touch her even, but always with restraint. She was the purity of knowledge, and he did not want to spoil that purity. Nor did he wish her to know the power she had over him.

But there were nights like this night when he doubted his ability to maintain restraint. She was very beautiful.

"You are warmer now. We should return to the camp."

She stood immediately and began to walk.

"On the horse, Kamillah. I will not have you walking."

"You will not have me on your horse. I despise the touch of you on my skin."

All the tenderness he had felt only moments earlier rushed away like low tide, with a surge of fury flowing in behind it.

He closed his eyes briefly. Spoke directly to those who had aided him thus far in his journey toward more power.

She walked only a few more steps, then jerked backward as though burned. She gasped and reached tentative hands into the air before her, then sucked in another breath when they appeared to collide with something.

She turned back to him, lips parted. "How are you doing this?"

Something solid had blocked her way. He breathed a prayer of gratitude to the Watchers. "You doubt my power, even still?"

She said nothing.

He needed more. Needed her to submit, to bow to him, to acknowledge the power he wielded. He raised a hand and called forth an incantation older than Parthia, older even than Persia, back to the glorious days of Babylon and the secret rites of the most ancient of Kasdim. A spell to inspire fear in even the strongest of women.

Kamillah's mouth opened wider, opened and closed like a fish's gills as it lay in the sand. Her eyes bulged and she clawed at her throat, as though his hands were gripped around it.

The words of the spell choked her, invisible and lethal.

She thrashed in the unseen hold, eyes begging for mercy.

Zahir let it go on for another heartbeat, then another. Another.

Finally, he waved a hand, whispered a word, and released her.

She fell to the ground, heaving in great gulps of air. Her fingers dug into the dirt and her shoulders shook, hair cascading so he could not see her face.

"Get up, Kamillah." He wanted to see her face.

She rose—slowly but without hesitation.

Ah yes, he had her now.

He had warned her that if she ever tried to leave him, his allies of the spirit world would stop her. He had allowed her to glimpse them on occasion, to remind her of her place. But never had she felt the physical yet invisible hand of power upon her body until tonight.

And in her eyes he saw what he wished to see.

She was his now. She belonged to him in every way that mattered.

CHAPTER NINE

REZA

"*You* are mad, Zahir."

I swept a scroll and the rocks that held it from the table inside my command tent, and one stone bounced off the chest of Galel, one of the three loyal soldiers clustered around the table and eying Zahir for his reaction.

Zahir's face purpled, his jaw tightened, but he said nothing.

The day before we had reached Bethel, the southern city that Misha declared the location of the next piece. Beyond my tent in a valley of the hilly country outside Bethel, the two factions that had been slowly dividing into rival herds were just beginning to stir in the morning fog, to stoke fires and heat water, awaiting instructions.

I jabbed a forefinger at the crudely drawn map now on the ground. "What you ask us to do—these are not the actions of honorable men."

Zahir spoke to my men. "It seems the mighty general has a distaste for what must be done to achieve victory. This is the man you would put on a throne?"

The tribunes fidgeted and looked to me.

"Achieve victory?" I mocked Zahir's tone even as I questioned him. "You speak as if the people of Bethel have come against us. They are shepherds and farmers, with no quarrel against us!"

"They are Judeans. What difference—"

"They are *people*. That is the difference. Or has your own lust for power obliterated any sense of morality you once had?"

Zahir motioned to my tribunes, two fingers that waved them from the tent. "Leave us."

Again, the nervous movements and eyes on me.

"They are not yours to command, Zahir."

He advanced on me, fist raised. "This entire expedition is mine to command!" Spittle flew from his lips. "It is you who is the usurper. And you will die for your traitorous ways.""

I laughed. "Then you will find yourself with no soldiers to protect you, and many who will see your body lain alongside mine."

Zahir pressed two fists against the table and leaned over it, glowering toward my position on the opposite side. "You overestimate your support, General."

"Do I? It is not only the soldiers who align with me. Some of your own Kasdim, certainly the Chakkiym, and even most of the traders have seen what kind of man you are and believe that Parthia might be better served by cooler heads—both on the throne and leading the Advisor"s Council."

At this reference to Misha's father, Simon, Zahir snarled and circled the table toward me.

Two of my men stepped forward, swords held parallel to the ground at the height of Zahir's chest.

The mage stopped abruptly with a glance at Galel's sword skimming the gold stitching of his purple robe. "You are a fool, Reza. Even you are committed to the finding of the last piece of the Nehushtan—do not think I am deceived about your true goal—and this is the only way to retrieve it."

"Then it will lay where it has lain for seven hundred years. For we will not slaughter the innocent in any quest for power. Not one of us."

Zahir nudged Galel's sword away from himself with a single finger, and his tone became conciliatory. "This is what I am saying, Reza. They are not innocent. They are Jews. They have done nothing but foment trouble from the time our Babylonian ancestors first rightfully claimed their land."

I sighed, heavy with frustration. In truth, I had no better plan. Our scouts had returned from Bethel late last night, with news that the locals were suspicious and unfriendly, as if they had something to hide.

I had longed to speak to both Misha and Kamillah about our mutual goal, but though Misha had gone with the scouts, he had not returned with them. They reported that he was spending the night in Bethel, attempting to get more information.

And Kamillah? She had not left Zahir's side since Panais. I had not gotten a chance to speak to her, to apologize. She spent the days of travel south riding beside him or even on his own horse, with his arms circling her and her face set like stone, refusing to even look at me. She spent nights in Zahir's tent.

Clearly, my unforgivable actions toward her in Panais had sent her running for the protection of her mentor. So I was alone in my evaluation of our next move into Bethel to retrieve the Nehushtan's final piece. The final step of a plan that benefitted myself and my friends and would betray, and perhaps destroy, Zahir.

But I could not agree that a cluster of Jewish shepherds were worthy of death simply because they were Jews. I inclined my head toward my men. "Escort Zahir to his own tent. I will speak to the troops in one hour with instructions."

Zahir's glare on me as the soldiers pushed him from the command tent was more than angry—to me it seemed like evil itself, if such a thing was possible.

Alone, I bent over the map of the city, drawn in haste by the scouts in the night.

Where were those guardian spirits that followed us and battled unseen against Zahir's Watchers? We could use some invisible help today.

I sketched some plans, discarded them, and sketched anew.

Less than hour had passed when the sound of argument drew me from my tent.

The morning's heavy fog had not lifted, but I could see far enough to know that the trouble that had been threatening for many days was about to erupt.

My sword was in my hand in an instant, its smooth coolness too familiar, too comforting.

Hostility had cleaved the camp into two factions, facing each other with jeers and yells.

I pulled aside Galel, still nearby after the confrontation in the command tent. "Update, Galel."

"Word has spread, General. The men know you are refusing Zahir's strategy." He coughed and spit into the sparse grass. ""Some insist that you go too far, that in making yourself over Zahir, you claim authority over Phraates as well. They say they will not be part of your rebellion."

"Rebellion." I turned the word over in my mouth, not liking the sound of it.

The yells had broken out into a skirmish. A half-dozen men, men who considered themselves brothers-in-arms only a few months ago, scuffled in the dirt in the center of the camp.

"Enough!" I forded into the brawl, waving my sword at the unarmed men still in their tunics. "We have enough to do to keep our people safe——"

But it was too late. Perhaps it was the fog, thick and portentous. Perhaps it would have happened even in a rosy dawn.

Instead of the small scuffle breaking up, it rose to a clamor that called to every fighting man in the camp, and within a few heartbeats, a true and bloody battle had begun.

I fought alongside the men who had pledged me their loyalty. But I fought against others who had followed me into other battles, when our cause was defense of our homes and families.

My sword sliced through fog, sliced through men. Overhead black birds of prey already circled, summoned to the battlefield by their instinct for blood.

Through it all I screamed for an end. I screamed for unity among brothers. My face was wet with tears as much as sweat and blood.

And it was not the soldiers only. Traders had taken up arms, and even some of the Kasdim grabbed up swords as if in holy war against sedition.

Where was Kamillah in all this? I prayed that her confinement to Zahir's tent would not see release today, not this bloody morning.

How many men had I killed already? My own men, once.

My Panais vow to find another way, a way not bathed in violence, mocked me now. There was no other way.

I took a small injury to the upper arm, a glancing sword-blow that drew blood but only slowed me for a moment. I needed to back away from the battle, to get perspective and find a way to end it with as little further damage as I could.

I limped to the edge of the fray, was met by Jabari, who waved me toward him.

His breath came in sharp gasps borne of exertion, and he pointed to the battle. "It was planned hours ago, General. It is Zahir's loyal Kasdim that riled some of the men into fighting against you."

"The Kasdim!"

He jabbed a thumb into the fog behind him. "A few Kasdim who are not so certain bring word to four men. They are building a plan to end it. They sent me to find you."

I nodded into the fog. "Take me."

He walked ahead for thirty paces, then dropped back to walk beside me. "Where are they, Jabari? Why so far—?"

But Jabari's dagger point was at my side.

I reached across my body to draw my own sword.

"Do not try it, General. Keep walking."

"You, Jabari? You would take the side of the mad mage?"

"He is loyal to Parthia, sir. To the king I have sworn to protect." He jabbed the dagger in little harder. "As have you. Or so we thought.'"

Jabari had spent long nights in the tents of those who planned my takeover of the throne. A traitor among us all this time. It was no wonder that the two sides had grown increasingly more hostile as Jabari reported our plans and actions to the others. To Zahir.

"Where are you taking me?"

"Not far."

It was no answer, but I did not press him. Better to let him feel my confusion, and to ready myself for whatever was to come.

A steeper hillside appeared out of the fog, with an opening gouged into its side. Jabari stripped me of my sword, shoved me into the shallow cave, and stood at its entrance, dagger in one hand and sword in the other.

I faced him, more able to see him in the clear air of the cave. The small space reeked of animal but was empty. Jabari's face held none of the fear or uncertainty I had hoped for.

"You will kill me here? Do you think that will help your cause? Those who oppose Phraates will only find another, and my death will inspire."

He pointed to my arm, still bleeding. "You will not die an inspiration. You will die of that wound at the outskirts of the camp, and I will report that I saw you run in fear from the battle."

"The wound is not a death blow, Jabari. Perhaps you want to come closer and see if you can make it so."

"It is not for me to make an end of you."

"Zahir."

"He insists on doing it himself. Says it will be an offering to Ahura Mazda, who watches over Parthia and keeps her safe."

"So where is the mad mage?"

"He will be here soon." Jabari pointed at the floor of the cave, nearly covered in the dung of whatever animal made it a home. "Sit.""

I sat, to conserve my strength, and to tend to the wound that could keep me from fighting Zahir and the traitor with all the force I could muster.

Jabari went to the mouth of the cave, stood outside it perhaps to provide Zahir with a landmark in the lifting fog.

I dressed the wound with supplies from my pouch, then found a cleaner place at the wall and leaned against it. To wait.

I had no weapon but my hands and was about to face Zahir who could kill with magic.

Where was my destiny now? I had tried to rise up, to be the military leader my people needed, to make a difference in this bloody world. But I had failed. And now I would die in disgrace, in dishonor. I had not made peace, not bettered the world for my people.

I am sorry, Father.

My coup was over before it ever began.

CHAPTER TEN

MISHA

The sun was past its zenith by the time the scouts finally left to report to Reza and Zahir. Misha shook his head when they motioned for him to join him, then climbed upward to a perch on the highest hillside of Bethel. The three tunic-disguised soldiers crept from the town assuming they were unseen, but they were clearly visible from the hillside. Did the shepherds who roamed the hill also watch their departure?

Misha turned from the scattered homes of the village to scan the flat pasture atop his hill. Knee-high grasses, copper-colored and crackling dry, swayed in the fresh breeze against an azure sky and the far-off bleating of sheep carried to where he stood, hands on his hips as he studied the landscape.

It had to be the High Place where Jeroboam had set up his altar. A tiny thrill ran through him, that familiar excitement of figuring out the unknown.

But who could say whose altar was the one he sought? Abraham had met with his God here and built an altar to mark the place. His grandson Jacob, in his flight from his angry twin Esau, had seen a vision of angels descending from heaven here and had also built an altar, naming the place Beth-El, "House of God." Clearly the spot was a center of power, as Kamillah would say, and no wonder that when Jeroboam decided to set up his alternative places of worship, he chose this spot at the southern-most part of his ten-tribe kingdom.

Perhaps it was Abraham's altar, or Jacob's, or even Jeroboam's that held the third piece. Or perhaps somehow all three were one and the same. But here on the hillside that stretched toward the horizon in three directions, no altars could be seen.

He started walking, hand shielding his eyes from the lowering sun.

Zahir would want to send soldiers to scour the village and hillside, with little regard for the people. If Misha could locate the piece first, before Zahir exerted force, it would be better for everyone. Zahir believed that wholesale destruction of anyone in his way was the best manner of handling inconveniences.

Not to mention that Misha would then have all three pieces and be ready for the next part of his plan. To Nisa and Mother. And to help Reza, even if his closest friend had ceased to trust him.

A knot of anger twisted around the lighter spirit of the hunt. If Reza didn't trust him, believe him capable of handing the Nehushtan over to Phraates to win Kamillah, then why should he remain loyal to the man? Why not do what he expected and gain Phraates's favor and Kamillah in one swoop?

Ahead, a cluster of shepherds came into focus, their white-and-black flock scattered among shorter, greener grasses. They were on alert long before Misha was within range of speaking to them.

"Greetings." Misha held up a palm, tried to look harmless.

Three of them had spread out among the flock as he approached. None returned his salutation. Eyes wary and mouths tight, they watched him stroll across the pasture.

"Beautiful day, eh?" The chatter was ridiculous, but he needed to gauge their level of hostility. Was it simply their flocks they were protecting, or something else?

Still no answer.

"I am journeying through on my way to Jerusalem. Your village seemed a good place to rest and your hillside too lovely to resist."

The shepherd closest to him, also the burliest, cocked his head. "You are not a Judean."

Misha gave a light laugh. "Perceptive. It was the voice, I suppose? No,

I am from Parthia, though my mother is Judean. I have come to make a visit to her old home."

What would this rural shepherd, one of the poorest of society, say if he knew Lydia's "old home" was none other than the palace of King Herod?

"Perhaps you should be journeying on, then." The spokesman poked his staff in a roughly southern direction.

Misha grinned. "At this hour? Surely you have some hospitality in your village? I have heard so many stories at my mother's knee of Bethel." He waved an arm casually across the plateau. "Abraham and Jacob, seeing their visions, meeting with the One God, HaShem. It's a holy place, no? I would love to see their altars." He brought his attention back to the men, pushed forward despite their furrowed brows. "And even perhaps Jeroboam's altar? That would be something to tell my own children!"

"There is nothing here to see." The brusque statement, delivered with no small amount of hostility, made it clear that casual visitors were unwelcome. The three were tightening their defense now, unworried for their sheep, rejoining in the center of the flock, a united front.

"Come, now. There must be some small pile of rocks somewhere, something for the local legends to be hung upon—"

"It is time for you to move on, stranger." This time the staff was lowered like a Roman's pike.

Misha shrugged as if the shepherds had merely commented on the weather. "Too bad, then. But I will remember the beauty of your town, all the same." He waved a friendly good-bye, then started down the hillside toward the village.

It wasn't going to be as easy as he hoped.

Village life was slowing at this hour, with only a few people still about, and the well of the central village nearly deserted. Misha headed there first, his eye on a pretty girl drawing water.

She eyed him subtly, with a shy smile that invited conversation.

Misha pointed to her jug and winked. "You must have come out here just for me, a poor thirsty stranger, yes?"

Her smile widened, white teeth and pink lips, directed toward the depths of the well. "You are welcome to a drink." She held up the jug and braved a direct look at him.

Misha smiled into her brown eyes, flecked with gold to match the sunlit highlights in the brown hair that peeked from her head covering.

Ah, but now that she observed him directly she was not so shy after all. He knew that look well, had seen plenty of girls offer it.

She sidled closer and handed him the jug with a lingering touch. She smelled of honey and baking bread.

The water went down cool and sweet, and Misha's belly rumbled.

The girl laughed. "Perhaps you need more than water."

"Nothing you couldn't provide, I am certain."

She raised her delicate eyebrows, then nodded. "Stay here." She was back in a few minutes, a basket of yeasty bread in hand.

Misha tore a piece from the loaf, chewed slowly, and leaned back against the stone wall of the well. He directed his attention to the hillside, where the shepherds could barely be seen.

"I wandered around up there for a while, hoping to find the places that make your small town famous. I was surprised to find nothing to mark the spot." He patted the lip of the well beside him, encouraging her to sit. "But perhaps that is so curious travelers like me have to beg for a guide to show them Bethel's secrets."

The girl sat on the edge of the well, letting her leg brush his, and laughed. "My father tends sheep up there. He would not like to see me leading you anywhere."

"Hmmm. Pity." Misha reached for her basket, tore another piece of bread. "How will I ever find it, then?"

"Something tells me you could find it with a little bit of direction."

He smiled. "And where would I find—?"

But she was already pointing. "Do you see that small grove of trees, there, to the left?"

He followed her hand and nodded.

"Walk directly west from there, all the way to the far crest of the hill, just before it begins to drop on the other side. You will see a clearing— the area was once burned and strangely has never recovered." She smiled prettily. "I'm afraid you will be disappointed, though. There is nothing but a pile of rocks." She adjusted her head covering, letting more hair escape. ""The town is much more interesting, I should think."

"Ah, I have no doubt of that. But my mother would never forgive me if I did not make a pilgrimage to our father Jacob's famous altar."

He waited for her to contradict, but either it was indeed Jacob's altar or she did not know the lore. Either way, he had his direction.

He stood, and she jumped from the well's edge to stand beside him. "You will come back before dark falls? We will be happy to have you stay the night—"

"We shall see. Perhaps I will need to continue my journey."

Her face flickered with a moment of unease, distrust perhaps. Who ever insisted on journeying at night when hospitality was offered?

He glanced around the well area, saw no one, then leaned to give the girl a peck on the cheek. "Thank you for the water, the bread, and the company."

Her face flushed. "I hope to see you again."

He bowed and made his escape, with only a slight jab of guilt at the flirtation. The girl had nothing to truly tempt him. She had none of Kamillah's brilliant mind or startling beauty.

If he could find the final piece before it grew too dark to see, he would be on his way before Zahir even gathered men to approach the town.

The shepherds were still with their flocks to the north of the girl's copse of trees. Misha crested the hill, then angled to the west and walked with the orange heat of the sun in his eyes. The girl's instructions had better be accurate, for he could see little with that glare.

But then the hill started to drop away in front of him, and the clearing was there, just as she promised. A charred and blackened rectangle as large as a village house, as though some inner fire kept it smoldering, smokeless but infertile, through generations.

And the pile of rocks—he had expected some haphazard remnant of an altar, but even from a distance he could trace the outline of an altar, though smashed and cracked in many places.

He approached cautiously, slowly. Was it the sacred space where Jacob's angels had passed between heaven and earth? Or was it Jeroboam's abomination, cursed with the burnt bones of false priests?

His attention was so fixed on the stones, falling into shadows and beckoning him forward, that he did not hear the approach of others until it was too late.

"You there!"

He spun at the sharp bark of a command, to face the group of shepherds he had met before. Was the biggest of them, the nastiest of them, father to the sweet girl at the well?

"You are not welcome here." He advanced on Misha, close enough to see two rotting teeth and the dirt-crusted collar of his tunic.

Misha put on his most innocent and reassuring smile. "I was only having a look—"

They were not interested. The leader grabbed Misha by the arm. The shepherd's sharp and dirty fingernails dug into his skin.

He tried to keep it light. "Must be buried treasure here, then?"

But the man was accustomed to fighting off wolves. He was behind Misha in a flash, pinning his arms behind him. And the hard-fisted blow to Misha's ribs was anything but casual.

He doubled over into the pain and the air rushed from his lungs.

The shepherd yanked him to standing, left him vulnerable to the next blow by one of the other men.

The one behind him pulled him into an unfriendly embrace. The stench of a man too long with the sheep and the scratch of his beard against Misha's cheek nearly gagged him.

Both of his friends had joined the attack now and pummeled Misha's jaw, his ribs, under his chin. The big one finally let him go and he dropped to the blackened ground, only to be kicked in the belly.

He lay still after the last kick, praying they would think him dead. It was the smart thing to do, though everything inside him boiled in outrage and he wished for a friend or two to fight beside him against these worthless peasants.

The beating stopped. He kept his eyes closed, his breathing as even as possible.

He felt himself lifted to a shoulder. So they wouldn't leave him near the altar, even if they'd killed him.

The jarring step of the shepherd beat like a drum against his head, and before long the darkening skyline went completely black and winked out, lost to his consciousness.

CHAPTER ELEVEN

REZA

I waited for what seemed hours for Zahir to come and finish off my pathetic attempt at greatness. With nothing but the cave wall to look at, I memorized every crack and fissure, traced each trickle of dampness from source to destination.

The sound of the men fighting faded as the hours passed. Had one side or the other been destroyed? Or had they found a way to forge a truce, at least for now?

I would never be a king, clearly.

But as the time passed, instead of filling me with more despair, the thought seemed to lighten whatever had been suffocating my spirit for weeks.

I would never be a king!

No, I had no wish to die at the end of Zahir's sword, or worse—as the target of his magic. But could there be a third way—a way to avoid both death by Zahir and crowning by my father?

The words of Simon seemed to whisper through my tiny cave.

"You are called to be the man you must be."

Of late, I had assumed that calling to be my father's plan. But was it possible I could break away from the expectations? Was destiny the thing you were born to do, not the thing someone else decided you must do?

The mist had burned away and the sun had long since set. But in my cave, I felt as though a beam of clarity had illuminated everything I ever was, and promised light for the path into what I could become.

A sound at the mouth of the cave. My new resolve would soon be tested, perhaps extinguished.

A muffled moan, some whispered commands. It did not sound like Zahir entering with his spells and his sword.

I slid my body upward, back braced against the wall, until I was standing. Fighter's stance, legs braced, arms raised. I would not make it easy.

"Reza?" The harsh whisper did not reveal the speaker. "General? Are you in here?"

I stepped forward, arms still raised at chest height, hands flexed and ready. The figure outlined against the dim light beyond the cave was only a silhouette.

"Who is there?"

"Bassam, my lord. And Walid."

"What of the one who was guarding—?"

"Jabari will waken eventually. We knew you would not want him killed."

I nodded, even though they could not see me. "Zahir?"

"No doubt headed this way. The fighting has stopped and he'll find it safe. We need to get you out of here."

They had mounted my rescue because they believed me their future king and capable of bestowing favors. What would happen to the loyalty of my men when they learned of my decision?

"Where?"

"The safest thing is to sneak you into Bethel. Talib found a tavern at the edge of town. A dozen of your best men will meet you there. Form your personal guard."

Personal guard. The words of men protecting a king.

But I would deliver the disappointing news after we were safely away from this cave.

"Lead on."

We skirted the encampment, keeping a wide distance. I held up a hand before proceeding beyond the camp. "Has anyone seen Kamillah during the madness? I'd like to get her out of there."

Even in the darkness I could see Bassam's shake of the head.

My heart seized. "What has happened?"

"Nothing, nothing, General. She never emerged from Zahir's tent, not during any of the fighting, or even after."

I exhaled, my chest still tight. Why her sudden attachment to Zahir? Or did he somehow control her even more closely than ever?

We continued toward the highest rise south of us, which Bassam and Walid assured me was the hillside above Bethel.

It would be the High Place of Misha's history, no doubt. Would he meet us in the village, perhaps in the tavern?

Or had he already found the third piece and taken advantage of the day's chaos to slip away with the entire Nehushtan, back to Nisa, to his mother. To his prize.

The promised dozen men were already in the dimly lit tavern when I arrived with my two rescuers.

They stood immediately, silent and serious. Many of them wore bloody bandages and the reek of battle was on them all.

They had fought for me.

It would only be the beginning of my disappointing others—the real blow would be to my father when we returned. But it would start here.

I motioned for them to sit and found a place among them at the long, splintered table. The innkeeper brought me wine in a crude cup, sloshing it onto my hand when he clapped it onto the table.

I drank deeply, trying to fortify myself.

"I am in your debt, all of you, for today."

At the chorus of disagreement, I raised my hand. "Hear me out. I have news that is not what you wish to hear, I fear."

Every eye around the table focused on me. I leaned forward, in an attempt to leave the innkeeper out of our conversation.

"It is clear to me that the men we have brought from Nisa will never stand together. Not after today."

A few fists thumped against chests, in silent solidarity with what they believed to be my cause.

"But something else has become clear to me. I am not the man to lead this revolution."

Bassam started forward. "You are the rightful—"

"That may be, Bassam. But that does not make me qualified. Nor obligated." I placed my palms flat on the table. "Nor destined.""

"So you will turn tail and run? Leave Zahir to put together this thing that will give him power—?"

"No. Not that." The cold anger in my voice surprised even me. "I do not know what the future holds for the Persians, whether we will regain our empire from the Parthians or not."" My voice rose above the musty silence of the tavern. "But I do know that if this Hebrew piece is as powerful as everyone believes, it should never be in the hands of someone like Zahir."

Cups pounded the table in response to my passionate statement.

"So what then?"

Yes, what then? In truth, I had been thinking of nothing else since my men rescued me from the cave. Zahir would not cease to hunt for me until he found me and killed me.

I had turned over the idea of grabbing Kamillah and running. To Egypt, to the safety of her home. It was the only place she would run with me. But I had no assurance that I could break Zahir's hold on her.

No, there was nothing to be done except the same thing that I had been pressing toward for weeks now. Find the pieces of the Nehushtan, use the power to break Zahir. Return the piece to Nisa. Only now it would be to deliver it to my father, to empower someone else to lead their people, if such a thing could be done.

But today had changed one thing—I would not work side by side with Zahir to find the third piece. No longer did I suffer the delusion that he found me irreplaceable and would let me live until the piece was found. Wherever it lay, and I prayed that Misha could figure it out, we would have to find it with subterfuge and in secrecy, or I would have to face Zahir head-on.

And I would have to kill him.

I nodded to the men, who had waited through my reverie with patience. "There is little time. After today, we have identified ourselves as traitorous to Zahir and to Phraates. We must find the piece before Zahir does and return it to our people in Nisa."

"How? We have no idea where it is to be found, where to look."

As if summoned by Bassam's words, the door to the tavern banged open and the figure of Misha hung outlined in its frame.

But he was not the cunning and triumphant mage we needed. He staggered against the door frame, grabbed for air, and fell to the dirt-packed floor.

"Misha!" I jumped from the table and knelt at his side. His face was sallow in the lamplight, except for the purpling of bruises along his jawline and a bloody gash against his lip. I slapped his cheek lightly. "Misha!"

The innkeeper loomed. "I don't want any trouble—"

"Get me some watered wine, man!"

A moment later I was bracing his shoulders against my arm and holding the cup to Misha's lips, dribbling the liquid between them.

He stirred against my arm and sipped at the wine.

"Misha, can you hear me?"

My men clustered around, each one peering over me to watch the mage.

His eyes flicked open. He sucked in a desperate breath and struggled to get free.

"Easy, friend. You've had an accident."

Even with a split lip, I could see his ironic smile. "Accident? I've had a beating."

He got his fists under him, pulled himself to sitting, and surveyed the room. "What are you all doing here?"

"It's a long story. I think you should go first."

He sighed and gingerly touched his face. "How ugly?"

I shrugged. "At least I can be sure of Kamillah's affections now."

Misha's eyebrows rose at my uncharacteristic joke. "Get me to a chair. And get me some proper wine."

We traded stories of the day late into the night, the men adding details of the fight I had missed while trapped in the cave. In the end, after all the news and all the facts, it was clear. We who sat in this tavern, all twelve of us, were the only thing that stood between Zahir and his goal of fantastical power.

And we would not let him have it.

CHAPTER TWELVE

MISHA

*M*isha crept through hillside grasses, no more than shadows scratching at his legs under a moonless sky. The burned-down torch in his right hand gave little light, but the other in his left was ready for the right moment.

The silence of the night remained unbroken. Misha raised his gaze to the tree line to his left. Reza had trained his men well. There was no way to tell that they followed, armed and ready.

But dawn would be upon them all too soon. It had taken too long to put their plan together. And if Reza's new friend had been suspicious, her father had been even less cooperative. Only the collective strength of Reza and his soldiers at Misha's back had convinced the shepherd that the town's best chance lay with them. Of course, the shepherd Eliakim did not know the entire plan.

The burned-out clearing was barely distinguishable in the darkness. Misha swung his torch away from his line of sight and squinted across the level hilltop. Yes, that was the place he remembered, and the pile of rubble that must have once been an altar. Whose altar, it was impossible to know. But considering the shepherds had guarded it so fiercely, something must be there.

He glanced at the trees again. Were Reza's men there watching him?

Waiting for him to work some kind of magic, to reveal the third piece with only a wave of his torch?

He touched the smoldering torch end to the other well-soaked cold one, then turned away half-closed eyes at the burst of light. A single torch could be seen for miles. He would have to rely on the protection of the soldiers.

He circled the pile of stones, tried to get some feel for the dimensions and angles of the altar, some logic to apply to where the third piece of the Nehushtan would have been hidden for all these years.

His father's synagogue readings came back to him from unused and dusty places in his mind... "*The altar split apart and the ashes poured out.*"

But this pile was nothing but cracks and fissures, alcoves between boulders and gaps inside of porous rocks. Perfect places for snakes to hide. Misha shuddered and shoved the torch into a large gap. No beasts slithered out, but that proved nothing.

How long did he have? Thankfully, the clearing was just over the crest of the hill, so the town below would remain ignorant of the lone torch bobbing around their precious altar. Eliakim knew only of Reza's men, hiding in the trees in "protection"" against Zahir. Misha had warned Eliakim that Zahir's men would approach soon, determined to desecrate their altar and kill any in their way. He had feigned ignorance of Zahir's specific plan but offered the protection of Reza and the soldiers, to keep their altar safe. Would the people even know that Misha had stolen it?

He pushed away a twinge of guilt and thought of his mother. Of her pale lips and sallow cheeks, her hair fanned out over her bedcoverings as she said good-bye to him. And if Misha didn't take the piece, Zahir certainly would, so there was no way to keep the people's treasure intact.

Besides, they didn't even know what they guarded.

He brought the torch low to the ground and circled the rocks. Where would the split have been? Would it be marked by paint on a foundation stone, perhaps? But paint could have worn away.

Thoughts of his father's readings and his mother's smile had made him melancholy. Homesick. And reminded him again that his desperate fight away from his father's beliefs had only led him closer to his father's God.

How many times had he traced a path around the rubble? Perhaps if he made it seven, the rocks would tumble like the walls of Jericho and reveal the treasure within. He smiled. What would Father say of Misha's remembrance of that old story?

"You there!"

Misha let out a heavy breath and turned to the voice.

"What are you doing?"

Was it one of Eliakim's shepherd clan? "Just a traveler. Looking for a place to bed down in some safety for a few hours." He cringed at the sound of his own voice, which carried too loudly and too far across the silent hill.

How much time had passed since they had convinced Eliakim to send the town's fastest rider to Jerusalem? Twelve miles there and twelve miles back, plus time to convince the Romans and priests to send men to arrest Zahir. The plan depended on precise timing. Misha did not have the slack for interfering shepherds.

The voice came into the circle of Misha's torchlight. Bushy brows drew together over squinting eyes. He gave the altar only a glance, but his protective stance was clear. "You can't sleep here. Go down into the village—"

"I don't want to trouble anyone. I'll be on my way before daylight—"

"We don't like strangers wandering around up here."

Clearly. Misha raised his free hand, palm facing the man. "Perhaps I will be on my way tonight, then." He pointed south. "This way to Jerusalem, yes?""

The man said nothing, only scowled and watched Misha until he turned away and started along the ridge of the hill.

How long did he need to walk to satisfy the shepherd that he was truly leaving?

Years ago, during a palace demonstration, he had seen Zahir disappear in a puff of bluish smoke. It was too bad he didn't have some of that magic tonight. Even his pair of metal rings were hidden in his belongings, still with the Chakkiym. Although a pass of one ring through another would do little more than distract.

To his right in the copse of trees, Reza and the men no doubt watched from the shadows, wondering what he was doing. He kept moving until a glance backward told him the clearing was no longer in sight.

He waited. Counted off a few minutes under the star-laden sky. Kept his torch low. Then headed back.

He was still a hundred paces from the altar when the alarm sounded —a whooping call that brought more than a dozen men from over the shadowy hill to run at Misha with malice in their faces.

Misha held his torch out at chest height, but he knew even before he heard the answering battle cry that Reza's men would not remain in hiding.

He could feel them flooding out of the trees even now, swarming up to stand at his defense behind him.

If Zahir's faction arrived anytime soon, the attack they had planned would be as surprising as a sunrise.

CHAPTER THIRTEEN

KAMILLAH

*K*amillah was not asleep.

It was late into the night before Zahir returned to his tent after the camp split into two angry factions. And he did not return in good spirits.

She waited, muscles tense and ears trained to the sounds of the night for any call from Reza or Misha. Neither had come for her when the fighting began, but if the situation grew dangerous, surely they would not leave her to Zahir?

But then, why not? Neither had approached her since the night she ran from Panais, the night Zahir showed her how easily he could kill her and then dragged her broken spirit back to his tent. She had not dared to defy him since. She spent her days trying to block all thought from her mind and her nights praying to Isis that he would stay on his side of the tent.

Zahir swept the tent flap aside, stalked inside, and let it fall. He ran a glance over her where she lay on a mass of sleeping cushions, a small lamp lit on the ground near her head. "Do not turn those cold eyes on me, woman. I need none of your antagonism tonight. There is enough of it about."

She propped herself on an elbow. "Yes, it seems even your men are seeing the truth about you."

He slid across the luxurious tent and bent over her.

From outside she could hear the crackle of the camp's central fire, fed with blackening dung chips. But though others were only a breath away, she had no thoughts that anyone would come to her rescue should she cry out.

Zahir smiled, that wickedly indulgent smile she so despised, his slick tongue glinting in the lamplight and lips stretched thin. "Then let us hope that truth spreads even to your friends, since it is the truth that there is nothing they can do to defeat me."

"No?" She could not resist a prod of mockery. "That is not what I hear. You were not so successful in putting down today"s rebellion."

He dropped to his knees before her, but the position was anything but humble. He stroked a smooth finger along her arm, from wrist to the inside of her elbow, then up to her shoulder.

The air of the tent felt close, stifling, as though the fire had been stoked here rather than in the center of the camp. Damp sweat on the back of her neck seemed to touch her stomach with nausea.

"No need to concern yourself with anything so common." The words were almost kind, soothing. Somehow he had entered in a foul mood and her barbs had only served to soften him.

"Besides," he leaned close enough to whisper against her ear, close enough for her to smell the spicy scent of him, "that *rebellion* as you call it has left you bereft of friends. Your precious Misha has not returned from Bethel, and it would seem Reza has taken the curs loyal to him and also abandoned you."

She tried to hear nothing, feel nothing.

"Do not be hasty, Kamillah." His coldness seemed to envelop her. "You will *always* have me. For if I do not have you, then you will be dead. Make no mistake."

Kamillah turned from his voice in her hair, pulled away and closed her eyes.

"But you will always have me."

"Then I have nothing."

Had they truly left? Misha and Reza both, moving toward the final piece of the Nehushtan without her, leaving her to Zahir?

An emptiness started to grow within her, a spreading black void in her chest.

But it did not unfold long or far. As though a tourniquet had been applied, she tightened against this news, letting it strengthen rather than defeat her.

So. She was alone. Again. So be it. The only thing that mattered was knowledge, because knowledge gave one power, and power was all she needed.

She could not break away from Zahir. Could not outrun him or even deceive him. The only thing that would win her freedom was sheer power, and if Reza and Misha would not help, then she would find it herself.

She pulled herself to her feet and crossed the tent to a small stand that held a jug of water. "So they have moved ahead without you, surely to be first to find the piece. And still you camp here, too tired from the exertion of the day to move yourself?"

Behind her, he grunted his annoyance. "Dawn will be soon enough—"

"Will it? Do they not have the other two pieces already? Should they find this third, what is keeping them from disappearing with it?"

He laughed, the sound short and clipped. "Ah, there you are wrong. The other two pieces are here in the camp, left safely in the hands of the Jewish sect. But I do not intend to let those men, nor the pieces, out of my sight."

She poured a cup of water and sipped, then turned to face him. The malaise of the past few days was falling from her and she felt the physical release of it. The welcome return of cunning thought, sharpening into a plan. "Still, it would seem prudent to move toward Bethel as soon as possible."

Yes, Bethel. One more center where she could draw power into herself. And if her blossoming plan held, where she could lay her hands on all three pieces of the Nehushtan and flood herself with power enough to break Zahir. No one would win her from Phraates.

As to what she would do with the restored talisman, she would think on that later. After all, Misha and Reza had both abandoned *her*.

Zahir was on his feet now as well, running a hand through his thick hair. "Perhaps you are right. Those two have always considered themselves one step ahead of me."

She smiled and sipped at her water again, eyes trained on Zahir over the cup. The schemes running through his mind were practically visible. *Break camp. Proceed with stealth. Send scouts to find Reza's men. Surround them...*

He left the tent without another word to her.

Kamillah set the cup down with a *thunk*, crossed to her basket of clothing, and pulled a head covering from the pile. There was little time to waste.

Outside, Zahir was already occupied with shouting orders to the remaining soldiers, of whom he seemed to have become general.

Kamillah slipped through the alleys formed by tents, even as men rushed to pull up pegs, until she reached the large tent of the Chakkiym. She called a soft greeting and was welcomed inside.

The men slept and snored in various positions through the tent, but Gaspar lifted a hand to her, beckoning her closer. She kept the tent flap drawn back, allowing in what little firelight and moonlight that could reach them. The tent smelled of dusty parchment and dusty men.

"What is it? Another attack?"

She bent to her knees beside his mat and shook her head. "No, there is no danger. But Zahir is moving us to Bethel. Reza and the other soldiers have already gone, and Zahir does not want to wait."

Gaspar's eyes flickered in concern, and he dropped his head for a moment, the wiry white hair catching the moonlight. "And Misha?"

"He has not returned from his scouting trip to Bethel."

Gaspar nodded. "Still he pursues this foolish idea, despite what his heart, and the star, tell him."

Gaspar's voice was melodic, even in sadness. Kamillah could imagine that voice in singsong prayers to his God, and the thought wrapped her in comfortable warmth. She touched Gaspar's blue-veined hand, weathered by the years, and smiled. ""I will help you pack."

Guilt stabbed her in the wake of her words. Misha would understand what she meant to do, even if Gaspar would not. But perhaps he would rather be rid of the occultic pieces anyway.

Within the hour the camp was on the move, and the pouch that held the two pieces of the Nehushtan had migrated from Gaspar's saddlebag to Kamillah's without his knowledge.

Zahir chose to ride ahead, thankfully.

Kamillah urged her horse to follow the soldiers and magi, keeping herself in the center of a group of soldiers who were only too grateful to have her under their special protection.

A chill breeze rose up as they moved toward Bethel, climbing slightly to that hilly town. The wind yanked at her hair, and she pulled in deep breaths of the coldness, letting it sharpen her wits to a fine point.

Dawn was just below the horizon when they rounded a bend to find a strange tableau playing out on a hillside—a silent and unmoving span of black silhouettes against the dawn-pink sky, soldiers and shepherds, weapons and torches, seemingly frozen in time.

Zahir held up a hand to stop their progress and the company halted, silent witness to the bizarre scene above.

At the edge of the group of silhouettes, one figure moved.

Even from this distance, she recognized the cocky walk of Misha-aku.

CHAPTER FOURTEEN

REZA

*W*e had hidden ourselves behind every strewn rock, flattened bodies into hillside grasses, tried to blend into the darkness that would soon lift. All of it to protect Misha in his task—and to take Zahir and his men when they inevitably arrived.

The plan had been a good one. If it had not been for these accursed people of Bethel, who guarded their desecrated altar as if it were the riches of the ancient King Croesus.

Now, as more of them raced up the hillside from the not-so-sleepy village toward where Misha stood outlined against the sky, there was nothing to do but signal my soldiers with a low, sharp whistle and flood onto the hilltop to defend him.

But as we leaped to our feet and raced toward the burned patch of grass, I called for restraint among the men. There was no need to cause harm when it was not warranted. Memories of Panais were still fresh.

We circled Misha from behind, forming an arc of protection at his back, ready to strike but motionless against the lightening sky.

Misha, not surprisingly, was already attempting to charm his adversaries. "You are all courageous in your defense of your town, as you should be." His voice was placating, his hands raised in innocence. "But you must believe us that we are here in *your* defense. Another comes to take what is not his. We have met with your men—Eliakim has sent ahead to Jerusalem for help, and my men are here for your protection until that help arrives." At this he spread an arm to take in those behind.

I swallowed a moment of irritation at the way he claimed my soldiers for himself. But it was perhaps the best strategy. At the mention of Eliakim, the angry mob seemed to hesitate, to question among themselves.

They did not have long to debate the truth of Misha's words.

From behind them, at the base of the hill near the dusty road that entered the village, a battle whoop sounded, and Zahir's men rushed us all, swords and daggers brandished.

Caught between the two factions, the men of Bethel took only a moment to decide their best option was to flee.

And so another battle between brothers began.

But we would not be alone for this one.

Something in the air shifted. It seemed at first a trick of the light at the end of a long night, a gray dawn too quickly realized. But it was not the sun, not the horizon. The air had thickened with it, with shapes and forms that seemed to writhe and twist above our heads.

All of us, regardless of loyalty, paused to take it in. No doubt even the Kasdim who waited at the bottom of the hill watched as well.

I found a pattern in the shifting light-shapes—some of them appeared to be traveling both upward and downward—as though they ascended and descended an unseen ladder. A trickle of fear shivered down my spine. Were they armed? It was difficult to make out their outlines, so blurred and fragmented.

But there were others, others attacking those who traveled, until the air above the entire hillside was cleaved with a battle between the heavenlies.

Their battle was our own, and as if the general of both sides had signaled to both Zahir and to me, our men suddenly erupted in violence.

I gripped my father's sword in my hand yet again and raised it to my enemy.

We thrashed and jabbed, slashed and gored. Blood ran in the darkness, men cried out in fear and pain, and above us the parallel war waged on.

So this was how it was to be.

Again I led my men in violence, in this destiny that could not be denied no matter my efforts. My training, my years of preparation, they filled my head and my sword arm and even my heart with the natural and deadly instincts of a warrior. I relaxed into it, let it sweep me into itself, lost myself to the need and the beauty.

Where was Misha? Had he found the third piece yet? Would he unite it with the other two while we all battled here on his behalf and be halfway to Parthia before the last of us fell?

And Kamillah? I spared a breath for a prayer that she held steady behind the wall of Kasdim below us.

It would be a gray day, for dawn seemed long in coming. Or perhaps time had stretched thin, victim of the unearthly war that raged above our heads. I could not gauge what happened there, nor even if one or other of the spirit armies fought in our defense. Perhaps their battle had nothing to do with ours.

But thoughts of war—of both men and angels—fled a moment later. An instant of indecision, of hesitation, and I felt the sharp tang of a sword point in my thigh.

Hot blood slid against the clammy chill of my skin. The pulse in my neck, in my chest, matched the beating of the blood of the wound.

Fear and anger boiled up to give me strength, and I dispatched my attacker quickly. But when I tried to take a step backward to assess the battle, my leg betrayed me. I went down.

It was a strange sensation, this realization that today would not end as I had imagined.

What *had* I imagined? Zahir's eyes going cold and lifeless under my own sword? The Nehushtan in my hands, giving me power to become the next king of Persia?

Whatever it had been, my supposed destiny, it drained away from me now as surely as my lifeblood.

But with that knowledge came a sort of relief, and I felt myself smile where I lay in the dark grass.

I would not fulfill another's thoughts of destiny for me after all. In the end, it had been my choice. To stand, to fight.

I would not be a king.

But this, this surprising alternative, was perhaps even better. To give my life in defense of my friends.

On my back now, I had all the time I needed to study the strange war above. But my eyes seemed too tired to focus on the whitish shapes twirling and shifting. So tired.

I let them close. Let the darkness come.

CHAPTER FIFTEEN

ZAHIR

*H*ow could it have come to this?

Zahir stood apart from the fighting, watched the battle play out on the ground and in the air, and tried to push away the cold twinge of fear.

The fool, Misha, was up there finding the final piece—the only thing that stood between Zahir and ultimate power. And the usurper Reza, with his fiercely loyal men who would see him on a throne—if Reza had his way, Zahir would be groveling before the Jew Simon. Or worse.

No. There was no way he would allow it. The three pieces would be united in his hands alone, and then he would see just how much power it held. Enough to become the star-promised World-Savior Himself? Certainly at least enough to make himself indispensible to Phraates. No matter how capable a general Reza was, the numbers were not in his favor. There could be no victory for him on this hill. And when it was over, Zahir would ensure that every soldier loyal to him lay dead in the grass.

But the coldness snaked through him again, refusing to let him look away from what he truly feared. It was not the soldiers who blindly followed the would-be tyrant Reza. It was the beings who seemed to fight for him in the air. Not Zahir's own spirits, the ones that whispered and promised and assured him of their own loyalty. The others. The frightening others.

Would that he could direct them. Any of them. But this battle above had little to do with him, he sensed, and he had no idea how to gain their attention, nor if he even wanted to. Before they broke camp, he had tried to breach those that protected the Chakkiym and had been rebuffed with a physical jolt akin to what he had seen Kamillah receive when she tried to run from him outside Panais.

He kept his eyes trained on Reza. Refused to acknowledge what transpired above. It was beyond his understanding, beyond his control, and therefore not worthy of attention.

Was the general injured?

Zahir sat taller on his horse, lifted his chin. Cursed the predawn gloom that did not allow him to be certain.

Yes, yes! That was Reza staggering backward. Falling to the ground!

Despite his usual caution in the face of battle, Zahir surged forward. He could not allow his enemy to die with thoughts of glory on the battlefield. He would stand over him and watch the light go out, remind him that all he fought for had been worthless, a waste.

Ignoring the angry swirl of spirit beings above him, Zahir charged up the hillside into the center of the battle.

CHAPTER SIXTEEN

$\mathcal{T}$he situation had changed in the blink of an eye, it seemed to Misha. One moment he was creeping quietly along the crest of the hill, and the next he had been found out, defended by Reza's men, caught between the soldiers who backed him and those who charged upward at Zahir"s command, and caught between the impenetrable earth and a war in the sky.

All of it was distraction, though. Designed to keep him from his true objective—the third piece.

He was so close now. The Chakkiym waited below with the other two pieces he had safeguarded with Gaspar, despite the old man's protestations. If Misha could only find the third, he could grab the other two and *use* the distraction of this fantastical battle to escape. He would be gone before it ended.

And what of Reza and Kamillah?

The temptation that was never far from him tickled at his mind even as he poked his torch at every crevice of the dismantled altar. To return to Nisa with the Nehushtan, and after seeing his mother healed, deliver it to Phraates in return for the prize of Kamillah...

He shook the thoughts away. The piece would go to Reza to decide its fate. Certainly. There could be no other way. Misha allowed himself a brief laugh at the thought of Kamillah's reaction should he make any other choice. He would probably not live to claim his prize anyway.

But he must not think beyond this moment. Men fought and died even now to give him this chance or to take it from him. The future lay in his hands, in his mind, in his ability to decipher.

Decipher. What had the parchment said? Altar split. Ashes poured out.

Perhaps, like Panais, the third piece was not lodged in a crack of the altar at all. Not hiding inside, but under.

If the One God had struck down from the heavens to split an altar apart, surely there would have been a great indentation in the ground itself.

Perhaps the split would have *pointed* to the place. Like the lampstand with the forked base on the cavern wall under Yathrib's Temple of Amun-Re, pointing to a simple wooden chest.

Seeing every fissure with new eyes now, he circled the rubble again, torch held close enough to blacken the stones anew. Above his head the mad battle he did not understand raged on, and below the blackened space soldiers still fought.

There. So simple. A deep chasm between two large rocks, an unnatural gap, nearly in the center.

Something whispered in his mind that there was little time. Was the battle going against him?

He needed to dig. Had nothing to dig with.

The torch was unneeded now. He shoved it deep into the gap between the stones, waited for it to sputter and die. Yanked it out.

Grabbing the shaft as close to the smoldering end as he dared, he used the lower, slightly pointed end to scrabble in the hard-packed dirt.

Too long. This would take too long.

He bent to the task, sweat building along his neck and forehead. Used one hand to feverishly sweep away the dirt he dislodged with the torch in his other.

You are looking for power in the wrong place.

The voice was audible, and yet not audible.

Misha sucked in a breath, looked around, saw no one. He returned to his digging.

You will not find what you seek in the dirt.

Unwilling, yet knowing he must, Misha looked up.

A spirit-being, vibrating along the edges of its form, whitish-gray and with a fierce countenance, stared down on him.

Misha's stomach nearly rebelled, and the blood seemed to flee his limbs, leaving him chilled and shaking.

There is no need for fear.

The being spoke, there could be no doubt, but there was no movement around what Misha would call its face.

You are looking for power in the wrong place.

"Where, then?" The question came out as a shout, the plea of a desperate man. To have come this far and not finish the quest... He waved an arm around the altar, inviting correction as to where he should dig.

Not where. Who.

"You speak in riddles. Tell me where to dig."

Not dig. Go.

The words of Zahir's stolen parchment returned to him. Their search should not be for a ruler holding an object of power, but a ruler who was Power itself. Dominion over all people and all of creation, not because of what He possesses, but because of who He is.

Misha shook his head and returned to his digging. He must find it, must find the third piece. For his mother. For Reza. For Kamillah.

A moment later his improvised shovel hit something solid.

Panting, he scraped faster, harder. The outlines of something long and cylindrical appeared under his groping fingertips.

He had found it.

More digging, more focused disregard of the voices and the battles around him.

And then it was in his hands. The third piece. At last.

And now you must destroy it.

CHAPTER SEVENTEEN

KAMILLAH

The figure of Zahir, racing up the hill, startled Kamillah. Was he truly running into the battle? It seemed unlike him, and a flicker of worry touched her chest. Nothing good could come of this. The man's hatred for both Misha and Reza had only grown since they left Panais. Chances were that he pushed forward to harm one or both of them.

Did she care, knowing they had left her behind? She tossed her hair behind one shoulder and lifted her head to the madness in the sky above.

Yes, of course she cared. For them both. They had each found a place in her heart, in their different ways. Misha, with his laughter and his lighthearted outlook on all of life. Reza, with his steady protectiveness.

But she must also think of herself here in the last hours of the night. Two of the pieces lay between her thigh and her horse's flank. The third was on that hillside. If she had all three, no one would own her. No one would stop her from returning to her people, to her land.

Her horse pawed the ground, and she shared his impatience. Why could she not see better what was happening? Did she dare break from the Kasdim as well and move into the battle? The spiritual forces in the air seemed unconcerned, unaffected by what happened on the ground. Would they accost her?

But why had they appeared at all? If not to fight alongside the humans, or against the humans, what was their purpose? And how did they not strike every soldier on the field both mute and still?

She nudged her horse toward where Gaspar sat alongside his own mount.

He nodded to her but then returned his attention to the fight. "It is not right. Fighting each other. It makes no sense, but that is what this senseless quest has brought us. From the time we stopped following the star we have been doomed to this."

"But why do they fight above us and not with us?"

He turned quizzical eyes on her. "On the hill, you mean?"

"No—not the men. The—spirits—or whatever they are.'"

He glanced back at the battle, then into her eyes. "What do you see, child?"

A tremor of panic tunneled through her. "You do not see them? The ghostly, shining things that clog the air above the soldiers, waging their own war? They are like men, but not like men."

Gaspar's breath escaped his lips in a slow whistle. He turned to his little cluster of Chakkiym, making sure they were listening. "There is more at stake here than we even imagined."

Nods bobbed all around and Kamillah scowled at their secrets. "What is at stake? Why do I see them?"

Gaspar's forehead wrinkled. "I have no answers to either of those questions, child. But you can be assured that this party will not leave Bethel unchanged."

"I am not the only one who sees them."

He lifted his eyebrows but said nothing.

"Reza and Misha. Even Zahir." She pointed upward. "He has tried to come against you all but found them protecting you.'"

"Yes?" Gaspar broke into a smile, the happy grin of a child who has been told he is his father's favorite.

She frowned. "They do not protect me, however. They hold me prisoner to Zahir."

Gaspar shook his head. "No, child." He waved a hand toward the battle he did not see. "Look again. You said you are witnessing a battle.'"

She glanced into the air but then quickly looked away, eyes pained at the strange brightness. "Yes."

"A battle requires two sides. There are some who hold you prisoner, perhaps. But there are others who would fight *for* you, if you should let them."

He was right. There had always been two factions, as though the men of their caravan had split along unseen lines that had been there since they set out from Nisa. Was it true? Did Misha's One God see her, too?

The idea was enough to give her the courage she needed. She urged her horse forward.

"Do not be foolish, my dear!"

But she was already leaving Gaspar below. "You said they would protect me." She called over her shoulder but did not hear his answer.

Halfway up the hill her fears were realized.

Reza was on the ground, on his back, unarmed. Zahir strode toward him, as if the battle did not exist around him.

But then Zahir jerked backward.

She knew that strange sense of being impeded by the very air.

Yet it was not the air. This time she saw the shining one who blocked his way, who shielded Reza.

She urged her horse upward faster, skirting the fighting but heading toward Reza.

He was injured. Perhaps dying. She had two pieces of the artifact with a miraculous power to heal. And by now perhaps Misha had the third. She had to reach him.

But her pursuit was cut short by a sound that even the Chakkiym must have clearly heard. A thunderous *whoosh* like the coming together of a thousand candle flames into a single pillar of fire.

And with the ground-shaking noise, the brightness of the battle of the air increased a thousandfold, until every mage, every soldier, every person under the sky of Bethel cried out and crumpled to their knees.

CHAPTER EIGHTEEN

REZA

*T*he light pricked at my eyelids.

I wanted to brush it away, to shield my eyes from it. But my arm would not obey my mind, and even my mind did not obey itself.

Was this death? Was there only light after death?

But the sound—the sound shook every bit of me until I felt the pebbles dig into my shoulders, the grasses scratched my arms. Not death then. But what?

I forced my eyes open once, twice, but the sky was on fire.

I turned my head, my gaze traveling along the ground until it reached the purple robes of the man I least wanted to encounter while lying injured on my back.

Zahir.

I lifted my gaze to his face. Why did he stand apart? Why did he not finish me, as he would have done in the cave where the traitor Jabari had kept me?

He held an arm over his head, as if to stave off a flock of angry vultures that would fly at his head, and leaned toward me, as into a fierce wind, but he did not take a step. And then instead of charging me, he fell to the ground.

Whatever was happening in the sky, and I still could not bear to look at it, had felled every man on the hillside.

Only one figure seemed to move among the battle. I saw the white of her robe, the lovely glint of her Egyptian skin, even as she crawled through the grass toward me. Our eyes met, and I reached a hand toward her. She carried something, slung over her back and weighing her down.

How did she move forward when all others had fallen still? Were they only paralyzed with fear and she the only one with courage?

She reached me at last, grasping my outstretched hand in her own warm fingers. I had not realized how cold I had grown.

We had not spoken since that awful night in her tent, but her eyes held no anger, no resentment.

"Reza, how bad is it?" She looked me over, searching for wounds.

"My leg. Not deep. But the blood…"

At her stifled cry I knew it was as bad as I had guessed.

She was ripping at the pouch she carried, ripping it to pieces.

I closed my eyes against her ministrations. She tied off the leg, just below the groin and above the wound. She would not be strong enough to tighten it sufficiently.

But then I felt the surprising bite of the bindings digging deep into the muscle of my thigh.

"Hold this, Reza." She guided my hand to something. Some kind of rod she had inserted into the ripped fabric and used to twist it until it stopped the flow. Smart woman. Such a smart woman.

I blinked my eyes open once more, glanced at the rod she wanted me to hold steady.

A gush of air escaped my lungs at the sight of it. The bottom piece of the Nehushtan. The rod that Misha's forefather Moses would have thrust into the desert sand so the Israelites could look upon the bronze serpent.

"Do you have it, Reza?" Her voice was low and urgent.

I nodded.

"I am going to find Misha. If he has the third piece, we can heal you!"

I nodded again, if only to release her to her futile errand. The chances did not seem very favorable that such a miraculous thing would happen.

And then she was gone, and I was left to wonder again at the brighter-than-noon light above me in the sky not yet blanched by the sun.

The clash above us had peaked. It could not last. Every cubit of the sky from horizon to horizon screamed with light and soundless fury.

One more blinding flash of white lightning, one more thwump of sound that rocked my chest. And then a splitting of the light, as though half the combatants had been sucked upward and half had seeped through the cracks in the ground.

The darkness that followed, even though it was nearly dawn, felt like there had never been such a thing as light in all the world.

And I felt bereft, as though something had warred for me, for my protection, but now had fled.

Zahir was there, standing above me. Ready to end me. His face loomed large, the smug smile I loathed hovering as he bent to examine me. He would take his time.

My hand still gripped the lower piece of the Nehushtan against my thigh.

It was an easier task than I would have imagined to slip it from its fabric noose, pull it backward with what strength I still possessed, and slam it against the side of Zahir's skull.

CHAPTER NINETEEN

MISHA

*M*isha clutched the top third of the Nehushtan to his chest in the moment before the sound and light and unearthly battle ended with the force of a massive wave washing over the hillside.

He had heard the instruction given to him by the strange being. *Destroy it.* But how could he, when he had come this far, and when the ability to heal his mother lay within his hands?

But there was no denying what had taken place here. A battle between angels and demons, outside the realm of human understanding yet somehow involving him and these three pieces.

He rose from his knees, peered through the darkness, and surveyed the madness below.

Men lay dead and dying, to be sure, but most of them seemed simply stunned. Had they seen all he had seen?

Below and to the south, movement caught his attention. Wagons thundered along the road from Jerusalem, with soldiers trotting behind.

And then Kamillah was there, scrambling up the hill toward him, dirtied and laden with something slung over her shoulder and resting against her back.

He ran for her, caught her up in his arms before she fell. "What is it?"

"Reza." She panted and inclined her head down the hillside. "He is injured."

Misha's pulse quickened. "How badly?"

But her eyes were on the piece in his hand. "You found it!" She pulled away, lowered her pouch, and clutched it to her chest. "I have the middle piece here. Reza has the bottom. Come! We must put it together to help him!"

She and Reza had the two pieces? How—?

"Misha! Come!" She yanked at his hand and started down the hill.

They reached Reza in moments where he lay in the grass.

Kamillah gasped at the sight of him, unconscious with the rod in his hand.

Zahir lay beside him, eyes closed and blood oozing from a wound on his temple. It was not clear if he lived.

"Reza, why did you remove it?" Kamillah pulled the rod from his limp fingers, jammed it through a cloth bound around his leg, and twisted the fabric tight. She quickly unwrapped the middle piece from her pouch and motioned Misha forward.

Too much happened at once. From below, the soldiers they had summoned from Jerusalem climbed the hillside, a few older men, priests perhaps, trailing them, their eyes wary on the battle that seemed to have stopped for no reason.

Misha waved them forward, secured his new find inside the pouch under his robe, and circled Reza's prone form to stand between his friend and the fallen Zahir. What would happen if the priests saw the Nehushtan? Surely they would recognize it at once and demand its return. He and Kamillah could not put it together until it was safe.

He gave a half bow of greeting to the group and pointed to Zahir. "Here is the man you have come seeking. It was he who began this." Misha swept a hand over the carnage of the hillside. "He was intent on desecrating your altar, in search of something."

The priests scanned the hill, the soldiers, looked upward to the crest of this hill as if they wondered if their altar was still a pile of rubble. One of them stepped forward. "And how came you to fight him? Who are you?"

Misha shrugged as though the question were nothing, but his mind whirred with possible answers, none of them credible. "We are part of a trading caravan, passing through Judea, south toward Petra. The soldiers accompanied us to protect the merchandise, but some of them were persuaded that they could kill all of Bethel's good people and take whatever treasures they might find." He gave a little laugh and a shake of his head. "Although what treasures they believed a backwater village with nothing but sheep could provide, I cannot imagine."

The priest's eyes narrowed and he glanced toward the fallen altar, but he seemed to find it more prudent to let it drop rather than ask more questions. He flicked another glance at the soldiers, and two of them obeyed his unspoken request by hauling Zahir to their shoulders and carrying him downward to their wagons.

"He will be taken to Jerusalem, where it will be decided what to do with him." The priest tilted his head to get a better look at Reza, still on the ground behind Misha. "I hope your friends are not too badly hurt."

Misha smiled, shifted to better obstruct his view, and bowed again. "We will all be fine, I assure you. It seemed our duty to protect your land from the worst of us, and I apologize on behalf of our company."

The priest gave another narrow-eyed glance to Reza, to the rest of the hill, and to Misha, then pursed his lips in definite suspicion and nodded once. "You should come to Jerusalem as well. Give testimony to what went on here."

Misha sucked in a breath. "We will send the company on their way, but several of us will come to you in Jerusalem very soon."

"Hmm." The sound was more of a frustrated grunt than an agreement. "Ask for Dov." He thumped his chest. "At the Temple Gate."

Misha nodded. "We will see you soon, Dov."

He watched them descend, not daring to turn back to Reza and Kamillah for fear that in the light of daybreak the Jews would see the Nehushtan. But at last they were at the bottom of the hill and climbing aboard their wagons.

Misha whirled to the other two, not knowing what to expect.

Kamillah still knelt on the ground beside Reza, and his friend seemed alert, if weak.

"So." Reza tried to push himself up, but Kamillah restrained him. "Here we are, each with a piece of what we have long sought.'" He touched his fingers to the rod against his leg, and his half smile turned to a grimace of pain.

Kamillah's gaze met Misha's.

Each of them, with a reason to keep the Nehushtan from the others. To use it for their own needs.

Kamillah was already unstrapping the pouch from her shoulder. She gave each of the men a long look, then opened the pouch. "I am choosing to trust you both." She slipped the center piece, with its coiled bronze snake, out of safety. ""Choosing to believe that neither of you will use this to bring harm to me."

Reza grasped her free hand and squeezed. A look of understanding, perhaps reconciliation, passed between them.

Misha bent to his knees beside his friends, pulling the top piece from under his robes. "I am choosing to trust you both as well. You know why I need it." He looked to Reza. "But it would seem that right now, you need it more."

Reza inhaled and shook his head slightly. "A flesh wound, nothing more." He trained serious eyes on Misha. "But I would trust you even if I did not lay here bleeding.""

They each held a piece now, Kamillah and Misha cradling theirs in trembling hands, Reza clutching the piece at his leg.

"Well?" Misha dragged in a nervous breath. "Shall we?"

Kamillah placed her piece against Reza's belly, then slid the end against the bottom piece. The cracked rod fit together perfectly, and she held it in place as best she could.

Misha could hear her shallow breaths, as if she expected the Nehushtan to burn her fingers or blind her eyes.

He moved next, placing his piece at the top break of Kamillah's, sliding it to fit just as she had.

They waited.

Would the angels return to touch the staff with power, make it a living thing that could remove the ills of the world? Would they hear whispers of the ancients, falling in the desert around the lifted staff, seeking healing and the removal of their guilt?

The sun had at last lifted its top edge above the horizon, and the flooding of the hillside with that first light seemed like a healing balm being offered.

But Reza shook his head. No miraculous healing, no stitching together of his wound under the bloody rags. No deliverance from pain.

Kamillah leaned forward on her knees and wrapped her entire hand around the point of connection between the bottom and middle pieces, as if her body could forge a link between the two.

Misha followed her example, and both of them watched Reza's eyes, watched his leg.

Nothing. There was nothing.

A growing coldness in Misha's chest came with this truth. He should have been hot, angry that after all this danger, and with both his mother and Reza in such need, that the Nehushtan was nothing more than a legend. But it was not anger he felt. It was confirmation.

He had known. He had always known.

Since the day they left Nisa and his father had said he must follow his calling.

Since the day the star had told him he must leave.

And earlier, at the altar above them, when the angel had told him to destroy it. He had known.

The Nehushtan was dangerous not because it was powerful, but because it was not. It held no power and yet men continued to seek it, to worship it, to let it distract them from truth and life and the way in which they ought to go.

"I don't understand." Kamillah's voice caught with emotion and her hand shook around the rod. "Do you think it needs to be fused in some way?"

"No." Misha rocked back on his heels and let the top piece drop from his cold fingers into the grass. "No, it can do nothing for us.'"

"That makes no sense, Misha!" Kamillah's voice always grew strident when she was frustrated. "The–the beings, the angels—they have been helping us, fighting for us. Why would your God send them to us if not to help us find the piece, heal your mother, help Reza?"

Misha gripped Reza's shoulder. "They have been protecting us, yes. Against Zahir, against the demons he has joined himself with." He inclined his chin toward the Nehushtan, now in three pieces again. "But not for this. They wanted something else for us." He lifted his head toward the eastern sky. "It was the star all along. The star we should have been following. Not this foolish quest."

"But your mother, Misha." Her voice still held a trace of anger, but it was borne of sadness, he knew. "And Reza."

"If the One God chooses to heal them, it will be of His doing. Not ours."

Surely that was too much for his Persian and Egyptian friends to accept. And yet they both nodded like pious Jews.

Misha took notice of the rest of their party for the first time. Without leadership, Zahir's loyal soldiers had given up on their pointless skirmish. Men huddled in the grass or wandered down to where the Kasdim clustered at the base of the hill.

Kamillah followed his gaze and sighed. "So, what now?"

Misha turned back to her, eyed the pieces that they had traveled so far and risked so much to discover. "The others—the demons—they have wanted us to hunt it. Wanted us to find it. To turn us away from the star, from finding the Messiah. Does that not tell you what must be done? It must be destroyed."

"You truly believe this Messiah exists?"

He seized her hand. "All my life I have fought against my blood, rebelled against my heritage. But now I must know. I must know if all of it is true—the prophecies, the scrolls. A Jewish Messiah to rule the nations."

Kamillah smiled. "The biggest puzzle you will ever try to solve."

He nodded. She understood. More than understood – she believed in him, saw him for something more than he was.

"And I am ready, at last, to acknowledge that perhaps my father was right all along."

A familiar voice drifted up the hillside. "Ah, those are words a father does not often hear."

Misha whirled at the sound.

How could this be?

Not twenty cubits from him stood his father, with an arm wrapped around his mother.

A wave of heat rushed from his head to his feet, chased by a chill that shook him. "What? How have you come—?"

Father smiled and released Mother.

She crossed the remaining distance between them quickly. "HaShem has brought us." She pulled Misha into an embrace.

He held her to himself, his eyes on Father below. "You are stronger."

She laughed and pulled away. "I am healed, Misha."

"I—I do not understand."

Father climbed to join them, glanced at Reza who still leaned heavily on Kamillah. His brow furrowed. "Reza—"

"I am well, sir. It will heal."

Misha watched the exchange, unable to think. "Who brought you across the desert?"

Father slapped him on the back. "As your mother said, Yahweh has brought us."

"How did you find us?"

His father laughed, a pure sound in the morning light. "For a man who is always seeking power outside himself, you are slow to accept it when it presents itself." He shrugged. "We were in Nisa. And then we were here." He jabbed a thumb down the hillside toward the village below. "In Bethel. And your mother was well."

Misha shook his head. "Just like that? Transported all these miles—"

His father's face grew serious. "HaShem has some greater reason in this, Misha. The Messiah, the scrolls—"

"Yes." He studied the group of Chakkiym still clustered at the bottom of the hill. "There is much to learn in Jerusalem. Much we have already learned. We will seek the One whose star has been leading from the beginning." He kicked at the pieces of the Nehushtan on the ground. "But first there is something we must do."

CHAPTER TWENTY

REZA

*T*he appearance of Simon and Lydia on the hillside seemed to me almost a natural occurrence after everything we had witnessed these past weeks. Why should they not be brought in an instant to where their son waited to fulfill the task his God had in mind for him?

Thinking of my own father and the task he had set for me, I summoned one of my men to aid me and took my leave of the reuniting family to speak with the rest of the soldiers. For all the weakness the injury had brought me, it already seemed improved. My strength was returning faster than I would have thought possible.

There would be no Nehushtan to aid my people in a bid for the regaining of our Persian kingdom. And I would not be returning home to pursue such a place for myself. If my fight against Zahir had taught me anything, it was that I must follow what I felt to be my own calling.

I waved one of my officers to me.

He trotted over, scowling at my injured leg.

"It is nothing. Bring the others."

Moments later I had my five top men around me. "It is time to return to Nisa."

There were glances all around, and surely they found the Bethel hillside an odd place to terminate our quest, regardless of what had happened here.

"Can we not wait until you are healed, General?"

I shrugged. "My injury is of no consequence. Because I am not going with you."

Questioning looks, but they waited for me to elaborate.

"Accompany the Kasdim and any traders who are ready to return to Nisa. Keep them safe. And give my father a message." I took a deep breath, the weight of my words heavy on my tongue before I had even spoken them. "Tell my father that I am not the man to lead his revolution. Tell him that I go on to Jerusalem to seek a power greater than my own, greater than even Persia. I must learn if this prophesied world ruler has been born. For if so, there will be no Parthia to overcome. No Persia to fight for."

"But sir—" Bassam's scowl was a precursor to the reaction my father would doubtless serve them when they delivered my message.

"That is all, Bassam." I nodded my approval to each of them. "I trust you will see this mission safely concluded when you return our people to their homes.""

I left them there, gaping, to return to Misha and his family.

To Kamillah.

For in truth, I would go to Jerusalem for more than the reason I had given my men. I would go because my friends were going, and I would give Simon and Lydia and Misha my protection. And I would go because one way or another, I must know where Kamillah's true affections lay.

CHAPTER TWENTY-ONE

KAMILLAH

*K*amillah had resisted the urge to lay her head upon Lydia's shoulder since the moment the woman had appeared.

Yes, appeared. Some sort of miraculous journey. Was there any more proof needed that this God of the Hebrews, whom they insisted was the One God, held power over angel and demon and over nature itself? Since she and the others had left Nisa, they had been kept safe by this power.

The answers she had long pursued, since the days of her youth in the Temple of Isis, all through her three levels of training as a mage in the courts of Phraates, were they answers that were held in the palm of the One God and His Messiah? Was it He and not Anubis who held the real power over life and death, over the destiny of the soul?

She was as hungry for knowledge as Misha. Hungry for truth she could take back to Egypt, deliver to the priests and with the gift, justify her return. Knowledge was of ultimate value in Egypt, and surely they would desire news of a World-Savior, whether he was the prophesied Messiah of the Jews or the savior of Zoroaster.

They stood in a cluster, Simon's arm around Misha's shoulders.

Lydia touched her arm, waking her from her reverie. "You are thinking of home?"

Kamillah smiled. The woman should have been a mage, so adept was she at reading the thoughts of others. "I am thinking that I have seen more power displayed by your Hebrew God than in all my days in Egypt. And I must know the truth."

Misha exhaled heavily. "The stories you have told me, Father—stories of the days you and Mother met in the palace of Herod—it concerns me to see you return to Jerusalem. If the news is to be believed, he has only grown more mad since your days in his palace."

Reza rejoined them, limping exceedingly and leaning on his sword. He nodded solemnly. "You shall have my protection."

The little band looked at him for a moment, then broke into laughter.

Reza grinned. "This?" He waved a hand at his thigh. "This will be healed before we reach the outer gates."

Kamillah circled to stand beside him, allowed him to lean on her.

Reza grew serious. "I meant what I said—each of you has my protection. But I cannot allow violence to control me again." He lifted his sword, examined his reflection in its marred and bloodied surface. "That is not who I am."

Kamillah warmed to his words of self-declaration, just as Misha's desire to find answers had resonated deep within her.

Both of these men, they had grown even dearer to her in these weeks of travel and danger. She could not keep them both close and at a distance at the same time. She must resolve her feelings, before she could return to Egypt.

Misha was gathering up the pieces of the broken artifact that still lay discarded at their feet, as if it was not the thing that had brought them all this far.

"It is time."

They met at the half-dismantled altar on top of the hill.

Kamillah stood slightly aside, but she would do her part when her time came. Until then, she watched each of the participants as if it were a drama played on stage.

At Reza's request, his men had gathered wood from the cluster of trees on the hill. The Chakkiym brought oil from their saddlebags.

Simon and Lydia stood nearby, arms around each other's waists, watching as the next generation did what needed to be done.

Misha stepped forward first. Laid the central piece of the Nehushtan that he had unearthed from the cave below the Temple of Amun-Re in Yathrib onto the pile of oil-soaked wood on the altar. Then stepped back, as if he had placed an offering to his God. And so he had.

Reza limped to the altar's edge then and laid the bottom piece of the Nehushtan, the rod delivered from the crack in the earth that formed a gate to Hades in Panais. The rod that had saved him from Zahir and reminded him of a destiny greater than even kingship.

And then it was her turn. Kamillah brought the top piece of the Nehushtan, so recently dug from the earth beside this very altar, and the piece that had shown her at last that power was not to be found in objects but in a Source too large for her to fully understand.

It was a victory for all of them, the laying down of what they had long sought and the recognition that their true quest lay elsewhere, in the place where the star had been leading them all along.

But a part of her felt a hollowness in the victory, for though she had identified the Hebrew's One God as more powerful than Zahir or any demons in league with him, still Zahir lived. And as long as he lived, he could exert his influence over her.

She would go to Jerusalem with the others, to find answers, to find the World-Savior. But she would go for another reason, one she would not share.

She needed to see Zahir destroyed. If not by the Jewish officials or their Roman authorities, then by her own hand, as she had suffered at his. One way or another, if she were to be free, Zahir could not be allowed to live.

It was Misha who touched the torch to the oily kindling, as it needed to be. More than any of them, this was his journey, this finding and then releasing of the Nehushtan.

The flames licked at the twigs, took hold of the oil, then roared to life around the pieces of the Nehushtan.

What parts were made of wood blazed into orange-black embers within moments.

The bronze snake would take longer. Perhaps it was her imagination, but it seemed to writhe and hiss as the fires tried to consume it.

They watched until it was unrecognizable. Only a molten lump of bronze that would never again tempt Jews—or Egyptians or Persians—to worship its supposed power.

And then they turned away as one and drifted down the hill.

Within minutes belongings had been separated, the soldiers and Kasdim were on their way north to take the Incense Road back to Nisa, and the now much-reduced band of travelers had set their faces south toward Jerusalem.

Kamillah shared Misha's horse and they walked alongside Simon and Lydia, with Reza leading the way and the group of ten Chakkiym riding behind.

The sun had fully risen now, the strangely lengthened hour of dawn over at last. And yet somehow, even in the brightening sky, the singular light of the Morning Star still shone, beckoning them toward Jerusalem, toward truth.

To an adventure greater than any they had yet encountered.

EPILOGUE

HEROD

*H*e would kill them, kill them, kill them all.

The streets of Jerusalem would run with the blood of every usurper, all his enemies, all of them.

Herod stalked the veranda of his palace, watching the city of Jerusalem spread to the south and east below. The coolness of the night breeze tickled the sweaty places beneath his hair and under his arms. Back and forth. The rhythmic movement sometimes served to dull the pain.

Not tonight.

The pain would not be put off tonight. His flesh decayed grotesquely in the most private of places. And all the kingdom knew of his disgrace.

What did they whisper in the alleys and synagogues? Did they say that he deserved it, that he had taken too many wives, too many young men? How dare they, when he had built up Judea like not even their precious Solomon and kept them in the good graces of Rome after the Hasmoneans had brought near ruin upon this city?

But they were all alike—all trying to thwart him, all trying to steal his throne. Praying to their God that the maggots would take all of his flesh, or that their prophesied Messiah would at last arrive, or that one of his own sons would finally succeed in slipping poison into his wine.

But he had shown them he was not to be trifled with, had he not?

Two favorite sons executed before they had a chance to kill him. Another in prison, awaiting only Caesar's approval for Herod to execute him as well.

And while every street corner seemed to boast a new Messiah, there had not been any he could not make disappear if the pretender grew dangerous.

Whom could he trust? Who would never betray him?

Only Salome. Only his sister had been beside him since the beginning, since the early days of friendship with Mark Antony, before Octavian had become Caesar Augustus. Before his beloved Mariamme had... He did not allow himself to think of her. Not anymore. Thinking of her on the gallows caused the voices to roar in his head.

What else? What else must he accomplish before the end? For the end was coming, there could be no doubt. The excruciating pain, for which the physicians had no relief. The creeping decay of his flesh that could not be halted.

He must secure his dynasty. That was all that remained. He held the reigns of kingship at Rome's behest and with Caesar's favor, but it had never been easy. Thirty-six years of politicking and placating, of bribery and begging, with the blood of a dozen traitorous friends and family members on his hands.

But he had built into this country a legacy of magnificence that would never be forgotten. Mighty fortresses, luxurious palaces, the great port of Caesarea. The massive Temple Mount that would surely stand for thousands of years. All of this had been generated by his hands, and must be credited to his family now.

It must be Antipas, all of this must go to Antipas, and Herod must make certain that his dynasty was intact before the end.

Yes, it was time to draw up another will. With money left to Rome's coffers and no question about succession.

And if any more contenders for his throne emerged—be they sons or Messiahs—he would destroy them without mercy.

Nothing mattered anymore but the legacy.

ROYAL BEAUTY

THE INCENSE ROAD

BOOK THREE

TRACY HIGLEY

ROYAL
BEAUTY
THE INCENSE ROAD
BOOK THREE

KAMILLAH'S STORY

CHAPTER ONE

KAMILLAH

*T*he journey to Jerusalem could not go fast enough for me.

Perched as I was on a horse with Misha, trying to maintain an appropriate distance from his broad chest and encircling arms, the ride would be uncomfortable. Awkward. Wonderful.

No more camels now. We had sent them all back to Nisa with the soldiers and Kasdim.

We traveled away from the carnage and revelations of Bethel as one party: the ten Chakkiym, Misha and me on a single horse—his mount— so his parents, Lydia and Simon, could share mine. Reza rode alongside the two of them, recounting the battles we had seen in Panais and Bethel to Simon, who was still an old soldier at heart.

In the many days in Nisa that I had watched Misha's relationship with his parents and with his closest friend Reza, there had never been doubt that he felt a certain jealousy over Simon's fatherly affection for his friend. But I felt none of that tension in the man sitting so close behind me on this early morning walk up to Jerusalem. In truth, he seemed in jolly spirits and more than once feigned a reason to grip the reins tighter around me or encircle my waist as if he feared my falling from his horse.

I swatted his arm away, but not before Lydia caught a sidewise glance at us. Her eyes met mine and a small smile tugged at the corner of her mouth. I could only imagine what she must be thinking.

But this was no trip for pleasure, and there was no time for foolishness.

With the rising sun warming us across the green sheep-strewn fields on our left, the slow *clip-clop* of the hooves on the hard-packed road beat a rhythm that could have been sedating, lulling me to a sleep well earned after the night we had spent. But I focused on the swirling puffs of dust at each hoof fall, forcing myself to think on what lay ahead. Birds chirped their morning songs, entreating the world to join their carefree spirits, but I counted each pace and wondered when we would see the city rising above us.

Misha seemed to read my thoughts. "We should arrive well before noon."

"And then what? Can we simply ride into the city, asking to be directed to the Messiah?"

I felt him shrug behind me. Could smell the sweat of the night's battle on him and the smoky-charred scent of the burning Nehushtan.

"Surely if one such as we hope has arrived, others will know of Him. The priests, the rabbis. The teachers of the law. Even Herod."

He spoke casually, and perhaps he felt nothing but cavalier, now that the days of hunting the Nehushtan were over, his mother was healed, and he had reconciled himself to his father's faith and the task of delivering the scrolls.

I, however, felt nothing but tension. For my quest was far from over.

Somewhere ahead of us, perhaps even now awakening from his unconscious state, was the man who I doubted could be kept under Jewish lock and key.

What would happen when Zahir awoke and found himself not on the hillside of Bethel with the three pieces of the Nehushtan almost in his grasp, but in a wagon bound for a Jewish prison? Would we find his captors dead along this road? Would Zahir be waiting around a bend, crouched behind a boulder, hidden within some trees?

No, I could not relax like Misha. Could not banter and laugh like Reza and Simon. Even the Chakkiym behind us murmured with excitement, approaching the famed city they had studied but never seen. But I must focus on my enemy. Until Zahir was dead, I would not be free.

A scuffling on the road far ahead pulled our attention forward, and we slowed as a group.

My heart thudded against my robes. Was this it, then? Had Zahir escaped already and come for me?

The dust obscured the party coming toward us, but it was too many to be only Zahir. At least a few horses cantered north, riders sitting tall. And others ran alongside.

We were more than a dozen in our traveling party, but we lined up along the side of the road to let them pass. Though I do not think any of us believed they were going to pass.

Soldiers. Romans.

They pulled up horses and circled, their animals snuffling and pawing at the ground. The foremost of them, a slight man with a hooked nose and narrow black eyes, looked us over as if we were an invading army.

"Who leads this group? Where are you going?"

Interesting question—at least the first of them. It was met with a few moments of silence, as if each in our group was asking himself the question again.

And then it was Misha who spoke. As I knew he would.

"We are scholars from Nisa, traveling to Jerusalem to meet with others, to see what we can learn of the ways and beliefs of the Jews."

The hooked-nose soldier scowled. "We were told you were traveling merchants, whose party broke apart and began to fight each other after some would have pillaged the town of Bethel."

Misha's left arm tightened around me, the hand gripping the reins, and his other hand rested possessively on my knees hanging over the side of our horse. "A mixed group, sir, yes. Scholars, traders, even some soldiers to protect us, though you can see we bear no military intent now." He nodded backward toward the Chakkiym, every one of them gray-haired and probably quaking atop his horse.

"Even so, Parthians are not typically welcome to travel Judea without reason or escort."

Misha shrugged one shoulder. "Perhaps you and your men would like to take on the task of escorting us, then?"

I could hear the grin in his voice. *Not now, Misha.* He would have us in a cell alongside Zahir if he did not maintain some respect.

The soldier was finished with friendly conversation. "You are wanted for questioning concerning the matter in Bethel this morning."

"I don't know what answers—"

"Enough, Parthian."

At this insult, Simon leaned forward and opened his mouth.

Misha's hand on my knees lifted slightly, palm outward—an unobtrusive signal to his father. It was not the time for them to declare their Jewish blood. Not yet.

And Misha's mother—she was the daughter of a Jewish Hasmonean princess, even if the blood of Egypt's Ptolemies also ran in her veins.

The soldiers were circling behind our party, herding us like sheep toward Jerusalem. "You will come with us to the city. And you will answer questions."

Misha shrugged again and smiled at his parents and Reza. "Sounds like a hot meal and a free bed to me, friends. Shall we go?"

But if Misha truly had illusions that we were simply being escorted as guests into Jerusalem, they were soon dispelled. The soldiers kept a killing pace, their pikes lowered as if to skewer any of us who would slow them down.

My only encouragement was that if Zahir lay in wait in the shadows, he would have to break through the band of Romans to reach me.

The city walls of Jerusalem appeared in the hazy morning above us within the hour, stark and foreboding under a grayish sky.

What were Lydia and Simon thinking? Feeling? To return after all these years to a place where they had seen both terror and victory, where they had found love?

Our Roman guards herded us around the massive platform on which the Jews' famed Temple rested, to the southeastern side where a tower clung to the corner of the platform and rose above the city, nearly equal with the height of the Temple itself.

Lydia called over her shoulder to Misha and me. "Herod's palace."

I could hear the tension in her voice, a tightness that spoke of past horrors.

The centurion at the head of the pack heard her comment and half-turned on his horse. "Not his palace any longer. He has built one much grander." The Roman's tone was derisive, almost mocking. "The king cannot pass a latrine without making plans to improve it."

Simon leaned forward on his horse. "If not his palace, then—"

"The Antonia Fortress is now used only for court proceedings."

"We are being taken to trial?" Simon's question had us all listening carefully.

The Roman shrugged. "You are being taken to cells under the fortress. That is all I know."

Simon tried to question him further, but the centurion clearly had little knowledge and even less interest in easing our minds.

At the arched entrance of the lower levels of the fortress we were relieved of our horses but thankfully allowed to keep our possessions. The Chakkiym, feeble as some of them were, slung pouches of belongings over their shoulders. Misha kept a casual hand on his pouch with the scrolls secreted inside, as if it held nothing more than a change of tunic.

Lydia whispered something about "horse stalls" as we were shoved into a darkened corridor and pushed along by Roman pikes.

A prison guard responded to the presence of the soldiers and swung open four cells in succession. Misha and Simon were thrust into the first, then Lydia and I into the second. We kept our heads at the iron bars, watching as the Chakkiym along with Reza were divided into two groups and driven into the last two cells like sheep. Reza was wisely remaining as docile as one of the old magi. There was no use in putting up a fight yet. Not until we had a plan.

The centurion gave garbled instructions to the guard, then the soldiers departed and the guard disappeared, leaving us all in the damp chill underground, with very little light.

We talked between us for some minutes, speculating on our fate, but there was little to do but wait and we soon settled into our cells, sitting with our backs against the wall and fighting off rodents that scavenged for any food their new cell mates might have brought.

"So," Lydia began when all grew quiet, "you and my son."

I stifled a smile in the dark. "Yes?"

"Do not give me your 'yes,' young woman. I have eyes."

Could she not speak a bit more quietly? Misha's cell was not so far off.

I tried to suggest the tone by answering nearly under my breath. "We have—grown to know each other better—"

Lydia followed my lead, and her laugh was gentle. "Hmm. Yes, it would appear so."

"But I hardly think such things important right now. We need to find a way to get out of here."

"Perhaps you have some magic you can work? Some tricks you have learned—"

"I should think your influence would be greater than mine in this city."

Lydia was silent. "I fled this city as an enemy. I have no influence."

"But you are of Hasmonean blood—a royal line! Surely if we could get word of your identity to the priests here—"

"No."

The word was delivered quietly, but it was undergirded with the iron will of a woman who had seen danger.

How could I convince her? I knew some of her history from Misha, but still—could she not do us some good here?

"You speak of identity. It took many years for me to find mine." Her voice had the softness of reminiscence about it.

Perhaps if I let her remember, she would gain strength.

"Yes, Misha has told me of how you discovered your parentage, not long before you left Judea."

"I do not speak of my parentage as my identity. Not really. I had to find myself in someplace other than my genealogy. It was not until I saw myself as a daughter of HaShem that I found peace."

I bristled at the strange words, so suggestive of my time on the hill in Bethel.

But I let her speak. Let her share her stories of her time in Herod's palace as maidservant to his wife Mariamme, before they had all discovered her royal blood. She spoke of Salome, Herod's sister, and the dark powers she seemed to command. Of the unthinkable cruelty of Herod who had executed the wife he loved because of a false rumor. Of the madness his acts had birthed.

"These are not people to be trifled with, Kamillah. We cannot simply assert ourselves and expect fair treatment." She shuddered in the cold cell. "If Herod were to learn that Simon and I were here—if Salome knew Misha held the scrolls—I do not want to think of what they would do to destroy us all."

Two guards interrupted us, one pulling a rickety wagon on misshapen wheels that clunked as it rolled along, jostling its contents that appeared to be food for the prisoners.

Misha was at his cell bars. "What is to be done with us? We have done nothing wrong!"

One of the guards shrugged a shoulder and shoved a cup and a hunk of bread toward Misha. "They don't tell me nothing. All I know is we got a bunch of Parthian spies locked up, waiting for whatever it is they do to spies."

My stomach lurched at the word. In any city, in any land, spies were executed with little thought to the ramifications.

The two proceeded to our cell, and as if they were twins born in the same moment, they each looked us over from head to sandals and back to head, then grinned, half drunk and leering. The first glanced at the second and nodded. "Best-looking spies we've seen, eh? Even the old one.""

Lydia huffed beside me. "Take your filthy minds and mouths away from us."

"Ho, ho!" The second laughed. "And spirit. Maybe we don't give these two over when they come for the rest, eh, Ithiel? Maybe we 'lose' them somewhere in the Antonia, what do you think?"

Lydia was at the cell bars beside me now, knuckles whitening around the metal and jaw set in a hard line. "Just try it."

I had another idea, however. "You two are ignorant of whom you address."

I felt Lydia tense.

"I am an Egyptian emissary to Parthia, daughter of Rahim Ptolemy of Alexandria. An ally of Judea and of Herod." I delivered this information with all the haughtiness I could summon in such a place.

As one, they both shrugged. "Who?"

I deflated and sagged against the side wall of our cell. Part of me had known it was pointless, but still I had hoped.

The guard elbowed his twin. "Got ourselves an Egyptian pretty. I thought she was too pretty to be one of those barbarian Parthians."

The other nodded. "Wait, wasn't the sorcerer asking about an Egyptian girl? Isn't that who he wanted brought to him?"

I was back at the bars in an instant. "Who? Who wanted me brought to him?"

Guard One grinned at my concern. "We got us some interesting story here, Ithiel. A Parthian sorcerer jailed up for trying to steal from villagers, and his Egyptian concubine trying to say she's some kind of princess."

Zahir. He was here, in the Antonia. And already with guards in his pocket. My fingers trembled on the bars and I gripped tighter, forcing down the bitterness rising in my throat.

"How much you think he would pay us to bring her?"

"Pay us? I don't want his gold—I want a spell to get rid of the swelling in my feet. Giving me too much pain these days——"

"I am a sorceress as well."

That got their attention. They both jerked back toward me, eyes wide.

"And if you think your feet are giving you pain now, wait until I am through with you."

CHAPTER TWO

KAMILLAH

*S*omeone was following me.

Fists clenched and jaw tight, I doubled back on my route through the night-dark city, crossed a narrow intersection, skirted an open square, and slipped into a murky alley, walls reassuringly close yet shadows that could hide anything.

Did they think I was stupid?

My release from the prison cell, with the others left behind, had been too quick, too easy. After my declaration of my Egyptian heritage, word had come down that because I was not Parthian, I was being released with all apologies of the king's court.

Ha! From the stories Lydia had told me of Herod, the man did not apologize, even through intermediaries.

And now the shadowy footsteps behind me, dogging my route through the night.

I braced my back against the rough stone of the alley's wall and watched the narrow entrance to my hiding place. I forced my teeth to unclench but could still feel the blood pounding in my head.

Every part of me wanted to step out of the alley and show this pathetic shadow what an Egyptian princess-turned-Persian mage could do to him. My fingers twitched and a spell came to my lips, so easy to speak into the night.

But Misha's angels—somehow knowing that they were there, just beyond the realm of my seeing—stopped me.

My hesitance tightened my gut, made me shake my head in self-chastisement. How was I ever going to kill Zahir if I could not even cast a simple spell on some hapless prison guard sent to follow me?

And how was I to get my friends out of that prison before the verdict of espionage came down and their executions were ordered?

The flash of an image, of Reza and Misha hanging side by side on the gallows, left me nauseated.

Instead of a spell, then, I sent out a tentative, whispered prayer to Misha's One God. A plea for help sent to me the way it always appeared for Misha.

Nothing.

Now who was the stupid one? I exhaled a breath of self-disgust. Even my half-believing made no logical sense.

More slipping through streets, taking sharp turns.

My follower had not yet appeared. I slid along the wall, jagged edges of stone snagging at my clothing, and I leaned my head far enough to peer around the corner. I allowed myself a small smile. He had been so easy to lose. They underestimated this woman.

Now where?

The evening grew late. Homes would soon be shuttered, families unwilling to open doors to a stranger. I could not spend the night in the cold, protected by nothing but my own cunning.

I had money in my pouch. The myrrh I had purchased in Petra, and other less valuable purchases from along the way. But it would not serve to draw too much attention, and it was not enough to buy my friends out of the Antonia Fortress. I slid a hand into my pouch, felt for the myrrh, closed my fingers around it for a moment, wanting the security of it. When I removed my hand, the scent of it traveled to me, stirring such a powerful longing for home that I had to swallow hard against the salty tears.

Something scuffed in the alley behind me—a scrounging dog perhaps, or something larger.

I stepped into the empty square, still half visible in the dusk. At least I could get to a more populated area.

The Antonia loomed behind me, and I tried to get my bearings in this unfamiliar city. The Temple's platform stretched far across the city from the fortress, on its other side. Surely more people would be there.

I hastened in that direction, my senses rubbed raw and alert to the tiniest change in my surroundings. A woman alone at night in the streets of any city, even if she possessed some level of power, was not a good thing to be, especially in this city with head uncovered and hair loosed. I needed to find shelter.

After a few minutes I slowed to a walk, breath shallow in my chest. Despite my run into the Panais night, I had spent too many years a pampered scholar in the Nisa palace. I was unaccustomed to running.

I crossed into a narrower street, with houses that blocked my view of the fortress, and was disoriented.

Behind me, a man stepped from a doorway and barked some sort of invective. Was it directed at me? I picked up my pace once more, navigating the uneven bits of pavement and refuse strewn in the street.

Not well enough, however. One lip of stone, cracked and jutting, caught my sandal and I went down, knees cracking against the unforgiving stone.

My hands shot forward, blocked my face from hitting the ground. The scent of the myrrh was still on my palm, and I breathed in home once again before lifting my head.

A small girl watched me from a nearby doorway, eyes white and wide in the darkness, hair tangled and one forefinger stuck in her mouth. The soft glow of candlelight behind her framed her tiny body, every wisp of unruly hair set afire by the warm light.

I reached a hand toward the girl but did not know why.

I pulled myself to standing, brushed the scattered dust and pebbles from my robe, and examined the damage. My knees throbbed, but a quick lift of my robes showed no blood staining my skin.

The girl turned away and disappeared into the house, leaving an ache in my belly. Time to move on.

I was shivering with cold now, clutching my pouch to my chest for warmth and perhaps some protection as it felt like the only thing between me and disaster. The city passed in a blur of black and brown and beige, all shadows and uncertainties.

More calls echoed from men I passed. They thought me a prostitute. But where were the pious men of Jerusalem I had heard so much about?

Men like Lydia's friend David. The boy she had befriended on the ship from Alexandria when they were both practically children, who had grown into a man in the palace of Herod where she served.

David.

Could I find him? Surely he would help, not only me, but Lydia and Simon and the others!

The plan quickened my steps again, propelled me around the Temple's walls toward its main entrance. Would people still be there, safe people to ask?

Thoughts spinning ahead into my plan, I did not see the man who blocked my passage along the wall until I nearly careened into his chest.

I drew up, sucked in a quick breath, then ducked my head in apology and stepped right to move around him.

He stepped into my path and blocked me once more.

With the towering wall on my left, there was little room for maneuvering.

"Excuse me." I said the words softly and toward the ground, hopefully in the tone a respectful Jewish woman would use. Though I was not dressed as a respectable Jewish woman, and we both knew it.

"Where are you hurrying to?"

"I am meeting some friends." I pointed toward the Temple entrance. "Just ahead there."

He moved closer, hands extended as if he would grip my waist. "I could be your friend."

The deep urge for spell casting swelled over me again and I lifted my chin, looked him squarely in the eyes. "I don't think so."

He grinned, his teeth a dull yellow in the rising moonlight.

I kept my gaze directed at his, letting the power flow through me.

But his eyes shifted, his attention moving to something behind me.

I turned, breaking my hold on him. Another equally leering man stood at my back. From his nod to the other it was clear they were acquaintances. Even partners, perhaps, from the way they both inched toward me, pinning me in the empty space between them.

There was no time for waiting on Misha's protectors now.

It fell to me, as it always did, to protect myself.

CHAPTER THREE

KAMILLAH

*T*his whole situation was unacceptable.

Between me and my impossible goals stood two stupid men who thought to make sport of a woman walking alone through the night.

Well, they were in for a surprise.

I whirled back to the first fool who had blocked my path, raised my arms until my palms were held in front of me, facing him. I began the words of a spell I had seen cripple stronger men.

The words were sweet and familiar on my lips and issued from me in a low stream of sound that curled into the air on tendrils of power.

It was the eyes first, always the eyes that spoke of fear, and I reveled in the fear I saw in them, widening first at my words and then no doubt as he felt the power burrow into his chest.

He struggled to look away, to glance over my shoulder at his friend, to give a tight incline of his head—the signal to flee—strained and restricted as if I held his head in a vise.

I released him. Lowered my arms, quieted my words.

He ran.

I did not have to turn to know that his friend ran with him.

It had felt good, the releasing of power. And yet as I hurried along the wall, guilt also snagged at me, an unformed and nameless regret I did not understand. Perhaps if I had waited. Had not insisted on my own strength, Misha's God would have answered.

But it was time to return to my objectives.

I needed to rid myself of Zahir, who held more power than I and had already gained allies in the prison where he was being held.

Before I could worry about Zahir, however, I had to find a way to get my friends out of prison.

To do that I needed to find Lydia's friend David—an impossible task in a city no doubt full of Davids, and with little else to go on.

There were few people milling around the entrance to the Temple at this hour. I would waste no time. I approached a woman slightly older than myself, holding the hand of young child, a battered woven basket over her other arm.

"I am looking for someone, trying to find his home."

She eyed me up and down and pulled the little boy closer.

"His name is David. His wife, at least she was his wife many years ago, was Halima. He was a woodworker, a mason in Herod's palace. I do not know if he still works in that trade…"

Her eyes narrowed. "You do not know much."

I sighed and glanced around at the dispersing citizens. "Can you help me?"

"My advice is to find yourself your own husband. Not go asking after someone else's."

I moved on.

After three more repeated requests, I leaned against the half wall of a stone fountain and folded my arms. This was not working.

"I knew a boy like that once."

I lifted away from the fountain and turned.

Filmy eyes blinking, an old woman stood behind me. She made strange clicking sounds with her mouth.

"Once?"

Her palm extended outward, fingers rubbing.

It took me a moment to realize she wanted payment. I shook my head. "After you give me information."

She pursed her wrinkled lips and the clicking stopped. Then a shrug. "He lives in the Mathias district. Near the new palace."

"I will need more than that."

She proceeded to give me directions, gnarled hand pointing.

I tried to memorize each turn, each landmark.

And then there was her palm again.

I obliged her with a few shekels from my pouch, thanked her, and headed for the next street before I forgot everything she'd told me. It took the better part of an hour to get reasonably close, with more encounters in the streets with brazen men. I barely slowed at their calls.

And then there was nothing to do but start knocking on doors and asking. The narrow street where I began stretched out into darkness, each home spilling warm light from the cracks around shuttered windows. I interrupted the evening of three families before I found some hope in the fourth house.

"David and Halima? What do you want with them?" The wife's half-squinted eyes accused me of trying to steal Halima's husband before I'd even found him.

"We have a mutual friend from years ago. She wishes me to pay him her regards."

"Hmmph."

"Can you tell me where they live, please?"

She debated a moment longer, then shrugged. "Two streets over. Third door on the left."

"Thank you. I will be certain to tell Halima of your helpfulness."

"Hmmph. Leave me out of it." And the door was closed.

Minutes later, I was knocking on the third door on the left of Halel Street.

It opened gently, and the lamps within outlined the trim figure of a man who seemed roughly Lydia's age. His hair was still dark, though shot through with streaks of gray. He smiled at me, the smile of a man taking pity on an unfortunate soul, and kindness filled his eyes.

"How can I help you, child?"

I was no child, and we both knew it, but the reference was a compliment since a woman my age should not be alone in the nighttime street.

"Is your name David? Did you once work in the palace of Herod as a mason, many years ago?"

He smiled again, softening the hard lines of his face. "Many years ago, and occasionally still, though Herod has less use for me since his new palace construction has finished."

I exhaled. But I was still unsure. "And did you have a friend—there in the palace—"

"David, who is at the door?"

He half-turned, then looked back to me and opened the door fully. "Please, come in. You should not be outside. It is cold."

Again, the kindness. I nodded in acceptance of it and stepped into the warmth of the lamp-lit home. It smelled of bread and herbs and olive oil and glowed golden in the evening. The tension of the past hours seemed to melt from my body the moment I crossed the threshold.

David's hand was at my elbow, guiding me to a chair beside a beautifully wrought table. "We have a guest, my dear."

A matronly woman appeared from around a corner, then stopped short at the sight of me.

Men were usually kind to me. Women, not so often. This one eyed me up and down with the look of a threatened lioness guarding her pack. She was sweet looking and still pretty, despite the years.

"You are Halima?" I smiled and bowed my head, attempting a deference I did not feel but desiring to put her at ease.

Her eyes narrowed. "Have we met?"

I looked back to David, who had lowered himself to the chair in front of me and watched me with interest.

"Did you have a friend in the palace, two friends really. Lydia and Simon?"

David laughed and slapped his knee. "So many years since I have heard those names!"

Halima sank into a chair beside her husband. "You know Lydia and Simon?"

"They are here."

David's glance shot toward the door. "Here?"

"In Jerusalem, yes. In the Antonia Fortress."

A veil of concern dropped over his face. "What do you—?"

"In cells in the lower levels."

He jumped to his feet and started pacing. "Why did they come back?" His voice lowered, as though he muttered to himself. "Even after all these years, they must have known Herod would not allow them freedom. And Salome—she would see Lydia strung on gallows." He stopped his pacing and glared at me. "And you——you bring danger to my family by coming here!"

"I do not think Herod knows they are in his prison. I need your help. To get them freed before he does."

David yanked the chair backward and dropped into it once more. "Tell me everything."

I did not tell him of the star. Not yet. I only told him of the battle at Bethel over the Nehushtan, of Zahir's arrest and our subsequent detention, and of the scrolls and the Chakkiym's desire to return them to Jerusalem, believing the time of the Messiah to have come.

"Yes, everyone in Judea seems to think the time has come, thanks to the prophecies of Daniel. A new Messiah appears on every street corner each morning."

I shrugged. "They are not my stories, obviously. I leave the interpretation of Jewish prophecies to Jews. I only know that my friends are in danger."

"A danger you have brought here with you."

"I am sorry. Lydia spoke so fondly of you, and knowing no one else in the city... But if you wish me to leave—" I half-rose from my chair, taking a chance.

"No. No, sit."

I remained, though David's expression was far from welcoming.

His wife's was even less so. "David, you cannot allow her to stay! Think of Adina!"

"I am thinking of nothing else!" David raked a hand through his dark hair. "But it is Lydia! And Simon. How can we not help?""

The door scraped open in that moment, and all three of us lifted our heads to the young woman who entered. She was a beauty—full red lips, high cheekbones, and lovely almond eyes.

"Adina!" Halima stood and circled us to clutch at the girl's arms. "What are you doing out in the streets so late?"

Adina, perhaps eighteen years of age, smiled questioningly at me, then looked to her mother's wrath. "It is fine, Mother. One of the kitchen workers walked me home. I only wanted to see you both before Shabbat begins tomorrow." She looked to me again. "Hello." The greeting was spoken in confidence, a girl with maturity beyond her years.

I stood. "My name is Kamillah." Speaking it aloud, I realized neither David nor Halima had asked for it. "Your parents and I have mutual friends, and I came to deliver a greeting to them."

Adina seemed to notice David for the first time, sitting with his head in his hands. "Father, what is it?" She hurried to his chair and crouched before it. "Bad news?""

He cupped the back of her head with his hand. "She has come with news of Lydia and Simon."

The girl gave a little gasp and turned, wide-eyed, to me.

David sighed. "They are here in Jerusalem, in Herod's prison, though it appears he does not know what a treasure he holds."

"But why—?"

"A long story. But we must find a way to help."

The older woman huffed. "Foolishness!"

"Halima!" The air crackled with the tension of David's rebuke.

I closed my eyes, lowered my head. In only a few minutes I had caused pain and upheaval in this house. But what choice did I have?

They talked in low tones, then, the three of them, leaving me out of the conversation. And I had little to offer.

Adina, it seemed, worked in the palace as maid to Salome's daughter, much like Lydia had once served Herod's wife Mariamme. But it was not career advancement or the relative wealth of high placement the girl was after. It was information. Her father belonged to a group of zealots who kept an ear to the ground at all times, waiting and watching for the right time to restore Judea to independence, to wrestle it from the greedy grip of Rome. Adina had been placed in the center of the hornet's nest to carefully listen to the political news freely spouted before servants who were not expected to have ears nor intellect. All that she heard she reported back to David, who took it to his fellow zealots. It was a precarious position, and if Adina were ever exposed, it would certainly mean her death.

And thus their panic over my appearance. Any connection between this family, between Adina and traitors such as Lydia and Simon, could mean execution for the young girl.

What had I done?

In the end, it was decided. Adina would return to the palace immediately and find out all she could about Lydia and Simon, and the others trapped with them.

"And Zahir," I added.

All eyes turned to me.

"He is the cause of all of this. We need to know if he has been released, if he can cause more harm."

And I needed to know how to destroy his hold on me. But this they did not need to know.

David donned a cloak to walk Adina back to the palace, kissed Halima on the top of the head, and nodded to me. "I will return soon. Halima, make sure our guest is comfortable here for the night." He smiled at his wife, as if to take the sting from his words.

"Thank you." I spoke the words to all three of them, for their hospitality and their help.

Halima busied herself as soon as the door closed behind father and daughter, gathering a blanket and unrolling a sleeping mat near the fire. "I am sure it is not what you are accustomed to—"

"It is wonderful, Halima. Thank you. I have come from spending many nights in the desert among soldiers. Your beautiful home is a welcome respite."

"Hmmph." It seemed to be the universal grunt of displeased Jewish women.

She bent over a pot at the fire. "Some lamb and lentils remain from our meal." She scooped the mixture into a dish and handed it to me.

Between bites I asked her about David's mention of the prevalence of Messiahs. "How will you know if you have found the right one?"

"Oh, we will know."

"The star seems to indicate that the time is now."

"What star?"

I set the dish in my lap. Did she truly not know of the star? "Regulus, the king star. Circling Jupiter, the king planet, like a crown. All of it inside the constellation of the lion. It signifies that a great king has been born in the land of the Jews."

Her brow furrowed in displeasure.

"Everyone is talking of it, as far away as Parthia. How can it not be the topic of every conversation here, in the very place where this new ruler resides?"

Halima stood, nostrils flaring. "Because we do not bow the knee to idolatrous star worship as you pagans do."

With that our tentative truce was broken. She took the half-full dish from me, set it on the table, and thrust the blanket into my arms. "You may sleep by the fire for tonight. But do not think that we can keep you here through Shabbat. It would be too—" She faltered, seemingly at a loss for words.

"Pagan?"

"Hmmph."

She disappeared into the back room, and I made myself as comfortable as possible on the thin mat, wrapped in the scratchy blanket.

Sleep did not come quickly. I gazed into the smoldering firelight, burning low but hot, and saw only the face of Zahir, somewhere in this city still plotting something, even though his Nehushtan was nothing more than a lump of molten bronze and ash. Could I bribe someone to let me into the prison so I could kill him? But if I were that close, he would bend me to his will. Perhaps bribe someone to poison him?

If Halima could read my thoughts, she would no doubt toss me into the street, confirmed in her opinion that anyone who worshipped gods other than hers was suspect.

And what of Halima's God? Lydia and Simon's God? Even Misha seemed to have surrendered at last. I had seen wondrous things, to be sure. And if the star was correct, and the World-Savior had been born a Jew, perhaps it was true indeed that the Jews" God was the one truth.

But could I trust this God to protect me from Zahir? To release me from the dark bonds the mage had formed around me? Or was I better off dreaming of bribes and poison?

I fell into fitful sleep before David ever returned, the blanket scratching against my cheek and the firelight dying until the room lay black and chilled.

I awakened with a jolt. Took in my surroundings and searched for memory of where I was.

The door was scraping shut, the watery light of dawn behind it. Adina stood in its shadow.

"Adina! You have returned already."

David and Halima joined us a moment later.

Halima crossed to her daughter. "What is it?"

The girl's pale face shone in the wan light and she panted as though she had run all the way from the palace. She thrust back her head covering and glanced at me. "He knows they are here."

I was on my feet. "Who knows?"

"Herod. And Salome, too. Someone saw Simon and Lydia ride in with a Roman escort. Recognized them." She sank into a chair, still breathing heavily.

A chill ran along my veins. I had never met Herod, or his evil sister, but Lydia's stories had been enough to make me wish never to set eyes on them.

David closed his eyes and leaned his head back.

I could not tell if he was praying or giving up.

"It is only a matter of time, then. He will see them executed as soon as possible. Herod has never been one to give up a grudge. And I believe his sister would personally slit the throats of everyone who has ever crossed her."

Adina shook her head. "But I do not think Herod knows they are in his prison. Not yet."

"How can that be?" It was the first question I had asked, and the three turned to me as if they'd forgotten my presence.

"It was reported that they received a Roman escort into the city."

I huffed. "Yes, at the end of their pikes."

"Apparently, the witness did not see it that way. Herod seems to believe that Lydia and Simon have made an ally of the Romans and have been brought here to oppose him in some way."

David grunted. "The man's paranoia knows no boundaries."

"But there is one more thing." Adina's voice trembled, and she looked to her father. "Salome knows somehow that they have brought the scrolls."

"Somehow?" Halima's voice hardened. "I can tell you how! Through her dark magic." With this declaration her glance went directly to me, and I felt the heat of it. "Nothing good can come of this."

David nodded, then pulled his daughter from the chair and into his embrace. Over her shoulder he also looked to me, with all the fierceness of a man who loved his daughter more than life.

"You have to leave."

CHAPTER FOUR

KAMILLAH

The walls were closing in on Misha.

One more night in this stuffy, manure-smelling cell and he would lose his mind.

How could his father sleep? Simon had made a small pile out of loose straw, wrapped his cloak around it, and now slept with his head pillowed as if in his Nisa home, among all the luxury and beauty Lydia had created.

Was Mother also sleeping in the next cell? He slid to the bars, listened for her breathing. Even a soft call of her name might wake her, and she needed the sleep.

And where did Kamillah spend the night?

It had been a shock when the guards came, yanked Kamillah through the iron gate, and clanged it shut behind her. At first they feared the worst, but enough of the guards' explanation filtered behind them to realize that she was being released.

He could still see the look on her face as she turned and searched him out before being pulled through the doorway. The look said a thousand things—determination to help them all, desperation that she would not see them again. Fear that she would not see *him* again, he dared to hope.

He and Reza had two cells between them—his mother's and another with some of the Chakkiym, but they had passed messages back and forth late into the night, tediously trying to concoct a plan to get out of this disaster. They had whispered along the walls until the guards yelled at them to shut their mouths.

And now they slept. Or tried to sleep.

He needed to get his parents out of here before Herod learned they were here. Deliver the scrolls to whomever needed them. Find the Messiah, if He truly existed.

And then what?

Best not to think that far.

How long until dawn? He leaned his head against the cold bars and attempted once more to keep his eyes closed.

The attempt must have worked, for when he next opened them, the darkness had lessened and the sound of workmen outside the prison signaled the start of a new day. His eyes burned with a grittiness and his belly grumbled at their missing provisions, left strapped to their horses.

Father stirred, then lifted his head. "Any news?"

"Nothing."

"How is your mother?"

"I have heard nothing from her, either."

His father crawled to the iron bars and put his forehead against the metal. "Lydia?"

"Hmmm."

"Ah, good. You slept."

After a moment of silence, his mother's voice carried to them. "Strange way of congratulating me on sleeping, by awakening me."

Father grinned at Misha. "She is well."

How did they do it? Maintain their good spirits, their confidence, when every circumstance worked against them? Misha did not bother to ask. The answer would be what it always was—a trust in the One God that rendered all circumstances nothing more than a few lines in the adventure of their lives, an adventure whose outcome was sure.

But for this morning, the clack of a dozen or more sandals on the pavement outside the prison cells did not bode well for this part of the adventure.

A group of pious-looking Jews entered. Not Roman guards or servants of Herod. Surprising.

One of them got out in front and surveyed the line of cells with a disapproving glare. "Who speaks for this group?"

Again, Misha stepped to the bars. "My name is Misha. These are my parents. We are scholars and have traveled here to seek news of the Jewish Messiah." It seemed the best approach, as these were clearly religious leaders.

"Bah!" The foremost of them spat the word like a curse. "When did Parthians ever seek a Jew for anything but to kill him?""

From the end of the cells, Gaspar spoke up. "We have seen his natal star and followed it here. For years have we studied the stars for news of the Long-Awaited One."

At this, the man's face purpled with rage. "You dare to speak of our Messiah in the same breath as your dark sorcery?"

Gaspar's voice was soothing, pleading. "Even your Psalmist, your great king David, wrote of the stars that speak of—"

"Enough!" His rage nearly rattled the cell bars. "I will hear nothing more!" With a flourish of robes and a swirl of anger, the man and his entourage swept from the prison.

Misha broke the silence that followed with a swift kick at the iron bars and a curse delivered onto their heads.

"Misha!" Mother's scolding sounded obligatory and halfhearted at best.

The morning wore on, grating on nerves and hearts. Misha and Reza traded more messages, but there was little that could be done until someone came for them, someone they could convince of their innocence.

When a figure finally appeared at the doorway to the horse-stalls-turned-prison, it was not one they expected, nor one that any of them, least of all Mother, desired to see.

"Salome."

His mother's quiet voice from the cell beside him was undergirded with granite, cool and confident even though she was the one behind bars. How had Salome learned of their presence?

"Lydia." The woman slid into the prison as if floating on water, her graceful dark robe trailing behind her. No sorceress in Nisa could have outdone the effect.

She was still youthful- looking, with masses of dark hair piled atop her head in the Roman style, braided through with gold threads. Bracelets jangled at her wrists and a ruby winked from a gold circlet cinching her upper arm. But the tight slash of her lips spoke of years of hardness.

Her attention was all for Mother, and she glided to the second cell without a glance at Misha or Father.

"I never believed I would see this day."

"Nor did I."

Misha pressed his forehead against the bars to better see her face. Smiling and cold.

"It pleases me that it should be in such circumstances."

"I am certain it does. You are unchanged."

What would have been a compliment to most women after the passage of more than two decades sounded more like an insult on his mother's lips, and Misha bit back a smile, heart surging with pride.

Salome tilted her head as if to better examine her prey. "Ah, but the years have not been as kind to you, have they?" She waved a thin finger toward his mother. "The lines of time weigh heavily on your face, I fear."

Mother laughed. "I would not trade all the years of joy that have etched my body for one year of your misery."

A storm cloud seemed to pass over Salome. Had it grown suddenly colder in the prison?

"But now it is you who will experience misery, yes?"

"What is to be done with us? We have done nothing wrong. Not now, or even all those years ago."

"Nothing wrong? You were a thief then, and are surely one now, at the very least!"

"Mariamme's jewels? Is that your accusation? They were given to me, and we both know she would have wanted me to have them."

Salome leaned close, her venomous voice striking the air. "It is not for petty crimes that I will destroy you, false princess. We both know you carried something of greater worth from this city. And now you are back, and it can be for one reason only—to complete your betrayal of my brother and to somehow place power where it does not belong. Well, I will not allow it. If I cannot see you on the gallows for legitimate crimes, then I will find a way for death to eat you from the inside, until you crumble in upon yourself."

A moment of silence followed this diatribe, and then his mother's reply graced the air in a tone as dignified as Salome's was vile. "A death much like your brother is facing, then?"

"Arrgghh!" Salome's shriek could have awakened the city. She smashed a fist against the bars of Mother's cell and called down curse after curse upon her.

Beside him, Father stood at their own bars, intoning a prayer under his breath.

At this, Salome whipped her head in their direction.

She could not possibly have heard Father. Something else more powerful was going on, and the hair on his arms and neck prickled, reminding him of the desert nights and the battles of the heavenly beings.

Three angry strides and she was before them. "So you have returned as well, soldier." She curled a lip. "I cannot even remember your name.'"

Father had not stopped praying and did not even look at Salome.

"And this is clearly your spawn, from the looks of him." She leaned in to study Misha.

He pulled back, away from the dark pools of nothing in her eyes.

"What's wrong, boy? Heard stories of the powerful Salome, have you?"

Misha smiled, feigning an amusement he only barely felt. "I have heard stories, yes."

She snarled at him—an actual feral snarl as if she were possessed by a beast. "I will see you all on your knees before myself and my brother in the throne room before the day is out. And then we shall see how far your confidence and good humor——and your prayers—will take you."

She whirled in a puff of dark fabric and chilled air, and then she was gone.

Father ceased his praying and sighed. "Lydia?"

"I am well. She cannot touch us, Simon. Do not fear."

Misha glanced at his father, eyebrows raised in a question. He did not need to hear an answer. Father's face showed that he did not share his wife's conviction.

Reza's shout bounced from the prison walls. "Is everyone all right?"

Mother answered. "Yes, Reza. Thank you, dear. Nothing to worry about."

But they had all heard Salome's warning, and it was not long before she made good on it. Within the hour, two guards were unlocking cells.

"What is happening?" Misha shook the bars while one fumbled with the latch on his mother's cell. "Where are we being taken?"

The other guard shrugged. "Orders to take you up, that's all."

"Up? Up where?"

The man jabbed a thumb toward the ceiling. "Up." His tone implied that Misha was a fool for asking, but clearly the part of the fool was already being played.

Two stupid guards for nearly fifteen prisoners? Misha glanced at Father, signaling a message to think on the talk of escape they had passed through their party late into the night.

But it was not to be all of them, after all. The Chakkiym and Reza were left in their cells, and only Mother, Father, and Misha hastily gathered up their belongings before being herded to the prison exit.

The wailing calls of the Chakkiym echoed after them. Misha glanced over his shoulder at Reza, standing grim faced behind his bars. Would it be the last time he saw his friend?

Reza nodded once, a message of courage and perhaps a farewell.

Misha returned the nod and wished for a moment to speak with him.

But the two guards were grunting at them to move, and moments later they were blinking against the sun, newly risen over the city walls. After the stuffy staleness of the underground stalls, Misha sucked in deep breaths of the brisk morning air and eyed the sky in appreciation.

A low ramp led upward to the outside of the Antonia Fortress, and they were prodded along in front of the guards, toward double wooden doors twice the height of a man.

Once inside the fortress, both his parents slowed and gazed around the front hall, taking in the place where they had once lived. Was it much changed? It seemed more military than palatial now, so perhaps there had been more luxury in those years.

Still, it was an enormously impressive building, especially for the Jews. Why had Herod seen fit to move from it? But he was an obsessive builder, they said, and could not stop improving the architecture of the country, so perhaps his new palace was even grander.

And if Salome's threat was carried out, they would soon see the throne room of that palace.

Still, there were only these two guards…

They were directed to walk along a colonnade that bordered a huge open courtyard, filled with small palms, bright red-flowering shrubbery, and a central fountain filled with scummy water that appeared not to function.

Along the back wall of the courtyard, still moving toward they knew not what, Misha fumbled in his pouch, then pulled out his bronze rings. Turning to the guards behind him, he held them up. "Ever seen anything like this, men?"

They slowed and frowned. "What you got there?"

"Have you not heard?" He twirled the rings, drawing their gaze. "I am a sorcerer from Nisa, with power over all metals.'" He showed them the three rings separated, back and front, pulled apart. "I can turn bitumen to gold, you know. Make solid metal pass through itself." With that, he clicked the rings together once, twice, and then spun them to show them joined.

At this wonder, both guards halted, slack-jawed and wide-eyed. "Do it again."

Misha shrugged, glanced at his parents, and shifted slightly to step away from them, all the while twirling the rings in his practiced hands.

Mother turned her head to study a narrow door set into the back wall of the courtyard, exactly where he had expected it to be from her description. Their late-night conversation might bear fruit after all.

When the guards' attention was fully on his hands, he performed the illusion once more, to their repeated astonishment. "Here," he held out one of the rings, ""examine it yourself. See if there are any gaps."

One of them snatched it from him, and both of them peered over it, turning it round in their stubby fingers.

Neither saw the flash of movement behind them, as Mother and Father disappeared into the wall.

He held out a hand for the rings' return, then performed for them again, taking his time with the flourishes. "What do you suppose magic rings like these might sell for, eh?"

Clearly the thought had not occurred to the two men. They glanced at each other, grins splitting their faces. Surely they thought it an easy task to relieve their prisoner of his treasure.

"But," Misha held the rings aloft, "you'll need to catch them first!'" He tossed the rings high and backward into the courtyard behind him, then heard the satisfying *plop* of them falling into the nasty fountain.

With a grunt and a curse, the two guards hurried toward it, probably both hoping to beat their partner to the spoils.

It was a loss, the rings he had kept close since childhood, but it was a loss he could live with.

A moment later he was in darkness behind the door, groping his way down a narrow flight of steps, hands on the walls on either side, heart beating in his throat.

"Father? Mother?" He risked a whisper into the gloom.

"Here, Misha."

"They won't be far behind." He could not count on the guards being ignorant of this door to the underground storage area. It was a route his mother had taken more than once in escaping this place, but the intervening years might have made its use common.

"Hurry!"

There was no light underground. Either the rooms were no longer used or torches were only brought occasionally when something was needed. Either way, it made travel difficult yet safer.

Mother led the way, warning of turns in the corridors before they reached them, as if she had never left or had a map of it all hidden away in her mind.

And then they were bursting into the morning sunlight, through a door that opened into the street below the fortress.

They drew a few stares of early shoppers. Mother grabbed Father's hand and pulled him along the wall of the fortress. "We must get lost in a crowd."

Minutes later they were crossing an open market in the bright sunlight, weaving through stalls of hanging meat marbled with fat, past folded fabrics in all shades of red and yellow and green, boxes of aromatic spices and cages of squawking pigeons.

On the other side of the market, they descended a wide set of steps to another street set on a lower level, turned a corner along a stone wall, and finally Mother stopped.

They all took deep breaths together.

Father slapped Misha on the shoulder and laughed. "So those rings finally came to good use after all."

Misha grinned. "And you said all my magi training was worthless."

Father scowled but the look was good-natured. "Worse than worthless, though we will leave it at that for now."

"We need to get off the streets." Mother was ever the practical one.

Misha patted his pouch. "And what of the scrolls? Now that we are here but separated from the Chakkiym, where do we deliver them? Who can we trust?"

Mother nodded. "Off the streets, and with someone we trust." She studied the faces of the passersby. "I have only one friend in this city. We must find David.""

CHAPTER FIVE

REZA

*N*othing had gone according to plan.

Reza had come to this city for two reasons: to protect his friends and to find the truth. Now they had been separated—Kamillah taken first, then Misha and his parents.

That left Reza to protect the Chakkiym alone.

He paced the cell, exhaling his frustration and no doubt annoying the rest of the men.

"General," Gaspar's voice was soothing, "your marching does no good. Sit and rest and be ready for whatever is to come."

"It helps me think." The old men could afford such inaction. What else could they do?

One thing was certain. If the Jews saw even this group of old men as a threat, they would put a Parthian soldier like him to the sword without a thought.

"Who has an extra tunic?" He surveyed the scattered men in the cell with him, most of them thin and bent. "Something that will fit me.""

They looked at him blankly.

"Balthazar." He called through the bars to the next cell. He was the broadest of the group. "Pass one of your tunics through to me.""

The man complied without asking questions.

Reza stripped his soldier's uniform, donned the tunic, then distributed his discarded clothing to several of the men to secret away in their own pouches.

He nodded at the transformation. "I am one of you now." The statement stung. How many times had he wished it so? "Do not speak of my being a soldier.""

Gaspar laughed. "We shall all be jealous of our young scholar, with so many years ahead of him to study."

Reza bit the inside of his cheek. Gaspar was right. He looked out of place among them and it would only draw attention to his physical strength.

He had no time to contemplate it further. Guards arrived and were barking orders at them all to gather their belongings. "Off to see Herod, you are. That is what happens when you talk of seeking another king."

Good. Perhaps they would reunite with Misha, Simon, and Lydia. And Kamillah—where had she gone after being released?

It took a few minutes for eleven of them to be shuffled and prodded from the prison and up the ramp alongside the outer wall. He strapped his pouch over his head, but sadly, his sword had been taken from him before they entered.

Reza kept his head down and was rewarded with the appearance of an ash pile. Without missing a step, he scooped a handful of ash as they passed. Moments later he transferred half the ash to his other hand, then bent his head and ran his hands through his hair. It was slightly greasy— the residue of burnt animal fat perhaps—and smeared easily through his hair. A few more surreptitious swipes through his hair and he glanced at Gaspar beside him.

The man nodded once, a barely perceptible indication that the ruse was effective. Reza was now a gray-haired Chakkiym.

He dusted his hands together, then wiped them gently along the sides of his tunic as they crossed through large doors and into the fortress. Was Herod here, or were they simply passing through?

The courtyard was like no military station in the Parthian Empire. But then it had once been a palace, so the opulence could be explained. Still, such a setting must make soldiers soft. He straightened his shoulders unconsciously at the thought, then bent them again, remembering his supposed age.

"Move it along, old men!" The guards had lost patience with herding such a group, it seemed. One of them poked at Gaspar with the short wooden rod he carried.

Gaspar stumbled at the unexpected jab and clutched at the arm of another mage, Melchior, to steady himself.

Reza increased his pace, threaded through several of the men between him and Gaspar, and took up a position at Melchior's back.

They descended a broad flight of steps and exited the fortress to the west, onto a busy street. The guards barked louder, sharper commands, perhaps fearful that they might lose their charges.

Reza studied the crowds, the alleys, and the horizon, pierced by three massive towers. The towers likely marked the location of the palace. Was it possible to coordinate an escape? Could he get a message through the group? If they all turned on their captors, would it be enough to free them? And how would he corral ten old men through the city, without drawing too much attention?

Gaspar tripped again.

The guard was on him in a blink. He crashed the wooden truncheon onto the man's shoulder.

Gaspar went down.

Reza shot forward, blood surging and fingers itching for his sword. His arm was raised over the back of the guard's neck before he knew his own actions.

The Chakkiym Balthazar caught the arm in the fraction of space before it made contact.

Reza turned on him, but the older man's warning expression slowed his anger.

"Gaspar is well, Reza." He inclined his head toward the mage, who was already moving along as though nothing had happened.

Balthazar was right. The best chance for these men to survive lay in his remaining unnoticed.

But he couldn't help the low growl in his throat.

A few minutes of forced march and they had reached the outer wall of the massive palace enclosure. They entered a central gardened court-yard through a huge stone arch, and all of them slowed to take in the lofty colonnades that bordered the east and west sides of the courtyard, each leading to multi-tiered buildings at either end that were twins of each other.

The courtyard itself was a marvel, with groves of small trees, ponds with bronze fountains, and small canals running throughout to provide water to the entire complex. Like an oasis in the desert, it was a pocket of sumptuous Greece placed in the center of austere simplicity.

They were herded to their right, toward one of the twin buildings. A few minutes' walk took them to the marble staircase, and they entered through the pillared front portico as if they were visiting dignitaries, which in a sense they were, even if Herod was too ignorant to realize it.

They passed through smaller courtyards within the palace, and Reza caught glimpses of a bath complex to rival any in Rome, spacious banquet halls, and enough chambers to house hundreds of guests.

They were apparently expected in the throne room. The wide doors were opened to them at once, and they were ushered into the chamber that was entirely silent, despite the scattering of servants and royalty.

Herod lounged on a gilded throne at the head of the columned room, with two servants nearby and a stately woman hovering at his left shoulder, her dark eyes trained on the newcomers.

Even in repose, the king was formidable. Despite his age, his build was strong and his features still handsome, though the full, sensuous lips and languid movement spoke of a certain moral laxness.

He straightened slightly at their arrival and passed a curious glance over the group. "So, these are our foreigners, come to persuade us that they are devout Jews."

Reza kept to the back of the group. It would be better for Gaspar to take the lead here.

"No such thing, King." Gaspar stepped forward. "We are from Nisa, capital of the Parthian Empire. This we do not deny.'"

"And you are a powerful mage, I am told?"

At this, the woman who must have been Herod's famed sister, Salome, leaned forward slightly, gaze turning to malice.

Gaspar inclined his head. "We are trained in the ways of the magi, yes. But we have come seeking *your* knowledge, not content with our own."

"Yes? And what knowledge is it that you think we have discovered?"

"We have studied the stars for many years, my lord. Watching for signs of great events, of great men."

Reza cringed. The Jewish people believed the eastern fascination with the knowledge of the stars to be evil.

But Herod leaned forward, clearly intrigued. "And have you seen something written of me, there in your eastern skies?"

Gaspar cleared his throat and studied his sandals for a moment. "We have seen a star rise in the east that indicates a new King of the Jews has been born. We have come to pay homage." He raised his eyes. "A newborn son of yours, we assume?"

It was a tactical move. They all knew Herod's sons were old enough to vie for the throne, and be murdered for their trouble.

Herod's face darkened and his brow creased. He gripped the armrests of his throne, and some of the madness they had heard about flashed across his eyes.

Salome was at his elbow in a moment. "It is as I said, brother. They bring their evil magic into this place, with lies meant to disturb you. We shall have them executed at once—"

Herod held up a hand to stop the flow of her words. "I would hear more of this new king."

Gaspar swallowed, and his voice was now a bit weaker. "Your Messiah, we believe. As was prophesied by your prophet Daniel, who lived his days in our land."

Reza inwardly applauded Gaspar's continued tact. Everyone in the room knew that Herod was not truly Jewish, but only part of the conquered Idumeans who had been forced to convert to Judaism centuries ago. He had won his place as king only through his early years of shrewd diplomacy toward Rome, before his mind had fractured.

Herod flopped back against his throne with a huff. "Messiah?" He looked to Salome, his full lips turning to a pout. "Must I hear constantly about Messiahs? Every day——"

"All lies, my brother. Your dynasty will rule Israel forever. The liars must be silenced."

She was smooth, this sister. Reza had heard some of Lydia's stories. The years had not dimmed her manipulation nor her intensity.

"But he says there is a star."

The petulant whine sickened Reza. This was their king?

Herod studied Gaspar. "What of this star, mage?"

"It is not so much the star itself, King, as its movement among the other stars. There is significance there that speaks of the birth of a King of Jews—"

"You see, Salome? This one is different. Not some rabbi shouting in the streets that he is the Promised One. A babe."

Salome smiled, the calculating smile of one who knew power. "Yes. Only a babe."

"And where is this babe?"

Gaspar's sandals shuffled uncomfortably on the marble floor, and the rest of the group shifted with him. "That is what we had hoped to ascertain from you, my lord. We assumed that if a new king has been born, certainly you would know of it.'"

But clearly Herod did not know of it.

He snapped a finger at an elderly man hovering nearby. Some sort of advisor, perhaps. "Bring all the scribes and the chief priests. Assemble them here after the noon meal. We will hear what they have to say about this new Messiah."

The advisor half-bowed and hurried from the throne room.

Herod waved away the eleven of them, as if they had served their purpose. "They must go. Take them."

The Chakkiym and Reza sat in the dimly lit chamber, some sort of dining hall at one time perhaps, with frescoes of vases overflowing with fruits and flowers. The older men quietly discussed the confrontation with Herod and what might come next. Would they be treated as spies, still? Threatened with execution? Or had Herod believed their reason for entering Jerusalem?

Gaspar seemed agitated with a sort of nervous excitement. "If they bring their priests, the teachers of their sacred writings, we can tell them of the scrolls—that we have brought more prophecies of their Daniel, intended for the end of days."

The day grated on, with no food or water brought. Had they been forgotten? But finally a guard appeared at the door and gruffly ordered them back to the throne room.

Gaspar was the first to his feet.

Reza touched his arm. "Easy, friend. It does not serve to appear so eager for a king to replace this one."

Gaspar half-smiled and shrugged. "You are right, of course."

A crowd had formed in the throne room. Apparently word was spreading of the foreign magi who had come to search for a new Jewish ruler. To one side, clustered between two blue-painted columns, was a group who could only be the religious leaders and experts Herod had called. They eyed the entering magi with a mixture of pious distaste and awed curiosity.

Herod and Salome were in their former places at the front of the hall.

Reza could not help a straightening of the shoulders, a slight swagger in his stride. They had nothing of which to be ashamed. Were they not the ones who had seen the star, understood its meaning?

"Well?" Herod summoned the leaders with a flick of his hand. "What say you about this new king who has supposedly been born?'"

The group of them moved forward as one, giving wide berth to their fellow scholars as if Reza and the rest of them carried contagion.

"There is a prophecy, my lord." The speaker was a squirrely little man, with an unnaturally high voice.

Herod was clearly in an impatient mood. "Speak up, then, man. Tell what you know."

"Our prophet Micah gives this foretelling, my lord: 'And you, Bethlehem in the land of Judah, you are by no means the least among the leaders of Judah, for out of you will come one leading as a shepherd, who will feed My people Israel.'"

After delivering this strange piece, the little man bowed and backed away.

"That is all?" Herod exhaled. "So Bethlehem, then?"

Salome stepped forward and bent to his ear again, though she made her voice easily heard. "So close, brother. Bethlehem is only a few miles from here."

Herod ignored her and summoned the magi forward. "It appears that if this Messiah is to be born, it will be in a village rather than a palace."

His tone was derisive and he shrugged one shoulder. "Does not sound like much of a king to me."

Gaspar was shifting his position, sliding closer to the expert who had spoken of prophecy to Herod. Reza tried to signal Gaspar to remain where he was, but the mage was intent on delivering the news of the returned scrolls to Jewish priests.

Herod raised his eyes over their heads and scanned the chamber. "Go, all of you. I wish to speak privately to our visitors."

Gaspar was visibly crestfallen.

The throne room emptied in moments. Salome remained.

Reza shifted uncomfortably on his feet. Witnesses would have been preferred. Perhaps Herod intended to summon guards from the wings and have them all cut down right there, for daring to imply that a child born unknown to him would usurp his place on the throne.

But Herod leaned forward and spoke in a conspiratorial whisper. "Surely you have heard that I am unwell."

The magi glanced among each other, none willing to assent.

"May my lord live forever," Gaspar said dutifully.

"Hmmm. Yes. It does not appear that will happen. But I do wish to leave Judea in capable hands. And there has been some—question—of whose hands that should be.""

Reza nearly snorted. Question? The man had seen two of his sons strangled, and the next in line could feel no more confident of his succession.

"If there is someone better to take my place, surely I should learn of it as soon as possible, yes?"

Hesitant nods bobbed around the group of them.

"Tell me, when, exactly, did this star first appear to you there in the east?"

Gaspar cleared his throat. "The phenomena was first observed nearly a year ago, my lord. Since that time, we have traced its movement—"

"I see. Still a babe, then, one would think. Though we cannot know if it rose upon his conception or his birth, can we?"

"Natal stars are generally thought to appear at birth, my lord."

Reza looked to the floor to hide his amusement at Herod's ignorance.

"And what of the other one of you? What would he say of this star, of this babe?"

"Other one, my lord?" Gaspar shook his head.

"The one brought back unconscious from whatever mischief he was causing in Bethel." Herod examined the group of them through squinted eyes. "I am to see him next, when I am through with you. What will he say to all of this?"

Zahir. Still alive, then.

Reza chewed at his lip. If Zahir were given the prophecy of Bethlehem, what would he do with it? He still sought ultimate power. Even without the Nehushtan, would he go after the Messiah-child, to somehow attach himself to this possible new world ruler?

"I believe a month ago he would have said the same, my lord. Zahir is a fourth-level mage—the highest order—and has been studying the star these many months as well. But there is nothing to be served in consulting him. He has gone quite mad with searching for some myth, an artifact of your people that does not exist."

Good man, Gaspar.

Herod sat back in his ornate chair, studying Gaspar as if unsure he was trustworthy. It mattered little. The king would bring Zahir and hear him out. Whether his own fragile sanity would recognize a fellow sufferer in Zahir's ravings was impossible to know.

Herod sighed heavily. "Very well."

Salome leaned forward, her paint-rimmed eyes fixed on her brother.

"You must go and search little Bethlehem, of course." Herod flicked both hands at them all, as if to sweep them through the double doors. "Find this new king. But""—his hardened gaze roved over each of them, no sign of madness now—"you must bring news of him back to me here in Jerusalem. If he truly is destined to be king of the Jews, then I must make changes to my will, must make preparations to honor him with succession.""

Wordless, Gaspar bowed to the king.

Reza hid a smile. The man was guileless and would have struggled to lie to the king's face, but his silent obeisance was neither refusal nor consent.

"Go then." Again the flicking of the fingers as if they were children. "Hurry off to Bethlehem, then hurry back."

They retreated from the throne room, then clustered in the annex, talking all at once in subdued muttering.

"We must find the priests and tell them of the scrolls."

"Why now, when we do not even have them, nor know where Misha is?"

"Or if he lives!"

"Perhaps the scrolls have already been destroyed. Or perhaps Misha has found a way—"

A female voice interrupted the murmurs. "I know where he is."

The group turned as one, mouths gaping.

A young woman, younger than twenty, stood quietly against the wall. How long had she been listening?

Reza stepped from the men and approached her.

It was hard to ignore her stunning beauty. She wore the head covering of the pious, but it could not hide all of her shining black hair, and the white of her servant's robes set off her long-lashed dark eyes and full red lips.

"Who are you?" The question emerged more harshly than he intended.

The girl pulled back against the wall, her lovely eyes widening, but more in condemnation than in fear.

"My name is Adina. I am maidservant to Salome's daughter."

"And what do you know of Misha-aku of Nisa?"

"As I told you, I know where he is."

Reza smiled at the slight coolness in her voice, the lift of her chin. She might have been a servant, but she did not speak like one. "And where is that?"

Her voice dropped to a whisper. "He and his parents are in the home of my parents, who are old friends of Lydia's and Simon's.'"

Reza's heart leaped. He had not actually believed this girl knew anything.

Gaspar pushed forward. "Your father—he is Lydia's friend David?"

She smiled at Gaspar, seeming to find him a friendlier face than Reza. "Yes. He and my mother, Halima, have welcomed your friends. The woman, too."

Reza sucked in a breath. "The woman? Do you mean Kamillah?"

"Yes. The sorceress."

"She is not—" Reza waved away the offense. "You will take us to them?"

Adina glanced left and right. "I cannot leave immediately. I have duties."

Reza nodded once and pointed in the direction of the huge entrance they had passed through hours ago. "We will wait in the central courtyard. Come and find us when you are finished."

Her eyebrows lifted at his authoritarian tone.

"Please."

She smiled, and the light of it was worth the humiliation.

Reza stalked away, leading the Chakkiym and chastising himself for being so distracted by her charms.

They waited through the heat of the afternoon, watched the sun set over the western hills, and drew their robes against the evening chill, but still Adina did not come.

The day had been momentous, but somehow most of it had been spent waiting. Why had they not simply gotten directions to Adina's house?

Finally, with the sliver of a moon rising between the three towers that backed the northern half of the palace complex, Adina appeared like an apparition out of the darkness. "You are ready?"

Reza unbent his legs from their cramped position on the cold stone of the courtyard and got to his feet to tower over the slight girl. "We have been ready for hours."

She huffed. "I should think you would be thankful to find your friends instead of complaining."

"I am not complaining. I am cold. And hungry. And tired."

She softened. "I am sorry I was so long. I can imagine it would be difficult for a man of your age to sit so long on the stones."

Man of his age? How old did she—? Ah, but the ash in his hair—she must think him as aged as the rest of the Chakkiym. He swiped at the back of his head, but it was useless without a launderer's cleansing powders and some water.

It took only half of an hour to reach Adina's house. She led the eleven of them like a shepherdess bringing her sheep home to the fold, and they crowded at the door of the small house, each one bumping and nudging to reunite with Misha and the others.

Adina entered first, and Reza followed, holding up a hand to stay the Chakkiym at the door. It would not do to frighten those inside with a swarm of newcomers. The warmth and coziness of the house hit him like a wave, and his shoulders shed the weight of tension.

"Reza!"

Lydia flew across the small central room to clasp him to herself. But Misha and Simon were there a moment later, slapping him on the back, grinning widely.

Kamillah crossed the room and grasped his hand in her own warm fingers and smiled.

David and his wife, Halima, were already herding the Chakkiym into the house, and with nearly twenty people talking and embracing at once, chaos reigned for some minutes.

It was heartwarming to watch Lydia and David together, reunited with as near a brother and sister as each had ever known. Adina slipped away to help her mother, who was working a lump of bread dough somewhat frantically at a low table.

"Do not think to feed us all, mistress. We did not come to presume on your hospitality, only to find our friends."

Halima glanced up at the respect in his tone and smiled. "You are welcome here for as long as you need, though I am not sure where to put you all—"

Reza shook his head. "No, no, we will find other accommodations. But we are so grateful for your daughter's help."

Did he let his glance linger too long on Adina? When he returned his attention to Halima, her friendly smile had turned a bit suspicious, and her narrowed eyes took them both in at once.

"Yes. She is a good girl. A good Jewish girl."

He nearly laughed. The implication was clear.

"Perhaps I could trouble you—"

She straightened, the attitude of hospitality returning. "Anything you need."

He ran a hand through his gray-powdered hair. "Earlier I felt the need to appear a similar age to the scholars I am protecting. I would love to wash the ashes from my hair."

He could not resist a quick look at Adina, and was rewarded once again with that big smile.

"I wondered—"

"Adina, fetch soap and water." Halima's voice had sharpened once more.

The girl slipped out of the house, snatching a small jug from a shelf on her way.

Reza nodded to Halima. "I will—help her."

He escaped the house, half-expecting Halima to chase him down with her dough-covered hands, but she must have felt the pressure of feeding the mass of them too keenly to intervene.

Outside, Adina was drawing a bucketful of water from a larger barrel beside the house. "Sit."

Reza lowered himself obediently onto a tiny stone bench she had pulled from the wall of the house.

Adina circled behind him. "Lean your head back."

Again he obeyed, closing his eyes at the warmth of her fingers in his hair and the coolness of the water she trickled over his scalp. This close to her, his head nearly resting on her chest, he could smell her flowery perfume and hear her soft breathing.

"How old are you, then?"

He smiled, eyes still closed. Bold question from a bold girl. She was a combination of Lydia's lovely spirit of service and Kamillah's strength. But there was a softness there, something Kamillah never allowed with him. Something Reza found very...... likeable. "Old enough to have resisted many charming women."

"Ha! You flatter yourself, Parthian."

"Persian."

Her hands paused in their working of the soap powder through his hair. "For a soldier, that was strangely spoken. Like a man more interested in family heritage than military conquest."

How had she discerned his heart so quickly, from only a single word?

He answered with only a sigh, and she seemed to find it answer enough.

The ritual was finished too quickly, and there was little excuse to stay outside under the stars. Halima would no doubt emerge any moment, prepared to break a jug over his head.

He took up Adina's hand for the briefest moment, squeezed her fingers, and looked into her eyes. "Thank you."

She laughed, the sound flooding the night with joy. "At least you smell better now."

He grinned. "Now if only I could wash the taste of ash from my mouth."

Her gaze dropped to his lips and her smile faded to something else. Then she shook her head and turned back to the house. "For that, I think we shall get you some wine."

CHAPTER SIX

KAMILLAH

I leaned against a far wall, pulled as far as possible from the ridiculous throng of people packed into David's house. The Chakkiym chattered with excitement over the nearness of their goal. Lydia and Simon and even Misha told tales of the missing years with David and Halima.

And Reza? I had not missed his furtive exit after Adina. I had waited for my heart to feel pained at the sight of it, but in truth it made me glad. This was a revelation to me.

The cause of it drew my attention a moment later.

Misha's characteristic laugh burst over the crowd, causing a pause of arrested conversation, and then more general laughter. It was a happy group. And yes, my – friendship – with Misha was loosening the bond between Reza and me.

So why did I feel so miserable?

No need to search my heart for that answer. It waited only a short walk away, in a cell under the Antonia Fortress. Or perhaps by this time, he had found a means to free himself.

What could Zahir accomplish if he joined his own form of madness to that of Herod's? I shuddered and braced my fingertips against the wall behind me.

Despite the success of this day, I was still a slave in search of a way to break free of my master.

The room quieted suddenly. Simon was banging a wooden bowl against the table to get attention. "We shall leave for Bethlehem at first light, men." He bowed in the direction of Lydia and then to me. "And women."

"Do not forget me!" Halima's hands were on her hips.

Simon laughed. "Halima, I distinctly remember you as a quiet girl. What has this man done to you over the years?"

David grinned. "She needed to get bolder to deal with me, I suppose."

"So," Simon took in the room with his glance, "we shall be a large party, all the better for the sake of safety."

"We will be followed." My voice barely registered above the general hum of the room.

All eyes turned toward me. "I was followed from the prison when I was released." I nodded in the direction of the group of old men. "Surely you were as well.'"

They traded glances, but clearly they had not thought to watch.

"Adina is always careful—" David was searching the room for his daughter, but she and Reza had not returned.

"With a group this size?" I shook my head. "It would have been impossible."

Reza and Adina chose that moment to return, and the silent room watched their entrance. Reza's eyebrows shot up at the attention, and his face reddened. He glanced at me.

I could not help a knowing smile.

"Adina, were you followed here?"

Adina looked to her father, evidently confused for a moment at the question. "I—I watched for anyone and did not see, but it was difficult— with all the men——"

Reza nodded. "So, we must assume that our movements are being noted and delivered to Herod. But what of it? We have his permission to search for the child in Bethlehem. Why should we fear his watchful eye?"

Simon and Lydia, David and Halima, and even Adina responded with varying grunts and sounds of disdain.

It was David who spoke. "You should fear anything and everything having to do with our *king*. The man has killed his own sons. There is nothing he will not do."

"We leave tonight, then."

Simon had reassumed command, and Reza nodded in deference to him.

I silently applauded Reza for his respect. With all the soldiers returned to Nisa and only the Chakkiym remaining, these were Simon's troops now.

"We'll leave gradually, slipping out one or two at a time through the night. We will meet up on the road to Bethlehem and hope we are alone."

Gaspar elbowed his way to the front of the Chakkiym. "We cannot leave without delivering the scrolls. Should something happen to us along the way, we cannot risk losing them."

Simon greeted this declaration with a moment of consideration, then nodded. "You are right, of course, Gaspar. I only hope we can find the right men to receive them. That they will understand and believe what we have brought."

The group divided quickly, Simon and David consulting with the Chakkiym and Reza about how the scrolls should be delivered as quickly as possible, and the three other women congregating in the kitchen area to take orders from Halima about provisions for the journey. I pushed away from the wall to join them, but a look from Halima stopped me. Apparently, women of my sort were not welcome in her kitchen.

Misha grabbed my hand and tugged me toward the door. "Let's get some air."

Indeed, it was growing close and warm in the house. Outside, I lifted my face to the cool darkness and breathed deeply.

"You were quiet in there." Misha still had my hand.

I let him lead me to the side of the house, where a stone bench nestled in a small garden. "There were plenty of voices without mine to join them."

Misha released my hand and moved the bench against the house. He sat and then slapped the bench next to him for me to join him.

Side by side, we studied the starry night.

"It was more than the crowd that kept you silent. Something is bothering you."

Ah, Misha. I thought about the first time we spoke, in the corridor outside the Vault, after he had used his cunning to pilfer something to help with his examinations. Even now he did not realize how intelligent, how perceptive he was. He could have passed without the help.

We had shared so much since that first day. Late night conversations on the wide range of our shared interests which others would have found dull. Traded glances of amusement at the arguments of the old Chakkiym. The occasional touch of his hand on my arm, my shoulder, my back. We come to value each other, to see the value in each other. Something I had never experienced with another.

"Where do you think all of this is going, Misha?"

His breathing caught and held for a moment.

I cleared my throat. "I mean, this journey."

"Hmm. To Bethlehem." He pointed. "It's about six miles south——"

"Very funny. I mean *after* Bethlehem. We came all this way for the Nehushtan. Well—you did. To heal your mother. But now the Nehushtan is destroyed and your mother is healthy again. What will we find in Bethlehem that will tell us what comes next?"

Misha was silent a few moments, still looking at the sky. "You think that I came for the power of the artifact. And I think that is what I believed at first. But I know now that it was always something more." He pointed to the star, still hanging above the horizon. ""I was always following, always being led."

"But to what? For what purpose?"

He folded his arms across his chest and leaned his head back against the wall of the house. "I do not know."

"Do you think your Messiah will have the power to break Zahir?"

"Zahir? Why do you think of *him* now?"

I gaped at him. "When am I *not* thinking of him? Do you still not understand who he is? What he can do?"

Misha smiled. "And do you still not understand what the One God can do? You have seen it with your eyes."

I leaned with him against the wall, suddenly exhausted. "I must have answers about the afterlife, about the gods. The answers will be my reason to return home. But I cannot be truly safe to return unless Zahir is broken."

He was silent again, as he always was when I spoke of leaving.

And tonight, sitting under the sable sky with him, I was not sure that home was what I wanted.

The bang of the door at the front of the house drew our attention.

Reza poked his head around the corner. "If you two are finished with your private meeting, we're putting a plan together in here and need everyone involved."

I was already on my feet and knew it was my turn for blushing. Fortunately, the darkness would hide it.

"We are coming."

Inside, they were pairing up. David and Gaspar would leave first, on foot, walk slowly toward the center of Jerusalem, and hopefully draw out whoever might be on watch. They would head for the house of the high priest, with the scrolls secreted beneath Gaspar's tunic.

The rest of us would escape out the back of the house, two by two, then circle around to retrieve horses and lead them as silently as possible out of the city, through the Zion Gate to the road leading south.

The women were packing up food, though little was needed since Bethlehem was less than a two-hour journey. "But you never know what we'll find when we get there," Halima said. ""A crowd this large—they may not be able to house us all."

Lydia nodded. "The inn there is not large. We visited once—with Mariamme." She smiled. "Alexander was born there." She glanced at Simon, a mutual memory shared between them, and Simon wrapped an arm around her waist.

The love between those two often made me jealous. Tonight, my heart felt strangely warmed.

David kissed his wife, clapped Simon on the shoulder, and extended a hand toward the door, inviting Gaspar to join him.

It had begun.

The first of us, Reza and Adina, crept from the back of the house as soon as David and Gaspar were clear. Halima frowned her disapproval at the pair, but Adina was needed to show Reza the way, and it would make little sense to anyone watching if Halima abandoned her guests. Reza and Adina, however, could be seen to have another motive.

Though looking at Reza's face, I was not sure the false motive was entirely false. He glanced toward me as they left, and only a little pang at his divided loyalty, or at least divided attention, jabbed my heart. I released it, for I had no true hold on him. Reza was steady and he was safe, and I once believed these were all the qualities I needed, the antithesis of Zahir. But since leaving Nisa, since facing both times of danger and times of laughter with Misha, I was beginning to admit that I needed something else.

We waited, none of us speaking much, as the minutes crawled forward. Finally, when it seemed the night was half spent, Halima stood and nodded toward Lydia and Misha. They would slip out next.

David's plan had been that if the house were being watched, the three pairs leaving would draw them out. Adina and Lydia would each take winding paths as they led the way through the city, hoping to lose anyone who followed, before circling back for horses and then meeting the others at the Zion Gate.

The rest of us would take our chances as two groups, with Halima and Simon leading the way.

I walked surrounded by four of the elderly Chakkiym and felt protected and cared for. But dawn felt close at our heels by the time we reassembled at the gate. A glance revealed everyone present, including David and Gaspar. The other magi crowded up close to hear Gaspar's report of the scrolls, with Simon at their shoulders.

Gaspar's head bobbed in excitement. "We roused them from their beds, several of them, and at first they were displeased at the affront by foreigners. But we soon convinced them of our sincerity, and they agreed that although from Parthia, we were God fearing and should be heard.'"

"They knew of the scrolls!" David's face was lit with pleasure. "Lydia's old friend Samuel had left a legacy here as well. But they assumed them lost forever."

"They received them with much reverence," Gaspar finished. "As well as the news of the star and our journey. If indeed the Messiah has come and the end of days is upon us, they will be ready."

Simon's arm was again around Lydia, their foreheads pressed together, and I sensed the end of a mystery they had spent half their lives protecting. My heart ached, but I could not say why.

We were through the gate within minutes, a large group headed south in the early morning hours, probably perceived as traders by anyone who observed.

Misha and I again shared a horse, his breath warm in my ear. The road was deserted, the sun barely scraping the violently pink rim of the earth on our left. Birds chirped out warnings in the scrubby trees we passed—olive and fig that struggled to thrive in the mostly barren soil outside the city walls. Rocks of every size dotted the rolling hillside, crouched in the half-light like predators ready to strike.

Despite the fear of Herod's soldiers preventing our journey or worse, the night's wakefulness caught up with me and I drowsed, my chin bobbing against my chest.

But we had not ventured many minutes before Misha returned to the conversation we had left outside David's house. "What do you propose to do about Zahir, if you are so certain you cannot return home?"

I lifted my head and inhaled, gritty eyes blinking. "Kill him."

Misha's arms tensed around me.

My confession had been too sudden, too honest—borne of the stupor of half sleep. "You do not approve."

Misha sighed. "I suppose it is not my nature to kill a man without just cause."

I stiffened. "You say this to me? To me, whom he has—"

"You never tell me *what* he has done to you, Kamillah!" Misha's voice had risen in pitch and volume, and I felt him struggle to bring it down. "You are as closed as a locked chest at times. I don't know how to—"

"He deserves to die."

The arms around me grew warmer, and he dropped his head against my shoulder for the briefest moment. It was acknowledgment, and pity, and even respect, all in one gesture.

My eyes blurred and I blinked away the emotion with a sniff.

"Still, Kamillah"—his voice was soft—"I do not want it to be at your hand. It would be his final triumph over you, for I know it would harm your soul forever.'"

"Guilt is better than bondage."

"Guilt *is* bondage."

We said nothing more for many miles. By the time the sun was fully risen, the village of Bethlehem loomed in our view, and the party was unconsciously gaining speed, excitement over the conclusion of a long quest speeding even the horses' hooves and bubbling through the crowd in murmurs and quiet laughter.

But at the edge of the village, we slowed and regrouped, talking of plans. Besides this long-prophesied town, we knew nothing more than what the star had told us. We did not know when the new ruler had been born, nor to whom. How would we enter this poor village, horses laden and jingling with treasure, heads turbaned in a manner foreign to all who lived here, and simply ask to be directed to their Messiah?

In the end, it was decided that Lydia should take the lead in asking discreet questions. Being at least half-Jewish and a woman, she might seem less threatening. She and Simon proceeded forward while the rest of us waited outside the town, our animals pawing at the dust in as much frustration as we felt.

Misha and I waited beside our shared horse, watching his parents disappear into the haze.

"Why did we bother with stealth?" I pointed ahead. "There is no hiding in a town this small, especially for a foreign party of our size.'""

Misha nodded. "All the same, we have given ourselves an earlier start on this mission than Herod's lackeys might report. It might be helpful— we do not know what we will find here."

I studied the flat-topped roofs and scraggly palms. "Do you truly think there is power here? Enough?" I asked the question softly, but Misha understood.

"If we have indeed found Israel's Messiah, then, yes. But I do not believe that power is something to be grasped and wielded as a weapon. That is Zahir's philosophy.'""

The sun rose fully, its drowsy warmth falling on us like a blanket, and we wandered to boulders and the shade of roadside trees to find more comfortable places to rest and doze. My own eyes were drooping heavily, my back against a rock beside Misha, when the sound of an approaching horse dragged them open. I elbowed Misha in the ribs and scrambled to my feet.

Lydia and Simon slid from their horse wearily, but their eyes were bright.

"Not much, but we have heard of some shepherds who tell a strange tale of a night some months ago when they were visited by a host of beings in the sky."

We exchanged surprised glances all around. Our spirit companions had been here as well?

Simon nodded at our unspoken question. "These beings spoke to them, told them of a Savior born here in town."

"If we hurry, we can catch them coming back from the night watch on the southern outskirts of the village." Lydia's voice was tight with the excitement we all felt.

We mounted as one and urged our beasts forward. There was no reason, nor time, for secrecy now. We were a party of eighteen, headed straight through Bethlehem, in search of a Savior.

CHAPTER SEVEN

KAMILLAH

I do not know what I expected. In all the time we had traveled, for the days we had anticipated this single day, I had not formed an image in my mind of what it should look like to find a Jewish Messiah, perhaps a World-Savior, located on the plane of earth with the hands and feet and heart of man.

But surely, surely I had not expected this. Not this tiny community of poor shepherds and farmers, eking out an existence among the rocky, scrubby hills below a great city. Not this ordinary house, with an ordinary man at the door—one who eyed the visiting crowd with suspicion and curiosity.

One of the shepherds, Eliakim, had led us here. His quick pace defied his small stature, and the tempo of his speech was even faster as he regaled us with the tale of a hillside night broken open by the sight and sound of a thousand angels. But for all that glory, he took us to an unassuming home with a flat-topped roof and mud-brick steps that hugged the side of the house, with the light of a small central courtyard spilling around the hulk of the man in the door frame.

Joseph. His name was Joseph, and he was father to the Messiah. Or so said the shepherd.

But how could such a thing be?

He was well built and clearly strong, with the look of a man who worked with his hands. A trimmed beard lined a strong jaw, and the furrowed brow was of one who held protection of his family as serious duty.

Introductions of everyone were hastily made, but Joseph's eyes lingered on all that was foreign to him—the turbaned heads of the Chakkiym, the look of Greece and Persia in the features of Lydia and Simon, and lastly me, dressed as no respectable woman of Israel with my dark hair flowing down my back.

"Who told you to come all this way?"

Joseph's question was a valid one, and we traded glances to see who would answer.

Simon spoke, perhaps thinking that as a Jew he might have more influence. "We are scholars and assayers of the night sky. We have seen his natal star from our home in the east and have come to pay homage to him."

At this, Joseph's eyebrows shot upward, and it seemed Simon's explanation had caused more concern, not less.

"To what end? He is a common child, born of common parents. There is nothing he can do for you."

My stomach twisted. I needed this child to be more. So much more.

Not only power to break free of Zahir. Also truth, truth I had been seeking all my life.

And if I were honest, even a place to belong. Not in this house, not a physical belonging. Something else—a belonging to a bigger truth that one could take to any part of the earth.

But even as I breathed deeply against the tension Joseph's words had brought, I saw in his eyes that he was withholding something from us. The words he had spoken were not as factual as he would have us believe.

Simon tried again, this time explaining his role in the long line of guardians of the scrolls of the Jewish prophet Daniel, to be opened in the last days. Of the secrecy of those scrolls and the journey that led us here, of our encounters with the spirit beings who protected us from the powers of the air.

At the mention of our sentinels, Joseph's glance flicked to the shepherd Eliakim, whose head bobbed with happy verification.

"You cannot all come at once. You will frighten my wife."

After much jostling and murmurs, somehow it was Reza, Misha, and myself who were invited first into the house.

"You three have made this journey happen," Simon said. "It is right that you go."

We had brought gifts, all three of us, though they seemed out of place now and perhaps would even be an offense. But we hastened to remove them from the pouches slung over our horses, to clutch them in damp palms, to ready ourselves for whatever should come next.

And so I followed the three men, heart hammering and mouth dry, still unsure of what it all meant.

"We have guests." Joseph's voice echoed across the tiny courtyard that spilled over with an abundance of greenery and flowers. The space was warm and private and bathed in the coral glow of morning. Sitting in the center was a young mother who looked up from where her young child toddled around her feet.

She was younger than I, though in even my briefest glance I sensed perhaps she was wiser.

But it was the child I came to see, and the child I could not take my eyes from.

He had seen his first birthday, I guessed, but not long ago. He was chubby and petal cheeked, with ruby lips and a wild shock of dark hair that poked comically from the crown of his head like a young Gaspar. And he was laughing.

His laughter was like the sound of all children laughing—infectious and delightful and charming.

We stood, all three of us, without a word or a sound and simply looked at him.

And then he looked at us.

In that moment, all minutes and hours and all of time itself was lost to me. I fell into the gaze of this child and knew something so new it had no words.

What had I thought? What had I believed before this moment?

I went to my knees before the child, because he was a child. Because he was a king.

"I—I brought a gift—" My voice wavered and broke, and my extended hand trembled.

The boy reached for the tiny box, patted it twice, then smiled at me.

Warmth flooded all the places of my heart that Zahir's treachery had frozen.

The mother reached for my gift. "His name is Jesus."

I heard Misha's intake of breath behind me. The name had meaning to him, though I knew not what.

She opened the tiny box, and the sharp and spicy scent of the myrrh floated around the three of us there on the ground.

Her eyes went to mine. She knew the spice. Knew its use.

Why should two young women with a baby between them talk of death? Of burial?

Because he was a Savior, and the very essence meant sacrifice. This I knew, and as I looked into the young-old eyes of his mother, it was clear that this she also knew.

She snapped the lid closed with a pensive smile and a slow nod of understanding between us.

I lowered my gaze to avoid her thoughtful eyes.

But the child was not troubled by the promise of the myrrh. No, the child tottered over to me and this time patted my cheek with a giggle.

I could not help but smile, to touch his own soft cheek and forget all my questions—of power, of truth, of belonging.

Kneeling before Jesus, all my questions disappeared.

CHAPTER EIGHT

MISHA

*M*isha fumbled at his side, at the pouch where he had deposited the gift he had brought. Kamillah had given hers, so it was the appropriate time for giving, but he could not take his eyes from mother and child and was too distracted to retrieve the treasure he had brought.

From the moment they entered the courtyard, the mother had watched them. He could not describe the look upon her face as Kamillah knelt before her son. *Thoughtful joy*, perhaps. She had wide, full lips and a generous smile, but her eyes were sharp and intelligent and missed nothing.

She was perhaps the most *alive* person he had ever met, lit from within by something extraordinary, as if she had been privileged to know something more of life and man and history than even the wisest mage Misha had known.

What was it that made this place seem like hallowed ground?

The courtyard was a chaotic jumble of color—mossy-green pottery amidst a profusion of flowers in golden amber, dark-hued russet, and lively indigo. Glossy leaves, as darkly purple as the deepest violets that grew up around their heads.

Like a bit of Eden, re-created here in the center of fallen Bethlehem.

Yes, yes, this was what had pressed on him since they entered.

This place, this child. Somehow, HaShem walked among them here as He had in the Garden with the first man and first woman.

And then Misha was on his knees beside Kamillah.

Tears coursed down his cheeks, tears of gratefulness, of humility. Of confusion and of longing. Of knowing and of mystery.

HaShem walked among men once more.

How could such a thing be?

Misha's gift was in his hand at last, thrust forward for the mother, a small and inconsequential acknowledgment to a truth too large for his heart to hold.

He had chosen it for its value, hoping to please the Messiah with his generosity. It seemed laughable now, but he gave it just the same.

The woman opened the frankincense, smiled, and sniffed the aromatic crystals. They would burn clear and pungent and fill the house with the scent of temples.

Incense, long used as a fragrant offering for the gods, would never be put to truer use. For how many years had he sought the approval of older men? Seeking to feel worthy before his father, Zahir, Gaspar? All of that frustration, all of the anger and bitterness and confusion, it all fell away in the presence of a child.

Kneeling before Jesus, Misha felt himself valued beyond measure by a God who would stoop to love even a fool like him.

CHAPTER NINE

REZA

*J*oseph stood apart from his wife and child, apart from the three visitors, but not out of disinterest. Reza recognized that posture—a man who had been given a charge that overwhelmed him, who must remain watchful at all times.

He was a powerful man, with rough-worn hands that perhaps had shaped the many pieces of stone in the courtyard—benches, a half wall, a decorative column. But for all his power, he had a vulnerability, and that vulnerability sat and toddled in the center of his domain.

It was this very vulnerability that gave Reza pause. He had come to see for himself if the star they had followed would truly lead them to a ruler of the nations, a king to put an end to all other kingships, to render national disputes irrelevant and military coups absurd.

But it was just a small house in a small town, with a young family working and loving and living an unremarkable life.

How could he return to his father with news of this underprivileged child, and insist that he would one day rule the world?

A sense of frustration filled him, of a long journey that had come to nothing. How had he imagined that a Jewish baby would be the answer to a Persian problem?

Misha and Kamillah were both on their knees, as if they wished to join the child's play. Kamillah he could understand, as she was a woman and had a nurturing spirit even under all her intellect and strength. But he had never known Misha to be engaged by babies.

The two had given their gifts, and it was awkward for him to stand behind them without also giving his, so he stalked forward with his jingling pouch.

The sound of its contents, and the pouch itself, implied that it was filled with coins. The idea of handing over a sack of money seemed suddenly awkward. As if they were paying for the privilege of laying eyes on an ordinary child.

He unstrung the knot and dumped the contents into his large palm.

Perhaps it would seem less like a payment to the parents if he let the child play with it.

He leaned between Kamillah and Misha, both still on the ground, and extended his palm to the boy.

The child did not reach for his hand as Reza expected. Instead, he looked into Reza's eyes.

It was a look both innocent and knowing at once. A look that called for protection at the same time it promised to deliver.

And Reza was on his knees beside his friends.

Hand still extended, filled with costly pieces of gold, he felt like a pauper offering nothing more than cinders.

So many years, searching for his destiny, questioning his purpose. Growing up in the shadow of fighting men, trained to go to war, to defend and protect the innocent.

His glance went briefly to Joseph, and a flood of understanding nearly brought him to tears.

Yes, this was a treasure worth everything to protect. Worth a lifetime of training, if only needed for a single moment. He could give his life to this one ambition, this one intent.

His gift was fitting. This was a king. A King of kings.

Kneeling before Jesus, Reza found his destiny.

CHAPTER TEN

MISHA

*M*isha stood on the Antonia Fortress roof at dusk, watching the city's lights flicker into existence as if one by one he could see each woman light a lamp over her child, each husband stoke a fire for the evening's meal. A breeze lifted the hair at his neck and took the day's heat from him.

He leaned against the half wall, high above the massive Temple Mount that Herod had built around the sacred temple. It was the vantage point from which a younger version of his parents had watched this same city, wondering about the Messiah to come and trying to avoid Herod's madness and Salome"s hatred.

With thoughts of Herod and Salome came clearer vision, from his rooftop through the darkness to the new palace with its three spired towers, then farther south to the Herodium. The artificial mound grew before his eyes, with yet another fortressed palace rising in the center, where Herod would one day be buried.

Then to the Alexandrium Fortress, which sprung up before him in Samaria, and on north to the magnificent port of Caesarea. Past lavish cities built in the Greek fashion, his vision soared and swerved like a hawk in flight, seeing over all of Judea, all of the land into which Herod had poured his fortunes to build a legacy to his own name.

Like the hawk, Misha circled back to Jerusalem, city of God, and settled once again on his rooftop above the Temple.

The darkness was floating in from the east now, settling over the city like an inky liquid, smelling of heavy musk and tasting of the bitter dregs of wine. It pressed upon him, this darkness, until Misha felt he could not breathe.

And still it rolled, in waves over the city, an unnatural darkness that swallowed rather than hid, that devoured with a low thrumming sound that buzzed against his chest.

It brought evil, this darkness.

He could see each occurrence, as he had seen every flame of the city.

A child, taken by a demon and writhing on the ground, mud in her hair and in her eyes.

An old man, tearing his skin into bloody strips, already scabbed from years of the same.

All the while they watched. They Watched. Urging on a blackness that was as luminous and bright as it was dark.

Misha saw all the way to Bethlehem, his sight now more like a sure-shot arrow than a meandering bird. All the way to the road leading out of the village.

Ten old men, turbaned and stooped, snaked from the village in a long line, marching in step with each other, sightless and wordless.

They marched to Jerusalem, one plodding step at a time, each step taking them closer to doom. In through the Zion Gate, up the dusty and crowded road, through the courtyard of Herod's palace.

His extended sight followed them into the throne room, lit by the flames of a single brazier at the front. A single line of wise old men, approaching the throne.

Herod stood before them, nodding them forward. In his hand he held a jeweled sword, polished and glinting in the lamplight, its sharpened point held outward at chest level.

And one by one, the Chakkiym walked into that sword.

Misha tried to cry out, tried to lift a hand, tried to warn them. But there was no sound, no stay.

Each one walked forward until the sword plunged through his chest.

Then dropped away to make room for the next in line.

Though his own voice made no sound, the puncture of flesh and the sucking out of the sword echoed through the throne room. Misha tried to cover his ears, but his arms would not obey.

When every one of the ten Chakkiym lay dead at Herod's feet, the king smiled.

A voice materialized out of the darkness behind him.

"There is one more, brother."

The smile faded and Herod lifted his gaze to the double doors of the throne room.

A figure, thrown into relief by the brighter light without, stood outlined in the doorway, chin lifted high. He took measured steps toward Herod. Not sightless like the Chakkiym. No, this one was aware and he was unafraid.

Father.

With a shock like an icy plunge in the north Jordan River, Misha sucked in a breath and shot from his bed, still in Bethlehem.

A dream. It had only been a dream.

No. This was more.

This was a vision.

CHAPTER ELEVEN

REZA

*R*eza awoke to the sound of chaos in the room he shared with six of the Chakkiym on the outskirts of Bethlehem.

All of them, to a man, were panicked. They sat on mats, paced the room, panted on their knees, clutched their chests.

"What is it?" Reza jumped to his feet, scrambled for his borrowed sword, swung a circle around the room. Checked the door.

"What has happened?" He saw no danger.

It would appear that not even the men knew. They glanced among each other, wide-eyed and slack-jawed.

"You saw it, too? Yes? Yes! And you?"

Nods all around.

A moment later, Misha burst through the door. He scanned the room quickly, as if counting heads, then doubled over, hands on his knees.

"Our brothers?" The Chakkiym clamored at him.

He held up a hand, then straightened. "All are well. Awoke as apparently you did, from the same terror."

Reza growled. "Someone better tell me what is going on."

"A vision, Reza." Misha's face was drawn and pale. "All of us with the same dream. Of Herod executing the Chakkiym."

Was such a thing possible? It was the shared dream he doubted, not

Herod's ability to carry out the bloodshed. But the proof stood before him.

He shook his head. "We must leave this town. We are like targets here. Herod's soldiers need only ask around—"

"We will meet in the inn." Misha spoke to the whole room. "Gather your things as quickly as possible. We still have time before the sun is up, but not much, I would guess."" He nodded to Reza, the unspoken responsibility for these men shared between them. "Hurry."

Misha disappeared, and Reza sheathed his sword and turned to the Chakkiym.

They were not soldiers, but they could make admirably quick work of packing up for a sudden move.

Or perhaps the horror of their dream sped their hands and feet.

He felt a slight twinge at the realization that each of them, and even Misha, had experienced this vision. And he had not.

But he was not a scholar, was he? He was a soldier. So be it.

They gathered in the inn only minutes later, met by the rest of the Chakkiym, white faced and nervous, along with Misha and his parents, David's family, and Kamillah. The inn had not been large enough for all of them, after the ten old men had their chance to pour their treasures at the feet of the child and wonder at what he was to become, so Joseph found friends willing to lend an extra room. But now they were together again, and decisions must be made.

Reza took charge of the conversation before anyone else had a chance. "Obviously, we are not returning to Herod as he wished. We will head south." It was a military operation now, and in that he had the most experience. Except for perhaps Simon, but those days were past.

"We'll circle around the Salt Sea and into Petra again. It will be the best place to meet up with a caravan heading back to Nisa."

There were nods around the room from the Chakkiym.

And frowns from the others.

"Jerusalem is our home." David stepped forward, his wife and daughter behind him. "We are not leaving."

Lydia clutched his arm. "She cannot go back to the palace, David!"

"No." He nodded. "But there is other work to be found in the city." He smoothed Adina's hair. "Or perhaps we will finally get her a husband."

Reza huffed, ignoring that threat, for now. "Another job, or even a husband, will not protect her. Protect *you*. Herod knows you have helped us, knows you have betrayed him. You will be safe nowhere."

Simon elbowed his way to David's side. "Lydia and I are not leaving, either."

"What?" Misha circled on them, shoulders hunched. "Nisa is *your* home! We must return at once."

"Son, we discussed it in the night. Your mother and I have been away too long. And we realize that we have been waiting. Waiting for this day. Our place is here, with our people. For whatever is to come."

Reza started to speak, and Misha would have joined him, but Kamillah put her hand on Misha's arm. The quiet gesture silenced both men.

"Misha, I have unfinished business here as well."

She spoke of Zahir, surely. She had never intended to return to Nisa, but neither could she go home with the specter of Zahir still holding power over her.

Her words wrenched a hole in Reza's gut. Someone needed to lead the Chakkiym back to Nisa. It could only be him. But it meant leaving Kamillah behind. His eyes strayed to the family he had just met. He would be leaving Adina behind as well. The thought caused more pain than he would have expected.

And Misha? He knew before he even looked at his friend that Misha would not leave his parents, or Kamillah.

But he had to protect the men, and more importantly, he had to remove the threat to the child. Get them all out of here before they brought more attention, did more harm.

He cleared his throat, nodded once, and turned to the old men. "Gather your horses. We leave immediately." To the rest he said simply, "You must also leave Bethlehem. Before Herod uses you to find the child."

There was a moment of hushed silence as everyone took in the implications of the parting. And then action, movement, bustling all around him, but Reza stood planted in the front room of the inn, staring at his feet.

Kamillah was at his side first, as he knew she would be. She pulled him aside, to a quiet corner of the quickly emptying room.

"You are good and strong and loyal, Reza."

He met her eyes and found them already shining with tears.

"Always you have done your duty, even now when it hurts you."

"I am a soldier."

"You are a soldier, yes. But that is only one part of you. You must not forget the scholar inside."

He chewed his lip and looked away.

"Reza, I am so grateful for your friendship, for your protection over the years. I could not have asked for more in a brother."

There it was, then. At last, her true feelings.

He swallowed hard and took a last look into her eyes. "And I would die for you, as I would for my own sister."

Tears spilled to her cheeks but she smiled. In these few simple words, everything was said between them that needed to be said. He would love her always, but his desire for her as a wife had more to do with her ability to be a queen. Everything had changed now.

He glanced across the room to where Misha stood arguing with his parents.

"I must say good-bye to the one who has been a brother to *me*." He smiled. "Take care of him, Kamillah. He needs more than a sister."

She laughed quietly and dipped her head.

A quick embrace of Simon, who clapped him on the back a bit too roughly, betraying emotion.

A kiss to the hand of the sweet Lydia, who had returned to beautiful health and laid a soft hand on his cheek.

And then Misha.

Reza faced his lifelong friend and his heart felt like stone.

Misha shook his head. "Not forever. You can come back. We can send word—" His voice broke.

Reza grabbed him in a most unsoldier-like embrace and hugged him fiercely. "Yes, yes, not forever," he murmured against Misha's neck.

A kiss to each cheek, and he spun away before he disgraced himself further.

David and Halima were outside in the darkness of early morning with Adina and the men, standing among the horses. One of them had brought Reza's horse as well. Halima was transferring every bit of sustenance she had packed to the pouches of those departing.

Reza bowed to Halima, grasped David's arm, and nodded good-bye, then turned to Adina.

Awkward, there in front of her parents, knowing he would not see her again.

He bowed. "It was a pleasure to make your brief acquaintance. I will remember you as all that was lovely about this country."

She blushed, glanced at her parents, then stood on her toes to kiss him lightly on the jawline. "Good-bye, Persian."

The others emerged from the inn to say their quick farewells and whisper prayers over the mounted party.

And then they were off, leaving Bethlehem in the lingering darkness behind them, the stars winking out one by one.

CHAPTER TWELVE

KAMILLAH

I struggled to conceal my emotions as Reza left.

For so long I had refused to let either of these men into my heart. Despite my resistance, they had both succeeded in making me love them in some way, even if my feelings were clouded in confusion and refusal. Reza's departure seemed to clear some of the clouds, but it saddened me as well.

I turned to Misha, but he was even more emotional than I to see his friend disappear into the dusty morning, so I gave him his privacy and huddled in the early morning chill with Simon and Lydia and David's family.

"We may not be leaving Judea," Simon said, "but we need to leave Bethlehem. For the safety of the child."

Lydia nodded, her eyes teary. "We should warn them."

Misha joined them now. "Of what? Of a dream?"

Simon circled an arm around his son's shoulders in silent empathy over Reza. "Of a dream, yes. A vision. Something tells me they will believe it. And they should know that Herod is aware of the child, aware of the threat."

"Because of us." I couldn't help the observation. The guilt had been simmering under the surface since we left Herod's palace. "If we hadn't come, Herod would have known nothing."

Simon turned to me, put his hands on my shoulders. "That may be true, princess, but do not forget that it was HaShem's star that led us here, and HaShem's mighty unseen armies that protected our journey. This was ordained, this discovery of the child. The Holy One has reasons we cannot understand but must always trust."

I swallowed the ever-present emotion and turned away. I hoped he was right.

Simon clapped his hands together once. "Gather your things quickly. We will go to Joseph's home to give them the news, and then we will be off."

"To where?" Misha was shaking his head. "Where have we to go besides here?"

"We will worry about that once we have removed ourselves, and the threat, from this town."

We dispersed to the rooms we had been given in the inn, then reunited minutes later in the front room and walked as one across the village. The rising sun pinked the sky with colors too soft to believe that danger could be a stone's throw from this precious family. But I had seen much violence amidst beauty in my life and knew better than to trust the sky.

Joseph received us with a somber expression and silent nod.

"You should send word to those shepherds as well." Misha's voice was tight with anxiety. "They were happy to lead us here with very little convincing. They might do the same for others."

Again, the nod. Joseph was not a man of many words.

I stepped between Misha and his father. "May we see the child once more before we leave?" It was a bold request, considering we had just explained the danger we had brought.

But he held the door wider, revealing Mary standing just behind it with Jesus in her arms. She had heard our conversation. Her face was pinched with fear.

I reached a tentative hand toward them both, but she did not pull away. I stroked the child's hair, disbelieving the revelations of yesterday for only a moment more. Something in the very touch of this boy was different.

What would it be like to watch him grow to manhood?

I snatched my hand away before the thought could become a desire. I did not belong in Bethlehem.

"Kamillah." Misha's voice was soft and his hand on my arm was gentle. "We must go."

We said our good-byes and returned to the inn, paid the innkeeper, gathered our horses, and turned our heads toward the southern road, which seemed the safest direction to walk away from the town, at least until we made a plan for whatever would come next.

Halfway through Bethlehem, our plans were abruptly cut short by the sudden appearance of a small cohort of soldiers.

That they had come for us, or for the child, was immediately obvious. If nothing else, from the leveled points of their swords and the way they fanned out to block our outlet from the town.

Simon took the lead. "We are foreigners, passing through to return to our home. Is there some problem?"

The centurion laughed. "You are more memorable than you assume. The Antonia Fortress has not yet stopped buzzing over your escape yesterday."

"What do you want from us?"

"Where is the new king you came to seek?"

Simon spread his arms to the town, swept his gaze around it. "Do you see a throne room? Servants and guards? Does this look like a place where a king would reside?"

The centurion's eyes narrowed. "Do you refuse to tell me?"

"I have nothing to say."

The soldier scanned the rest of us, as if to see if any would step forward in betrayal.

The sense of belonging I had felt with Jesus yesterday still clung to me, enveloped me. I would not give him up even if that sword point pierced my chest.

At our silence, he flicked his head at his cohort, who quickly circled our party, weapons pointed inward.

"Go." He spoke only the one word, but his meaning was clear. We were returning to Jerusalem. To Herod.

Our march toward the city was a copy of our first entrance two days ago, but with more hostility on the part of our escorts. They urged us faster, muttered ethnic insults about our slowness, and more than once a soldier leeringly volunteered to give Misha's horse a rest from the weariness of carrying me by transferring me to his own.

The trip was long but the tension held and none of us spoke. What would Herod do with us when we reached the city? Misha had whispered a bit of the vision they had all shared in the night, and it was enough to make me shudder with revulsion and not a little fear. I asked him if he saw me in the dream, but he would not answer.

Inside the city limits, there was to be no pause to water our horses, and no intermediate stop at the prison cells beneath the Antonia Fortress. We were herded directly to the courtyard of Herod's palace, ordered from our mounts, and prodded through the massive front arch of the southern building complex to the receiving area outside the throne room.

My first glimpse of the inside of the palace astonished me. While his people lived in relative poverty, Herod had constructed a home to rival the great palaces of Egypt, Greece, and Rome. Everywhere were statues in the Greek style, vessels of silver and gold, porticos and pillars and an abundance of greenery. It was finer even than Phraates's palace in Nisa.

I should have been paying more attention to the inhabitants of the room than the décor.

Herod sat on his platformed throne at the head of the room, flanked on one side by a woman who could only be his sister, Salome, and on the other by Zahir.

I wrapped arms around my middle at the stab of violent nausea. Why did it not surprise me that Zahir had gone from prisoner to adviser in only a day?

Zahir's cold eyes bore down on me even from this distance, his gaze fixed on me alone as if Misha and the others were nothing more than mist.

I felt myself drawn forward by the invisible cord that always ran between us. Until I stood at his feet, head bowed before him, heart thudding with panic even as my blood ran with fury.

Herod's voice raised my head.

"Where are the rest of you?" It was a plaintive question, like one posed by a boy who had not gotten his wish. "I told you to bring all of them."" He spoke over our heads to the centurion behind us.

"My lord, we inquired in the town, but these are all that are left. The others have apparently returned to their homeland."

"I told them to come back to me! And you two"—Herod's gaze darted to Lydia and Simon—"you weren't coming back either, were you?"

The older couple said nothing.

Beside Herod, Salome barked out a laugh. "They wouldn't have dared."

Something flared in Lydia's eyes, a bit of anger mixed with rebellion.

I silently cheered her, but to speak her defiance would certainly mean her death.

Simon must have felt it, too, for he stepped slightly in front of his wife. "We were not aware that the king had requested our return." The tone was respectful, though considering the way the three of them had left the palace, chased by guards, the statement was ridiculous.

Zahir leaned toward Herod. "This is the one I was telling you about —the one causing the problems in Nisa, stirring up talk of this Messiah, a new king to overthrow you."

Beside me, Misha tensed and nearly started forward.

I touched his arm in restraint.

Herod raised his eyebrows. "Is he? Our own Simon, who was such a competent soldier and palace manager until he ran off with my wife's maid?"

He was baiting us. Lydia was much more than a maid in this palace, and he knew it.

But we all kept silent. The unholy threesome before us, a combination of power-lust, madness, and evil, kept us cautious.

"So what is to be done with all these spies, half of them foreign, who display more loyalty to an unknown baby than the king of the Jews rightfully installed by Caesar Augustus himself?"

Zahir bent to Herod's ear and whispered something.

The king threw back his head and laughed.

I felt a roiling in my stomach.

"No." Salome had slipped into a throne beside Herod's, a throne presumably for his absent queen. She bore down on us with a malevolence more powerful than even Zahir"s. "No, give them to me."

Herod glanced at his sister. "Still nursing the old grudge, eh? How many years since the little maid got the best of you?"

"Twenty-five." The answer came quick and angry, as though she had been counting the months and the days as well.

Herod flicked a hand toward his sister. "Very well. You take them. Do what you wish." He waved the centurion closer. "But this Bethlehem threat must be dealt with. Take your men back to the village."

The man's shoulders visibly dropped at the prospect of another journey southward.

"Find this so-called Messiah baby and kill him."

The seven of us audibly gasped as one.

The centurion nodded. "And if we are not able to find this one baby, my lord?"

Herod scowled.

Zahir bent to his ear once more.

He smiled at his new adviser and shrugged at the soldier. "Then kill them all. All of the squalling brats under two years of age. That ought to give us assurance."

Another nod, and the soldier was gone, dismissed to his horrific duty.

Lydia stepped forward. "Herod, this is an evil—"

"Silence!" The king's tolerance had come to an end. "I am sick of this whole affair and want to return to my bed!" He stood, the effort seemingly painful. "Zahir, you will attend me in the afternoon when I return. I have more to ask of you regarding Parthia and her military plans."

Zahir's satisfied smile drifted over to me.

I silently thanked Misha's God that Reza was gone. At Zahir's request, Herod would have surely tortured him for any secrets he might hold.

Herod left the throne room through a nearby door, almost invisible against the painted borders of the wall.

We were left alone with Zahir and Salome, and I did not know which direction to look first for danger.

But Salome held sway in this room, regardless of how far Zahir had climbed in a day.

She did not take her eyes from Lydia. "Leave us, Zahir."

"My lady—"

Still, those icy dark eyes were fixed on Lydia. "My brother may find you useful, mage. I find you distasteful. Leave us."

Zahir growled in his throat, stepped off the platform, and headed toward the double doors at the back of the room. He slowed as he neared me, leaned his shoulder against mine, and brought his lips to my ear. "I will see you outside, in the grove of trees in the central courtyard. You will come to me when you are finished here."

I twisted my head away from his mouth, my vision blurring with hatred.

And then he was gone, and it was Salome who commanded our attention and our fear.

She had stepped from the platform as well and circled the little group like a wolf around a huddled pack of sheep.

"So." She smiled with satisfaction. "It has taken all these years. But I have had time to practice. Time to grow. What have you done in those years, little maid, except to grow old?"

Lydia raised her chin. "I have had time to learn humility, to learn that I am but a servant."

Salome laughed, still circling. "At last."

"But not your servant, Salome. Nor Herod's. I am a servant of the Most High God."

At the reference, the royal sister's face darkened, her lips a tight slash across her pale face. "Parthia did not take the Jew-blood out of you, I see."

"On the contrary."

Something in the way Lydia spoke the simple words, undergirded with iron, seemed to disquiet Salome. Her measured steps briefly faltered.

She returned to the base of the throne platform and stood before us, like a queen herself, and raised her head to the heavens, eyes closed. "For twenty-five years I have yearned for this moment."

The room grew suddenly cold. A chill breeze blew from somewhere, and the flames of the single brazier sputtered and died.

Misha grabbed my hand, his fingers as icy as my own.

David circled arms around his wife and daughter.

But Lydia had stepped forward, squaring off against Salome. "And for twenty-five years, I have given you no thought at all."

Salome's head snapped forward and a hiss escaped her lips. She raised both arms, palms flat, eyes boring into Lydia.

The cool breeze whipped into a freezing wind, a torrent around our heads, snatching at tunics and whipping my hair against my face. I gripped Misha's hand as if he alone could keep me from this darkness I well knew. It was the sucking void that Zahir could summon, though somehow even stronger.

Misha was pulling me, was leaning into the blast and moving, one labored step at a time, toward his parents.

I risked a glance at Lydia. Simon had joined her, grasped her hand as Misha held mine.

Misha grabbed Lydia's other hand, and we were suddenly four together.

I felt a tug on my free hand. Adina, clutching at me, with her parents joined on her other side.

And now we were seven.

And in that place between Misha and Adina, I felt a surge of power run through me. I reached for it with my mind, with my spirit, but it was not within me. It was only flowing through me, like water through a channel, from Adina to Misha. Perhaps from David all the way to Simon.

My legs threatened to fail me.

Misha's firm grip kept me upright.

The Power. The power I had been seeking all my life. This was it. *This was it.*

I had known it must exist. Seen glimmers of it at times in the eyes of Simon and Lydia. Had searched for it, knowing only this power could defeat Zahir.

And now, here it was flowing through me and I could do nothing to harness it, nothing to store it up in a reservoir for use against my enemy.

But it was more than raw power, was it not? The feeling was somehow wrapped up in all that profound sense of belonging I had felt when I knelt before Jesus. It was all the same. The love and the power.

At this revelation I sucked in a deep breath, filled my chest with a purity of air that existed somehow outside of Salome's presence, and drew my shoulders back. Courage and passion and a fierce hatred of all that was evil filled me up, and I could almost feel it radiating from my eyes like a beam of light focused into all of Salome's darkness.

And Salome staggered backward.

Her eyes were not on me. Still she obsessed only over Lydia.

But Lydia stood as tall and fierce as I, and down the line every one of us held the same stance.

We advanced on her, slowing closing our line of defense into a half circle around her.

Salome went to one knee, threw an arm over her face, and screamed.

Lydia sighed. "A thousand years in His eyes is like a day that is finished. Like a watch of the night. Did you truly believe that even twenty-five years would find the Most High powerless against *you?*"

"You!" Salome still covered her mouth with her forearm, peering up at Lydia. "*You* should be powerless against me.'"

Lydia shook her head. "Still you do not understand. I was always powerless. I still am. But I am never alone."

The woman's glance shot to the rest of us.

"Not them, Salome. Do you not see? I belong to the Most High God, and His power flows through me, to defeat any enemy that comes against Him."

The words burrowed into my soul, even as they found a home in Salome's. But while she covered her ears at the words and screamed curses upon Lydia's head, I opened my heart at last and felt the blessing of the One God fall on mine.

Not for the power. The power would never belong to me. I would never be more than a channel. But what a glorious calling that was!

We left Salome there, still cursing and weeping on her knees.

Lydia led the way.

CHAPTER THIRTEEN

KAMILLAH

The huge wooden double doors of the throne room swung closed behind us, but not before a figure waiting outside the chamber whirled and looked past our exit to where Salome still huddled on the mosaic throne-room floor.

The look of confusion on Zahir's face was one I would have paid a thousand drachma to see three months ago. Today, his discomfiture barely touched my conscious mind. Already he was becoming nothing more than a man in my eyes.

The group of us glanced at each other, no doubt each wondering if we could simply walk out of the palace. I felt a palpable anxiety to get back to Bethlehem before Herod's soldiers.

Misha was at my back, staring down Zahir over my shoulder. His days of obeisance to his mentor were over.

I nodded to Simon and Lydia, and to the rest of them. "Go. I will deal with this. With him."

They seemed unsure, so I nodded again. "You have an urgent message to carry. You must go."

Misha had not moved. He spoke quickly to his parents. "I am staying with her."

It was the permission they all needed, and they turned as one for the palace entrance.

Adina hurried ahead of David and Halima as though she would be happy to never step within its walls again.

Lydia slowed and took one backward glance toward the throne room. In her eyes I saw a past laid to rest, a settled confidence that her days of faithfulness were not over, and that her God still worked His power through her.

And then they were gone, leaving me to face Zahir with that same power available to work in me.

Misha tried to step in front of me, but I held him back with a touch. "There is nothing here that can hurt me now. And I must do this alone."

Misha smiled slightly, the proud smile of a teacher for a student.

I did not miss the irony.

I faced Zahir, with Misha fading into the background somewhere behind me.

"You cannot stop us, Zahir. Surely you can see that." I inclined my head toward the throne-room doors. "Salome herself watched us walk away.""

He shrugged. "I care nothing for the rest of them. Including him." He speared a glare toward Misha. "He was never good for much besides sneaking around."" He circled me, close enough to touch. "It's you I want."

I stared ahead, ignoring the warmth of his breath on my cheek. "You speak in riddles. You did not make this journey to secure me. You already had me in Nisa."

Still he circled, never taking his eyes from my face. He held his precious rod in his hand once more and scraped it along the stone tiles as he walked.

I tried again. "I do not understand your schemes. You came to align yourself with a new world ruler, if such a person existed. If not, you told me you planned to return to Phraates with the Nehushtan and make yourself even more valuable to him than you previously had managed. Instead, you've lost the Nehushtan, aligned yourself with Herod who is no friend to Phraates, and want to see the child murdered." I looked at him at last. "If you are not careful, you will have no friends nor power remaining when this is over.""

His circling pattern shifted slightly.

Why—? He was weaving a spell around me! How had I not seen it immediately? It was an entrapment spell, meant to root me to the floor until he finished with whatever malicious intent.

A flicker of concern flamed in my chest but was soon extinguished. In its place, a rush of joy and insight.

Zahir chuckled and stepped back toward me along the invisible web he wove. "Do you not see, brightest pupil? The murder of the child—it is a test. Only a test. If he truly is to be the World-Savior, how can he be killed? This is how I will know. And Herod, Herod is nothing to me. A tool in my hands. The man is insane."

So. Zahir still craved the power he believed the child would give him. He would not stop hunting Jesus, even if my friends reached Bethlehem in time with their warning.

But I would worry about that later. Right now, I had only to deal with Zahir and his decade-long design on me that now culminated in his measured steps across the floor of Herod's palace.

"And me, Zahir? How do I fit into this test of yours? Why am I so important?"

He scraped his divining rod once, twice across the floor at my feet in a sort of X, then smiled down on me. "Because you and I together can accomplish so much more."

"You have plenty of willing protégés in Nisa who would gladly join your schemes." I resisted the urge to glance back at Misha. "I ask again ——why me?"

He stepped close and used a bony finger to slide my hair behind my shoulder. "You have more power in you than any of them. You simply do not know it."

At his touch, a shiver swept over me. Part repulsion and part fearful attraction to this power he'd held out to me for years like a ripened fruit.

"I am leaving you, Zahir." The words surged up from an unknown place within me. "I will not be your hostage any longer.""

His soft breath of amusement angered me.

"We have been here before, Kamillah. More than once."

I could almost see the pattern he had woven in stone around me. In the eye of my mind it was as visible as any mosaic or fresco.

Without doubt, without hesitation, I took a step, then another, and another, until I was well outside his design. I spun to face him.

Zahir's eyes were murderously black. He scanned the floor, as if he too could see the outlines plainly and searched for some inadvertent gap that had allowed my breach.

He struck his rod against the stone floor again, then swung it toward me.

In this strange dance, I was facing Misha now, who still watched from the background.

He started forward to intervene.

I shook my head.

Zahir's rod pointed toward me like a Roman pike, but he did not thrust it toward me. Instead, he whispered a few dark words and dropped it to the ground.

I flinched, expecting the impact, but the sound was soft. The blackened rod curved and flexed, then moved of its own accord across the floor.

A glossy black cobra. Thick as my forearm, with yellow eyes and a hissing tongue. It undulated along the floor toward my feet, seeking the bare skin of my ankles.

A long-ago story from my own history flickered to life behind my eyes. Had I heard it from Misha? From Simon? Or perhaps as a child. The story of a Jew in the courts of my homeland, demanding freedom for his people, unafraid of the diviners and their rods turned to snakes.

With a whisper of my own, a prayer to Misha's God, I bent to the snake and grabbed it just below the head.

I kept my eyes on Zahir, but under my grasp the smooth scales of the snake firmed and hardened and its body became polished wood once more.

Zahir was shaken. But not defeated.

"You see, Kamillah?" He swept across the antechamber to me and wrapped his hand around his rod, just below mine. "Do you see the power you have?"" His free hand swept the space where his spell had not held me, and he shook the rod under our mutual grasp. "I have always known you had this great potential for power. Your blood flows with Egypt's secrets and your mind is filled with those of the Kasdim. Together we can rule a new Parthia, and with this child, perhaps even the world."

I closed my eyes and exhaled. "For all your gathered wisdom, you understand nothing, Zahir. I have nothing within myself. No power." I opened my eyes and stared into his. "All these years I have wanted nothing more than to be away from you. And yet, I could not break free. Not until I finally accepted that the power would *not* come from within me, and could only come *through* me as a channel of the One True God."

Zahir staggered backward as if struck. Just as Salome had done.

"The Hebrews' God? You have given up everything for a tyrant who will allow no other—"

"There is no other."

"Kamillah, listen to reason." His voice was pleading now. "You are a very powerful mage—"

"I have no power, I tell you."

He waved a hand. "Call it what you will. You are a channel, or you are powerful yourself, it makes no difference."

I laughed. "It makes all the difference. The only difference."

"Then we are all channels!"

I nodded, thinking. "Yes, perhaps you are right. But if so, then I know the power that flows through you is dark and evil and sets itself up against the Most High." I stepped away and held out a hand to Misha.

He was by my side in a moment, grasping my warm fingers with his cold hand. Had he feared for me?

He needn't have. For at the very last, when I walked away from Zahir, it was not with a fantastic show of long-accumulated power. Not with spells or incantations, nor illusions and ancient secrets. No legendary artifacts.

I simply walked away. Because I could. Because the Power that could turn snakes into wood, could heal mothers across space and time, and could whisper from a star and command a host of unseen angels around our heads could also simply take my feet across the marble of Herod's palace and leave the great mage Zahir growling in impotent rage at my departure.

CHAPTER FOURTEEN

ZAHIR

*Z*ahir watched her go. Watched her slip from his grasp, and knew it was final, that she would not return. The day he had long feared had arrived. He could not hold her any longer.

And why?

His unseen path across the marble floor—he could trace its outlines in his mind, knew it was a strong and certain spell he had used before. But this time, no power had flowed along its lines, no answer to his calling down of authority.

The doors of the throne room burst open.

Salome strode through the doors, the black lines of kohl around her eyes now smeared and running in tracks along the paleness of her skin. But it was not grief in her countenance now.

It was rage.

Zahir took a step backward, suddenly fearful that the spell he had woven into the marble would hold him instead.

She swept across the lines without slowing. "You!" A bony finger jabbed at his face. "This is your doing, foreign mage.""

He raised a hand, willing it not to tremble, and gripped his rod with the slick palm of the other. "I assure you, I have done nothing." Yes, nothing indeed.

"Do not lie to me!" Her voice shook and spittle flew from her lips. "You used your dark powers against me, to block my own abilities!""

Zahir exhaled and searched the corridor for an ally. But where would he find an ally here?

Salome advanced on him, still pointing. "Do not think I am stupid to your tricks, mage. You would see me destroyed, see yourself standing at my brother's side, adviser to the king, eh?"

At this ridiculous accusation, he straightened and found his voice. "I am chief council to the king of the entire Parthian Empire, woman. What would I want with your puny Roman puppet of a brother?"

Rather than intimidate, his insult seemed only to inflame. She inhaled a mighty breath, closed the distance between them, and snatched his diviner's rod from his hand.

He had only a moment to realize her intent before the jeweled head of the rod crashed against his skull.

He went down. His cheekbone smacked the floor somewhere near the center of his entrapment spell. The jolt sent sparks along his limbs and knocked out three teeth.

He half-rolled to his back and raised a hand above his head to block the next blow. It cracked his forearm.

The pain roared, but behind it, whispering, were only questions.

Where were his Watchers? Why did they not strike her down?

But even as he heard the questions, he also heard the answers. They were here. The Watchers. But they bore no loyalty to anyone but themselves.

And for today, they poured their power through another channel.

Salome, sister of Herod the Great, wielded Zahir's rod like a hammer brought down on a stone that was no longer useful, a brick to be smashed into rubble and then swept aside.

Two more blows and it was done.

CHAPTER FIFTEEN

MISHA

*M*isha could barely keep pace with Kamillah as she flew from Herod's palace, through the courtyard, and into the city street. Her dark hair streamed out behind her, the wind catching it and brushing it across his face.

"Kamillah, you were remarkable in there—"

She gave one quick shake of her head, thrust a hand in the air to stop his praise, but did not slow. "Not me, Misha. It was not me."

He smiled. He need not ask her to explain. It was all becoming clear now, to both of them.

And rushing from the palace of Herod with her, on a mission that meant everything to both of them, he had the sense of stepping back in time, stepping back into the life of his parents. They fled this same city, this same king and his sister, twenty-five years ago.

And spent the last twenty-five years loving each other well.

Would that he be so blessed.

But now was not the time to think of a future any farther off than the immediate need for horses and for speed.

The horses were quickly located and they were soon pounding along the southbound road to Bethlehem.

"Do you think the others will still be there?" Kamillah's question was nearly a shout to be heard above the hoofbeats.

Misha shrugged and shook his head. "We are not far behind them."

"And the soldiers?"

She knew that he had no answer, so he did not bother. Her question was his question. The only question. Misha's tunic clung in damp fear and his throat felt like the desert they had crossed.

A gradual awareness came over Misha of a third set of hoofbeats behind them. He glanced quickly over his shoulder and confirmed. Someone was chasing them.

"Kamillah!"

She jerked her head at his shout.

He inclined his head backward.

She looked back at the single rider and her lips parted in surprise.

Misha dug heels into his mount. Their pursuer was a single rider only. Not a cohort. They still had a chance—

But Kamillah was slowing. Circling her horse.

"What—?"

"Misha! It is Reza!"

Reza.

Misha reined in his horse and brought him around.

Reza flew toward them, one hand raised in salute. He was at their side in moments. He pulled up, breathing heavy, but then pushed his horse forward again. "Come. I will explain as we ride."

He explained as best he could, above the pounding horses and at a pace they could not keep up for the entire six miles. And then he explained more fully when they slowed to give the horses a breath.

Reza had found someone to escort the Chakkiym back to Nisa. Someone he had happened upon at the gates of the city, whom he cited as being placed there by the Most High God to enable him to return to Bethlehem with the news he also heard at the city gate. That Herod was sending soldiers to kill Jesus.

"Misha, your God provided another so I could bring this news—"

"But we already knew. My parents and David's family have already returned to warn them."

Reza's face fell. "Then I am of no use. I do not understand."

Misha wished he could reach across the space between their horses to encircle his best friend's shoulder. "Not everything is plain at once. We must trust."

"There is other news as well." Reza's glance went to Kamillah. "Zahir is dead."

Kamillah's eyes fluttered briefly, then she nodded and set her face toward Bethlehem.

They reached the village within an hour of Reza's joining them and found the others hastily making preparations.

Joseph had conscripted help from two village boys, who were packing a wagon with goods from their home. His steady, silent watchfulness over the whole process lent an air of calmness, though Mary's pale face and wide eyes in the doorway where she clutched the child to her chest were enough to break Misha's heart.

He touched a gentle hand to the child's back and studied Mary's face. "We will get you away from here safely."

She nodded and smiled, the courage coming back into her eyes.

He scanned the area in front of the house. "Where are the others?"

She inclined her head toward the center of the village. "They have gone to buy supplies. They should return—oh, but here they are now."

The group rejoined them with hasty embraces and explanations of Reza's return.

Adina stood apart, but Misha did not miss how she watched Reza with shining eyes, or how Reza's glance kept returning to her even as he spoke to the others.

The wagon was packed, the supplies were purchased. Nothing was left but to leave.

Except no one knew where the family should go.

They crowded into Joseph and Mary's tiny courtyard, several voices speaking at once, offering suggestions.

"We could return to Galilee." Joseph's voice was low and commanding.

Simon shook his head. "You did not see the murderous intent in that man's eyes. It would take his spies no time to learn of your family and trace you back to your home."

"Egypt."

All eyes turned to Kamillah.

"It is *my* home. But it could become yours." She smiled at Mary. "Alexandria is a good place to raise a child. Education, culture, and the sea."

Joseph snorted. "Pagan—"

But she turned on him, chin lifted. "Alexandria has more Jews than Judea. Beautiful synagogues and righteous men to teach him."

He dipped his head in surrender but sighed. "How can I possibly take a single wagon, with a woman and child, all the way to Egypt?"

Misha stepped to Kamillah's side. "You will not be alone. We will take you."

Joseph gave a tight smile of gratitude, but they both knew that even four adults on such a long journey was taking a risk.

His father put an arm around Misha's shoulder. "Lydia and I want to make our home in Jerusalem. But my wife has been longing for a visit to her birthplace for many years. We will travel with you."

Mary covered her lips with her fingers, but a small cry escaped. "Thank you."

Reza turned to David. "Sir." He swallowed hard. "There is a matter I wish to discuss privately with you."

David eyed the rest of the group, a half smile on his lips. "Yes. Yes, somehow I am not surprised." He extended a hand toward the front of the house.

Reza proceeded him.

Misha glanced at Kamillah. How would she react to the conversation they all knew was about to take place?

But Kamillah's eyes were crinkled with a smile of true happiness. She watched Reza and David disappear, then turned to Joseph to discuss the route they should take in their flight to Egypt.

Father drew Misha aside. "Son, are you certain about this choice? This is surely not the way to reach the next level of your training, and Zahir will—"

"Zahir is dead."

"Ah."

Misha gripped his father's arm. "But you must know by now that all of that means nothing to me."

His father's face was unreadable.

Misha studied the courtyard floor. "You were right, Father. You were always right. About the One God, about Zahir. The scrolls. The star. The Messiah." He met his father's amused gaze. "As usual, right about everything."

He enfolded Misha in an embrace.

"I know that I am not one of you, Father. Not Chakkiym—"

His father pulled away, hands still on Misha's shoulders, brow furrowed in an unspoken question.

"The dream. I was not in that terrible line of men."

"But you were there, were you not? Watching from the side, perhaps, but still there. Still needing to make your choice."

Misha looked to the little family, heads still bent in conversation with Kamillah, who was laughing and touching the baby Jesus's cheek. He nodded. "Then I have made my choice. The choice to follow in my father's footsteps."

Father smiled. "Ah, and I pray someday, Misha-el, you will hear your own son say the same words. Especially the part about his father always being right."

Misha laughed. "That day is a long way off, I am certain."

His father's eyebrows rose and he tilted his head toward Kamillah. "I am not as certain as you."

He exhaled. "Father—"

"Do not play innocent with me, son. I have watched you respect your friend Reza. But she does not belong to him."

Kamillah chose that strange moment to lift her eyes to his, and the look she offered in that moment weakened his limbs.

Yes, Reza was talking to David even now about Adina.

But perhaps it was time for him to talk to Kamillah.

At that happy thought, Reza and David burst back into the courtyard, a single word on both their lips.

"Soldiers."

CHAPTER SIXTEEN

HEROD

*H*e could hear them screaming.

But this was impossible. Not all the way from Bethlehem.

He rose from his bed, where he had escaped after the encounter with that awful couple, Lydia and Simon, who had haunted his dreams for more than two decades.

Barefoot and in only a short tunic, he padded out of his bedchamber, past the guard always standing at his door.

"My lord?" The guard's glance traveled from Herod's head to his feet. ""Do you have need of something?"

Herod laughed. And laughed again. And again.

"Need. Yes. I have need of peace. Can you find that for me?" He patted the boy's cheek. Was he eunuch? Difficult to tell at this age. ""Can you find me a piece of peace?" He laughed again at his own joke, then continued down the wide corridor.

He would go to the dining chamber. Yes, that was a good idea. He would get the musicians to play some music, to drown out all that awful screaming.

There was Salome. What was she doing on the floor, at this hour?

She knelt beside a body. Who was that? Yes, that foreigner—what was his name? Zahed?

Herod stopped beside her.

She looked at his bare feet, then up to his face.

But it was not Salome behind those eyes he knew so well. Someone else was there. Someone he did not know. Ah, well. He moved on, toward the dining chamber. For the screaming was growing very loud now.

It wasn't just the babies. Though babies could scream, he knew. But there were others. Somehow he could hear Aristobulus drowning. Aristobulus, his late wife's younger brother, High Priest and possible usurper. The gurgling sounds of his drowning could still be heard some thirty years later.

And his beautiful Mariamme. The snapping sound of her neck in the gallows. He could hear that, too.

And the boys. The two sons Mariamme had borne him, strangled in their beds with that odd burble in their throats. Such a strange sound.

He would be joining them soon. This he knew. It would not be long before the decay would be complete. His flesh and his mind would join each other, somewhere far beyond saving. Even now they both were being eaten, eaten, eaten away.

Yes, too much noise. A little music was just what he needed.

CHAPTER SEVENTEEN

KAMILLAH

*N*ever in all my years of subjection to Zahir and the spirits he seemed to command had I felt such fear as I did that night.

We hid, all ten of us, plus the child, in a back room of the village's inn, kept safe by the innkeeper who was friend of Joseph's. The wagon and our horses waited behind the inn, for the signal from these kind friends that it was safe to flee.

Misha gripped my hand in the darkness, and I knew he felt the fear as well.

And yet under it, there was somehow peace. We had come this far, traveled through cities and deserts, fought battles underground and in the heavenlies. How could the One God not continue to protect us all, and most importantly, the Messiah that He had sent into this broken world?

And when the innkeeper came, face white and hand waving us out of the cramped storage room and through to the back of the inn, Misha did not let go of my hand.

The soldiers were still in the village, moving from house to house, looking for Jesus.

We had whispered to Joseph, Mary, and Reza of the horror Herod had ordered if they could not find the babe. I wished we had not told them. To see Mary's face at this news of her neighbors and friends was a fearsome thing.

And now, running for the wagon, I could see her face turned to the village, to those she left behind who would soon feel a grief we all prayed she would be spared. It was an unfairness that struck at the heart and could not be looked upon fully or we would all falter in what we knew to be our calling.

We must take Jesus to Egypt. And it must be tonight.

Blood pounding and throat constricted, I ran alongside the others in a half crouch. Misha finally released my hand, and I climbed aboard the wagon with the other women. Misha, David, Simon, and Reza mounted horses, and Joseph took the reins of the wagon's pair.

It had happened in the flash of an eye. One moment we were in the storage room, the next we were bumping along under the stars, racing south out of Bethlehem toward the unknown future.

I held Mary's hand now, small and cold and trembling in my own. The boy slept on her shoulder, mercifully, and did not raise a cry at the rough handling or the jostling wagon.

I squeezed her hand to draw her attention from the village as it receded.

She bit her lip and looked away. "They are giving their lives for my son." The words were barely audible, floating out behind us toward Bethlehem. Tears welled and spilled down her cheeks.

I ran a hand over the babe's head, and words came to my lips that felt like prophecy. "Yes. But he will not forget. And one day, he will do the same for them."

She closed her eyes at my words, hardly a comfort, and yet somehow we both knew them to be true. Somewhere in the wagon, secreted away with Reza's gold and Misha's incense, was my gift of myrrh that had spoken this truth before I even knew what it meant.

We made camp alongside the road that night, not wanting to leave a trail in any towns along the way. It was only the beginning of a very long journey, and best we put some distance between us and Bethlehem before we made ourselves known anywhere.

We had a few makeshift tents and bedrolls for the women, the men bundling clothes to cushion their heads from the hard-packed earth. Watching the group come together to say good nights, I realized that each of them had someone they belonged to. Lydia and Simon. David and Halima. Mary and Joseph. And now even Reza and Adina.

As if reading my thoughts, Misha took my hand and led me away from the little crowd, farther into the starry night.

We walked in silence for some minutes until Misha sighed and then spoke. "We have come a long way from the palace of Nisa."

I smiled, though he probably could not see it in the darkness. "Indeed."

"And I am glad. I would not return to my ignorance, for all its luxury."

"Nor would I."

"Ah, but you were never ignorant, Kamillah. Always the brilliant scholar. The mysterious Egyptian beauty." He laughed. "I would not return to Nisa because in Nisa you never spoke to me."

I bumped his arm with my own. "That is not true. Do you not remember the Vault? Where I caught you sneaking away with some trick to pass your examination?"

He turned me to him, continuing no farther into the night. "I remember. I remember how you spoke to me without condescension, in a way that I did not deserve."

"You have never seen yourself as you truly are, Misha."

His eyes were dark with an uncharacteristic intensity that stole my breath. "Kamillah, I know what I am. What I have been. I have lived for myself, for the next challenge, the next laugh. I have disrespected my heritage, cheated and stolen and amounted to nothing of worth. But I promise you, I can change. I can be more like Reza, more——"

I put my fingers over his lips. "It is not Reza I want, Misha."

His eyes closed briefly, then opened with a depth of emotion I had never seen.

I gripped both his hands. "Reza is a wonderful friend, to be sure. A man to be trusted and relied upon. But Reza does not make me laugh. Does not make me want to embrace adventure and live a life outside the narrow boundaries of what I can understand with my mind. That is you, Misha-aku. Only you."

"Misha-el." He smiled, a bit of sadness mixed with joy. "My name is Misha-el."

I nodded.

"But Kamillah, I know it is hard for you to trust." His attention was on our clasped hands, as though he could not look at me. "You have so much to offer. Others have only seen the merest shell of who you are and wanted to exploit it. I promise you—" His voice caught and he looked away. "I promise you that I will see all of you, but still be worthy of your trust. And that you will never be alone.'"

I said nothing. Waited for him to look into my eyes again.

When he did, I let him see my heart.

With a laugh, quiet and low in the darkness, he cupped my face in his hands, slid his fingers back into my hair, and kissed me. Tentative at first, then with the strength of a man who knew his heart and knew the heart of the woman he loved.

We returned to the silent camp hand in hand and parted beside the tent where the other women had already settled.

Under the soft moonlight, Misha crossed the scrubby grass to the men on the ground, then turned to lift a hand to me.

I returned the good night, took a last glance at the sky, and slipped into the tent.

And somewhere far above, a silver-white star shone down on us all.

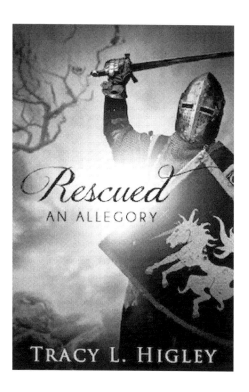

ALLURING... FASCINATING... AND MYSTERIOUS.

The Seven Wonders of the Ancient World still reach out to us, with stories waiting to be told.

From the **Hanging Gardens of Babylon** to the **Great Pyramid of Egypt**, each of The Seven Wonders Novels takes you into an adventure of history, mystery, and romance.

NOTE: Each book in The Seven Wonders Novels is a stand-alone story and they can be read in any order.

Start your adventure through the Seven Wonders of the Ancient World with *Isle of Shadows...*

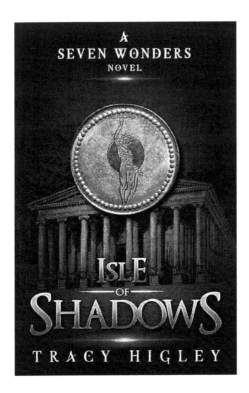

What will freedom cost her?

Enslaved in an Ancient World of Money and Power, Tessa Dares to be Free.

Raised as a courtesan to wealthy and powerful men, Tessa of Delos serves at the whim of the corrupt politician, Glaucus, on the opulent isle of Rhodes.

Ten years have passed since she was forsaken by both the gods and her mother. To survive, Tessa abandons any desire for freedom or love, choosing instead to lock her heart away.

But when Glaucus meets a violent death, Tessa grasps at a fragile hope.

Only she knows of his death.

And if she can keep the explosive secret long enough, she can escape.

But time is running out. Another treacherous politician emerges from the shadows, in a bid to seize power over Rhodes.

And this one is claiming Tessa for himself.

What will freedom cost her?

Buy Isle of Shadows here

HOW TO HELP THE AUTHOR

I hope you enjoyed *The Incense Road!* If you're willing to help, I would really appreciate a review. It doesn't have to be long or eloquent – just a few lines letting people know how the book made you feel.

Click here to leave a review on your favorite retail site.

Dear Reader,

I hope you enjoyed *The Incense Road* trilogy. It's been a fun ride, and I hope you'll join me for another, like *Isle of Shadows*, the first of the Seven Wonders Novels.

What I'm really hoping for, however, is that you'll become part of my "Caravan" - my affectionate name for my community of readers. I love showering readers with goodies, like free short stories, behind-the-scenes videos of me on location of my book settings, sneak peeks at new covers and plots, and deep discounts on books.

Want to be a part of this community?

Just get your copy of *Rescued: An Allegory* at the link below. It's a short story that I believe will touch your heart. I'll also send you some thought-provoking questions that go along with the story, that you could use for a group discussion or personally.

CLICK HERE for a free short story, and to join my Caravan!

And in case you're curious, here's more than you want to know about me…

I've been writing stories since the time I first picked up a pencil. I still have my first "real" novel—the story I began at the age of eight during a family trip to New York City.

Through my childhood I wrote short stories, plays for my friends to perform (sometimes I had to bribe them), and even started a school newspaper (OK, I was the editor, journalist and photographer since no one took that bribe to join me). Then there were the drama years of junior high, when I filled a blank journal with pages of poetry. {Sigh.}

In my adult years I finally got serious about publishing fiction, and have since authored thirteen novels in thirteen years.

When I'm not writing, life is full of other adventures—running a business, raising kids, and my favorite pastime: traveling the world.

I started traveling to research my novels and fell in love with experiencing other cultures. It's my greatest hope that you'll feel like you've gotten to travel to the settings of my books, through the sights, sounds, smells, colors, and textures I try to bring back from my travels and weave into my stories.

I'd love to hear your thoughts about *Star of Night*, or ideas you have for future books I might write. Get in touch with me at tracy@tracy-higley.com.

Now, onward to another story!

BOOKS BY TRACY HIGLEY

The Seven Wonders Novels:

Isle of Shadows

Pyramid of Secrets

Guardian of the Flame

Garden of Madness

So Shines the Night

The Time Travel Journals of Sahara Aldridge:

A Time to Seek

A Time to Weep

A Time to Love

The Books of Babylon:

Chasing Babylon

Fallen from Babel

The Lost Cities Novels:

Petra: City in Stone

Pompeii: City on Fire

The Coming of the King Saga:

The Queen's Handmaid

The Incense Road

Standalone Books and Short Stories:

Awakening

The Ark Builder's Wife

Dressed to the Nines

Broken Pieces

Rescued: An Allegory

Printed in Great Britain
by Amazon